THE RAINBOW RUNNER

JOHN CUNNINGHAM

TOR

A TOM DOHERTY ASSOCIATES BOOK
NEW YORK

This is a work of fiction. All the characters and events portrayed in this book are fictitious, and any resemblance to real people or events is purely coincidental.

THE RAINBOW RUNNER

Copyright © 1992 by John Cunningham

A Tor Book
Published by Tom Doherty Associates, Inc.
175 Fifth Avenue
New York, N.Y. 10010

Tor ® is a registered trademark of Tom Doherty Associates, Inc.

ISBN: 0-812-51359-2
Library of Congress Catalog Card Number: 91–36514

First Tor edition: April 1992
First mass market printing: February 1993

Printed in the United States of America

0 9 8 7 6 5 4 3 2 1

To Nina, John, Richard, Mary,
and all of theirs.

PROLOGUE

RAIMONDO SAT looking hopelessly at the four-barreled derringer lying in his left palm. What was he supposed to do with it? Kill who? How? The cheerful desert sun smiling through the dirty window only increased his despair.

The swaying of the train added seasickness to his fear. He began to wish he was dead. Better drop dead here than be tortured and strangled in Los Angeles. They had said, handing him the gun in San Luis Potosí a thousand miles ago, just pull back that little thing and press that little thing and it will fire. Which little thing was which? He had forgotten, he had never really understood, he had had no time to practice shooting it. Ramon, sitting beside him reading his dirty Latin classic, had been given a nickel plated peashooter but thought his fishing knife was enough protection.

They were coming down toward the Colorado to cross

into California, and they would be in Los Angeles that night. He was committed. There was no escape.

The ancient day coach, tacked on to the end of the train from El Paso to carry the motley poor, swayed and stank, its scatter of Anglo white trash farting, coughing, and groaning all around him, getting drunk or trying to sleep. It was debasing, it was not suitable to a professor of law who was almost pure Spanish. The lurching back and forth wasn't so much because the desert roadbed was rough as that the journals of the old day coach were worn out and the wheels slammed from side to side on the axle.

He was a fool. His brother was a fool. In a fit of folly they had volunteered to deliver a treasure worth half a million pesos to the Los Angeles rebels to be sold for the Revolution. The golden monstrance with its load of jewels was right over his head, in a round hatbox rocking back and forth in the luggage rack. Sixteen pounds of gold and jewels. Why had those devils robbed the church? How could the Revolution prosper with that kind of behavior? One of the thugs in Mexico City had killed a priest and then, disguised in his cassock, had stolen the monstrance right off the altar during benediction, right in front of a hundred old women.

To rob God! The thing must be cursed by now. Surely he and his brother would be killed. Sacrilege! It was all Ramon's fault. Ramon had talked him into this.

What in the name of God were they doing, he a peaceable professor of law, his brother a Latin scholar, mixed up in this revolutionary brawl of sweaty peons? Patriotism, was it? Idiocy! What was patriotic about being shot in the back of the head?

They would be met in Pasadena in a few short hours, and then taken to the City of the Angels by their unknown compadres of the revolution. But suppose something had gone wrong? Maybe those mythical leaders of the Los Angeles cells, Paz Faz and Gavira, had been betrayed. Maybe they would be met by the city police, informed by some traitor, and shipped back to Mexico to be shot against some wall. Or worst of all, that terror of the Mexican government, Palafox, the Los Angeles consul, who had trapped dozens of the rebels and sent them south to be executed. He had never seen any of these people. How would he know who to shoot, even if he knew how to shoot this thing?

He watched the hatbox rolling back and forth gently in the rack as the car swayed. "It's going to fall and smash," he said.

"Don't bother me," Ramon said, his nose in *Suetonius,* "I'm getting to the good part where Julius Caesar dreamed he raped his mother."

"If it gets smashed, they'll kill us."

"Please shut up, Raimondo. It won't get stolen up there, that's the main point."

Raimondo glanced sideways with hatred at his fat twin brother. About to be killed, and here was the little fool reading *Suetonius* in the Latin. Just because the rebel bosses had wanted a couple of gentlemen, not thugs, to cross the border with that cursed monstrance, here he was with the damned train drawing him closer and closer to the final terror, with a gun in his hand he had no idea how to use. He wanted to strangle Ramon.

"Why do you read that crap?" he said, the rage in his voice squashed under the pressure to keep it down. "You'll bring us to hell with your dirty mind. *Suetonius!* You should be saying your prayers instead of chuckling over that filthy stuff!"

Ramon's laughter shook his round little belly and his double chin. "Relax! There you sit, you puritan, with a pistol in your hand, the professor of law himself, scared to death—"

The coach gave a lurch and down crashed the hatbox into the candy wrappers littering the aisle. It lay there rolling gently in the trash with the round lid popped open like a dying clam and the old sheet they had wrapped the monstrance in spilling out.

"Jesus," Ramon said, his laughter dead in his throat.

"It's broken," Raimondo wailed. "You fool, how will they sell it now? You jackass, I told you not to put it up there!" He knelt in the aisle and snapped the hatbox shut. He picked it up and hurried down the aisle, lurching from side to side as the coach slung around a curve.

They locked the door of the tiny washroom. With the roar of the train in their ears and the smell of vintage urine in their noses, bumping against each other, they unwrapped the treasure. Raimondo put the monstrance on the toilet seat. The sunlight coming through the little window flashed and glowed on the gold and jewels, making the diamonds surrounding the little crystal box of the pyx in the center sparkle as though they were alive.

The base was a solid gold pyramidal complex of beads and ogees three inches high. From that there rose a golden cross a foot tall. Behind this cross, as a background, shone the wide sunburst, its golden waving rays outstretched. On each end of the cross's arms grew a heavy fleur-de-lis; in each corner of the cross, where the beams joined, an oval grew outward, and on the end of each of these another fleur-de-lis, so that these eight flowers growing on the cross formed overall, as of a heavy golden lace, a squarish diamond. In the outward-curling *C*'s of the side-leaves of these fleurs-de-lis, and in the center lyrate blades lay jewels in blue enamel beds, large and small rubies, sapphires and diamonds, and in the ovals of the corners, pear-cut emeralds. Large stones dominated central positions, surrounded by small ones, the whole making a blaze of color behind which sprang out the shining gold of the sun's ta-

pering rays, whose wavy edges seemed to make the whole
sun tremble in the light.

Raimondo inspected it minutely. Nothing was broken
off, none of the jewels had been knocked out of its setting.
"Thank God it's all right." He sighed deeply and stood
looking at the monstrance, almost bemused by its beauty.
His fear was gone. Something about it had restored his
sense of perspective, the humility of reason. After all, he
thought, they were only two small tools of the Revolution.
They were not the important ones. They would do their
duty and deliver the treasure and the important ones would
take over. He was finally ready to accept whatever was going to happen.

"I'm sorry I called you a fool, Ramon," he said, and
patted his brother on the back. "Everything will be all
right."

He carefully wrapped the treasure in the sheet and put
it back in the hatbox. The brothers stood for a moment,
friends again, swaying in the rattling, lurching train, rushing through the desert toward their end.

THE RAINBOW
RUNNER

CHAPTER ONE

THE PARTNERS always kept locked the half-glassed door to their office. Neither of them had ever been shot at, Jacko thought as he felt in his pocket for his key, but it was always a possibility.

The door said, "O'Donohue & Horton, Import-Export," and a card, hung permanently on the knob, said "Back in two hours." They lost no street trade because there wasn't any. All the investigating business came by phone from the lawyers, except for spying on the Los Angeles Mexican anarchists on behalf of that smooth child of tyranny, Señor Lorenzo Plutarco Sepeda y Palafox, the Mexican consul, referred to by the cynical anarchists as El Magnifico. Jacko took no sides in the squabbles south of the border: business was business, and if the anarchists had paid him to spy on Palafox he would have done so as gladly as he spied on them.

In many ways this spying for Palafox and his friends the L.A. police was a game understood by both sides. There were certain rules. The chief rule was to keep the game going. The L.A. police understood that if, in courtesy to the Mexican consul, they deported all the anarchists to sure death in Mexico, they would only get duty harder than routine surveillance, so they went easy.

Understanding this, the anarchists provoked the police very little and spent most of their energy talking and raising funds. For his part, Jacko held back from Consul Palafox any intelligence which might force his friends, the police, to do something radical and upset everybody. Why cut off the income by being too successful and killing the job? The Spanish-American War had taught him one truth: What the world needed most was a permanent standoff.

Everything was going well. But ¿quien sabe? Someday it might happen—Crash! would go the glass, bang bang would go the pistol of some drunken Mexican revolutionary, creating his anarchic heaven on earth out of two dead investigators.

He paused to listen to the voices beyond the door, his partner and the spy. Dirty jokes. As he pushed the key in the lock he looked at the reflection of his face in the frosted glass. He thought the homburg hat gave him a dignified and somehow dashing air, but he might be wrong. He cracked his poker face with a smile to ease the severity of his rather hawky nose and sharp eyes. Ah, that was better, more genial. He went in, relocked the door and glanced around.

The hired spy Chagoza was sitting on the windowsill, his butt presented to Los Angeles from five floors above Spring Street. Chagoza's black shirt showed none of the nervous sweat that streaked down his dark olive cheeks into the ends of his black moustache. He was always afraid of being seen coming into the building.

In through the window, on the fresh, clear air of a Los Angeles May day, came the smells of traffic, a mixture of manure and auto exhaust, and a confused roar of the clopping and clacking of heavy hooves, the grind of chaindrive Mack trucks, the heavy rumble of iron-tired drays. Above the battle whirled flocks of gray and brown pigeons, flashing in the sun. Whole farmyards of sparrows fought and fluttered over treasures in the dung.

Mike, smoking one of his stinking cigars, sat in the "client's chair," which had so rarely had a client in it, tilted back against Drawer G-L of the tall oak four-drawer file. This drawer contained three clean shirts and a discarded black holster. The green leather of the chair went well with Mike's burnt-sienna hair (two shades lighter than Jacko's own) and the reddish tweed of his sport suit, and well enough with his plump red cheeks and curly red cupid's mouth. The sport suit did not go at all with the confidential agenting business and the elderly lawyers who still, a few, wore morning coats or Prince Alberts.

Jacko looked over Mike's outfit with narrow care: Norfolk jacket with more than the usual pleats on the front, the belt a little more than usually low, narrow knickers and wool socks of the latest style, with little loops below the knee bands, through which ran a leather strap to keep the socks from falling down on his shoes. Very natty, the whole outfit brand-new. And where had he got the money, with the agency broke?

Jacko hung his hat on the deer-horn rack and flopped down in his black leather very dignified judge's chair behind the table that did for a desk. "Sorry to keep you waiting."

Mike smiled back at him. His patience was soldierly; he was brilliant at waiting for orders.

"Relax," Jacko told Chagoza. "What's the story?"

"Their name is Rivera. They are brothers. They are coming at eight o'clock on the train from El Paso."

"And they have a monstrance with them?"

"Absolutely."

"In one piece? Not broken down?"

"Not that I heard. They had no way to melt the gold, on the run from Mexico City. The jewels, who knows?" He sighed. "They say it is beautiful. It is worth—who knows? Millions?"

Jacko smiled. "Of sentimental value only, Chagoza, just an old museum piece. Nobody else would want it." He had no intention of letting Chagoza know that several museums would pay a quarter of a million for the thing. He had bought and paid for Chagoza, but a traitor once, a traitor always. Not that Chagoza was smart enough to get away with it. In Chagoza's eyes greed died reluctantly. He stood up to go and held out his hand to Jacko. "My fee, señor?"

"Just a minute. Where are they arriving?"

"Pasadena."

"Oh? Why not Los Angeles?"

"Paz Faz and Gavira are afraid of you and Señor Palafox, that you might arrest the Riveras in Los Angeles station. They know Señor Palafox has the power, as Mexican consul. He is such a friend of your American police."

"Who told you all this?"

"Nobody told," Chagoza said. "I heard it at the meeting last night at the Torero Club. The one run by Paz Faz and Gavira."

"What do the Riveras look like? Does anybody have a photograph?"

"I don't know, señor. There is one member who knew them when they lived in San Luis Potosí." He shrugged with elegance. "You wish me to find out from him?"

"There isn't time." Jacko turned and looked out of the window at nothing, compressing his lips in twitches as though swearing in his head. "How the hell am I going to know who they are if I don't know what they look like? I can't go bawling 'Rivera' through the train."

4

"Well, they are *cuates*."

"Twins? Okay. That'll do if they're sitting together."

The hand came out again. "If you please, señor, *tengo mucha prisa*."

Mike said, "You want me to jump on his stomach?" and laughed. "That'll take the hurry out of him."

Jacko gave him a look that sank his laugh into a bog of gloom. Why laugh, after all the trouble jumping on stomachs had got him in the Philippines? Mike's great gift, his infallible key to happiness: his exceptional inability to learn from experience.

Jacko pulled out his wallet and gave Chagoza two twenties, leaving himself one five and two ones. "*Muchas gracias*, Señor Chagoza." He had to make up for Mike's rudeness. "Your help is invaluable, as usual. I am most grateful for your excellent report." He unlocked the door.

"At your service, señor," Chagoza said, smiling and folding the bills into his back pocket. He gave Mike a sideways sneer of total contempt and went gracefully out, like a matador turning his back on a defeated bull.

Jacko locked the door after him and sat down in the judge's chair. "Cheer up, Mike." Mike looked up from his sad pool of gloom and smiled weakly, gratefully. Jacko lifted the black receiver of the telephone out of its little yoke.

"Central?"

"Number, please," came the cultivated whine.

He gave Palafox's number. Mike began humming "Smiles" to himself and sat looking out the window at the pigeons sailing around. If it wasn't "Smiles" it was "K-k-k-Katy, beautiful Katy, meet me by the kitchen door" or falling down the back steps or whatever it was. Unforgettable favorites of the woebegone dislocated Irish.

"Mexican consulate," the receiver said formally in his ear. Palafox had to run his shop by himself. After trying to sound like a very forbidding secretary, he would go call his usual cheerful self to the phone.

"¿Cómo está usted, señor?" Jacko made a point of speaking Spanish to the Consul. It made for good feeling, and kept his own Spanish in shape, as Señor Palafox was a man of considerable culture and many words. Too much listening to the broken Spanish of the Los Angelenos made him begin to talk like a Mexican hillbilly.

"Fine," Jacko said, replying to the consul. "And yourself?"

All Mike could hear of Palafox was *scrawk-scrawk.*

"Muy bien," Jacko said. "The Rivera brothers arrive tonight at Pasadena. Paz Faz and Gavira are planning to take them off there instead of at Los Angeles because they are afraid we would grab them at the L.A. terminal."

Laughter from Palafox.

"Suppose we grab them before they reach Pasadena," Jacko said, "say at Pomona, beat Paz Faz to it."

Scrawk-scrawk.

"Muy bien, at noon," Jacko said. *"Hasta la vista."*

He hung up and looked at Mike. "Palafox says Mexico City confirms it's worth $600,000. The reward by the Mexican government, or the Church, rather, that they're squeezing it out of, is $60,000. We are to return the monstrance to the priest at Guaymas, for Palafox, and collect the $60,000 for him. We get $12,000 of that and all the travel expenses."

"Why doesn't he go get it himself?"

"Don't be dumb, Mike. The rebels have taken all of Sonora except Guaymas. If he got stuck in Guaymas and the rebels took it, which they probably will, he'd be the first they put against the wall. You know how they hate the consuls."

"Twelve thousand dollars isn't much to split," Mike said.

"What's the matter with you? It's money from heaven. Thank God it'll keep us going until we find out why the lawyers have quit calling us." He thought for a moment, watching Mike. "It must be somebody spreading rumors against us."

He couldn't ask the lawyers directly. They would smile and deny any knowledge, and laugh at his back, watching him go down the drain, the sadistic bastards. The only attorney he could ask was Linebarger, and only because they had been teammates at USC.

"Why not grab the whole $60,000?" Mike said. "What could Palafox do about it?"

"I knew you'd think of that," Jacko said. "You want to go into hiding? Get your throat cut? Grow up. We go to Palafox's office for the details at twelve. Tickets to Guaymas and the other stuff."

He gave the city attorney's number to patient Central.

"When will Linebarger be back? ... Ten minutes? ... Tell him to call O'Donohue. It's urgent."

He went to the window and leaned out to get away from Mike's cigar smoke for a minute. He looked down at the rising conflict between the autos and the imperiled carriages and wagons, mixed with the raucous clamor of bulb-horns and klaxons, topped by the clanging of the streetcars butting their way through the chaos.

There was still plenty of manure on Spring Street, cleaned up by an army of white-uniformed pushbroomers who with their scoops trundled two-wheeled ashcans along the streets, enraging several million boisterous sparrows. Its healthy perfume relieved the stench of the exhaust, but it was fading each year as the noise increased and women's dresses grew slimmer at the hips and tighter at the ankles, until they had to mince along like toy dogs. No wonder they wanted the vote, and had got it in Sacra-

7

mento, he thought. Now they would probably take to trousers in another rebellion.

He thought of Mike's suffragette wife, another chronic irritation, who brassily showed herself in a skin-tight bathing suit, pleased to shock the world, and went striding around, if anybody only five feet tall could be said to stride, with her hobble skirt split halfway up the sides so she could march in women's rights parades.

"How are you doing for money?" Jacko said, looking idly at the new suit. "I've got $138 in the bank and six bucks in my pocket and I've got to help my father with an interest payment. Maybe we ought to split our reserve fund to tide us over."

"I'm doing all right," Mike said, admiring his country-tweed knees. "Let's leave the reserve alone."

Just how was Mike doing all right?

The telephone rang. Jacko picked it up, listened for sixty solid seconds, and hung up; stood like a statue for half a minute and went back to the window, breathing slowly until the shock and the anger died down.

"Well," Mike said, "did the grand inquisitor find out why we're going broke?"

"He couldn't talk about it on the phone. I'm going to meet him at eleven-thirty." He watched Mike's face out of the side of his eyes. It was stiff as a board with smiling deceit.

"No idea, eh?" Mike said. He smiled as though it hurt.

Jacko stood up. "Not a clue," he lied. He unlocked the door, went out, locked it again.

He walked down the dusty, silent gray hallway and punched the elevator button with his thumb, stood looking at the pointed tips of his shoes.

Linebarger had said on the phone: "The rumor's around that Mike's been blackmailing your lawyers' clients. Nat-

8

urally you wouldn't know. The screwee never does." So that's where the new suit had come from.

He punched the elevator button again. Silence from below. Was Harold sleeping? He jammed the button into its little socket as though he were squashing somebody's eyeball. He heard the crash of the bronze ground-floor door. Ah, Harold had waked up. Far below, the accordion gate closed with a rattling crash and the long whine began as the elevator struggled into its painful ascent, wobbling along its tracks.

Where had Mike gone wrong? Where had *he* gone wrong? Oh, yes, it had been glorious, as king of the relay team at USC, fifteen years ago, to save Mike's befuddled ass. Jacko, the kindly father type, protecting hungover Horton from the vengeance of Linebarger and the others of the team. Help me! Horton had all but wept, fleeing into Jacko's arms from the mad pursuers, who were going to kill him. "I didn't mean it!"

No, he hadn't meant to get drunk the night before, didn't mean to fall down in the cinders and lose the race, so appealing in his honest panic, like a child. How could Jacko, the kindly team captain, not have protected him?

Adopted him! From then on, Jacko had been his loving big brother, deciding everything. Mike had wanted to dump USC six weeks before graduation and join Roosevelt's Rough Riders to seek glory in Cuba, and had asked Jacko's advice. Jacko had stalled him, saving his degree. They'd gone for glory in the Philippines instead, shipping out of San Francisco with MacArthur's five thousand California volunteers. Then transferred to the Sixth Infantry when Jacko had got his commission and wangled a sergeant's stripes for screw-up Horton whose record of AWOLs and getting drunk with the local monkey girls hung forever from his neck like a dead chicken. The only reason the Army kept him on was because of his courage, no doubt of that, and the bums among the volunteers needed an example when chasing gooks in the bamboo.

Then to Company I of the 26th Volunteers, into the half-assed G-2 there in Iliolo until June of 1900, when O'Hearn was murdered, and then by the grace of God home when the enlistment term ended, but not before the investigation of Mike's water tortures, which left Mike reduced to private. Home again across the sea, Mike wagging his tail at Jacko's heels, adoring him for saving his ass from five years in the stockade. And because Mike was competent under direction, Jacko had taken him into the new agency which he had set up to take advantage of what he had learned in G-2 counterintelligence, and the flock of lawyers he knew from USC.

To do the dirty work, Jacko thought, and his insides shriveled as he clenched his teeth. He was ready to bite himself and throw up at the same time. Blackmail! If the house falls, he thought, you yourself have pulled it down. You fed him the dirty work; didn't you teach him the dirty work? Then why blame him? You let him stay a baby forever for your own glorification as the great friend-father, to have a slave at your heels. Noblesse oblige, as his grandfather said, in a world without nobility, is nothing but the pride of Satan. The smirk of the devil's charity.

He could see, far below, the roof of the elevator rising slowly up the shaft, as though the building were having heartburn. The counterweight, like a memorial slab from a floating cemetery, descended majestically down the opposite wall of the shaft in a pas-de-deux with the rattling cage; the cables, black in their grease, slapped each other on the back.

Blackmail! He's wrecked you, but you wrecked him with your pampering. You let him grow from the bruises and contusions of boyish fraternity pranks to jumping on water-swollen bellies in the Philippines, to breaking the jaws of the Torero anarchists for the sheer fun of it, here in this City of the Angels. The time the chink chopped his leg half off with the cleaver, Mike had just laughed, caved in the chink's forehead with a baseball bat, and left him dead with one eyeball lying on his cheek. Protected by Jacko O'Donohue in one court after another.

The cage hove in sight, its golden bars rising in the dark shaft like the glorified bones of the resurrection. Harold's old gray face, fixed in eternal resignation, the opaque gray eyes veiled half-blind with contemplation of world doom, looked through the bars at something just above Jacko's head.

In that head was appearing the military court in Leon, on the island of Panay. The vision was clear, the hum of the ceiling fan, the hallelujah chorus of two hundred flies, supping up the sweat of faces white and brown, the scratching of a clerk's pen, the last of the beautiful pastel dawn fading out in a haze of blinding dust. He was on the "stand," a chair facing the three-man court, not charged with anything, a witness.

Q. Was not the water cure resorted to by the soldiers for the purpose of securing information?

A. Yes, the practice was prevalent in the Scouts, and around Iliolo.

Q. The Gordon Scouts?

A. Those are the Gordon Scouts.

Q. Did you witness the burning of any towns by the United States soldiers?

A. Oh, yes.

Q. Just state what towns you saw burned.

A. The town of Tigbauan, the town of Oton, the town of Alimodian, the town of San Miguel. It was not the town of San Miguel, but houses along the roadside—

11

barrios—and we burned that old string of houses there.

Q. How many houses did you burn at that time and place?

A. I could not say how many we burned. The troop was traveling right along, and we did not make any observation after we lighted a house.

Q. Why was that barrio burned?

A. To intimidate the natives. We came across the bodies of two American horses that had been ridden by soldiers that had been fired upon.

Q. What other barrios and towns were burned?

A. We burned a good deal of the country as we were fired upon. It was the practice if a column was fired upon to burn the buildings.

The cage stopped with a grunt, as though struck in the belly, and bounced on its cable a full foot below the floor level. Harold swung the fore-and-aft control handle through its arc, and the cage jumped eighteen inches into the air and bounced again. Two more thumps and Harold had it right enough, within two inches. He shoved the accordion gate to the side with a rattling crash, and seizing the latch of the bronze floor-door and staring with remote world hatred into Jacko's eyes, gave it a heave and slammed it open with a terrible crash.

"Watch your step," Harold said through clenched teeth. That was all he ever said, except Going Up and Going Down. He never chatted. He had learned to keep his teeth clenched together to keep his plates from falling out every time the elevator came to its soul-shaking stops.

He slammed the doors behind Jacko with a grin of vicious pleasure. "Going Down," he said, and the cage jumped a foot into the air. He calmly reversed engines, throwing Jacko's stomach into his throat, and together they began the long, slow, trundling descent.

Jacko sat on the red plush seat, his head bowed. Now he was listening to Mike, sweating on the chair.

Q. How did you administer the water cure?

A. Their stomach was filled up with water from a bucket held up and a hose going down in their mouth, and then was jumped on.

Q. What was the effect upon these natives of giving this water cure?

A. They would swell up—their stomach would swell up pretty large—and I have seen blood come from their mouth after they had been given a good deal of it.

Q. Do you know what information they got the first day?

A. It was in regard to the killing of Lieutenant O'Hearn. After. After we had found his bones. The bones of O'Hearn.

Q. Did the natives confess that O'Hearn was burned before he was murdered?

A. They confessed. He was tied to a tree at seven o'clock in the morning and was tortured by cutting with bolos and by slow fires until five o'clock at night. So the natives confessed.

The cage descended slowly in the ice-cold shaft, darker and darker. How could he not have defended Mike? It was orders, orders. What he could not defend had never been questioned: Mike's joy, jumping up and down like a little boy on a bed. But they had not tried to convict Mike of Joy.

Slowly descending, he thought of the Four Last Things: Death, Judgment, Heaven, Hell, which every Irishman, even to the last generation, knew forever. In that Court, there would be two trials, one on the issue of Orders, one on the issue of Joy.

Why had the rotten bastard betrayed him? And his other enemy, his beautiful slim blond wife, who had killed his child.

I'll get them both, he thought.

CHAPTER TWO

WITH JACKO'S slamming of the door still in his ears, Mike sat like a lump, tilted back in his chair, his stout cheeks sadly slumped, his cherub mouth a broken bow. He could tell by the fierce icy look in Jacko's eyes after he talked to Linebarger that Linebarger had somehow found out about the blackmail. Why hadn't Jacko said anything? What was Jacko plotting against poor Mike? Or was he?

With Jacko on guard, he had played freely in the world, jumping, laughing, beating up bastards, no fear with Jacko there. How luscious it had been, to jump on those squashy bellies and hear them squeal, the dirty little bastards. The old song came up from the pit of yesterday, to the tune of "Tramp, Tramp, Tramp the Boys are Marching," and he heard again like surf in a shell the drab platoons humping along the flour-dusty Iliolo roads, getting shot at out of huts. Those had been the days, masters of all they surveyed, except their dead, as the poet said:

Damn damn damn the Filipinos,
Pockmarked kakiyak ladrones,
Underneath the starry flag,
Civilize 'em with a Krag
And return us to our own beloved homes.

Why was he always the one in trouble? the despised?
Why should he have to be helped out of messes all the
time?

Jacko and his millions of oranges, him and his noble
lace-curtain ancestors, him and his money, him and his
fancy mansion on Bunker Hill, while poor Mike, twice the
man, had to live with his scrawny little wife in a lousy
apartment house. Him and his rich friends, him and his
lousy airplane. Good good good! he'd had to sell the stinking airplane. Hurray for that! the bastard. And now he
might be thinking about jail for Mike, his friend.

Suddenly he laughed with relief as the solution flared in
his mind like divine revelation. The $60,000 reward, why
not take it all? They'd go down to Guaymas together and
swap the silly monstrance, and somehow Jacko would
miss the returning boat, get drunk and fall in the water, or
something. That was the way. Why should that fat f——g
Palafox get anything at all?

With $60,000 he could kiss Los Angeles goodbye, and
as for blackmail and jail, South America would receive
him in her warm, lovely breast.

Thinking of breasts, he had a vision of beautiful May,
Jacko's lovely. Another thought came, that while May
scorned poor Mike, she had never yet hung up the phone
on him, or slammed the door on his frequent platonic visits over the last six months. Platonic, yes! How could old
Jacko object to a little platonism, which they'd studied so
hard at USC? If she had never cut him off, then wasn't she

16

hanging on to him, in a way? Was she then so noble a woman? He smiled.

Jacko, he thought bitterly while visions of jail put fear in his stomach, I'll have you for dinner and your wife too, you bastard.

He had to run, sure, to stay out of jail for that black-mail. And if he had to run, he might as well take every-thing with him. Jacko was smart, but Jacko was trusting, and that would be his downfall.

He leaned out the window and saw Jacko coming out of the building. Farewell, Jacko, he said to the smart gray hat and spat down five stories, carefully aiming. He watched the blob wavering in the morning thermals. Nope, nope, missed, a southwest eddy caught it and it landed on the head of an old gray horse wandering by, attached to a wagon. Too bad. Better luck next time.

He went back to Jacko's throne and asked Central for Jacko's number.

"O'Donohue's residence," came a clear Boston voice, with a ghost of dead brogue hovering over the flat *a*'s. It was that damned old crone of a maid.

"Let me speak to Mrs. O'Donohue," he said suavely. Mike Horton could be as gentlemanly as anybody, for a reason.

"And who is—"

"Michael Horton."

"A moment, please," said the old snob.

A moment passed. Then:

"Hello?" said a low, sweet, almost timid voice, like a shy young girl.

Mike smiled. He would never get over the wonder, how May could be so gentle and sweet, answering the phone, all the time those lovely eyes like a layer of blue ice fro-zen on an adding machine. But could her lips be hot and luscious? Would he ever find out? The truth was, he didn't really care much. As far as sex went, he found that giving some bum a good bust in the mouth and watching him spit out his front teeth was far more romantic, though of course women had never quite bored him.

His careful, delicate, distant flirtation with Jacko's wife was just a sort of game with which he tantalized himself, almost like poking a tooth with his tongue to see if it hurt. It was a test of his powers of tact, like picking the lock of a door he knew he would never open. A game of teasing. He was too wary of Jacko ever to think of her in a bed. Sometimes he thought they had almost become friends. And it was true, there was something in each of them that echoed in the other, he didn't know what.

Yet she was something beautiful on Jacko's shelf, that could be taken down now, not for love, not for lust, but perhaps for revenge on Jacko for his own ruin. A compensation. Perhaps.

He smiled at the air.

"It's your faithful admirer, Mike Horton."

"So Lilly told me," she said in a voice that carried an inaudible coda, "you silly ass."

He didn't mind. Her somewhat affectionate contempt, always showing its edge, but rarely drawing the blood which would drive him away, only heartened his confidence. They knew where they stood, and each of them enjoyed standing there in their peculiar relationship, which she had never let develop, but never sought to part from.

"I found the one you wanted," he said.

"Which one?"

" 'Real Slow Drag.' I got the piano roll."

"I could use the record too."

"All right, darling," he cooed, but not too much.

"Don't call me darling. We are only friends, Mike. Only my lady friends call me darling. Or do you want me to hang up for good?"

He knew by now she'd never do that, as long as he was tactful. How many of her fancy friends did she have left to go shopping with, since Jacko went broke and the champagne wells went dry?

"I thought I'd bring it by, if you're going to be home," he said.

"I'm always home nowadays," she said with a twist of pain in her voice. "You know that. Where am I to go? With no money? And one loses friends fast, if one can't treat for lunch."

She was never stingy with her complaints, he thought. That was part of his hold, to be the towel she could cry sopping wet.

"I have good news," he said. "Jacko and I are going down to Mexico tomorrow to collect a reward of $60,000. We get $12,000 of that to split. Nice, eh? Somehow I think I can get the whole $60,000, May dear. I've been thinking of quitting the agency and going on my own. Maybe down in Buenos Aires. I speak enough Spanish."

"Leaving so suddenly?" she asked. "Who will bring me music rolls?"

"I can't talk about it over the phone." Curiosity always got them, the cats.

"How very interesting, Mike. Why don't you drop by with the piano roll? We can play it and you can tell me all your plans."

"I'll be there as soon as I can, dear," he said.

"I can't wait to hear."

He knew what she heard, now. The sound of a door opening, out of her prison. Would she really rise to $60,000? Why not?

He could sound her out on it, get her to agree. But then how was he to get the whole sum? At some point he would have to get Jacko out of the way. A Mickey at the right time would do it perfectly, knock him out for twelve

19

hours. And who would supply him with a few drops of it, but the old bitch down at the Sergeant's Saloon on Third? Why not find out now how much the old bag would screw him out of for it?

Plenty of time before Jacko got back from his old man and they went to see Palafox.

CHAPTER THREE

A T SPADRA, poor dying hamlet, Jacko turned the Stanley off the churning dust of the Pomona Highway, waddled across the Southern Pacific tracks and turned back west toward the orchards along the estate road. Passing the company warehouse beside the tracks, he waved to Fernando, who was bossing a dozen ranch hands unloading sacks from a freight car standing on the weed-grown siding. On the end of the enormous sad brown warehouse rose in flowery Victorian letters as tall as a man, weathered to the gray ghost of a name, ESTANCIA QUIÑONES, kept in honor of the original Spanish grant. Below, in faded yellow letters modestly half as tall, O'DONOHUE CITRUS, INC. This title represented the foresight of Jacko's great-grandfather, a well-heeled immigrant adventurer from Ireland, who by marriage into the family of the land-poor Spanish grantee brought happiness to a young widow, cash to her assets of beef tallow and hides, and eventually the whole six square miles of prime land, much improved by his efforts, to their half-Irish heirs.

Jacko slowed the Stanley to navigate the potholes past the gloomy warehouse. Like a line of ants under Fernando's contemplative supervision, the olive, tan, red-brown sweating friends of his childhood trundled dollies of sacks from the freight car to the growing debt-mountain: nitrogen, phosphorus, potassium to feed the army of three hundred thousand trees always a hair from starvation. He waved to his old friends, a few waved back, too happily fatalistic to resent his owning a Stanley, or, if they had known, to sympathize that he now had to sell it.

The years had aged, shaded, and sobered the old alliances, but he knew he was still one of them. He still came out and played ball on one or the other of the teams. With his arm out of training and control weak, he was no longer captain, but Fernando, now manager, with a tolerant smile let him pitch until he walked somebody, and then they all hooted him out to left field where he now belonged. But he still belonged, and could sit drinking beer with every-body after practice, just one of the Spanish-chattering crowd. Their Latin logic had no envy; if he had been born son of the mostly-Irish *padrón*, that was not his fault.

He left them behind and entered the ranks of the dead trees, the battalions struck down by the freeze of 1908. Jacko could hear again his father's voice beyond the heavy closed door, saying, "The year he married that Czechoslo-vakian strumpet, the year the bad luck began," and his mother's gentle remonstrance, "But, Vincent!"

All the heat of his resentment at Vincent's attack on his new wife had been slaked away in a year, as the slow slide of days scraped bare her act and left for the sweet and lan-guorous beauty a listless ninny, brought to life only by rage and greed. The safety of marriage turned her into a sloth, she would lie bathless in the bed he had abandoned

22

turning sourer by the hour; her eyes, no longer shadowed, shrank to moldy gray raisins in her pie-dough face. Across the dinner table she looked at him with the sniffling, nose-twitching, blur-eyed greed of a weasel measuring a baby chick. How right Vincent had been, about the strumpet, at least.

But the bad luck had been all Vincent's, the fatal end his "Eastern" investment in 1907, the year before the freeze, when Wall Street's roof fell in. That year's orange profits went up the flue along with the Knickerbocker Trust, wiping out their cash and landing them forever in the hole with the San Bernardino bankers.

"Everybody has to make a big fool of himself at least once," Jacko's grandfather had said of Vincent's investment. "I did it in 1880 when I built that stupid castle you live in, Vincent did it in 1907, and you began your performance when you came back from the Philippines and started your so-called business. But when will yours end?"

He drove the Stanley under the great, elaborately plastered arch at the *estancia* entrance, past the broken-hinged gates sagging open with the morning glory vines twining upward through their wrought-iron arabesques. Nobody had ever suggested repairing them because nobody had ever closed them anyway. The narrow rutted road began to rise very gradually toward the distant houses of the estate, hidden now by the orange trees, but marked by the *mirador*, the old watchtower, which stood on the ridge with the eucalyptus trees behind it.

His grandfather was probably sitting up there in the tower now, as usual, rolling his cigarettes and enjoying the fruits of his Irish father's avarice and love—the rich view, in the morning sunlight, of the Quiñoneses' royal grant sloping away to the east, cattle land which he himself had covered with an army of orange trees.

Here at the bottom of the gentle rise, the ice-cold air had

sunk and like a great wolf had bitten the trees to the roots. The dead still stood in skeleton ranks, as far as he could see to the north, in a narrow curving swath at the bottom of the ranch's great slope where the boundary creek was rushing with the winter's rain down from the San Gabriel Mountains. After the 1907 panic, Vincent could not afford the man-hours needed to cut them down and burn them, much less think of a new planting.

He felt smothered by the feeling of death all around him and fed the Stanley more steam to get away. Each time he saw the trees standing dead a memory of the cramping pain in his stomach returned, a shadow of the pain he had felt when he and Vincent and their hundred men had stood with shoulders sagging that bleak morning, with the futile black stink of the exhausted smudge pots fading away around them, and watched the frost-burnt leaves drop from the trees one by one like tears, or shower down in sudden gusts of warming winds from the far-off ocean.

He passed the other of Vincent's faulty inspirations, the old windmill, which stood as the failed test of a plan to create a network of power-saving windmills and wells. Its iron framework stood skeletal and silent among the dead trees, with the rotting pumphouse white about its feet like a fallen shroud. The wrong kind of wind, they said, too weak and gusty. The pump jack now was locked, the pale steel blades of the fan never turned. But sometimes teased by the frail night wind it would kick weakly against the iron bars, the pump jack in its prison house banging futilely with petulant clangs like mourning bells, while the fruit rats rustled in the dark.

Why in God's name didn't Vincent tear the relic down? Perhaps he let it stand as a prompting to prudence; as a cautionary reminder of fallibility. Jacko had never proposed the junking of the wreck. He knew what Vincent would say: Why don't you come out and help me do it?

24

Jacko hastened by. The threat of a hands-on involvement with the groves shrank him away like the peril of some fatal infection.

Now he came to the end of the desolation, and entered the great green choirs of silence higher up on the rise, where the trees stood beautiful and still, their deep skirts almost touching each other. Their fruit, both green and turned red-gold with cold spring nights, hung like lovely gifts, each singly presented, among the dark carved leaves, and all among them smiled the bright scattering of those small white bursts of blossoms, like children at a solemn cathedral mass chirping joyfully between the dark towers of their parents.

For Jacko life in the *estancia* had moved like a hearse. In the old days, when the family had been transplanted every spring from the house in Los Angeles to the groves, he had suffered patiently through the summer, playing in the dusty village street with the other children, or wandering with feeble curiosity among the men and women in the barns and workshops. The whole summer was one long suffocating wait for the family's return to Bunker Hill in the fall, to the brilliant excitement of the city. The only thing that had interested him at the *estancia* was baseball, his grandfather's passion.

Where the road to the workers' village turned off from the main drive up to the big house, he left the Stanley idling on the pilot burner and walked down the crown between the ruts, the grass whipping the shine off his shoes. On his right the majestic trees cooled him with their green morning shadow. All the earth around their skirts was cultivated clean, Vincent's precise economy.

Vincent's little one-room cube of an office building shone in the morning sunlight with the glowing white of peace and purity, its thick adobe walls for a hundred years born anew in whitewash every spring. An ancient orange tree, twenty feet tall, reflected a greenish tinge on Jacko's old baseball target (two vertical grooves the height of a man, the width of home plate apart) carved in the clay wall.

This was the first house on the place, built in 1822 by the seven Spanish soldiers who with General Quiñones had abandoned a Mexico ruined by independence. Beyond this isolated cube of purity lay everything Vincent commanded, the tall, open-sided barns of gray, weathered wood which housed the spray wagons, the gang plows, the cultivators, and beyond them the tangle of corrals for the mules and the stables for the horses, all of which Jacko smelled, on the fresh, clear morning air, with an inexhaustible pleasure. Horses, yes; trees, no.

He came around the corner of the little building, and standing in the sun, looked through the dark doorway. The sun glare on the white wall blinded him. He stepped through the doorway into cool silence, to be blinded again by the darkness of the old beamed ceiling, the ancient furniture against the blue-white plaster. Slowly the shadows were gently lifted by the light from the little windows embrasured in the three-foot-thick adobe walls. To the left stood the bookkeeper's desk where the old Chinese from Pomona sat once a week rattling his abacus. In the rounded fireplace, built into the corner of the room, the last weak flame of the morning fire flickered over ashy coals and smoking stubs of orangewood.

On Vincent's massive old desk, black as a coffin, one of his gray-backed ledgers lay open. His pen stood slanting in the inkwell, a sure sign of quick return. Beside the inkwell lay a blue-gray blotter with Vincent's slanting signature reversed on it a dozen times. A thread of blue smoke rose from half a cigar lying brown against the pearl of an abalone shell. Beside it, an empty porcelain cup, white with a blue rim, matching its saucer, a stain of coffee drying in the bottom. On a small table beside the desk stood, as staunch as a castle, a No. 5 Underwood typewriter, on which Vincent pecked out his own letters.

Jacko stood looking at the shadowed portrait of his mother on the wall beside the fireplace and waited. The thin face, the beaklike nose and hooded eyes were like his own, and might have seemed cruel except for the small, habitual smile which she had lost only when scolding or commanding in her unabrasive way the two hundred people who worked the place. With fitting self-distrust, the painter had not essayed the hands in detail; but the few suggestive strokes brought up in his own hand a physical return of the feeling of her touch.

She had not been the kind of woman who would rush with open arms to welcome him on his visits from the city; the demonstrations of her love were regulated by a respect, and even reverence, for physical contacts which so increased their meaning that a touch of her fingers on his arm was a complete caress, its sweetness distilled from her nature like perfume by the very parsimony of her display. Smiling with the patience of affection, he waited, his head full of the recollection of her, waiting for him in her patio, all around her its implacable geometry and military ranks of flowers. Indeed, the garden had been, was still a portrait of her nature.

Was he to regret how, little by little, he had grown away, filled with other more important things, which had died in turn? What he had left was a quiescent love which wished only to sit in friendly, comfortable converse with her, enjoying those qualities, deeper than maternal, which maturity now enabled him to perceive in her with such contented admiration.

She was the daughter of a Boston attorney, the son of one of those not too unusual immigrant Irish who had come over with money. This man had struggled upward in politics; had made quite a lot of money as a lobbyist; had sent his daughter to Dana Hall, a young ladies' finishing school of repute, and then to Paris for two years to study the violin.

These two years had ruined New England forever for her, so she said; she had been saddened to live with her mildly guilty contempt for it, and had resigned herself to the limits of a faded affection.

When Vincent, at Harvard in 1877, had invited her as his bride to California, she could hardly wait to flee. Los Angeles was anything but Paris; still, she loved Vincent, the groves, and her enormous Mexican family of workers, and when sometimes she thought of Boston again, she put the devil behind her.

He heard feet crunching sandy clods outside the door and turned. His grandfather came in, followed by his father, black silhouettes in the brilliant doorway. The sunlight struck three oranges held up in Vincent's big right hand. He gave Jacko a one-armed hug and went around the desk to face him, slightly smiling; sat down in the old high-backed Spanish chair and for a moment had for Jacko the appearance of a genial king, holding the three oranges like golden orbs. Vincent's face was composed, complete, having the immobility of an unchangeable contentment, yet full of grooves and wrinkles and heavy folds in the cheeks and along the mouth, the scars of long-interred disputes. Many fine lines across the wide forehead showed a nervousness on which he imposed the contentment of internal discipline.

His old grandfather sat down in the chair where the Chinese bookkeeper, now off duty, took a break now and then.

In his washed-out blue bib overalls he looked like some old pensioner. His round red face with its pooched-out cheeks and chin, sagging eyelids, was half-hidden by a white three-day-old stubble which he had decided to grow into a beard. He unlaced one of his broken-down workshoes, lifted his foot onto his fat knee and began massaging its instep.

"I know why you're here, my boy," old Thomas said. "Don't ask me again to sell that land. I'll never vote against your father, so don't start up. I wish to God this was a rocking chair."

"Give him a chance to say something," Vincent said. He put the oranges down beside the ledger and dug in his pocket for his jackknife. "I heard that car of yours. I knew what was coming. The old trilateral disagreement. So I went and got Thomas."

Jacko pulled a chair over and sat down facing his father.

"Don't sit there," Vincent said with all the peremptoriness of affection. "I can't see you against the light. Sit at the end."

He should come more often, Jacko thought as he moved, knowing that for a thousand reasons he wouldn't, and felt a passing ghost of guilt.

"You know I'm right," Jacko said, "you've both got to give in." He pulled out his wallet and laid the small sheaf of one thousand dollars on the desk. "I have to go to Guaymas tomorrow, so it's been a race getting this together. I'll have the other seven hundred and fifty when I sell the Stanley this afternoon. I'll mail it to you. I've got a job in Mexico that pays $12,000, but I won't get my half for a month." He began counting out the bills.

"What kind of nonsense is this?" Thomas said. "Running down into the middle of a war."

Vincent's eyebrows rose briefly and fell, his idea of a shrug. He sat watching Jacko count. The brilliant sunlight, coming through the doorway, reflected from the cool interior walls as a sort of nimbus about Vincent's face, so smoothly carved, the deep grooved shadows softened, highlights paled on the high peaked nose. A spot of reflected firelight gleamed flickering orange in the dark iris of his eyes, another on the white porcelain of the cup.

Thomas let go of his foot and pulled a sack of Golden Grain and a packet of Zig-Zag papers out of his overall ruler pocket and sniffed the sack.

Thomas George Lawrence O'Donohue had been born "O'Donohue y Quiñones," but the Spanish maternal half of this name had been dropped now for sixty years. He was eighty-three; the chair he complained of, Jacko had calculated, was about ninety-one. It was a large, primitive affair made of round sapling stock, shiny bare sticks, legs tied together by rungs crudely doweled into them. The seat and the wide, tall back were woven of thin strips of rawhide, as hard as wood. Thomas's father, Alexander, had bought this, and the others scattered around, in the plaza market of the pueblo of Los Angeles in 1822.

The Spanish Quiñones, disgusted with the rule of the lunatic Emperor Iturbide and the chaos of Mexican Independence, had abandoned their several tons of furniture in Mexico City in 1822 and emigrated to their frontier California land grant. At almost the same time, in Ireland, Alexander O'Donohue, great-grandson of a turncoat who had fought for Cromwell, fearing the pro-Catholic agitations of O'Connell, sold off the booty lands awarded by the Lord Protector and adventured to California, met the Quiñoneses and became their estate manager. Alexander's little offspring grew up half Spanish and half Irish.

The old man leafed up the lid of the packet of cigarette papers and zigzagged out a little sheet of the fine French stuff. He shook his round white head. It had been dark red, once, like Jacko's. This white hair covered the back of his neck so thickly that his head seemed to grow neckless out of his broad, thick shoulders. Most old men, Jacko thought, seemed to melt and shrink slowly away, but

30

Thomas had always stayed the same, thick, broad, and short.

Jacko laid the bills down in front of his father. "That's that. It'll pay the interest till I get back." He sat back and looked at the other two. "We can cut out this foolishness of paying interest if you let the collateral go. What's a quarter of a section out of five square miles? Let it go. You know I'm right. It's foolish to sell the Bunker Hill property just to save that quarter section. The Bunker Hill property is nowhere near its top, but the grove land is. So sell the quarter section. It's only logical."

"No," Thomas said. "I won't go against your father." While the bills whispered softly as Vincent checked the count, the old man sat remembering. He thought of Vincent bringing back the seeds for the eucalyptus windbreak from San Gabriel in 1873, almost the first from Australia. And himself, buying the first little orange trees, ten years earlier. And then he thought further back of his father and his mother and brother and sister in the rocking, bumping old coach, on the dusty road to San Gabriel when he was little, going to mass at the Mission, so far away they had to leave before dawn and got back by starlight. And all the cattle they brought up from Mexico, and letting the Indians steal what they wanted.

It was the death of the thousands in the drought of 1862 which had turned him from cattle to oranges. They had skinned the thousands and left the carcasses for the buzzards and the Indians, and later had nailed skulls to the fenceposts, that the skulls should stare in hatred at the barren summer sky. Nowadays, where the fenceposts had long rotted, his milk cows, kept for the village children, wandered through the groves grazing where they pleased.

"How long will you be gone?" Vincent asked.

"Two weeks, maybe three. It's a slow ship, an old freighter."

"Seven hundred miles of sweat on a greasy tramp. Why don't you fly? That Avro of yours would make it all right. They've got cars down there now, you know, you'd have plenty of gas to get back on."

Jacko looked carefully at Vincent's face for a flicker of irony. Was he mocking him about what he thought had been the folly of the plane?

"I sold the plane," Jacko said, trying to smooth out of his voice the stiffness he felt. "I told you that last month."

"Ah," Vincent said, lifting his chin, reined up by both the reminder and the reproach. "I'd forgotten. I'm sorry, Jacko. A pity. I liked the idea."

"I had the impression you thought I was an idiot to buy it."

"Oh, I did think it a shortsighted way to spend your *Times* windfall, but I like the idea of flying." He opened his jackknife, examined the blade, closed it, opened it again, laid it down, opened, on the ledger. He sighed. The eyebrows made their shrug.

"Well, you'd better get your money out of Guaymas in a hurry," Thomas grumbled, shifting around in the big chair. "By the time they get through with their stupid war, Mexico won't be worth a nickel. What have they got down there that's worth $6,000?"

"It's a fee for returning something to the Church. A monstrance. Stolen from the cathedral in Mexico City. By some of our Los Angeles anarchists, to finance their revolution. Or I should say their subrevolution. Supposed to be worth a $600,000. Gold and jewels of various kinds. Just another baroque monstrosity, I suppose."

"Another bloody gamble," old Thomas muttered. "Another pot of gold at the end of the rainbow. Why are you always running to the ends of rainbows?"

"You say you suppose it's a monstrosity?" Vincent said. "Then you don't have it. Where is it?"

"On a train, coming tonight. We'll board the train and take it."

Jacko shifted in the hard chair and sat up straighter. "It's the first decent piece of business we've had in two months. Maybe it'll change my luck. I asked Linebarger to poke around and find out why the lawyers have quit calling us. You remember Linebarger, the fellow I used to bring out to play ball when we were at USC? He's assistant city attorney now."

"City attorney! He's done well."

Jacko's face turned a fine pink.

Vincent noticed, turned half away in his chair to hide the stricture of compunction in his own face at the ill-considered reflection on his son, then swung back to exhaust his embarrassment in complaint. "How long does this have to go on? That I can't compliment your friend's career without offending you about yours?"

"I wouldn't say that I had done so badly," Jacko said. His mouth had tightened, his voice had a little difficulty coming out and he coughed. "Until now." His face felt hot and he was sweating around the collar.

He had to put up with it. He had to do his best to talk them into selling the land, if he wanted to keep on living his life in Los Angeles.

"I think it's that partner of yours who's killing your business," Thomas said. "He's changed. The last time I saw him, in town that time last year, I had the feeling he had become mean, although he still smiles a lot. A mean man is always discontented, or a discontented man is always mean, I don't know which. So they'll steal."

Jacko got up and crossed the room to his mother's portrait, stood looking up at it. "Never mind him," he said. "Sell the land. You're going to have to eventually."

"You should have dropped him after the war. War buddies don't mean anything. Why didn't you?"

Jacko opened his mouth to object. He stopped himself and sighed. "In a way, he's helpless. I felt responsible for him. The army made him shiftless."

"Helpless? He got a degree the same time you did, didn't he? A brute like that can always make a living, beating somebody up."

"Ever since the army he's looked to me for direction. His decisions are always wrong, really just impulses."

"You *let* him look to you for direction, he leans on you. Sucker."

Jacko went back to his chair and sat still, enduring it.

"I don't understand it," Thomas said. "How could you saddle yourself with this oddity, especially when you knew he was going downhill, after the Philippines scandal? A sense of noblesse oblige? You think you have to take care of this brutal incompetent just because of USC and fraternity brothers and all that juvenile hogwash?"

The old man had tolerated USC because it kept his grandson close to home. He himself had been sent to Harvard in 1849 by his father, Alexander, who had been told that Harvard was the oldest and most distinguished of American universities. Thomas, used to Spanish manners, had thought his father naïve. The one affection he had brought back, besides an Irish wife, was for his professor in Greek, old Apostolides, who had kept a pet chicken roosting on his shoulder and when dying had wept on being offered chicken broth, thinking it a decoction of his friend.

"Did you feel the need of a retinue for your lordship," Thomas said, "or a squire to your knighthood, a Sancho for your Quixote? Or just to have an ex-sergeant hanging around your defunct captaincy? Some of us have an unquenchable thirst for the company of inferiors. I hope not you."

"Please," Vincent said.

"He is good at the divorce business," Jacko said, "and anything rough, spying. Once in a while, breaking in for evidence."

"Breaking in?" Vincent said, startled. "You mean that you are burglars?"

Jacko considered the question. "Not really. Sometimes when the City Attorney wants evidence, he has some agency steal it. He can't steal it himself, the judge wouldn't admit it."

"You mean he would steal it if the judge would admit it."

"I suppose so. The thing is, if he buys the evidence from somebody else, it's legal, the judge allows it. That's the law. So Linebarger hires us. It's policy. It's legally okay. They need us to get convictions."

The old man banged his fist on the arm of his chair. "I detest your light-minded attitude toward such criminality. To you it is a game, a sport, a contest against the crooks. You are not sincere, you are playing at life. And you keep this Mike to do this dirty work. I can't believe you realize what you are doing. Get out of it. At least get rid of him, get out of the dirty side. Life is not a game."

"I *am* getting rid of him," Jacko said. "I made a mistake."

The old man sighed. "Mistakes. This Mike, your marriage. Where did all these mistakes come from?"

Jacko said nothing. The red of Thomas's face slowly grew darker.

"You know where they came from!" the old man suddenly cried, anger bursting out, hurt and confused because he didn't want to be angry. "It's the damned modern thinking! The playing around, the superficiality. It's that damned Edward the Seventh and his putrid court of pimps and false wits, that corruption of idleness and luxury that's become the fashion. A rotten, spoiled fatso that you people imitate, thank God he's dead. How could they call him the Peacemaker, with that ambitious little ass Churchill boosting the British navy to keep up with that lunatic Kaiser and the popinjay French with their new army? All heading right into a war anybody can see coming. Because the fools want it! They're crazy with wealth and power, they can't wait to begin killing people to prove how powerful they are. And George the Fifth concentrating the entire quarter ounce of his brain on the problem of killing fifteen thousand pigeons a year, I tell you, *there* is a really accomplished man!"

He slowed down and shook his head. "Power. Is that why you hooked up with this stupidity Mike Horton? To exercise your power over somebody?"

Jacko said quietly, "Will you sell the land?"

"Will you never give up?" the old man said, and subsided. His wrath was like the wind, rising and falling.

Outside, a pack of children ran down the dirt road toward their village, half a mile away. In a clearing among the trees, a couple of dozen small houses faced each other across the road. Playing in the dust, children and dogs amused themselves. Their fathers were usually invisible in the middle of the groves, up ladders picking in the trees, or following the mules pulling cultivators, spray wagons, down the middle of the trees, or laying bright metal irrigation pipes, or siphoning the water out of the big ditches down the rows. Their mothers too were invisible, rarely coming out of their houses. Three miles north there was another village.

"I saw most of them born," the old man said. "I know all the grandchildren. I'm not going to rip the ground from under their feet. No dice, Jacko, forget it."

Vincent leaned forward. "Jacko, why don't you give up, and come out here? God knows I could use the help. What are you building with this business? You sound like train robbers! The only real piece of money you've made was that reward for the *Times* bombing thing. How often do they have to blow up the *Times* building to make you rich? And you shot that on a third of an airplane. What an investment!"

"Don't let's start criticizing investments! What about you and the Knickerbocker Trust?"

"Don't be criticizing your father," Thomas said sharply. "If you want to criticize, pick on me, for building that damned palace you insist on living in, the king of Bunker Hill. Your father got caught in the panic of 1907, that's all. It wasn't his fault. But that damned palace was my fault, waste of money. In 1882 I thought I was rich. I thought I wanted to hobnob with rich grocers. I should have burnt the house for the insurance." He rolled up a cigarette tight and twisted the end. He got a kitchen match out of his overalls and scraped it alight on the floor.

"How is *your* hobnobbing getting along, Jacko?" He sucked in a deep drag off the cigarette and blew it out. "Maybe the desire to hobnob is an inherited trait. With your rich yachtsmen, your fellow airplane flyers, motor car racers, the wonderful people that I see you with in the society section. They're impressed by the house, hum? If only by the land value. Good for entertaining. Champagne. Not much champagne these days, eh, Jacko? I'm going to plant your landing field in soybeans next month."

"If we're going to discuss this," Vincent said, "let's do it in a friendly way." That was as far as he ever got with reproving his father. He rubbed his hands as though he were cold. He sat slightly hunched, turned a little away from his son. "It's just that—" He stopped; then, "It's just that we've all worked for the same thing, three generations, and now you've abandoned it, the first one."

They sat in silence. Through the little windows came the scraping sound of brake blocks on iron tires of wagon wheels, coming down the track; then the sudden fluttery blow of a mule's sneeze, the jangle of trace chains, and the four mules in harness went past the door, nodding their white-muzzled heads. Then came Fernando on the high seat, reins in hands, slapping them lightly, with indolent affection, on the rumps of the wheelers. Then the dozen varicolored partners of Jacko's youth, standing swaying in the wagon, hanging on to the slat sides, talking quietly, laughing, the lazy ones sitting on the tail, jean legs dangling, swinging in the slow dust. Slowly the creaking, the jingling, and tinkle passed down the road, fading music.

The cathedral silence of the groves returned; the sun shone through the doorway across the desk, reflecting on Vincent's grooved face, the empty coffee cup.

"It strikes me your business is a game, Jacko, playing at things. What will you build up in fifty years, compared to this?"

"This?" Jacko asked. "In fifty years they'll be building streets through the groves, and little houses. Why should I build up what I know will disappear? When they start building houses out here, they'll tax the groves out of existence, we'll have to quit."

"What's that got to do with right now?" Thomas said bitterly, and stamped out his cigarette. "Are you excusing some romantic sense of futility? Some philosophical drivel you picked up at USC? Too big a dose of Nietzsche and the rest of those dog-brained Germans? We should have sent you to Notre Dame."

Jacko said nothing. He felt no resentment at the old man's anger. As the Mexicans said, anger was the egg of fear. The old man was afraid of losing the groves, little by little. He was fighting off the first little.

"Why do we go on," Vincent said, "each gouging himself to split the interest on the loan? When we could sell the house on Bunker Hill and pay the Mormons off?"

Jacko sighed and shifted in the chair. "Why don't you sell it all out and go live by the sea in Santa Monica? You're old enough to rest."

"Sure, take a rest. And what happens to the two hundred people living on this place, where do they go? To live by the sea too?" Vincent turned away in his chair and back again. "The obvious thing is to sell that monstrosity you live in. Why do you insist on keeping it up?"

Jacko looked down. The "castle" represented the whole of his Los Angeles life, his root and anchor, the symbol of his substance, his style of life, that he would not surrender to the demands of the groves. In some vague way the big house had the feeling of his mother, as the groves had the feeling of Vincent.

Vincent's face softened. "An expensive sentiment." He picked up the knife and wiped it on the blotter. "The truth is, we should never have incorporated, got into this mess. At least in such a way, with three votes." He picked up one of the oranges.

"Even if grandfather voted against me and we sold the Bunker Hill property, I won't keep the groves when I inherit," Jacko said. He watched his father turn the orange around and around in his hand.

"I wouldn't either, in fifty years," Vincent said, "but now is now, Jacko. It's the people. Where should they go? Boyle Heights, with all those others?"

"Don't you ever get tired of it?"

Vincent picked up the open knife and sat looking at the orange. "Of course I get tired of it."

"Then why do you put up with it forever? The boredom, the same old dumb troubles, the stupidities the people always repeat, the eternal complaints, the ingratitude. Putting out money on a private hospital. You just get older, worn out, sick. They never give you any peace. And the trees. Nursemaiding the people, nursemaiding the trees. Don't you ever get sick of oranges?"

Vincent began cutting off a long helical ribbon of peel, starting at the blossom end. Jacko watched his father's hands, the deliberate, perfect execution of this feat. The ribbon came off without flaw, equal in width from one end to the other, curling toward the floor.

"And all for nothing," Jacko said.

Vincent silently peeled the other oranges. He handed one to Jacko and the other to his father. They sat in silence, eating the oranges.

Then Vincent said, "I would appreciate it if you would be sure to raise the $750 before you go to Mexico tomorrow. Begging those Mormons in San Bernardino for more time is a humiliation I can do without."

Jacko looked stubbornly at his knees. He could not explain to his father how the groves, the orange trees, brought a feeling of suffocation to his chest, a restlessness to get away, to the city where everything was fluid, active, nervous, brilliant, exciting even in failure, where life hurried by, not to be missed, events piled on events, faster and faster. The whole world, life itself, was going faster. But here, in the groves, nothing changed.

"Don't worry about the debt," Jacko said. He stood up. "This Mexican money will keep the Mormons from the door."

Vincent rose. He sighed and said, ending the visit, "Well, that's that." Then, reminded by departure of his manners, he said, "And how is your wife—May?" His voice was weak with unaccustomed hypocrisy, rising almost querulously on the name, as though he were pretending that he was not sure of it. He did it on purpose, Jacko thought, to maintain a distance he would never lessen. Vincent recognized his daughter-in-law only as a fraudulent institution, a quasi-wife, barely as a person with a name. It was an infection of prejudice Vincent had caught from Mary. She had detested the mixed marriage as a feeble-minded romantic gamble against all odds for happiness, and Jacko knew now she had been right.

She had found herself unable to be kind to May, to glaze over her disappointment and revulsion with a cheerful pretense, because her feelings were too deep for her to lie. He did not admire his mother for this, it was a virtue of defect, like the chastity of impotence. She could not lie even enough to blame May for his own stupidity in marrying her, in fact she did not blame her at all. She could hardly involve herself in blaming one whose existence she would have preferred not to recognize. It was an unkindness, rare in her, saddening to Jacko, who still understood that she could not, because of a rare weakness, overcome her feelings of revulsion.

Always the ghost of her wonder and worry about the eternally delayed grandchild had hovered over the steaming coffee cups of his dutiful visits and stifled their conversation, which at best had been, on her part, a flutter of evasions hovering over the all-important question of an heir, about which he could not tell the truth without the deepest offense to her. A ghost indeed, the thought of the tardy child still hung over the whole place as though it had died, rather than had simply been delayed. He supposed they blamed sterility; he had let the acceptable illusion stand for the truth they could not have endured.

One day he had come home unexpectedly to the "castle" on Bunker Hill. Hearing repeated heavy thumps on the floor above, he had listened at the door of the bathroom from which the sounds seem to come, and at the fourth thump had opened the door and seen his wife jump off the cover of the toilet seat, landing stiff-legged on the floor as heavily as she could. He had seen the blood on her bare ankle.

She had turned toward him, her face full of teeth in a snarl of pain and fury, a vision of a demon that struck him in the heart like a fist. He had shut out the face with the door, and stood with his hand on the knob setting his will like steel against his sudden outrage and grief, the ravening hunger to kill her that rose in him like a shriek. He had stood blind, outside time, holding on to his rage; then felt blood beat in his head again, and his vision came back. Through the roar in his ears came the sound of the flushing of the toilet, and he turned away before he murdered her.

He did not trouble to imagine how else she had been cheating him all the eight years of their marriage, with what whorish devices of self-sterility; but he knew instinctively, knowing her, why she had done it, and her increasing coldness over the years had been explained. He had not made the money she had expected. He had refused to become the manager of the million-dollar groves, he had made it clear that he would never work to make her more than comfortable. So she would have to wait for wrinkling years and years until Vincent died and her husband could sell the land. But that had not been her plan. Her plan had been to sell him a child if he would make her rich while she was young.

Slow death by penury, he thought in his rage, would suit her well. He would divorce her; he would pursue her, driving her from job to job, turn her into a two-bit whore eating out of garbage cans, and watch her die stinking in the last bed.

His rages did not wear well. The pain slowly dulled, he had learned to ignore it, even to smile coldly at himself, the fool she bought like a sheep by that fine body and bright, sly brain. Getting rid of her would be enough.

Because she had accepted so calmly, without comment, the end of his seeking her in bed after the murder, he knew that she too was now plotting to catch him out in a celibacy she knew might have proved too difficult for him. Adultery was the easy, cheap, direct way for them to ruin each other.

She did not intend to let him go without paying; he was determined to get rid of her for nothing. They vied, and failed, during a year of loud parties, to find means of leading each other into adultery by introducing into the house a series of charming sex baits. Now they waited, stymied, in the silent house.

From the time they reached their simple, implacable decisions, they had lived in the lavish house on Bunker Hill an even, peaceful life, preserving the innocence of the servants by speaking civilly and calmly about the daily news at breakfast and dinner table, while watching each other from remote internal distances, waiting for each other's passions to spring their individual traps.

Somewhere in the future, when he had got rid of the tramp, he would find the woman he should have married.

"So we still can't agree," Jacko said, "and we keep bleeding the interest."

The old man groaned and shifted in his chair. "This vanity about the house," Thomas said sadly. "Maybe it's that wife of yours. Is she behind your stubbornness? Does she insist on keeping it? Jacko, I am sorry for my evil bitter words. I hate to be angry. It's a sin to be angry. If it wasn't a sin, it would still be stupid. But I have to ask you one thing. Has she been false?"

"Please," Vincent said. "It's Jacko's business."

"His wife is family business, Vincent. Has she, Jacko?"

"Not yet. I am waiting to catch her."

"Why not get it over? Pay her off."

"Never. She has robbed me enough."

"Being robbed of a few years, that you can discount. Don't waste time. Find a good one."

"I don't want to go into that."

"Very well," the old man said. "I assume there are other reasons besides an irrational desire to win a battle without cost."

After a moment the old man turned sideways in the chair and looked at Jacko directly. "Listen, Jacko. The world is in a whirlwind. Don't be dazzled by it, or swept away. The big ones are so puffed up they do not see the bottom falling out from under their feet. I tell you because I love you, we have to stick more and more closely to the truth, to the Faith, to the old rules, the old values, the rock which has always stood. The new things are poison if they lead you astray, on strange roads, as in this sad marriage of yours. Liberal thinking! Everything is falling apart in this mad search for new things, the scientists poke and pry with their pathetic little curiosity, like apes, like this poor little Madame Curie who two years ago gets a prize for burning her fingers off with invisible powers.

"Leave this new craziness alone, meditate on the old truths. I tell you, what the wise have always known, the love of novelty is the mother of death.

"Now the millions can no longer live with anything old, but look for shiny new truths. They are so distraught with despair and lack of faith that they look for wisdom even between their legs, or drug themselves for what they think is an easy death, because they cannot stand the boredom of reality, which can only be relieved by love. They have already died in their hearts, and do not even know it. There are only the old truths, for us to widen and deepen with humility. What will bring the world to its senses? Meditation and love. Peace conferences? Pacts with enemies? Never. What might work is a terrible disaster, with millions destroyed, to bring everybody to their knees. A glory to God, if it worked. But how long would it work? We are all such fools."

Jacko sighed. He had heard it all before. He waited in silence a few moments before moving to go, out of respect for his grandfather's sincerity. Then he said, "I have to leave. I have to sell the car." He turned toward the door.

Vincent and Thomas rose and followed him. His grandfather gave him a hug and kissed his cheek, and smiling he kissed the old man's whiskers.

The father and grandfather stood watching the Stanley roll away down the slope through the white tree skeletons.

"He has no feeling for the grove," Thomas said, not by way of criticism, a sad fact.

"I know," Vincent said. "Nor the people either." He himself felt the trees almost as living persons. He would touch the leaves almost as other hands. He would contemplate the trees, standing there in their dresses of leaves, hands and arms of branches holding out their skirts of leaves and flowers for admiration, their fruit for praise.

The old man smiled, remembering. "He was such a good worker, all those summers." Then he said, with disgust, "Huh! And now he runs after rainbows." Vincent watched the car out of sight and turned back to the office. He would wait and watch the road.

In the car, passing again the great warehouse by the tracks, where the thousands of sacks of debt rose in the dark, Jacko thought: How can it be resolved? If grandfather dies, it becomes two votes, father's and mine, blocked. And how then can the deadlock be broken, before the debt eats us up? We can never repay, since the loss of those trees, out of income. We have to give up one thing or the other, either let the bankers foreclose on the mortgage and take the half-section of groves they hold as collateral, or sell the Bunker Hill property. Would a touch of resentment be too much to pay for solvency?

He passed the frozen windmill, its pump jack locked inside the little cabin to bang futilely forever in the faithless wind. That's the way we are, locked dead. The old man, out of what he thought was love, was balking like one of his mules, waiting for a miracle to change somebody, or something.

And they thought *his* business was a disaster! Jacko yanked down on the steam throttle in sudden anger, and the Stanley jumped forward like a hot goat, leaping and plunging over the potholes.

CHAPTER FOUR

T HE ALEXANDRIA stood yellow and square where it always would, proof against time, genial home away from home of the up-and-coming. From the entrance to the dining room, Jacko saw Linebarger, deep in the dim interior, ready for breakfast and reading the *Times*. At half-past eleven, the dining room was almost empty; Bill Linebarger liked to beat the noon crowd. The round tables, in blue-white shrouds, centered in their séance rings of empty chairs, stood as though now seating the spirits of dead patrons come late for a plate of nostalgia.

Now a waiter dressed in formal black and white came from the swing doors of the kitchens and stood looming tall and black over Linebarger, and Linebarger, folding his paper, sat hunched submissively, short and square, under his dominance. This priestly figure, with ancient badge of napkin over forearm, began transferring to the table from an immense oval tray of silvery pallor the burden of

Linebarger's breakfast of grapefruit, kippers, ham, eggs, four pieces of toast, and five kinds of jam, each dish covered by a silver helmet clapped on to defend it from the Sixth Street flies. The myriad tiny dents in these helmets, suffered in greasy kitchen wars, diffused about them reflections of distant light in velvety halos.

Linebarger viewed the distribution of these sacrificial offerings with head bent forward in an attitude which seemed to Jacko at once prayerful and vulturine, like that of some flesh-eating god. To Jacko, it was all quite religious in its smooth ceremoniality, easily reminiscent of his duties as altar boy at mass years ago.

Now the waiter bowed with an exquisite deference and backed off as from the Presence; and suddenly seeming to shrink magically to the size of a large, formally attired cockroach, sailed smoothly backward toward the kitchens.

Jacko sauntered up to the table. Having eaten his grapefruit and fish, Linebarger was by this time operating with knife and fork on his slice of ham, his elbows held close to his sides in equestrian fashion, knife and fork straight ahead, as though he were performing an appendectomy through a keyhole. The appearance of intense interest in the incision was merely the effect of the vulpine sharpness of his lower face, which contrasted with his rounded cheeks as the fox's sharp nose with his jovial ruff.

"Have a seat," Linebarger said without looking up, and poked a small square of ham into the small, dark hole of his mouth. "I was thinking of our social decline." He gestured with the fork toward the distant windows, through which came the horrific squawking of klaxons and beeping of bulb horns.

"I am thinking of *my* decline," Jacko said. "What's the trouble, Bill?"

"The trouble is that progress is getting out of hand. The great genie of science is refusing to go back in the bottle.

Out of the blessings of science and the simian curiosity of those white-coated bastards, we have created an overpowering, unmanageable demon. We ought to shoot the scientists before they wreck the world. Think of the thousands of tons of warships being built, of the thousands of tons of new smokeless gunpowder produced by Dupont, that servant of the people, of all the peaceful dynamite and other explosives granted us by Nobel, lover of peace."

"What the hell are you talking about?" Jacko said. "What's the story about the blackmail?"

"Oh, I didn't know you were in a hurry."

Jacko sat down.

"Too bad about your plane. You flew it so gracefully at that meet in San Fernando, at least until Herculano tried to saw off your wingtip with his propeller and you went into a spin. Congratulations on coming out of it. I understand not many do."

"The bastard was trying to kill me to win a twenty-dollar bet. He just can't stand to lose."

"Well, I guess that's what makes him the most successful smuggler in California. That'll teach you to go up against that big machine of his with your dinky little thirty-five-horsepower Green engine."

"The time before he bombed me with buckets of oil."

Linebarger laughed. "Poor little fellow! And there he is safe in his cabin."

"Screw you, Linebarger," Jacko said, getting up red in the face.

"Oh, sit down," Linebarger said, troweling boysenberry jam over a piece of toast. "Here, eat this. Cheer up and I'll tell you the dirt."

Jacko sighed and sat down again. "Shove your toast."

"How ungracious, Jacko. I won't feel forgiven unless you eat something with me. Last week I got a report on your bank accounts. Easy enough for us. Your balance was

$138. That's logical, considering nobody's called you for two months except that slimy fellow Palafox, as I happen to know. But Mike had a balance of $3,952. So what do you think about that?"

"Go on."

"Then, a while ago, a man came to us, the city, and confessed something nasty rather than keep on paying blackmail, to get us to stop the racket. We followed this up. We were watching the post office box the blackmailer used to get the money. He must have wised up that we were on to him, and got scared, because the demands stopped."

"So?"

"The connection is that you have been investigating this man, the complainant, for Adams and Forrestal, on a different subject, fraud. The blackmailing began just after you had closed your investigation. Which never turned up this fellow's perversion, just his fraud. At least it wasn't in your report. I checked that with Adams."

"No, I remember. Mike was on that."

"What's the implication?" Linebarger asked.

Jacko sat silent. "It isn't exactly proof."

"It isn't exactly a trial. But it implies something concrete enough, doesn't it?"

"Mike dug up the perversion and used it for himself," Jacko said.

"Okay?"

"Thanks. I wish there were more proof, more cases."

"Proof?" Linebarger asked. He leaned forward. "You've been ruined by what the lawyers think, not by a court conviction. That's the way it goes. Things get around the brotherhood. No attorney is going to hire your firm as long as Horton is in it."

"Sunk by a rumor."

"No, not by a rumor. By circumstantial evidence. Why are you defending him?"

Jacko said nothing.

Linebarger sat back. "You've got a long history of defending that turd."

Jacko smiled with half his mouth and shrugged. "Call it an obsession with reform."

Linebarger's fox face suddenly relaxed into a smile. "I've always thought reformers had a weakness for crime. They love it. They can't keep their hands off it."

"Neither can prosecutors," Jacko said, smiling, and stood up. "Thanks." He turned and left Linebarger wiping his smile with his enormous napkin.

Jacko stood again in the hall, key in hand, and read the black names on the frosted glass door, ripe for the razor blade to plow them off into little curls of folly lying on the floor.

He opened the doomed door. Mike, sitting in Jacko's lordly chair, the blade of his little red penknife hovering delicately over a broad thumbnail, looked up and searched Jacko's face with eyes questioning.

Jacko cleared his throat. Mike got up and moved to the clients' chair; Jacko, not to underline the usurpation, sat down on the windowsill. Looking at each other, they listened to the clang of streetcar bells and the occasional grinding squeal as a trolley went around the corner, showering a splutter of sparks from the overhead wire.

Jacko cleared his throat again. "They say, the lawyers, that you have been blackmailing people with bits of dirt you picked up on our jobs, and that's the reason they've quit hiring us, and the reason you've got $3,800 in the bank that never came from *this* business."

Mike's mouth suddenly compressed, and his eyes jumped open boldly. He started to leap up from his chair to make an outraged protest, was caught by the futility of it, sighed and sank back.

"Lies, Jacko," he said, without bothering to show much conviction. "How did you know about my bank account?"

"Why, Linebarger, as deputy prosecutor, just called up the bank and asked and they told him. What's your story?"

Mike smiled with a lip-curl of contempt. "Jackasses. That's gambling money, not blackmail. Where did they get the idea of blackmail? They don't like me, never did. It's a lie. I'd never do such a thing, even if it was legal—too dangerous. I've been playing the horses at Santa Monica."

Jacko looked at him sadly. "Mike, I can get your fingerprints on the application for the post office box. That's enough to jail you. But even suppose it's all just a mistake? It makes no difference. The lawyers *think* it's blackmail, and that's what counts. If they won't have you, we're through as partners. Get this: you're out, through, done, finished, the partnership is busted, as of now. Get out."

"Now wait a minute, wait a minute," Mike said, standing up, pushing a palm out, "not just so goddam fast. I got rights in this business. It may be busted, but not right now. There's the accounts receivable, maybe not much, and there's the Mexican job coming up, I got a claim on that the minute we took it. Besides that," he said, the blaring of claims softening to a half-smiling appeal, "you need me, Jacko, you need somebody at your back, if there's fighting. You can't go alone."

"He ruins my agency," Jacko said, to the wall, "and now he's concerned for my back."

Mike's face tightened, the placating palm dropped to his side. "All right, never mind my friendship. You can't do me out of my share of that fee. I got $6,000 coming."

"You've got a boot in the ass coming, fifteen years late. And maybe a few years in prison."

"Prison? Some friend! You can't screw me out of my money with threats. I got a legal and moral right to the reserve money."

"I don't want you with me on that trip."

"Then pay me off. Give your half of the reserve money. That's $2,500."

"I can't do that. I can't work broke."

"Well, can I?" There was victory in Mike's eyes.

Jacko stood looking at him. He could ruin Mike with the city; with a little work, he could put him in jail. The poor, stupid bastard.

Jacko turned away to the window. After all, he thought, looking down at the mob, the son of a bitch did have the right to the money.

His anger was cooling. With Mike out, he thought, he could start fresh. And suddenly he was sorry for him. He turned from the window and looked at Mike's smiling stupid cherub mouth. There Mike stood with victory in his eyes and the shirt off his back, ruined. What would the poor simple loony do for a living with nobody to tell him what to do? Hire out as a strongarm for some gang? Blackmail? He didn't even have wits enough to keep his own nest clean, and that was the pity of it.

Pity! Here he'd picked up this poor three-legged dog and taken care of him for fifteen years, out of a habit of addled compassion, a damn fool himself, hoping that the mutt would grow another foot. Thomas would have shot him through the head out of love and mercy.

"All right, Mike, but I go to Mexico alone. You'll get your money when I get back."

"The hell I will. I'll get it in Guaymas, the minute we get paid. You think I'd trust you after this?"

Jacko burst out laughing. "All right. I guess we can stand each other for another two weeks. I'll see you tonight for the train job."

As he locked the door on his way out to see Palafox, he remembered Mike's look of victory. There should have been some regret, after fifteen years, and some sorrow or shame for what he had done. He realized with sudden, cold clarity that the Mike he saw now was not the one he had imagined he was looking at for fifteen years. Somewhere along the line, or all along the line, Mike had changed by imperceptible degrees. A sharper man, no longer so helpless. It was himself, not Mike, that was the fool.

"Hurry up!" he bawled down the shaft in a sudden storm of exasperation.

Something poked the back of his shoulder. He turned around. Mike had come up soundlessly behind him. Mike smiled, one of his stinking cigars pooched out in his curlicue lips. He removed the cigar with a certain elegance.

"I thought I'd better come along," he said. "To protect my rights."

Jacko looked at him from a hundred miles away.

Mike's complacent smile died, leaving only tired gloom. "Oh shit, Jacko," he said. "Oh hell."

Jacko contemplated the look of appeal, of softness. Was this a con? Had it always been a con, this helplessness? He remembered something his grandmother had said: "Beware a helpless man! Inside him there's a hyena to eat you up." And the same for a helpless woman, thinking of May. Why was he forever the fool sucker for the helpless? Or was that the root of it?

They stood side by side listening to the cage rattle its golden bones up from the depths, a misfiring resurrection, the cables slapping their black applause.

Jacko refused to feel, to think, and stood like a stone.

CHAPTER FIVE

SEÑOR LORENZO Plutarco Sepeda y Palafox (El Magnifico), the Mexican consul for Los Angeles, had as his combined residence and office a suite in the fourth (top) floor of the Hotel Cordova, immaculate white at the corner of Eighth and Figueroa. Jacko, crossing Figueroa toward the hotel on the opposite corner, noted the stout figure of the Consul standing in a blaze of white suit at his sunny apartment window, high above.

Jacko gave a glance at the square, blocky faces of the Aztec gods whose cast concrete grimaces decorated the hotel façade at intervals—a dash of romance by the architects, who had made the gods look very contented, instead of traditionally hungry. Perhaps the Consul had chosen the Cordova because the old gods made him feel at home, appealing to a drop of Aztec in his own blood.

The reason for the combined residence and office was that it discouraged the Magonista anarchist cells from burglary. They badly needed money. If El Magnifico had an office separate from his residence, they would break into the office while he was at his residence, or into his residence while he was at the office, to steal his money, blank passports, his liquor, and indeed even his pajamas, as the Magonistas had need of everything.

As things were, with Palafox living in a fort on the fourth floor with access to the roof for sunbaths and .22 pistol practice (he was an excellent shot) and with the desk clerk and hotel detective blocking the way, not counting a robust and secretly armed elevator boy, there was not much hope for the Magonista burglars.

Palafox knew the Magonistas would never try to kill him in the street, no matter how much they hated him or how easy it would have been to do. If the Magonistas had killed him, God knew what kind of replacement that murdering Indian dog General Huerta, President of Mexico by virtue of assassination, would have sent to replace him. Better a devil they knew. After all, he was an old-line Porfirista with some sense of honor, left over after the great stone god Porfirio had fled from Madero's revolution with his large family and trunks to Paris, leaving the mess to that sniveling, lying little capitalist Madero. In turn, Palafox was left over from Madero after Huerta had murdered the poor little man.

This survival through the throes of presidential succession was not remarkable, and indeed all the Mexican consuls along the border had lasted well, as each administration, having done away with its predecessor, had still to employ the consuls in entrapping, extraditing (or kidnapping), and killing the successive cliques of rebels living in the United States. As always, the tyrants strove to preserve the bureaucracy, without which they could not tyrannize, no matter how insouciantly they might slaughter other politicians.

In the alley behind the hotel, across from the abandoned

56

stables where Palafox kept his magnificent Pierce Arrow, there was a steel back door to the hotel for which Jacko had a duplicate key. He led Mike through the basement, saluting in passing their friend the house dick, up the freight elevator, and down the hall to the Consul's 4C—knock-knock, pause, knock-knock. Señor Palafox, shining in his Palm Beach suit and glacé white pointed shoes, opened the door and led them through a little foyer to the front room, overlooking Figueroa.

The Consul's eyes twinkled with slightly sadistic humor, the three-carat water-clear diamond on his left little finger glittered superbly in the brilliant sunshine coming through the window. This effect was increased greatly, though secretly, by a bit of gold foil concealed beneath the diamond in the closed setting, just as some clever cutting concealed a bit of regrettable clouding of the stone. The large, quite genuine pearl in his tiepin gleamed and glowed like heaven's gate, as silky as his smile.

In a corner of the room, stuffed tightly into the angle like a poor relation shoved out of the way, sat a sardonic mockery of Palafox's graceful self, his half-brother Herculano Santana. Where Lorenzo Palafox was plumply nimble, mobile, gracious, smiling, constantly conducting an invisible orchestra while he talked, with both expressive hands, sometimes with arms, Herculano Santana sat like a great, squat block of rock chopped out by some Aztec god-carver halfway to human shape and then given up in disgust. The white light from the window struck sharp shadows across a face as set, square, stiff as the cast-concrete images stuck to the wall outside. His head, black hair *en brosse*, was square as a box, his bull neck as wide as his head, rising out of a welter of rumpled tan worsted suiting that wrestled with a body as stiff as a bottle. His chest was such a barrel that the heavy arms hung away

57

from his sides as though he were perpetually ventilating his armpits.

This figure, Jacko thought, might have been funny except for the feeling people got from the look on the big, dead block of a face, that Herculano might at any moment leap out of his chair and sink his teeth into their throat.

The god-carver had laid out this face with a T square and sawn it out of stone. The jaw was wide as the bottom of a bucket, the chin jutted forward with an effect of battleship aggression, commanded from above by a lipless mouth sliced straight across. This grim line was repeated by an exactly parallel straight black moustache as thin as a knife and precise as a death sentence, a bit of pretentiousness that made the mouth and the jaw seem all the more deadly.

Above this prissy accent a small, hooked nose peeked out from the wide expanse of olive cheeks, like the beak of an octopus waiting to rend and tear, and huddling close on each side of this merciless little beak were two small baby-blue stones for eyes peeking out of their holes, each surrounded by short, wide-spaced bristles of eyelashes as startlingly black, sparse, and distinct as those of a baby doll. Jacko knew that their expression of wide-eyed idiocy was entirely a genetic accident. There was nothing idiotic about Herculano, who was one of the first to find out how to pull a plane out of a tailspin.

"My half-brother Herculano Santana," Palafox said, waving an arm toward this fixture in the corner by the window. "But of course you have met! How foolish of me! In fact, if I recall, Señor O'Donohue, you once had the pleasure of a ride in his aeroplane, did you not?"

"Not quite that," Jacko said pleasantly, "but close." A year before, he and Santana had raced their planes to Santa Barbara on a small bet, planning to land on the beach where there would be plenty of witnesses to the victor. It had been neck and neck until they hit a head wind over Fernal Point, and Herculano's boxy cabin Avro began to fall back. Unfortunately, Jacko thought this a good occasion for a little taunting, fell back too, and pulled ahead again, grinning at Herculano alongside, and the next time he fell back in his stupid game, Herculano came at him with the obvious purpose in his dead-set man-eating face of ramming him, which he did, clipping off eight inches of Jacko's right wing with his propellor. The result was a panic-stricken crash landing on the East Beach at Santa Barbara, wrecking the plane and breaking Jacko's right thigh.

All he had meant to do, Herculano later explained with a death's-head smile, standing at the side of Jacko's hospital bed, was to scare him; but whatever his intention, Jacko had been forced to swallow a defeat in a suit against Herculano in which he could prove nothing. The landing runway he had cleared at the bottom of the groves, by the old skull fence, had gone back to thistles and morning glory.

Smiling at Herculano now, Jacko felt the pleasant warmth of his resolve to get double his money's worth out of Herculano, as soon as the chance came up.

One of Herculano's baby-blue eyes blinked at him and the knife-slit mouth quirked on one side in friendly recognition. Herculano didn't dislike him, Jacko knew, Herculano thought he was funny. One day, Jacko thought, he would kick the octopus beak nose through the back of Herculano's head.

"My brother has shown an interest in the monstrance," Palafox said, as though Herculano were ten miles away, or stuffed. "An altruistic interest, I should say"—laugh—"as he isn't commercially concerned with such small, uh, tomatoes. He feels that the reward will be what you call a

59

nest egg for me—what a charming metaphor!—in these times so perilous and uncertain for a Mexican consul."

He pirouetted toward a chair and waved Jacko and Mike toward two others beside a tabouret where stood three beers. After the usual *cómo estás* and inquiries as to families, the Consul poured the beers and they proceeded to discuss in quiet voices events of general interest, this to avoid an impolite plunge into business, which would have offended Palafox's penchant for endless diplomacy. They discussed the building of the Southwest Museum, the remarkable large bones raised from the tar pits out on the old La Brea rancho; the unfortunate freezing of Captain Scott at the South Pole; how, or whether, the new income tax law would affect the resident alien, that is, Palafox.

All through this, Herculano sat like a poor relation, silent and remote in the corner. Jacko would have thought he was dead except for the bright little eyes in their bristle of baby-doll lashes, moving with lizard jerks from speaker to speaker.

Jacko knew he was anything but a poor relation. Nobody had ever found out how much money Herculano was making out of his smuggling racket, because the take was all in Switzerland; but Herculano's wealth must have been immense to permit him to wear such cheap suits and so little of the jewelry which Palafox displayed to conceal his own spendthrift poverty. Poor rumpled Herculano was able, for example, to order by cable, credit unquestioned, the new model cabin Avro from the works of Sir Alliott Verdon Roe in England.

Who was paying the rent here? Probably Herculano. Who had paid for the Pierce Arrow? Probably Herculano. Why should not Palafox be a spendthrift? Who would not, with such a brother? For Herculano loved his little brother with a maternal passion so jealous and intense that few girls dared to flirt with young Lorenzo.

One proof of this had been the fate of a gentleman who had, one evening in a crowded restaurant, called Palafox a queer, making Palafox scream and chatter with rage like a monkey. Herculano had prevented Palafox from running for his pistol, instead repairing his reputation later that night by scattering the gentleman's body parts on his front lawn, each neatly wrapped in white butcher paper and labeled Head, Left Arm, Right Foot, Privates, Intestines, and so on. The slur on Palafox was never heard again.

"As to our immediate concern," Palafox finally said, delicately wiping beer from his small moustache with a large, immaculate pink handkerchief, "as I said, I will pay you $12,000 for the job, on your return here with the $60,000 reward. That is, if you survive," Palafox smiled amiably. "I think the fee is fair. The piece is worth $600,000, according to the chancery letter from Mexico City. The finder's fee would then be $60,000, which I get, of course, and your fee in turn for finding the reward, so to speak, would be $6,000, except that I am an unusually generous man by nature and the transaction will be a little dangerous. So I am making it $12,000, leaving me $48,000. I trust you are not only satisfied, but pleased— and I would be truly hurt if you weren't, and so would you, because if you objected, I would get somebody else." He laughed heartily. "Of course, I jest."

He left the room and came back with three more beers, ignoring Herculano. "You are to return this valuable piece of furniture to the Church of Mexico, precisely the church at Guaymas, where the parish priest is waiting for it with the reward money. Furniture?" He frowned. "Is that correct? Not chairs!" He smiled brightly again. "The monstrance. I take it, Señor Horton, you are familiar with the monstrance as a species?"

"An animal?" Mike asked. "Some kind of tropical animal?" He despised Señor Palafox and, with the instinct of a medieval jester, believed that by reducing himself to a fool, he could somehow elevate the Consul on a pin of mockery with perfect impunity.

The Consul smiled the cramped, narrow smile which, with him, expressed a desire to kill somebody, or at least to grind his toes into the floor with his heel.

"No, Señor Horton, it is a rather large, ornate—could you call it a very large setting for a jewel, so to speak, Señor O'Donohue? In this case, as described for me in the letter of the chancery, it is a sort of symbol of the sun, a sunburst made of gold, radiating golden rays from the center, in which, in a small glass box, or pyx as they call it, the Blessed Sacrament is sometimes placed to be exhibited to the people in churches at certain times for adoration. This sort of golden sun is about forty centimeters—what's that? fifteen, sixteen inches?—in diameter, on a gold stand. The whole thing is decorated with jewels. It is the jewels chiefly which make it of value, aside from its artistic merit. Do you have a comprehension now, Señor Horton?" His lower lip smiled, the upper one sneered. Mike looked confused, as intended.

"It has much added value as a museum piece. In fact as a museum piece it would be worth much more than the total value of gold and jewels, broken down. Yes."

"Have you been thinking of breaking it down?" Jacko asked. "If it is not an impertinence to inquire?"

"Hum. Well, one does think of such things, naturally. They cross the mind. But one would not destroy a work of art. Besides, it would be difficult to sell to a museum in this country. Perhaps less so in Europe. Especially in the Netherlands, which has always hated Spain and would be delighted to rob her of something, despite all poor Spain's effort to civilize that pathetic fringe of German rejects. Two virtues they are noted for, cleanliness and stubbornness, twin children of their mother the mud. Alas, how pitiful, that this little subtribe of retarded Teutons, driven into the sea by their superiors, those fat and jolly German barbarians, should have been forced to survive by shoveling up islands of mud to sit on. One suspects that Rembrandt had more than a drop of Spanish blood. How else to account for such grandeur of talent?

"One might try the Rijksmuseum," he went on with a dreamy expression, "or if what one asked was too much for those waterlogged misers, one could go to the Germans, who feel such a vast need for *Kultur*, perhaps the Museum für Kunst und Kulturgeschichte in Dortmund. My brother has dealt with them in his traffic of pre-Columbian bits and pieces. Europe is beginning to understand the value of these fragments—unfortunately just as my government is beginning to feel that having a cannibal for an ancestor is something to boast of." He laughed.

"But seriously, the provenance of the monstrance is certified, I have it all along with the chancery letter. It was made by Antonio de Arfe around 1540, and signed. A very famous goldsmith of Spain, he was.

"A work of a great artist, minor, of course, probably for a city parish church, but extremely valuable nevertheless. But not for sale, after all, and a trip to Europe to dispose of it is only an idle dream, an amusement for an afternoon."

"And what about a reward for the capture of the thieves?" Jacko asked.

"Frankly, señor, we are not interested in capturing them. What would we do with them? My government is fatigued with the cost of extraditions. Preferably, the thieves would simply be caused to disappear."

"You are not suggesting, I hope, that I—"

"No, no," exclaimed Palafox, "I would not dream of asking you to involve yourself in anything so—Well, perhaps another subject. Perhaps you would be interested in the provenance of the theft, so to speak.

"The Rivera swine were in Morelos looking for money from that other swine, Zapata, murderer and thief, the so-called Angel of the Poor, hang them all. You know he is the only rebel swine with money, because he controls with his army of monkey peasants and unspeakable Indians the whole state of Morelos, and threatens the rich *hacendados* to burn up their fields and barns and murder them and their families unless they pay him, the swine, *la extorsión*—" In his excitement he was having a little difficulty breathing.

"It infuriates me to think that that rampaging jackal of the garbage heaps"—pant pant—"Indian cannibal *bastardo*, son of a maggot, bred by a pustulated pimp's spawn"—pant pant—"I must stop, I myself enrage so that I will myself burst if I do not soon kill at somebody."

He gripped the arms of his chair as though to hold himself back from murder, panted some more, and finally swallowed heavily, gave a great sigh. "So much for the Magonistas. Church robbers. Swine. But do not permit me to start again.

"As I say, these Rivera thieves were down there begging money from Zapata, and he refused them, naturally. But he put them up to stealing the monstrance from the Cathedral to get rid of them. So they dressed up as priests and stole it right off the altar, right in front of a hundred old crones during the Forty Hours, and escaped to the north. And yes, we will be meeting them when the train stops at Pomona and put an end to their villainy."

"You mean we are to arrest—"

"No, you board the train, pretend to be Magonistas. You will tell the Riveras that I am waiting at the Los Angeles terminal to arrest them. You have come, you will say, to take them to safety in Los Angeles in an automobile—mine, of course.

"If we had a shooting on the train, who could tell what might happen? Better a little subterfuge. Then we can take them to some out-of-the-way place and—well—we will see. And of course you will give them the current password, which my spies told me last night. *'Sangre y pan.'* Strange taste, to say the least, blood and bread. Typical savagery. Cannibals like their ancestors."

"And then?" Jacko asked.

"Then, tomorrow morning you will come here and I will visa your passports and give you the letter from the Archbishop's chancery and expense money and the tickets and my letter of authorization. And then you will sail at eleven o'clock on the Mexican freighter *La Paz* with the monstrance to Guaymas. It is not very fast. It will take about seven days.

"She is taking a cargo of arms and ammunition which I had the good fortune to purchase here, to the Federal Army in Guaymas. Thank God for your great Winchester and Remington companies!

"After you have got the money, you will come back by the same ship, which will return for more arms. If the rebel swine have not occupied Guaymas before you get there, you will have no trouble at all."

"And if they have?" Jacko asked.

"Very unlikely! But let me caution you about this Padre Miguel who is holding the money. The police watch him. His housekeeper is a police spy, like most rectory housekeepers these happy days under the esteemed General Huerta, who suspects everybody, the drunken luna—Excuse me! I must have been thinking of Madero.

"Well, then, when you see this Padre Miguel, just take the money and get back on the *La Paz*, which will be returning for another load of rifles, ammunition, bombs, and so on to carry on the war."

"How about expense money?" Jacko asked.

"A thousand?"

"Very well," Jacko said, standing up. "We will meet you here at six."

"Better at the stable across the alley where I keep my car," Palafox said, also rising.

Jacko lifted a hand in farewell at the body of Herculano in the corner. No response. As he and Mike went toward the door, Palafox made a gesture of touching Jacko's arm with a delicate forefinger, without actually touching. "Señor O'Donohue, if I might presume, could you wait a moment? There is a tedious matter of accounting which need not detain Señor Horton."

"Of course," Jacko said. He saw Mike out the door. "Meet me at my house at five-thirty," he said. "And bring handcuffs." He closed the door and turned back to Palafox.

Mike stood in the hall looking at the closed door. Thrown out. What would they be talking about? Some plot to rob him of his split? Jacko, so courtly, so suave, with that greaseball. Suppose Jacko fell suavely off the ship one night? He smiled sadly, knowing he could never give the push. Still, many other things could happen.

Mike turned and ran down the hall, on the way to May.

Jacko, about to push open the door of the apartment to go back in, heard the brothers talking. Their words were muffled by the door. He quietly let himself into the little foyer and stood listening.

"Why don't you let me sell it in Europe?" Herculano was saying. His voice rose. It was a voice ill-matched to the powerful body, a tight, almost womanish tenor. "I could stuff it down some German's throat for half a million. Isn't that the chancery evaluation?"

"But, Herculano, my reputation! My career! A little fiddling and diddling with the customs, yes, I have helped you out, but—"

"Reputation! Who cares? With a half a million earning fifteen percent on whorehouse mortgages in Berne, who needs a reputation?"

"But my career? If I don't return the thing, how long do you think I would be a consul?"

"How long anyway, Lorenzo? How long can that old drunk Huerta stand? Look at all the dogs in the pack after him, those power-grabbers like Carranza and Obregón, that lunatic Villa. They will pull Huerta down and then all the Porfiristas like you will be finished for good. You want to shine shoes on Temple Street? Be a waiter in the Alexandria? Teach Spanish to amorous spinsters who have nothing better to do than ogle a bankrupt politician?"

"Herculano, I have never criticized you and your ways. Bless you, dear brother. But my honor hurts at the thought, I cannot—uh—"

"Can't steal?" Herculano laughed in his thick throat like a far-off gun, ack ack ack. "Don't hide behind that relic of a conscience of yours, you're just afraid of being caught. Who is to catch you? Who cares but the buggery Church? Listen, I have the perfect museum, the Schnutgen Museum in Cologne, they specialize in religious art and they are only open since 1907, in four years they haven't half filled their pathetic galleries, they are raving hot for acquisitions. Perfect!"

"I can't think, I can't think, Herculano, leave me alone. No, no, my honor rebels, I could not live with myself!"

"What is it the chicken says? *Crawk crawk crawk.* It is time you grew out of that hidey-hole, this honor of yours. Who do you think you are? Don Quixote?"

"Enough, Herculano, you have your way, I have mine. With $48,000, little as it is, I can buy a rich widow here in Los Angeles. Enough!"

Jacko backed silently out of the foyer into the hall, closed the door quietly, and then knocked loudly. The voices stopped. The door opened. Palafox stood in the foyer wiping his forehead with his pink handkerchief.

"Ah! come in, come in," he said, puffing up his chest and recovering himself with a smile turned glassy by Herculano's exhausting assaults on his conscience. "I trust all goes well with your assistant? Those cigars!" he said as they went back into the living room, where Herculano was seating himself again in the corner. "Cannot Señor Horton afford something better?"

Jacko almost liked Palafox. He felt rather a reserved but relenting personal sympathy, a tolerance rendering Palafox's pomposities and prejudices more quietly amusing than fatiguing. He liked Palafox in the same way he would have liked a caged and sleepy cougar.

"I asked you to stay, señor," Palafox said, "on a matter more delicate than mere accounting, and I hesitate to enter into it because it entails, or might entail, if I should inconceivably permit such to exist, an element of possible discourtesy; for if I were to raise any question, or even suggest the existence of one, about Señor Horton, it would unavoidably be a reflection upon yourself, a thing not even to be contemplated, and wholly contrary to that esteem in which you are so universally held.

"At the same time, a degree of prudence, inspired by the fact that we will be dealing with \$60,000, forces me to the very painful act—which may honorably be subsumed under my general duties—to inquire in a manner as delicate as possible, and with a total abhorrence and denial of any intention to offend, even in the most minuscule or negligible way, whether or not—" He hesitated.

"On the other hand," he began again, "perhaps I could make my point by saying that for myself I have the highest regard for you and most easily confide in you my complete trust; for knowing of your illustrious family, and that you are the descendant of that eminent family, the Quiñoneses, still so highly regarded by the upper classes of Mexico, and moreover having myself the honor of the acquaintance of your most esteemed father and grandfather, I take much relief and encouragement in trusting to you the burden of ransoming this holy object, and am grateful beyond power of expression that you have agreed to employ your courage and ingenuity, whose verity I know well from the past, in confronting certain elements of danger, but—still—How can I present my thought without trespass? Perhaps you realize it already."

"I am most honored," Jacko said, also in Spanish, "by your trust and value much those sentiments of respect you have shown to my family.

"As to your concern, which I venture is a certain doubt as to the qualities of my partner, I hasten to assure you that you need have no care that he may, being as you know, of a character more forceful than consistent, prove erratic, not to say false, in carrying out your commission, for he has always been most compliant to my commands; and while I sympathize and agree with certain aspects of your estimation of possibilities, that is, to put it in language whose directness, while always disagreeable, is nevertheless permissible in an exigency, that he might run away with the money, given the opportunity, I feel that I can rely on years of experience with him, that his devotion to me, if not to my standards of conduct, is fully sufficient to disqualify him from so dishonorable an act."

Consul Palafox gave a great sigh. "I am so relieved, Señor O'Donohue. Oh, you cannot imagine the difficulties of my existence in your amazing and complicated country!" He fell back into a chair and rubbed his forehead as though by erasing his wrinkles he could banish his worries.

John Cunningham

"Alas, life here for a simple man is a continual turmoil—dealing with such a bouillabaisse of attitudes, customs, morals, ethics, religions, cults, manners, accents! Your melting pot!

"It is such a relief to talk to one who has, to a certain extent, my own, my country's simplicity of belief, custom, and manners, and that iron respect for the surfaces of life which prevents our dissolution into the barbarities of the unconscious. It is so good to talk to a friend! even across our political frontiers.

"And on top of all that, for more confusion, here I have served three masters in two years, the great Porfirio, who blessed our country with such magnificent progress and so many railroads; then that small yet spiritually gigantic man, Madero, whom I learned to love totally in just a little week after Don Porfirio left us for Paris. Ah, Madero! the gentlest, most humane benevolent of Christians, and never mind his Ouija board, a veritable saint, who was so tragically eliminated in that automobile accident, in which so many mysterious bullet holes in the automobile later were discovered by General Huerta to have been shot much much earlier—and now that stern and loyal figure of discipline, our supremely esteemed Huerta himself, of whom it simply is not true that he is always drunk, who stepped in the breach and rescued our country and who is not a smelly, disgusting Indian at all, as that ridiculous rumor has it.

"Can you understand the difficulties of adjustment? The life of a Mexican consul in this country is one long puzzle, rendered sane only by our chief purpose—the rounding up of the enemies of the Mexican government, whatever that happens to be at the moment, and shipping them across the border so that they may be shot as soon as possible, or sometimes, to save ammunition for national defense, simply strangled.

70

"One element of signal good fortune penetrates the confusion—no matter what our Mexican administration may be, the enemies are always the same, that is, any opposition whatsoever. Alas, your country is so generous, and welcomes everybody, both sheep and goats. I could wish, without being presumptuous, that it would welcome fewer goats, that is, these exile rebels—there must be twenty thousand of them. But then, what would I do if they were not here to be pursued, to relieve the monotony of my sunbaths on the roof?

"Ah, well," he concluded, rising with a smile and offering his glittering hand to Jacko, "life is what it is, wherever one is, is it not? I thank you for your reassurance and I shall look forward with pleasure to seeing you at six o'clock."

"Until then, Your Excellency," Jacko said, shaking hands and making a suggestion of a bow. Why not, *excelencia*? Palafox was too astute to be deceived by flattery, but good-humored enough to enjoy it.

He left the building by the alley and turned left toward Figueroa, to head for home and get his daily report on May's goings-on from Lilly, the agent he had planted in the house as a maid.

He heard the rapid tap of heels behind him and glanced back. Herculano was pounding along, granite-block body on thick granite-block legs torturing the seams of his cheap suit. Jacko stopped and waited. Herculano came up and stood beside him, looking across Eighth Street. Jacko turned and saw Paz Faz and Gavira, side by side, leaning against the wall of a building, watching him. The face of short Gavira, a gloomy moon made of Monterey Jack, did not change, but that of Paz Faz, lean and handsome like his narrow dancer's body, smiled with a twist of mockery, as of one professional enemy to another.

"Anarchists," Herculano said quietly and spat on the

sidewalk in their direction. "Little shits. They are always hanging around here, dreaming of killing my brother. That's all they have, dreams." He stood silent. Then, "They are too little to kill," and shrugged his heavy shoulders.

He turned and standing close looked at Jacko. "I am glad you are Lorenzo's friend." The doll's eyelashes gave him a look of humility and innocence Jacko knew was anything but. Herculano moved a little closer. "I trust you, Jacko," he said softly.

First names! Was he being invited into a friendship with this sonofabitching murderer? What was coming? Trust from Herculano was too great a weight to bear. He would much prefer shooting it out with him to accepting a trust from him; the consequences of failure would be much less painful.

"I'm not exactly honored," Jacko said.

"Oh, come on," Herculano said, "after all, it was simply a sporting event, that little matter of the plane. Surely you don't hold anything against me?"

Herculano moved closer. "I know you will work for my brother honestly and loyally," he said, almost in a whisper. "I know that you will never deceive or defraud him. This is such a relief to me, I do not have to worry, as I would with other men. I have the greatest confidence. I know you will always protect Lorenzo, and will not fail to bring his money back to him."

There was something almost hypnotic about the soft little voice. Jacko felt as though he were being gently wrapped in barbed wire.

Herculano moved closer, until his eyes were only a foot from Jacko's. "I trust you absolutely, old flying *compadre*, never to do the least little thing that would hurt my brother in any way. I trust you because I know you are an honorable man."

"You owe me a plane," Jacko said.

"What plane?" Herculano backed a step. A tiny smile cracked the wax on his tiny moustache. "Good day to you, Jacko my friend, have a good trip." He bent his granite-block head on his stump of a neck in a tiny bow and turned away.

Jacko watched him cross Figueroa. Across the street, Paz Faz was grinning at him. Jacko walked on. Anarchists! Revolution! In Los Angeles the revolution was like the report of a very dull, slow game of chess, a mere symbol of a war whose cannons in the desert were a dream.

CHAPTER SIX

L ILLY, JACKO's hired spy, opened the massive front
door for little Becky Horton, and smiling warmly
showed her into the cold mortuary of a parlor. She
went back to the still open front door and slammed it
home with a terrifying crash. A morning gift to her mistress May, upstairs.

The sound boomed up the grand baroque stairway to
May's startled ears. She jerked upright in bed. A sizzling
rage rose in her head. That damned Lilly! Why did she always slam the doors?

She swung her beautiful legs out of bed, gathered her
peignoir over her peach and cream silk pajamas and stood
up. Eleven-thirty, ticked the little gold watch on her delicate wrist. Mike would be coming along any time now.
She headed for the door, heard the thump of Lilly's heavy
feet on the stairs, the grunts of labor as she climbed. She
put a hand to the high massed gold of her hair in a gesture
partly of fatigue at the impossibility of dealing with this

lump of an old Irish potato Jacko had foisted on her, partly to reassure herself of her own existence. When she touched her hair, particularly at the back, she knew she was still there.

Lilly came into the room, her grizzled head under its tiny white maid's cap bent down as usual, her thick barrel of a body puffing forward like a doughty engine, propelled by two stumpy piston-legs.

May awaited her with hatred, her upper lip lifted in contempt.

"There's little Mrs. Becky Horton below to see you," Lilly said, looking at May's slender bare pink and alabaster feet.

"You ass! I told you I wasn't at home! Why did you let her in?"

"Yes, ma'am," Lilly said.

Oh God, May groaned in her heart. She didn't care if Lilly knew she hated her, things had gone so far in this disastrous house that appearances no longer mattered. And Jacko wouldn't fire her.

May slipped on her mules with their puffs of eiderdown and hurried past her. Downstairs, she saw Becky sitting in the gloom on the edge of an ottoman, in her usual awkward show of social unease, and sailed into the great parlor, her peignoir flowing in the air behind her like a glistening cloud. She stood looking with a sneer at Becky's smart little morning outfit of verdigris wool with jolly belt and collar of a plaid taffeta, yellow and gray. She knew where Becky had picked it up, at the Mart on Ninth, the cheapest copier in Los Angeles, $10.

"I suppose I've come too early, dear May," said Becky, springing up like a bird off a twig, "but such a wonderful idea occurred to me." She hovered in the air a moment and then alighted again.

May forced a skull's smile, but did not sit down. She

glanced out the side window at the view down Grand Avenue. No Mike in sight.

"I'm so sorry, Becky," she said. "I was just getting ready to go out."

"Oh, then, I won't stay but a minute." Becky looked around the great room, dark in the majestic height of its ceiling. Cobwebs were quietly growing in the upper corners; it had been months since there had been a maid spry enough to disturb them. "Such a lovely house!"

"For two cents I'd burn it to the ground," May said.

The misery of this remark filled Becky with pity. She looked up at May, her large dark eyes lost their hard watchfulness and gently filled with commiseration. "I understand," she said. "Mike has told me about Jacko's problem with the interest, the pressure on him to sell this beautiful house. And that's why I'm here, about my idea. We could help some, you know, Mike and I, to tide things over. He's doing so well now in the business, and he doesn't have Jacko's burden of the interest."

"He's doing so well?" May cried. "What do you mean? Jacko says the business is on the rocks. Who's lying? Him or Mike? Do you think I'd have only one maid, and that fit for the dogs, if we had any money coming in? A maid like that is all Jacko can afford. Look at the place!" She waved a lovely arm though the air. "It hasn't been dusted for weeks! Smell the carpets! Nobody to beat them! Have you noticed the windows? What on earth do you mean, Mike's doing so well? Mike can't be doing well, if Jacko's broke."

"Oh, but he is, May dear," Becky said. She was disturbed at being so flatly contradicted and her eyes began to get their stony look. "He's doing *very* well. He's showed me his bank book, and even repaid me a bit. Oh, he's such a good man." This lie gave her a gagging sensation which she overcame by swallowing hard. She would

76

never share her true thoughts about Mike with May. Screw May—oh, yes, she knew such words, had learned them well at nursing school, but she swore only in the privacy of her head.

"May dear, we've been friends, our husbands partners, for years now. Do let me help."

Is she trying to needle me? May wondered. A sudden suspicion shocked her. Jacko, that evil bastard, had been lying about the business. He was hiding money away. And then she saw it—the plot to give him the grounds for divorce. She clenched her teeth and her lovely, tapering fingers curled into beautiful little fists. Never. Never. *Never.*

"And even if you *did* have to sell the house"—Becky's voice drifted in through the gray clouds of May's cold rage—"you could always come live with us in the La Touraine, get an apartment of your own."

May looked down at her. Becky's eyes were wandering around the room again, apparently drunk with admiration. Fool! May screamed in her heart. "My dear," May said, the perfect lady, moving like a pale white swan toward the door, "you must excuse me, I am late for my appointment now." She turned away upstage, swirling her peignoir.

"Of course," Becky said, springing up, "so thoughtless of me! I was so taken up with my idea. Forgive me!"

She hurried to the front door, where Lilly, having heard everything as usual with her spying for Jacko, opened it for her.

Pestiferous meddling little suffragette bitch Becky, May thought, how dare you come offering charity to *me*.

She sank onto one of the Belter couches. So Mike was doing so well! She had it solved now. Either Jacko was lying about the business, or Mike was onto something else to make money. If so, he hadn't told Jacko.

So now Mike had money! She thought more kindly of him, in a calculating way. What was this $60,000? She sat alone, hated by the house as she hated it. The devils in the walls with myriad eyes stared down at her, panting with hunger.

Looking through the window's thick plate glass, she saw Becky standing on the bottom step of the wide walk, framed by the two large cast-stone Florentine vases, full of pink-striped geraniums. Becky was looking up in adoration at the house. She looked so stupid that May could for once feel sorry for her.

Oh, what a fool, thought May as she watched from hiding like a baleful scheming cat. Mike had borrowed most of her money, the only thing he had ever wanted. Becky wouldn't see it.

Outside, Becky's eyes feasted on the aristocratic façade of this "châteauesque" house, the apogee of Queen Anne fantasy. The house was what the gentle part of Becky would have dreamed of having, if having were a hope. How she loved the high thimble-topped towers! and the surprise of turrets here and there, the little dormers peeking with crystal eyes from the skirts of enormous mother-dormers; the fairy work of wooden laceries entwined and garlanded from the narrow, fluted columns of the long verandas, like vines of frozen froth descending from the sky-high gables; even the soft effect of rounded shingles, like a gentle suit of feathers.

All this femininity delighted her heart without offense to her militant head and all the more that these soft vineal devices clung so lovingly to the proud, high bastion front, braving the heavens, as she herself had leaned against her father, her head in the hollow of his shoulder. To her, the whole house was a love affair in wood, and though she knew it was being scorned to dust by the rising new men like Wright, and all its feckless wealth of style abandoned like a fevered dream dispersed by modern day, it had for her a resonance of childhood which would not let her go, of all those quaint felicities of life so loved before the century turned from long security to rising wars.

Alone, she was free to be sad, free to be gentle. It was the fools, the liars, and the cruel that turned her hard. Perhaps the passion of her flight into the fore of the women's battle rose from her despair at the loss of what she loved; and even some hidden part of her sought to find, in sharing with her sisters the raucous masculinity of politics, an echo of the silenced man to nurse her heart. Her smile quivered as she turned away.

Inside this fortress of old-fashionable desuetude, May turned from the window toward the dark and stood slowly bowed by silence. She had no more friends; those frippery ladies who with their highly varnished carriages and hats like clouds had come with her to squander Jacko's money in the stores, they came no more; like shrieking geese when the corn is gone they rose from the barren field and flew away, to come no more. The silent street by day was quiet as by night, a great event the grocer's boy slowly pushing by his rattling cart, once in the solemn afternoon there came clopping by an empty hansom cab, no more.

She sat down, bored with waiting for lying Horton, and indifferently let the house-ghosts gather round. Not a tick, the big clocks and little clocks had long since stopped, killed. She could not stand the steady knocks of sound upon her ear which grew and grew as she would sit staring in the empty mornings, hammering louder and louder, the awful beat slowly rising and bearing down on her like a terrible black engine on tracks of roaring hell, the heavier booming rising to a shattering crash on crash until she twisted in her chair and shrieked in her head, struggling to reduce the ogre crashing to its beginning tick again, to start all over.

She looked around at the abandoned museum of furniture, seeing the pieces as mythical eagle-wolves, vulture-beaked black goats, furry spider-bears, all with yellow fangs, long spiky tongues, and slavering grins, waddling and grunting in upon her from all around.

She hated the whole house, everything left over like the mummified dead from the nineties and earlier; she hated the Belter suite, the darkness of this drawing room, shut in by the heaviest of velvet and damask drapes, and two complete sets of net curtains, stiff with age, across the big plate windows frozen in their frames.

The overcrowding and confusion drove her mad—the litter of little silver trinkets, the bronze Indian miniature tiger and the seven elephants, in dwindling sizes, the sea shells brought back by forgotten relatives from far lands, odd pieces of porcelain; tiny silver filigree baskets filled with tiny artificial flowers cluttering the whatnots and useless small tables, further loaded with carved onyx and jade. On the piano stood reticulated and scaling oil miniatures of Quiñones people whom even Jacko could not name, later daguerreotypes in oval silver frames, and even later sepia prints of endless O'Donohue relations, great-great-aunts and great-great-great-uncles and their plenitudinal descendency.

And then the fifteenth cousins lost in the depths of Mexico and Massachusetts whose births and deaths no one could recall, but whose anonymous faces, severe or pallidly smiling, Jacko kept like sacred relics, all ranged like a battalion on parade on the Damascus velvet which smothered the grand piano she was afraid to play, which sometimes terrified her when in the silence a mouse sped an arpeggio of twinkling feet across the dusty strings.

There were chairs enough crowding the room for three generations of ghosts, dusty palms lording it in the corners with hostile dying fronds bending over her like monster claws, and proud pampas grasses towering snobbishly in enormous porcelain floor vases.

She had lost the furniture war, but she had won another battle, long ago in the first hopeful years of marriage. Now gone were the "animals" (as she called them, instead of "trophies") from the library across the foyer, whose fur she claimed made her sneeze—the skin of the enormous Kodiak bear Jacko had shot in Alaska, snarling at her from the floor, nasty little eyes glinting at her redly in the firelight. Gone was the stuffed whole Mexican jaguar, stealthily stalking her along the top of a bookcase, the elk head sneering at her from high on the wall, the deer of piteous eye, the antelopes which had smiled at her so pathetically, like begging mothers, and most hideous of all, the six-foot sturgeon he had caught on the Rogue River, stuck on a board over the mantel, looking in its prehistoric armor like a frozen dragon.

All that was now gloomily turning back to dust in the attic towers far above, the only thing left of his exploits the moose head in the foyer, which he had insisted could not bother her nose because she only passed through the place; that and the case full of his shotguns, rifles, and pistols, in the corner of the library behind the fat globe. He never hunted any more.

She was sick to death of the yellow and purple stained glass on each side of the front door, casting the colors of gangrene on the parquet floor. The moose head, motheaten behind the ears, lorded it out of the shadows over the entrance hall, its broad horns spread like the wings of an enormous dark bat ready to pounce upon and ravish her every time she passed.

How sick a piece of luck it was, to begin with, to have been born in a New Jersey whose only fame was to fetch vegetables for New York, in a city like Newark, no more than a bacterial sprawl, and in the slums of that. She saw its scenes mostly as by night—wet black gleaming streets of wandering cats, her girl-self fleeing from one poor island of a lost streetlight to another far too far away, through a dark that tingled with danger; or if by sullen day, how she and other grimy brats would darkle in the crannies of sunk courts and cellars, hiding and seeking in a world waiting to be ruined. But mostly she remembered the nights, the cats, the juice of gutter garbage, slinking curs, the drunk-yelling damned sailors in saloons and stumbling floozies trooping to the oil-lamp-lighted old hotels.

Highest of all in her remembrance rose the black giant bulk of the Bakery, with its five floors and hundred brilliant windows gleaming in the midnight, humped like a great ocean liner glittering with life in a sea of death, hulked up majestically against the dark, with the wicked sickle moon hastening away like murdering time through a sky all raddled sick with torn dirty clouds. How bright, how warm the Bakery, full of big floury men, the sweet yeast smelling up the whole night town, the great bulk a giant engine rumbling alone alive in the dead city.

That was the field her father worked all through her childhood, two hundred illiterate Polish and Russian bakers, to many of whom he lent five dollars each Monday and on Saturday payday collected six or broke a nose. He never broke an arm to put them out of work.

The fools rarely failed, he grew rich, bought a fine brick house with trees and a carriage and pair. She went to the finishing school and excelled in elocution, so that when she was eighteen and her scrooge father was found one night in the gutter with his head squashed like a tomato by a gang of Polish bakers and the door smashed in and all the money in the mattress gone, she could save herself from the streets by smiling herself into vaudeville in New York and then into the movies. She had a presence; she had a beautiful body. Ten years before, she would not have been fat enough to please; now her sleeker shape was catching on.

On the old rooftop movie lot, men had treated her as a "hot blonde," with butt-pinching, constant propositions, and one instance of assault on the way to the bathroom, which she had cut short with a rabbit punch to the throat, learned in the Newark alleys; but her bowels never got the better of her head, as one disappointed producer had put it.

She was not a hot blonde. She had learned from her father never to give anything away at all; always to lend for a steep increase. Never give away! She never grasped the idea of trade. So she teased her way with cool smiles, moving from one producer, one director, to another, wearing them out. The dropped producers began to hate her, spread the word. All she knew was six for five or break a nose.

So she had found Jacko and took a new tack, selling her whole self for what she thought was a fortune. She had killed the child because it went against her grain to give it away when her dreams of the fortune had faded. Standing on the toilet seat she had long known that Jacko was a playboy and would never make her rich until his father died, and her face buried in a grave of wrinkles. That hadn't been in her dream-bargain.

Why had fate failed her? She never could find out, no matter how she puzzled her head. In these last lonely afternoons, she sat blaming the cats, the garbage, the Bakery, the Poles. She did not know that nothing comes except from something given up, the flower from the seed. All she knew was six for five or break a nose, that's all they ever told her.

Somebody twisted the wind-up bell on the front door. May swam up from the depths of her gloom.

Mike came in and stood with his high nose pointing about, as though sniffing the air for strangers.

"There's nobody here," May sighed. "Sit down and tell me about this money."

Instead, he came over to her chair, and taking her limp, lovely hand, raised it to his lips and kissed it wetly. Lilly could have heard the smack from the attic. May yanked her hand away in surprise and wiped it on her peignoir. "What on earth is the matter with you?" She looked furtively at the doorway.

"Never mind her," Mike said, "I saw the old warthog heading for the kitchen. I haven't got much time, I'll have to come right out with it."

"All right, out with it, whatever it is. Or I won't forgive you for forgetting my piano roll."

"Oh, God, that. Listen." He seized a purple ottoman by its tassels and dragged it close to her knees. He sat down and leaned forward.

"I have to be blunt." He tried to hold her hand, it slid away. "I am not a clever man, May," he said.

"Clever of you to say so."

"I could never fool you, May. I'm busted. The partnership's busted! I'm out! and I haven't got any time left to play any more of this piano-roll game of ours, nice as it was. I've got to make a move, and I want you to make it with me. I'll tell you the plain truth. I'm fed up with Jacko. I'm going to skin him on a deal. I'm taking $60,000 we were going to share, taking the whole thing. It's a reward for returning a thing they called a monster to people in Mexico. I'll share with you, to make it worth your while and come with me."

"What do you want with me? You never made a move before. Oh, I see. To hurt him. I wouldn't mind that, not at all. Why did he toss you out?"

He stood up and moved away. "Don't think less of me."

84

"How could I?" she said.

"I was caught blackmailing."

She suddenly smiled with real warmth. "Blackmail! So that's how you've been making money. Did you tell Becky?"

"Christ no, she'd split a gut."

"Becky told me you were doing well. So then, Jacko's not lying when he says he's broke."

"He's broke all right. I've ruined the agency, he says. He's talking about jail. So I'm going. Far away."

"Where?"

"Argentina. Beautiful country, May. You'll love it."

"I suppose you think if we both go, he's hurt double."

"Well, wouldn't it? Wouldn't it break his heart if you left him?"

She smiled, looking at Mike with amused eyes. "He'd die." Mike would never know how delighted Jacko would be if she left him flat. If there was one thing she knew about Jacko with a dead certainty, it was that he would never discuss his private life with anybody, except his lawyer or his priest, not even Mike. "He'd die, just pine away. But I've told you before, I won't leave him without a whopping settlement."

"You'll never get it. You're tough, but he's a lot tougher than you, once he gets over being sentimental."

Her smile had faded.

"So if you think," Mike said, "that waiting around to catch him in somebody else's bed is a way of screwing him for money, think again. He'd never do it."

"He's waiting to catch me at it," she said.

"So you're deadlocked. You'd better think of my $60,000. If you want out as bad as you've said you do, you'd do well to take me up."

"And what do I get, just half of your $60,000 and revenge?"

85

"I'll be setting up a gambling place in Buenos Aires. You'd up my credit as a man and give the place some tone. And we'll make plenty, down there."

"When do you get this money?"

"We get it together. I'll get rid of Jacko, then you and I go down to Guaymas on the ship and collect it there. Easy as that. I've thought it all out. I can get the Mickey from Sergeant Ciro's saloon on Third, me and his old witch of a wife, we know each other well. As for him, too well! He was master sergeant in the great Captain O'Donohue's company in the Philippines, with me ramrodding just a bloody platoon under Ciro's great red nose, damn him, giving me hell all the time for a fuck-up. But I get along great with Mrs. Ciro, and I can get the dope from her. I know how to get on the good side of these sexpots, pinch their ass or give it a good squeeze, especially these Sicilians like her, with their brains between their legs. All she is, is a piece of ass on wheels, and if you don't make her think you want to lay her every day, she thinks you're insulting her. That's why she hates Jacko, he's never made a pass, so she thinks he's pissing on her. So when I tell her I'm going to knock Jacko for a loop, she'll give me the Mickey, all right."

"You wouldn't double-cross me, then, Mike? Just take the money and dump me in Guaymas, after I've served for your revenge?"

"Why, May, if all I wanted was the money, why would I invite you at all to share it? I could just leave Jacko smarting with the loss, for revenge, if that was all I wanted."

She sat thinking.

"What other way out is there?" he asked.

She looked at the hideous furniture all around her, the dying palms, the ranks of forgotten relations on the piano. She gave a long sigh. "I'll call you."

"Don't put me in a bind," he said. "I have to buy those drops. And I have to meet Jacko in an hour."

"Don't worry," she said, and stood up.

She watched him as he walked up the street toward the Angel's Flight tramway, to drop down the cliff to Hill Street and the Grand Central Market. Champagne and a Mickey. The main point was, they would get the money down in Guaymas all in one payment. Guaymas? Why go all that way? Why not fence the monster, whatever it was, right here in Los Angeles?

After that they would see who would get to keep it all More than one could play at Mickies.

CHAPTER SEVEN

S ITTING IN the bright kitchen, Lilly poured Jacko another cup of tea.

"Now I couldn't hear everything that went between them," she said, "you know how it is when two such crooks and thieves are planning their crimes, the voices goes up and down, whispering the worst parts."

He had sneaked in the back way, coming over from Figueroa on Third, past Sergeant Ciro's saloon at the mouth of the Third Street tunnel, left up Cinnabar Street to the top of the hill and then through the abandoned back gardens of his house, down into the cellar like a thief, and up the back stairs to Lilly's kingdom.

He sat now smelling bread and the bright yellow scent of the linoleum, with the west windows full of the kind sun glinting from the nickel-plated doohickies and curly thingumbobs of the great black coal stove.

"Oh, the God's curse on them!" Lilly said. "But the main thing is that Mike says, 'I'm leaving the country, I'm going to get the whole $60,000 and start a gambling house in Buenos Aires, and I want you with me. That'll give me revenge on Jacko.' Can you believe it, the jackass thinks you still love her."

"As I thought I did when he was my best man," Jacko said. "He's not very observant. Always surprised when it rains."

He looked around the immense kitchen, big enough for two cooks and a salad man. Why did he have a feeling he was leaving it? Most of it was empty now, drained as the people drifted away, the big tilting flour bins under the counter empty, the pantry shelves and drawers left forlorn with all the heavy silver packed up somewhere in the attics, the coal box empty, and the great stove cold, dead as Queen Victoria, supplanted by the wretched gas thing in the corner.

Oh, he had loved, when small, to play with the grandmother stove's large family of lids, big and little, covering the fireholes, which he would lift with the hooking tool and slam and slide them around like hell's own flapjacks.

"How long ago did he leave?" Jacko asked.

"Ten minutes or so. She's to call him when she's made up the dirty bed of her mind."

Jacko smiled. "Strange kind of providence—he wrecks my business. Then he steals my wife for revenge and does me the favor of getting rid of her."

"She's desperate for money. She was down to a nickel the other day and I heard her cursing the poor thing."

"Well, I keep her poor in the hope she'll leave."

Distant heels rapped in the hall. "Listen!" Lilly said, half jumping up. "It's her! Is she coming? What if she finds us plotting together?"

"Take it easy, Lilly, she never comes in the kitchen. So you see Mike did me a favor by making me poor, didn't he? Now she'll desert me, and there's the grounds for the divorce. To tell you the truth, Lilly, I never did really think she'd go for adultery. Adultery costs money, for hotels and cabs and little restaurants for cozy chats and lovey-dovey lies and at her age she'd have to pay the rent. It was greed kept her chaste, waiting for me to betray her. God, what a mess."

"Tell me now what you'll do to get out of it."

He sighed deeply and looked into the dregs in his cup. "I see a ship at the dock, and a man and a woman getting out of a cab. He has a valuable jewel thing in a sack under his arm. They hurry toward the gangplank. And lo and behold, out from behind a big crate steps Jacko O'Donohue with Linebarger the assistant D.A. and accosts them. 'Where are you going with O'Donohue's wife? And what are you doing with that valuable work of art under your arm? You're under arrest, Mr. Horton, for theft, and as for you, Mrs. Grass-Widow-to-Be O'Donohue, you can visit your lover in jail, on your day off as hotel maid down at the fleabag Palace.' Once she's on that ship, I've got her for desertion. But now I've got to help her make up her mind to leave me, and to do it, dear Lilly, I have to fire you to put her in a rage."

"In a rage! Why, Jacko, she'll sing and dance to see me out the door."

"Not when she has to cook her own dinner and pick up the telephone for herself." He pulled out his checkbook. "Here's for the last week, Lilly. I'll call your agency and tell them what a great job you've done for me."

He stood up and, bending, kissed her soft, red, wrinkled apple cheek. "Take care, now, Lilly dear." He headed into the belly of the house.

He found May sitting in the half-dark parlor, staring glumly at the paper guests on the piano, who stared back in turn with the faraway eyes of the dead.

"Why so quiet, dear?" he asked, sitting down in his favorite Belter armchair. "Nothing to do? Doesn't the house need dusting?"

That roused her. She sat up slowly, uncurling like a cobra. "Do you expect *me* to dust this mausoleum?"

"I'm afraid you'll have to, dear," he said. He had got the "dear" business listening to Sergeant Ciro soft-soaping his wife in a sweet way that maddened her. It had to be said sweetly, lovingly, with the resignation of a martyr and a dying fall at the end. "I had to let poor Lilly go, just now. I'm sorry, dear. I can't pay her any more. All I've got left is six bucks in my pocket and $138 in the bank."

"You let her go?" She rose slowly from her couch.

"I'm so sorry, dear. It's up to you to manage now, I'm afraid. Dusting, making beds, wiping the bloody footprints off the toilet seats. I suppose you can cook yourself some eggs, that's easy. Here's a dollar. Run down to Hill Street and buy yourself a dozen. Keep the change, you'll need it." He unfolded his wallet, held out a bill. "I hope you won't be too lonely at dinnertime, dear, with the mice crawling around under the table nibbling at your toes."

She seized the bill. "You can't do this. You're lying! I know you have more!"

"I'm sorry I haven't, dear. I thought I'd have some from the check for the car, but I had to send the whole thing to my father. Debts first, of course."

"The check for the car?" Her eyes drooped with bewilderment. "You don't mean—"

"Yes, dear, I had to sell it. This morning. To help pay my father's interest."

"You sold the car!" she screamed. "You sold—Oh, damn you, damn you, damn your old father, damn your damned family, it was the one thing left, those rides in the park to get out of this prison, and now you—Oh, damn you!" She shook her fists helplessly.

"Now, now, dear," he said calmly, and crossed his legs. "Why don't you sit down and smoke a cigarette? It would calm your nerves, I'm sure."

"There aren't any more!"

"Oh, what a pity, dear, you've been starving for a smoke all morning? Well, dear, take your dollar and trot down to Hill Street and buy yourself a pack. And a couple of eggs for your dinner. I think Lilly stole everything out of the icebox. At least, I saw her leaving the back way with a big heavy sack over her shoulder."

"You pimp," she cried, sneering down at him, "you pathetic little queer. You goddam bastard son of a bitch, son of a whore, dog puke."

"What a vocabulary! so fresh and new, what *can* you have been reading? But please not the 'little,' dear. I don't mind the pimp, queer, bastard, and the rest of it, I can get used to them, I suppose, but, please, not the little. I'm not little. I'm quite large."

"I know your goddam game!" she shouted. It was an immense relief to swear, something she seldom did, only under the greatest pressure, like most ladies of quality. The hinder parts of Newark's memory sprang to her aid, her heart hungered for knives, guns, broken noses, the saving burst of mania.

He watched her, the distant relatives watched her, the walls watched her. What devil raged in all this alabaster loveliness?

"I know your goddam game! Starve me out, will you? Well, I'll show you. I'll show you." She turned around, looking wildly for something to show him with, something to smash, turned again.

"Show me what, dear?" he asked mildly.

"Aagh!" she screamed and dashed to the piano, swept her arm across the army of dreaming faces. Frames slammed down, toppled from little bamboo easels, slith-

92

ered, scattered clattering, glass tinkling, a Niagara of por-
traits tumbled to the carpet. She seized the tasseled velvet
drape and whirling hurled it at her husband. Unexpectedly,
it sailed like a magic carpet smoothly, beautifully as a
swan through the air and draped its graceful riches across
his elegant knees. He sat there composed, smiling ur-
banely, lacking only a cigar for a portrait of a Turkish gentleman.

She marched out into the hall. The front door slamming
shook the house.

He listened to the fading sound of her feet rapidly pat-
patting down the street. So she had made up the dirty bed
of her mind, as Lilly had put it, and without a doubt was
hurrying to the closest public telephone. And whose would
that be but Sergeant Ciro's, only three blocks away?

He went to the foyer, and stood under the moose by the
phone. He would wait a half-hour to give her time for her
dirty call to Mike, and then phone the faithful Sergeant to
find out just what she'd said, maybe a hint more of their
plans.

Bang! through the swing doors of the Sergeant's saloon
burst May, and stood looking around for an enemy. There
were only four lonely whores drinking beer in a corner, far
too early for trade but not for consolation, and an old soak
looking at them like lost love from under the grosgrain
brim of his moldy brown derby. And there the Sergeant,
leaning on his marble bar, half asleep. Everything smelled
cool, the beer faucet weakly leaking single tears, the fresh
clean sawdust on the floor smelling for the last time of old
oak forest glades.

The night-time workers would be waking up and crowding the place any time now.

May strode to the telephone on the wall, stuck in a

nickel. The Sergeant looked up groggily, rearing up from the bar like a huge bull walrus from the beach.

"Can you talk?" she asked the phone.

"She's in the darkroom," Mike said down the line. "All's clear." He laughed. "She's developing a blackmail photo and doesn't even know it. Ha ha ha."

"You're one of the cleverest men I've ever met," she said. Residues of her contempt dripped like acid down the mouthpiece of the phone. "I've made up my mind." The hike down the hill in those hobble skirts had exhausted her anger, and she had her composure back. "I can't wait forever," she said. She knew the Sergeant was listening, and cared not a fig. "I'll tell you what, Mike, I'll believe you've got the heart for the whole thing when you've done your deed tonight, and I'll take a chance on you and Buenos Aires, because then you'll have no way back. Burn your boats, and I'm with you. But remember this, Mike, I wasn't born yesterday. My father broke noses for a living, Mike, and I take after him."

"No fear, dear May. You have my absolute respect."

"And one more thing, you'll have to give up those cigars if we're going to be together."

"I will, I will, I swear I will!" he cried with joy.

Fool, she thought, hanging up the phone. What are you so happy about, waiting for a sharp stick in the eye?

Without a look at the Sergeant, she pushed disdainfully out through the doors and headed for the hill.

In the somber hall, as Jacko stood counting minutes by the phone, odd bits of ancient visions swirled slowly up, a company of ghosts of old defeats to bear away his marriage back to the land of poor uncovered graves where they in silence always lay. Above him, the moose stared with his glass eyes sadly into some spectral forest. For a moment, Jacko remembered the way the lily pads had dribbled from the moose's mouth just before he keeled over dead in the lake. Why had he shot the poor thing? Vanity of vanities, the prowess of a man with a bullet and no brains, the herculean dreams, the waxen wings of overweening youth; and then remembered how another bullet blew away the heart of a little yellow man in Iliolo, and how looking down upon the fatal welling blood he fell upon his knees with his face in his hands, and how then he got slowly up again with his own heart dead to death.

Poor moose, he thought. Oh, I'd give you back your lily pads if only I were God, but let's hope now He'll find them bigger for you, sweeter in the lakes of heaven. And as for the little yellow man, I beg, I beg, I beg, I beg, I beg your pardon, now and forever, world without end.

That was when the worm of sadness hatched within him, never sleeping, wrapped in the memory of the war. Like the skulls of once-fair women, horror revealed with the sloughing of the rotten flesh, came the realization that in the glorious crusade to kill the tyrant, the whole army had become the tyrant. Little by little the glorious face of war had rotted away and the lies of that greedy landgulping Roosevelt with his cooked-up crooked little war, and Jacko himself turned into nothing but a cop, hunting down Aguinaldo and the rest of the rebels, to create the Roosevelt empire.

A shrug for murder! nothing to be done, himself the real prisoner of war, locked to the duty of a dog. Conscientious! trained by the Church Militant to step in time from the age of four, duty came as easy as his commission, and he lived by the numbers, the unformed question only a vague, continual uneasiness in his stomach.

Somewhere at the bottom of his mind there was an unnamed crime, a crime excused as loyalty by all the world, but the same Church Militant that had made him dutiful had created an iron conscience that would not let go. What was the crime he carried in his gut, the gnawing worm? He could not find the name.

He went back into the long, dark parlor and stood viewing the wreckage of his blood-kin gallery, then slowly picked up the relics one by one and having smoothed the velvet catafalque upon the dead piano, set them again, as he had ranged his boyhood soldiers, in their precise, forlorn array.

He sat again in the Belter chair and waited in the dusk to call the Sergeant. He knew her well, he knew from her raging heels, the rapid, hurrying tap-tap-tap down the hill, that she had left him for good in the great slam of the door. Why wasn't he happy? She would come back to wait on the edge of her bed for her flight with her tin-plate lover tomorrow, eyes frozen away in the ice of her heart. Where were the tears for either of them?

Jacko sat remembering his little French cat, Merlette, with her long fur like a fine ball gown—or dust mop?— almost trailing the floors, as black as a blackbird. Merlette too was loyal and brave, and had peed delicately in May's slippers several times. Once she had decorated even more substantially her fine silk underthings in a drawer carelessly left open. And then she had disappeared, one day was no more. Jacko knew he was lucky to have no proof of what he suspected, for what he might have done to the two-legged bitch.

Merlette had almost driven May mad with attacks of fury and fear, as though she were being beset and persecuted by a devil in animal disguise. She thought Merlette wanted to kill her. She never knew that all the little cat wanted was to tell her to go away, as politely as she could.

But was she so wrong? What had been wrong? She was the victim of a nature she had not wanted, never willed, that saddled her life like a grinning ghostly giant ogre-frog on the back of a poor unknowing child.

Only ignorance, some vast emptiness of soul had brought down the blood upon her foot. He saw again the red print on the wood. He was too old now to evade, to blame, except to see his own self in ignorance and folly. She was a half-thing, killing in a viciousness she never asked to learn, could not unlearn. Gone, he could not hate her, sealed away dead by the crashing door. Gone, no more.

He looked at the dead on the piano, yellow faces, absent eyes. In all of them his blood had run, and theirs in him, she never understood. She could not feel the infinite tiny branchings of heredity, of red veins like intertwining delicate roots, a thousand thousand interminglings, far away, that tied together all the distances, calling silently across the continents and hundred years, web of the living and his dead. Like the house high above him, they held his life, and neither would he let them go.

How she had mocked the Belter suite, carved by the crazy old German in New York, bought by his grandfather off the ship in San Francisco in 1856. She could not know how his finger, when he was five, had softly run along the rosewood curves of all those delicately carven flowers, cresting the backs of the sofas and the chairs—those crests as light as surf, their perforations filling them with air and grace; how time after time, alone in the drawing room, he had felt out the cool smoothness of Belter's carving, building a private world as though of lost caves and dark woods, tracing the way from flower to leaf along the curves, penetrating through the traceries, so that the carved crest became a retreat known only to him and to the craftsman who had carved and polished it. How she had complained of the slipperiness of horsehair upholstery! never knowing how when little he had once loved to slide upon it.

What she did not see was the beauty of the ancient; that

beauty newly found must be with careful nurture worked to gold antiquity. Nor could she ever see the yellow of the faded photographs as turning paper into golden age, that years themselves accrued a beauty of their own.

Where are you? child, old bush-beard man, and roly-poly gleaming-eyed adventurer; staid aunt in primmest bonnet, hair pulled back as tight as torture; or heavy, round, eye-dreaming jowly mother of the awestruck little three, staring like baby owls at the camera's glaring evil eye. And you, *mi general*, smiling with power under grand gray moustache like eagle wings bearing away the saber nose, the pouter breast in martial blue emblazoned with memorials of merit, French, Austrian, Spanish, ceremonial sword at side, almost a wink of the eye, secretly mocking this self-majesty with the knowledge of his hidden decorations, the bullet pockmarks on the massive chest.

Two grim-lipped Irish brothers from Fall River, famous makers of four-hawser cables; then humbler Quiñones merchants, was it the Vera Cruz branch, or the Mazatlán? slightly grim one-sided smiles remembering old Porfirian deals; and several priests, mostly Irish, fat and somber, thin and gay, two bishops side-looking on their thrones with lip-worn rings on helpless hanging fingers waiting for obedience. And you, the smiling Boston nuns, how long invisible and gray in death, the hopeful virgin brides of Christ, seeking peace and finding war, humble in the image of their Mother, the Mother of God, enduring the world's hate in the ceaseless growing love of her Son, their Bridegroom King of Heaven.

And then the nuns of the other world, dead in Juarez's prisons. How far away you are, he thought, all you forgotten Quiñoneses, in that romantic, cruel, and faithful world, while I sit here a king of emptiness in dollar-land, the world of black or white, yes or no, good or bad, never a doubt, where doubt is heresy and not the crown of wonder.

Where unnatural women leap from toilet seats to kill their children.

How could he have so deceived himself, meeting her at that movie party at the Alexandria? Those were the days, before the movie companies discovered Hollywood, when they worked in vacant lots on Washington Boulevard, hurrying to and from the Alexandria on Sixth Street to change their costumes. The party was a grand celebration of some faded cinematic masterpiece.

She had been seated, half lying, in the pearly white of a satin gown, borrowed from wardrobe, on a fake French chaise longue, champagne in hand. And he, excluded from the technical talk, having winced away from the hotel buffet, had sat by her, wondering at her aloneness, not knowing that she was, for the movie people, a hopeless proposition.

But she knew him, had seen him, asked about him; about the miles of orange groves, the mansion on the hill, and liked his look, too, all handsome black and white in tails, and smiled and gently teased, which he found affectionate and friendly.

So he took her to the races, he took her to the fairs, he took her flying in his little plane, racing his friends and landing on the beach in Santa Barbara near the grand Potter Hotel, where all the rich of the East forgathered in the winter. She had found it very pleasing, if just a little boring, and the pair was much admired. Had they been sealed together, after all, merely by universal admiration? Oh, what a handsome couple! The verdict settled on them like a fate. She reigned a queen at parties on the Hill with his university friends, lawyers and business barons of the town; and she was pleased at the gentle compassion in his eyes when he returned her to her humble room in the cold hotel.

So they got married. He thought the alabaster goddess

would be a wife, not knowing exactly what a wife was, or even if he would want exactly that even if he did know. She thought all the money was free to his hand at any time, and never imagined, or anybody else, the crash of '07 or the freeze of '08. And not having much heat herself, she grew tired of impetuous passion, which bored her, and slowly put him off with the usual headaches.

Sitting now in the ancient Belter, he smiled to himself. He took the phone from its little black yoke and got the Sergeant's saloon.

"Yass."

God, it was Mrs. Ciro. He felt the usual strain of dealing with her dislike, expressed on his face by a small, grieved snarl of distaste. Why did she hate him? She had for him, for some strange reason, a flame of malevolence that burned like old Blake's tiger.

"Let me speak to the Sergeant," he said.

"Whosa datta callin'?"

"Jacko O'Donohue, Mrs. Ciro. How are you today?" And cursed himself for a fool. Why hadn't he said it was Santa Claus? She wouldn't have known the difference.

"Jackadonnahoo, hey? Thassa facka! Ima tellin you, shesa too beesy now. You calla somotha tima, hey? Naxa wick, hey fella?"

Goddam bitch, he thought, screw him up for no reason at all. "Thank you very much, Mrs. Ciro," he said, and hung up.

He put on his homburg and walked out the back through his wilderness of forgotten garden, so as to miss the ordurous woman who would be coming back up the hill.

Banging in through the batwing doors, blinded by blue daylight, the first thing Jacko saw in the dark brown gloom of the bar was the evil omen of Mrs. Ciro's black Sicilian eyes meeting his with a glowering stab, as usual.

Half Arab from the Palermo coast. Was she jealous of the
Sergeant's old army friends? Had he ever said anything to
offend her? There was nothing he could do about it but
smile with persistent civility, hoping for improvement. She
stood with tray upraised like an enormous discus seem-
ingly to hurl at him, and then he saw the innocent load of
steins on it, and then his friends rose into vision, chatter-
ing around the tables, lolling in the captain's chairs, shuffling the sawdust with their feet. Where was the Sergeant?

These were the night people from Main Street who slept
late in the mornings in the clean old hotels on Third and
Fourth, their thirsts waking up in this middle afternoon.
Now, licking their lips, they wandered in to lave their
throats in lager and enjoy a few hours of the cool of shadows and sawdust before they went to their nightly work.
Then, too, the time-offing teamsters giving their drays a
break, and the hay pitchers and manure slingers from the
big stables down the block, where the heavy clop-hooved
Belgians and Clydesdales thundered up and down the
ramps of their three-storied horse hotel to and from their
stalls.

There were the pawnshop people from Main and Central, the dealers in stolen clothing from the cross streets,
dishwashers from the greasy spoons and tamale joints,
cardsharps and plain dealers, stagehands from the gaudy
vaudevilles and the freaks from the sidewalk shows. There
was little Miss Helen Arrigari from her hole-in-the-wall on
Main, where she sat two feet tall in her baby crib, no legs,
with golden curly locks falling where her arms should
have been born forty years ago, and politely lectured any
passing gent or bum with ten cents for a fee on the politer
pursuit of sex, cautioning them to patience with the delicate sensibilities of the ladies, to contain that passion
which she knew (but how?) flared up in the male at the
sight of a stocking on a clothesline.

To her and her heavy, black-dressed guardian, Mrs. Forelop with her kind dragon smile, he bowed, sweeping off his homburg, delighting their hearts as usual.

Here a wave, there a smile, a pat on back, a punch on shoulder, he meandered through the quaffing, gabbling people to the bar.

And then the mighty Sergeant like a spewing whale rose through the trapdoor in the floor with another barrel.

"Heigh-ho, Jacko," the Sergeant said, thumping the barrel down.

"A private word with you?" Jacko asked, his elbows on the bar straddling a puddle.

"Treea beersa!" screeched Mrs. Ciro from the crowd.

"Yes, dear," moaned the Sergeant like a beached liner in the fog. "Just a minute, Jacko boy," he panted, getting the barrel up to the pumps.

Oh, the sociable humming of the friendly little flies, scooting down from the horse hotel for a drink, pleasantly licking their black-bristled little chops at the beer puddles, polishing tiny moustaches with clever little finger-feet, grooming their underwings with back paws, lifting a leg at a time; then, their coattails all tidy, they polished their hands like congressmen gloating on a deal and headed for another puddle to do it all again. Oh, the drunken flies of my youth, thought Jacko, waiting at the bar, grandfathers of mighty millions, in what heaven fly you now with crystal wings of glory before the God who made you?

"And what will it be?" the Sergeant said distinctly, close to his head, leaning over the bar.

"Was my wife in here phoning?" Jacko asked.

"I'll say she was, no mercy on my ears either."

"What did she say?"

"She was talking to somebody, some fellow I guess, saying she would go with him to Buenos Aires. Is it true, Jacko? You're breaking up?"

"She's leaving me, thank God."

"Like that, eh? Oh, I tell you, women can be terrible. Like my own devil."

"Tell me, why does Mrs. Ciro hate my guts?"

"How would I know? I don't understand women and I don't want to, God knows I got enough on my mind. She hates because she enjoys it, you ain't the only one."

"Foura beersa!" screeched the Sicilian, hustling toward them through the tables with her tray, hopping and grinning at the fusillade of pinches.

"Yes, dear!" the Sergeant cried.

She sailed up and slammed her tray on the bar, stood glaring at Jacko with her black evil eyes glittering like Saladin's scimitar. Jacko smiled at her. Oh, what a black-hearted hawk of a woman. How to be friendly? He could have kissed her hand as he kissed little Helen Arrigari's cheek, but without the affection he felt for the tiny crippled dwarf, he would have thrown up to have touched his lips to the Arab's scaly claw.

Besides, her kind was a glutton for hatred, savoring the sulphur smell of it like a devil's minestrone. Why deprive the lady of her pleasure in it?

The Sergeant slammed down the beers on the tray. "On your way, dear," he said, and she sailed off.

"Oh, what a woman," the Sergeant said. "I let these bozos pinch her ass to keep her hotted up for night, not that she needs it much. She keeps me alive like a Saturday serial. But she scares me, Jacko. What if she gets tired of me? Poison. Hollow rings for the old man's wine. Death at a distance. I swear to God if she wasn't so goddam glorious in bed, I'd bury her in the cellar for fear of my life. I think I'll start sleeping in a chain-mail vest. Oh, there's never a dull moment with them Sicilians, Jacko, they keep you young and lively as long as they let you live, boy."

Jacko turned and waved as he pushed out the doors.

Mrs. Ciro was leaning on the bar, one skinny arm akimbo, looking at him like a cannon, black eyes smoking. He shook his shoulders to get off the spell and made for the hill.

The heavy door closed behind him with its solid chunk of sound. He felt the house cold and empty above him. Where was she? Where could she go, without money?

He stood listening to the dead silence. How long since he had heard a clock ticking? She would be gone, and no need to pamper her any longer about the noise of the clocks. He went into the library, up to the poor old grandfather clock behind the globe, and keyed up his weights, then with a respectful finger started his pendulum. The old man said Tock gratefully, and his noble face gleamed with renewed pleasure. Jacko, smiling to himself, went about the house, gently starting clocks on mantels, walls, in the kitchen, in the halls, and slowly the house came alive again, all the clocks talking to each other.

Five o'clock! the grandfather bonged his basso profundo. Time pretty soon for Mike to arrive with gun and handcuffs. Time to pick out his own weapon.

He went to the gun cabinet and pulled out the pistol drawer. A neat .380 Belgian Browning, or the brand-new Colt .45 auto he had wangled from an Army friend on a phony survey. Which? The Colt New Service .44–40 was too big, but the auto was flat enough to hide under his jacket. But it was really a combat gun, best for a battle you could foresee, but not for a surprise. For the fastest shot, the little Colt Police Positive Special chambered for .38 Specials was the thing. He had had the barrel cut from four to two inches and the puny sight rebrazed. In the other pocket went the handcuffs.

He went back to the parlor and sat down at the piano to wait, picked out "Old Black Joe" with his forefinger. Sad,

sad the empty house, sad, sad, the overgrown garden. Who would fill it for him, bring another child? Or four or five. He could hear them chasing each other through the house, laughing, their feet running in the halls. He would rebuild his old sandbox, get a load of beach sand from Santa Monica. Throughout the house, to the out-of-tune twanging of "Old Black Joe," the clocks discussed all this among themselves.

Goodbye Mike, goodbye May. His mouth was a hard, thin set line. It wasn't revenge, it was just housekeeping.

> I'm coming,
> I'm coming,
> And my heart is sad and low,
> I hear the angel voices calling,
> Old Black Joe.
>
> Twang twang.

CHAPTER EIGHT

"**G**AMBLING, YES, I've been gambling, Becky, so what?" Mike said. He was standing in the living room of their apartment in the La Touraine Residential Hotel. This was a fashionable five-story white wooden building, which could have been advertised as ideal for fire insurance reclamation, with six fluted columns, two stories tall, forming an imposing portico. This genteel palace, boasting brilliant cherry-wood paneling and registration desk in its main lobby, stood on the very brink of that cliff which dropped from the south end of Bunker Hill into Fifth Street. Its height gave it an angel's view of the city, spreading out to the south, and to its tenants a feeling of transcendent superiority, as long as they looked at it. The bright sunlight, still pure, untouched by the city below the hill, struck down through the tall windows, making the dust motes dance and the felted olive walls green-gold.

"There's nothing wrong with gambling, Becky, but

Jacko doesn't like it, so we're through." He had made the explanation of the partnership bust-up short and sweet and spoken with authority, but his hands were trembling with fearful joy at his enterprise with May.

He looked around the room, which had grown detestable with paying for it. The place was dangerous with mission-style furniture, heavy enough to fell an ox or break a hip if you ran into it in the dark. The only comfortable thing in the room was the somewhat Louis XV sofa, threadbare on the curves.

"And what about this little jewel?" Becky said, shoving a wet eight-by-ten print at him. She had processed it for him in her little darkroom. There lay those two respectable, middle-class figures preposterously prone on the beach, apparently in intimate conversation, so stiffly stuffed into their fashionable proper attire that they would probably need a derrick to hoist them up again, dribbling trickles of sand from their gussets and furbelows. They looked like a couple of seals, a little spot in the middle of the negative.

Was Mike really that stupid? Was that fat, crinkled rubber brain of his perishing at last? And he was lying again, she could hear it in the sweet sincerity of his voice. The only time Mike was one with the truth was when he had been severely injured. "It's a great photo, Becky dear," he said. He smiled at his blackmail masterpiece, Mr. Meldane and Mrs. Varminter lying on the beach. "But eight by ten is too small, blow up that middle part until you can see them smile." The victims had to see their faces clearly, why else would they pay? And then he realized the folly of it. He'd be far away in Buenos Aires.

"Too small for what?" she said, like biting off thread.

"For the photo club! I'm calling it 'Love on the Beach.' "

She never laughed at Mike, his ego could throw terrible

tempers, but smiled with half of her mouth in a way that showed an eyetooth. A prize for this? There was something more to it, but she couldn't guess what it was.

He sighed, depressed at leaving all that easy money behind. But what could he do? Stay and risk jail? Oh, well, let Becky blow it up to keep her out of trouble. He looked at his watch. Good God, Jacko! he thought. He had to meet him in forty-five minutes with the gun and he still hadn't got the dope from the Sergeant's old bag of a wife.

Becky let the ridiculous picture hang at her side, dripping slowly on the Axminster.

She gave his fat-cheeky profile her dead-eye look. He was being brave; and if he was trying to be brave (she could always smell it when he was fearful) he was suffering and telling the truth. She was always, with Mike, betwixt nausea and the tenderness of distant pity; the tenderness rose now, the bitter smile died. Oh God! to be stuck with such a problem, to nurse him or kill him. No matter how deeply she might have learned to regret her marriage, nor in what barrenness of love it might have begun, marriage itself had created a sort of reluctant concern which might have been called at least an affection, on reflection slightly nauseating.

To hell with nursing and to hell with marriage, she thought, her nurse's privy vocabulary rising fitly to the thought of her bitter failure in both fields. Nursing and Mike! Would she ever make anything but mistakes?

"I'll carry on," he said, "I'm a good detective. I've got $3,800 in winnings and half of our reserve capital. That's almost enough to open my own office. And now this job for Palafox, that's a split of $6,000 more. How much have you got left?"

She thought of her black tin box with the delicate red stripe around it, under the bed, with its bonds and jewelry. There were four bonds remaining of the ten her father had left her. In early days she had lent six to Mike to expand the business, as he had explained it.

"What's left of the housekeeping money?"

"*Housekeeping money?* Are we down to that, the change from a chicken?"

"I'm throwing a party here for us all tonight, to celebrate this new job. Caviar and champagne. Now, no more sad thoughts, Becky darling," Mike said, reviving her animosity, his gassy ebullience and fake confidence giving her chills of apprehension. How close to the gutter were they?

"Let tonight be a celebration," he sang, his head full of a swirling humanitarian soup of specious good will toward mankind, "a party before we sail—Jacko and me, that is—in the morning. Let's have no criticism, let's forget the past, accept the breakup, be friends, and smile. Can I trust you to smile tonight?" He smirked gently down at her. She bit her lip to keep from cracking a flat hand across his grin. "Now give me the housekeeping money so I can buy the champagne and stuff, that's a good girl."

Good girl, was it! Bristling, she led him to the parlor, found her silver mesh bag, and counted out $19.45. "And don't forget we have to eat tomorrow, so bring some back," she said, seeing him out the door. Fat chance with that bugger, she thought, and immediately despaired of her vocabulary. Nursing training had taught her to swear like any slut, and she lived with one-half of her English doing penance for the other.

She went back into the darkroom to redo the print. She loved her darkroom and studio. In the studio stood her beautiful Rembrandt portrait camera, and the eight-by-ten Deardorff with its totally flexible front that she sometimes took into the streets for architectural views. Her still-life setup stood between the windows with their adjustable shades and tall light stands, and on a table beside it, her great collection of pots, vases, plaster casts, and artificial flowers.

Along shelves on the wall stood the fruits of her stone-collecting hobby, kept over from her courses in mineral-ogy at Xavier University in Cincinnati, where her father, devoted to Rabbi Isaac Wise and the Hebrew Union College, had sent her in an effort to broaden both their minds. These were rocks and crystals she had collected in the California mountains, even three geodes she had found in the desert hills.

Standing in her darkroom, she felt superbly efficient, dressed in her long rubberized apron, doing something only men ordinarily did. She had left the women to their breathy watercolors and was steeped in chemistry, the hard world of science. Her skill reaffirmed her conviction that women could do anything men could do, which reassured her as to all her feminist principles; but more personally, this development business made her feel happy inside, as though her body were swelling with song in a silence complete except for the gentle whir of the ventilating fan.

For all her bravado in parades, carrying posters, enduring hisses, boos, male laughter, and the frowns of stodgy women still hypnotized by male propaganda, the conflict tired her. Her suffragette image, that upright, vigorous, argumentative person was not all of herself. Her aggressiveness went with her riding and skill at moderate jumps, but not with her love for Steichen's *Camera Work*.

All alone she took the big red cars of the Pacific Electric out to San Bernardino, sixty miles away, and up the mountain to Arrowhead. Loaded with tripod and five-by-seven view camera and film holders, she trudged the paths of crumbling granite through the great pines by the lake, from view to view, looking for a Stieglitz scene.

She had never allowed a sense of futility to overcome her; if she felt depressed, she simply straightened her back and lifted her chin higher. If life was a matter of failed expectations like the nursing school and the marriage, to hell with them both.

She dipped her rubber-gloved fingers into the soup and plucked out the print. The faces were bigger, recognizable, now. The couple lay on a blanket on the beach probably north of Santa Monica. Large boulders gave them some privacy.

Another booby prize at the club show. She dumped the print into the washer and went back to the living room.

Had Mike ever loved her? she wondered. She looked at the chased brass fire screen with its large cupid with bow and arrow that she kept so brightly polished, concealing the black pit of the cold grate.

Something of her father's good-humored, wry rationality despised the question, which was the trap women had forever fallen into. It was a doubt of their self-worth, really, and she rejected it as having only doubt for an answer. She rose and went to the window, looked out over the city from her height on the hill. The modern woman shut her mind to doubt.

Yet she needed something more than logic, and she took refuge in the thought of her father, as he had been in his white linen suit and white Panama hat in Cincinnati when she was six, the year her mother died. She often thought of him when Mike made her feel alone. She saw him in profile, standing in front of the house on the hill, looking far over the river, cigar in one hand, stick in the other, affluent stomach protruding confidently against the eastern sky. Calm, slowly puffing his cigar. She could feel her head again resting on his shoulder, his warm hand on hers, and peace slowly flowed over her loneliness.

His smile had been a discipline, after her mother's death, she realized now. Everything in him had collapsed, he had fallen away from his Reform principles back to his

Orthodox childhood. He had turned the funeral arrangements over to the local Hevra Kadisha. He had torn his coat and sat the shiva for three days, and the Orthodox rabbi rejoiced at what he took for a return. But after only three of the seven days, he put on his shoes again and threw the coat away, and drove his buggy, even on the Sabbath, up to the Hebrew Union College, to reaffirm his attachment to Rabbi Isaac Wise.

And then, when he left Cincinnati in 1895, he abandoned even Wise, leaving him, the Reform, and the cemetery with all the dead of his family and his wife behind like the torn coat, fleeing west away from all reminders.

What did she know of his religion? A few vague recollections of her grandfather's house: the dining room with its fortress tons of black walnut furniture, exuding vapors of darkness to curl like vanquished Sheol wraiths about the radiant white tablecloth of the Sabbath Eve, all set with silver for the three generations waiting around it.

From the west windows came the last red of the sun, going down as her grandmother, invisible beyond the little girl's hand-cupped eyes, lighted the two white candles. She herself, after opening her eyes with joy on the suddenly blazoned Sabbath, lighted on her own little candle so as to learn the ways of a good, pious wife.

There on the shining linen sat the two little mysterious loaves side by side under their special napkin, and all around her the sense of the humming life of the whole family. She could hear again, soundless, the high, slightly strident voice of her grandfather's benediction; and then, remembered most dearly, the warm, gentle cap of the old man's hand on her head, which seemed to be that protection from the terrible spaces between the stars which she had been born needing. God, her grandfather prayed, was to make her like several women whose names she had forgotten, except Rebecca's. But who was Rebecca?

These images would grow out of overrunning seas of sadness, coming out of the dark like the light of the candles, the voice of the patriarch humming with the peace and joy of the Sabbath, breaking now upon them like a transcendent sun.

Why had he blessed her among so many children at that table, as she felt, especially? Even had she been merely the paradigm for all, his attention must have been still special, for hers was the only father who sat there the old man's enemy, black rebel for all his bowed head, brooding up courage for the break. Darkness, sunset, heart-flame candles on the brilliant cloth; joy, peace, the warmth of the breathing family all around her: gone.

She sat in the cool stillness of the apartment, high above the febrile breathing city, in her mind as though in a cold, dark room, looking back through a little door into an old world of light and warmth, hearing as in the broken language of the sea the warm and loving voice of the old man.

What the father wanted for his daughter was the safety of total secularism. "Nursing," he had said, "think about it. When I am gone, a living, security, respect, and doing good. What could be better?" He had found his secularism in Los Angeles. Now for three years he had lain among the Gentile dead.

She drew a deep breath. What women needed now were more parades, until they won. She looked far over the clean new city, bright as a garden, fresh as Eden in the brilliant air, and smiled at the golden future, full of new success for her and Mike with his new agency.

A party! Something very odd about the idea, yet if Mike wanted to celebrate the new rather than mourn the old, that was a good sign, wasn't it? Or was it? Sign of what?

She began pushing the furniture to the walls to make room for dancing, her small body straining against the

heavy weights. Mike always wanted to tango when he had
drunk champagne.

She knelt to roll up the carpet and paused. As she rested
on her knees as she had done in the nursing school, wash-
ing the floors of the wards, the dark descended and she
saw again the dead negress on the guttered white slab, her
flesh thin, hard and dried as jerky, the fatal swelling no
longer raw beneath the pubis. The old man professor ran
the scalpel around the skull with the easy skill of long
habit and with a neat, expert rip pulled the scalp inside out
down over the dark, shrunken face to get at the skull with
his saw. The old man, cutting and burrowing in the
shrunken gut pressed something too hard, a spurt of yellow fluid shot up out of the corpse and hit him in the face.
Wiping his face with a towel, he turned to the class laughing regretfully, both amused and apologetic at this unmen-
tionable deviation from autopsy protocol. When two of the
student nurses giggled, Becky sank down to the hexagonal
white tiles in a faint. The next day she sold her textbooks.
But this was only after several such trials, such as finding
in her bed, left as a prank by some medical students, a
man's arm, freshly cut off at the shoulder.

She sat back on her heels and looked blankly at the wall
in front of her. All that was long ago. Down from the
washed-out blue Los Angeles sky, vapid and threatless as
usual, the sunlight came through the window and fell like
fool's gold into the silent room. She sat at peace, feeling
the sunlight on her shoulder, warm like a hand.

CHAPTER NINE

INCONSPICUOUS BEHIND the Pomona station, the three sat slackly waiting in Palafox's 1909 Pierce Arrow Touring Special, Jacko and Mike in the front like chauffeur and footman, Palafox in the middle of the rear seat, an arrangement his dignity insisted upon. The moon was coming up over the buildings across the station plaza. The top of the car was down and their faces were stiff with a thin paste of dried sweat and highway dust gathered during the bumpy drive from Los Angeles.

"The train's never late," Palafox said, looking at his watch, "if it hasn't been wrecked," and laughed. His pure white suit loomed out in the darkening air as cool as snow. He wiped his face with his pink handkerchief, shoved it back in the pocket under the black holster of his heavy revolver. As an Honorary Sheriff of Los Angeles County, he was permitted to carry it openly. Jacko rubbed his dirty face and envied Palafox's disgusting composure.

The spiteful yellow of the railroad buildings had deepened in the dusk to a noble gray, the angles of the roofs of the buildings around the deserted station plaza thrust up like black axes into the lemon-yellow strip of fading sky. Bats flickered in and out of shadow with tiny shrieks of hunting joy.

"We should squeeze them for a few more traitors' names," Palafox said, "and examine the monstrance for damage. If there is any, I'll feed them their eyeballs. Some quiet place, Señor O'Donohue. You know this country. Your *estancia* is not far from here."

"We have an old pumphouse near the highway, quite isolated," Jacko said. "But no violence, señor."

Somebody turned on lights in the waiting room of the station, square shafts of orange shot into the blue dark of the plaza. The yellow-streaked western sky died behind the skyline of faceless black buildings. The cool dark air breathing on Jacko's cheek was full of the whispers of palm leaves, the bulks of all things were lost in shadows of themselves.

Then the station yard lights came on and everything snapped up out of the dark, palm trees, shops across the street, the baggage wagons standing abandoned, false as flats on a stage.

"I may have been described," Palafox said. "I'll wait here."

Jacko climbed down from the car and went through the station to the broad trackside platform, Mike following. The smooth steel rails shone dull gray; the top half of the moon had sneaked up over the row of flat black roofs across the way.

The platform began to vibrate. He stood up straighter, took out his gun and checked the loads. "What we want," he said to Mike, "is two men sitting together who look alike. *Sangre y pan* is the recognition signal."

"What's the countersign?"

116

"God knows," Jacko said. "We'll take them with the guns if we have to. You take the coaches from the rear, I'll go from the front, we'll meet in the middle."

The ground trembled. Invisible, the engine wailed and then the yellow eye of the black giant coming around the curve suddenly glared down the shining rails. The train slowed groaning and clanking past. Rows of yellow window squares flashed by above, light flickered on and off their faces. The orange light of the fires glared out from the belly of the engine, a great sideburn of steam blew out across the platform, and then the train, hissing, clanking, chuffing, squealed to a groaning stop and sank back, sighing exhausted steam. Mike was running for the last car. Jacko swung up into the steep steps of the first coach.

Inside, he walked swiftly along the paper-littered aisle, glancing down the ranks of green seats at the scatter of tired faces, pale in the lamplight. Three men, with seat backs swiveled so they faced each other, huddled over cards spread on the side of a suitcase; a woman and three children sprawled asleep; a woman nursed a baby. Single man in derby reading, single bearded man asleep.

He pushed through the heavy end door onto the gritty platform between the cars, pushed through another grimy door, looked down another rubbishy aisle, saw the same small scattering of people. No two men sitting together, much less looking alike. Mike came through the farther door.

"They're not on it," Mike said.

"Hell," Jacko said, "they must be in the Pullmans. How could Palafox be so sure they're poor? Nobody knows anything." He turned and they hurried back, dropped down the steps to the platform, ran to the front of the train. They walked swiftly through the three Pullman cars. No two men were sitting together, looking alike. They stood stumped in the middle of the aisle.

"Maybe they had a quarrel and are sitting apart," Jacko said.

"Or they didn't come," Mike said. "Or on another train. Or Chagoza—could Paz Faz and Gavira have been wise to Chagoza and fed him a lie?"

"If they were on to him, they'd have killed him."

The train jerked under their feet, Jacko caught a seat back to steady himself. "Get out and tell Palafox to follow the train to Spadra, it's only six miles. I'll keep looking. They've got to be on this damned thing somewhere."

As the train began to move, Jacko went back to the coaches and walked down the rocking aisle, this time more slowly. As he came to the man who was reading, another came out of the toilet at the end of the car, and Jacko stopped. Brown derbies, tight gray suits, white shirts, black string ties. The only difference was that the one seated reading was fat, and the one walking toward him was thin. Thin sat down beside fat. Fat or thin, they were alike even to the curve of their shoulders and the slant of their necks and eyebrows.

"Buenas noches, señores," Jacko said, advancing to them. "I believe the word this evening is *'sangre y pan.'* And you are the brothers Rivera, right? I am John O'Donohue, and I have been ordered to conduct you to Los Angeles."

They looked up at him, eyes sharp. "Who are you," the thin one said, "and what is this ridiculous talk about blood and bread? Who sent you?"

"Paz Faz and Gavira, who else?"

"And what is your cell?"

"El Torero."

The thin man's face relaxed a little. "All right. But explain to me why you meet us here, getting on at that town of Pomona, when it was planned we should be met in Pasadena?"

"May I sit down?"

"*¿Sí, cómo no?*" The other smiled. "My train is your train. You must excuse my brother, he is very suspicious." Jacko sat on the arm of the next seat. "We found out there was a spy in the cell. We couldn't take a chance that he heard we were planning to meet you in Pasadena and told Palafox. So we decided to back up one stop and meet you in Pomona, and take you by car into the city. That's all there is to it."

The thin one smiled warmly and stood up. "A pleasure to know you, señor. Forgive my suspicions. I am Raimondo Rivera, and this is my brother Ramon. And since it is too late for Pomona, and too dangerous in Pasadena, what shall we do?"

"There is a little village just ahead, Spadra, and the car will meet us there. If you will get your baggage together, I will ask the conductor to stop for us."

They stood on the platform at the end of the car watching dark orchards pinwheel by in the moonlight, waiting for the train to come to the trackside shed of the Spadra station.

"May I ask," Jacko said, "what is your profession, señor?" What had happened to Palafox's hayseeds?

Raimondo smiled. "I suppose you were expecting a couple of wild-eyed pickpockets," he said. "In Mexico, most of us are students or professionals or civil servants, the class strangled by Díaz and Huerta.

"I myself am a professor of law at the Instituto Científico at San Luis Potosí. My brother is a Latin scholar and editor of a scholarly journal in linguistics. From reading so much pagan literature, like the Ovid he is carrying, he has had to choose between becoming a lecher or a pessimist, and has chosen the latter, so don't expect much conversation from him." Jacko looked at his face, thin and refined, amused.

The train slowed, orange trees went by, the switch to the *estancia* spur clicked past beneath them, then the tiny Spadra station in its barren, dusty lot, and the train squealed to a stop. Jacko got down and helped with the two suitcases and a large hatbox. The tall cars rolled away behind them, the long line of bright squares shining down from the windows paraded off into the darkness.

"The car will be coming any minute," Jacko said. They stood in the moonlight, waiting. Across the tracks, the endless rows of orange trees began. A hundred yards down the line, the bulk of the *estancia* warehouse rose black against the moonlight glittering on the leaves of the trees.

"Who is that coming?" Ramon said, pointing his Ovid up the road. Headlights were bobbing up and down as a car jounced slowly over the potholes, and the Pierce Arrow pulled up. Palafox stepped down.

"*¡Que grandeza!*" Raimondo said, opening his eyes wide at the great car's glitter of nickel in the moonlight. "Anarchists in your country I see are unusually rich."

"Permit me to carry these," Jacko said, stooping and courteously picking up the two suitcases.

"And this," Mike said, picking up the hatbox.

"With your permission," Raimondo said, taking it back, "I will carry the monstrance, thank you. My responsibility is not over until I hand it to Señor Faz. I am sure you understand."

Jacko gestured toward Palafox, smiling in the headlights of his car. "And this is Señor Palante, the chief of counterintelligence of our cell."

"Ah, I had not heard of you, señor," Raimondo said.

"I must keep my activities very secret," Palafox said, smiling and shaking hands. "I work as a spy in the camp of the capitalist swine. It was I, in fact, and I am proud to say it, who discovered that Señor Palafox, that terrible fellow, was going to trap you tonight."

"Many thanks for your care, señor. I am happy we have someone so astute watching the enemy. A pleasure to make your acquaintance. Tell me, Señor O'Donohue, how is Paz Faz? And Gavira? We have never met, but we have had much correspondence."

"They're both fine," Jacko said. "If you will be so good as to seat yourselves in front with Señor Palante, who will drive us, you will have a better view of the city. The lights of the city at night are spectacular."

He opened the car door for them and climbed in beside Mike in the back. "Señor Palante, if you will be so good as to take that small road to the left, between those two rather broken colonial gateposts."

"We do not go by the highway, then?" Raimondo asked. "A secret route, perhaps?"

"Now," Jacko said, pulling his little Police Positive out of his pocket and showing it to the tail of Raimondo's eye, "please raise your hands, señores. You are under arrest for stealing from the Mexican government."

"You cannot do this!" fat Ramon cried. "We are not in Mexico, we have escaped! A crime in Mexico is not a crime here, in the land of the free. Is it?"

"I have my authority from Señor Palafox, the Mexican consul, who is also an honorary deputy sheriff of Los Angeles County. He is the gentleman who is sitting beside you."

"Palafox!" Raimondo cried. "Good God, that murderer, we are finished." Ramon made a lunge for the door. Mike caught his collar and hauled him back.

"Hands up, please," Jacko said, poking Raimondo gently in the back of the neck with the barrel of his pistol. "Don't be alarmed. All we want is the monstrance. Mike, put the cuffs on Don Ramon."

"Oh, hell," Mike said. "I forgot the damn things."

"You ass," Jacko said. He cuffed Raimondo and Ramon

121

together, right hand to left. "That'll have to do. Out, señores, and keep the hands high. I don't want any trouble."

They stood in the white moonlit dust of the road while Jacko and Mike searched them. Jacko pulled a little nickel-plated top-break gun from Ramon's belt. Mike got a four-barrel derringer from Raimondo. "You can let down your hands now, señores," Jacko said.

The twins stood desolate in the dust, all their pockets pulled inside out, hanging white in the moonlight like flags of surrender. What the hell are these two decent gentlemanly professors doing, Jacko thought, trying to be criminals?

"Please get back in the car," Jacko said.

"Three thousand miles for nothing," Raimondo said bitterly to his brother as he climbed in. "You and your plans."

"Are we in Pasadena?" Ramon asked, mocking him. "How could you fall for it?"

"Why did you?" Raimondo snapped back. "If you would get your nose out of your damned Latin classics, you might be of some use."

"Gentlemen," Jacko said, "take it easy. You could be dead, and you're not. Think of that. After we have inspected the monstrance, you will be freed and you can go on to Los Angeles and explain everything to Faz."

"He will kill us."

"Surely not. But if so, at least you may be comforted to have died among such good friends. Really, cheer up. Paz Faz will forgive you. Now, Señor Palafox, do you see the old windmill to your right there, in the dead trees? You can pull in beside it. No one comes by here at night, we will be perfectly private."

Palafox drove the Pierce Arrow off the narrow road, slowly down a bumpy aisle until it was forced to stop by bushes growing between the dead trees. He pulled up and turned off the lights. The moon shone cold on the dead white branches all around them, the pump clanked once against its lock as the blades above tried to turn in the night breeze. Palafox got an enormous flashlight from under the seat and shot the beam at the pumphouse.

"Douse that," Jacko said. "I don't want to alert anybody up the hill."

They climbed down from the car, the brothers stumbling awkwardly because of their handcuffs. Really, Jacko thought, why have you good and gentle people put me in the position of having to abuse you this way? Why couldn't you have been a couple of filthy bastards, so I could enjoy this?

"You," Palafox said to Raimondo, "which bag is the monstrance?" Raimondo stood silent, head up, body erect, refusing to admit humiliation.

Palafox smiled and picked up the hatbox. "I know you people. You talk justice and freedom. Freedom! What foolishness, what we want in Mexico is law and order."

"A law of dogs like you and Díaz," fat Ramon said, bristling. "Go on, kill me."

Palafox slapped him hard on the side of the head.

"Hey, hey there," Jacko said, shifting his gun. "Not while they're in my custody, you!"

"Let him kill me! Let the swine drown in my blood!"

"Listen to what the sausage says!" Palafox laughed. "The martyr, the hero. You liars! What would you dogs do with freedom? You anarchists are just like everybody else. Power-grabbers. Why don't you be honest about it, like Díaz?" He turned his back on the brothers. "Now show us the way, Señor O'Donohue," touching Jacko's shoulder gently.

CHAPTER TEN

THEY LEFT the car and tramped through the knee-high weeds toward the shack. Dry mustard stalks and brittle thistle crunched underfoot as they guided the handcuffed brothers through wild bushes springing up haphazard between the rows of skeleton trees. Ahead, the spindly frame of the windmill rose black against the star-lit sky. The pumphouse squatted in the moonlight, its walls of gray corrugated steel smudged here and there with dark growths of rust. Two crude little windows cut in the wall stared out of their prim wooden frames of flaking white like the eyes of an idiot.

Jacko shook the old wooden door. It stuck, warped in its frame, the foot of it embedded in a cast of mud accrued by petty winter floods. Shoving with his shoulder, he kicked the door loose and stumbled into the musty, oil-smelling dark, then saw above, in the far corner of the room, moonlight shining down through the rotten roof where the four legs of the tower came through.

"Give us a match," Jacko said to Mike. "There's a lamp in here somewhere."

Palafox flashed on his enormous "special service" Eveready and flicked the beam around the twenty-square-foot room. Black unknown shapes crowding the walls leaped out in the light and shrank away again. Jacko took the light and probed the beam along a workbench against the wall, found a dusty glass-bowled lamp, still half-full of kerosene. The wick flared orange in the draft from the door, shadows of strange shapes wavered, then steadied in rows of black smudge pots with their rusty stacks ranked along a wall; a battered bench with a heavy vise; a thicket of long pruning hooks, old split-handled shovels with eaten-out points, a bare-springed sagging bed, four barrels stacked teetering two-up, all a welter of brown on black.

Lording over all, filling a full quarter of the room, stood the four spindly steel legs of the mill tower splayed down through the roof, the cross-bracing throwing a shadow maze of x's and y's against the corner walls. A thin layer of dried mud covered the concrete floor, left by winter floods.

Jacko guided Raimondo by the arm to the near leg of the windmill, dragging Ramon along by his handcuff. "Sit on the floor," Jacko said, taking out his cuff key. He unlocked Raimondo's cuff, threaded Raimondo's arm around the tower leg, under the lowest cross brace, and cuffed his wrist again to Ramon's. They crouched together, in the center of the room, silent and withdrawn.

Palafox heaved the hatbox onto the table, shaking the lamp and the shadows, and stood with his back indifferent to the brothers, huddled on the floor close behind him. Jacko and Mike watched from the other side of the table.

Grunting with the weight, Palafox lifted out a bundle of white cloth, carefully unwound it, and gold suddenly

125

gleamed, jewels glowed and flashed red, blue, green, and glittering white in the warm lamplight.

"Ah," sighed Palafox and set the monstrance beside the lamp, put the hatbox out of the way on the floor.

As though put to sleep by the glowing brilliance of the golden sun, the three stood silent for a long time, and then Jacko gave a long sigh.

"It's a little cruder than I expected," Palafox said. "The value is reduced by the stones."

"What's the matter with the stones?" Mike asked. "Are they glass?"

"Oh my no!" Palafox said. "No glass faker would imitate such antique cutting. These are very old stones, not of modern cut at all, of course, probably old even in de Arfe's time." He smiled. "How foolish of me. Somehow I had imagined that everything would be of brilliant cut, or square, at least modern, which just shows the foolishness of imagination. In de Arfe's time, the brilliant cut had not been invented. Some of these, yes, these large ones, you see they are no more than polished, not cut at all, left almost in the natural state. Very likely Indian, these diamonds and rubies.

"Take this great diamond at the head of the cross, very old, hardly shaped at all, maybe brought from India by the Portuguese in Goa, perhaps taken at the massacre of the Mohammedans by Albuquerque. Or who knows, even four hundred years before Christ, brought by the subtle Persians in their caravans of dromedaries from Kalikat to Pericles of Athens, made loot by Caesar at Pharsalus, traded for Egyptian wheat by Diocletian, taken by raping Saracens to Spain, and by the swords of Aragon at infidel Granada, and so from hand to noble hand till saved from Joanna's crazy crown by some old greedy bishop, who brought it to de Arfe. How else?" He laughed. "They're all so old, these stones, they'd have to be recut to have any value nowadays. I mean, if taken out of the monstrance."

"What of it?" Jacko said. "Nobody's going to take them out of the monstrance, since it belongs to the Church. Let's pack it up and go, so I can free these gentlemen."

"On the other hand," Palafox said, tip of forefinger at mouth, "none of this would affect the museum value." What naïveté, he thought, looking up at Jacko. He brushed back his jacket and pulled out his heavy pistol, held it on Jacko and Mike. They stiffened, alert.

"Don't be offended, señores," he said, "this is purely defensive, no one will be hurt, not even these *chinches* on the floor. I have changed my mind. My brother Herculano has said I am foolish not to sell to a museum in Europe, and I have been thinking about his advice. What's more, I had a dream last night, a warning of the miseries of poverty, and I decided then to take it to a certain museum in Cologne that Herculano recommends. I have been the victim of my own foolish scruples! I will clean out my safe and my office tonight. Don't worry! I will send you your expense money in the mail. That should be enough for your trouble. Herculano is flying me to a certain port where I will sail in a certain ship leaving in a week." He smiled at Jacko. "You do not seem surprised, Señor O'Donohue."

Jacko relaxed against the bench. "I always had a feeling there was something unreal about your arrangement. It was ridiculous to believe that you would be satisfied with $60,000 by returning it to the Church, when you could get ten times that by selling it yourself."

"Well, the change has cost you nothing, after all," Palafox said. "I would apologize for disappointing you about the job, but how can you be said to have lost a fee of $12,000 when you never earned it? What have you lost? Only expectations. But then life itself, as we grow older,

127

might be said to be nothing but lost expectation, might it not? Who ends with what he hoped for?

"That is my problem, Juan, if now at parting I can address you as a friend; age, that creeps up on a diminishing career, when all my frail advantages begin to fade away. Alas for all my days of luxury with that most noble Don Porfirio, I am left now with a drunken Indian for a lord, my poor Pierce Arrow blunted with four years of wear and failing like my fortunes.

"How shall Huerta bear against the pressure of the rising tide against him? All his generals are old, their eyes and noses run like creeks, they can no longer see anything but their spectacles, smell anything but the mold on their moustaches, hear anything but their bowels; their armies are a horde of drunks, idiots, *enganches* shanghaied in the streets, pickpockets and pimps whipped out of the jails into uniform, driven like sheep, sure to desert at the first shot. When Huerta falls, where will I stand? We all flee in the end, Santa Ana to Granada, Porfirio to Paris, and Huerta, where? when the time comes. And I? Should I wear out a loyalty already worn too thin, stand by the dead, cast out by a rebel government to starve in the slums of Los Angeles? when I can sit like a king, or say a count, in the cafés of Paris? I think not. So farewell."

"By all means, take the monstrance," Jacko said. "Who has mentioned robbery here? Not I. Call it the spoils of war, or what you like, a change of mind if you prefer, and not the revelation of a lie, why should I care? It's not mine, never was entrusted to me. As you say, I have lost nothing, can claim nothing. So put your gun away. If you rob the Church, custom will surely give her consolation, she has been robbed every day for four hundred years, and one more pilfering is nothing but a feather on her tons of loss."

"With Señor Horton glaring at me," Palafox said,

amused, "I'll keep the gun out. But I am glad you understand. I regret leaving you here on foot, but you have two of them, and if you wear one out on the way to Los Angeles, you have the other. Good luck to you, my friend."

Jacko laughed. "And the same to you, señor."

He watched, amused, as Palafox lifted the hatbox to the table, took out the white cloth to rewrap the monstrance, and screamed, his mouth and eyes opening wide. His arms flung out, the hatbox and the gun fell to the floor, and he sank, trying to hold on to the edge of the table.

Jacko stood openmouthed, and then leaped forward. Ramon, his mouth a grimace of ultimate determination, with his free arm was stabbing Palafox's right thigh with a short knife again and again as fast as he could, bringing Palafox down, and Palafox fell backward, screaming, twisting, trying to beat off Ramon with his fists. The knife sank into his belly, he fell back, the bright blood growing like a scarlet rose on his white shirt. Mike's gun roared beside Jacko, Ramon collapsed, blood spurting from his neck, and Palafox's gun came up from the floor in Raimondo's hand, fired in Mike's face and missed as Mike fired again. Raimondo sank limp, Mike's gun came down on him a second time, Jacko knocked it up with his arm and it fired through the roof. Jacko chopped his fist down on Mike's arm and the gun fell out of his hand.

Jacko stood trying to drag himself out of the stupor of shock. Palafox stared up at him with eyes seeming to ask for some explanation, surprised as a child. He said in a low voice, "Not yet, not yet," and the low mound of blood pumping up from his belly sank and died. He slumped down limp beside Ramon, and they lay huddled on the dried mud almost as though sleeping in each other's arms.

Raimondo was struggling to breathe, a small red hole in his shirt front was blowing red bubbles in a quick stream. Jacko went round the table to him and knelt. Raimondo coughed blood. There was nothing Jacko could do about a lung shot. He knew the blood was rising as it rattled in Raimondo's straining breath. He watched, knowing the blood was pouring from the filled lung over the bronchial fork into the other, that Raimondo was drowning in it. Raimondo twisted, raising his hands, the bright blood frothed out of his mouth, he choked, then his arms and legs dropped slack and the highlights in his eyes slowly dulled away.

Jacko stood silent, looking at the three lying at his feet, from life to death in ten seconds. The lamplight trembled, the monstrance stood shining and glorious. A moth batted against the smoking lamp, fell fluttering to the table.

Jacko, cold and sick, turned his back. All around him lay death, the dead smudge pots, dead tools, dead bare-springed bed, dead windmill, dead mud, rust, silence, dark, and on the floor three dreams of life as by some magic spiraled in an instant far away.

Before him the monstrance shone in all its splendor, indifferent, serene, waiting for what? to be taken up by whom, now, on what journey? Out of him slowly rose a laboring groan of pain. "Oh Jesus," he said, "how could it have happened?"

"He had a knife," Mike said. "The little fat one."

"I know that, but where was it? You searched him."

"I don't know. I looked."

"In his shoe," Jacko said. "Slid down in the back of that high shoe beside his heel. You didn't look there?"

"No, for Christ's sake," Mike said. "How would I know he'd have a knife in his shoe?"

"How would you know! Good God! You stupid son of a bitch, why didn't you look? And the handcuff you forgot, you ass. If they'd been properly handcuffed, it couldn't have happened."

Mike's face turned red. "What's the difference!" he

130

shouted. "They're nothing but a bunch of lousy greasers anyway, so what if they are all dead? Haven't you seen a hundred dead in the fields at Iliolo? Are these in some way deader, or less dead, or a different kind of dead, that you curse me now when you ordered me to fire then? Yes, I forgot to look, am I God to know everything, to think of everything, are you God to expect me to? Up your ass, O'Donohue, fuck you hell west and crossways, shit on you!"

"Lousy greasers! You blockhead, you've got the sense of a goddam hog. You were going to murder Raimondo."

"Murder!"

"With that second shot I stopped, pure murder, you bloody butcher."

"You know the rule, keep shooting till they're down."

"He was down, damn you. You get stupider by the day. You bastard, you'd have emptied the gun in him. Thank God we're through."

He stood sick with disgust, and suddenly a realization came flooding down over his mind like the breaking of a dam: you're leading a dirty life, a really dirty life. How did you get here, in this place, with a murderer and three dead men that have no business being dead? How? What have you done, to have got so dirty?

They stood silent, shouted out, looking dumbly at the monstrance, letting the shock that had frightened and enraged them trickle away.

Then Mike said, "I'm sorry, Jacko." And he was, except inside something screamed with rebellion, at being sorry, sorry all the time. Yet where would he have been without Jacko? In Leavenworth for bursting Filipino bellies? In San Quentin for killing that chink? He knew he had just wits enough to know he couldn't really go it alone. His brain stabbed him with something else: in his heart he was already depending on May for advice and guidance, on what to do when they cut loose. Was that the real reason he had asked her? because he was afraid of being alone, without Jacko?

For a moment he felt like crying, oh, the decent, innocent days of the track team, the university, before his balls somehow got such an ascendancy over his brains. That was the trouble, the storms of lust that surged like surf over his mind, like when just now he'd wanted to shoot the greaser full of holes, pulverize him into hamburger. Why? A kind of love, it came over him in a passion, ever since the belly-bursting.

"What am I to do with that thing?" Jacko said, very tired, looking at the monstrance. "I wish to God I'd never heard of it."

"Yes, but it's ours," Mike said in a low voice. "All ours. Do you realize that? There's nobody left to put a hand on it but us."

"It belongs to the Church."

"Nobody but us even knows for sure the brothers came, or that they even had it. The whole thing is ours." And the whole thing was getting simpler, he thought, and his mind pulled itself together. No more Palafox to worry about. Just Jacko, to be slipped the Mickey tonight.

He began packing the monstrance in its wrappings, stuffed it into the hatbox. "Let's get out of here." He headed for the door.

"Hold on," Jacko said. Mike kept on going. Jacko followed, saw him stooping to crank the car. "Just a minute," Jacko said, putting his hand on Mike's arm. "We can't leave the bodies here."

Mike stood up. "The hell we can't," he said. "Do what you damned please, Jacko, I'm going to Guaymas with this thing in the morning. Get away from me."

Jacko grabbed at the crank, Mike yanked it away and raised it to strike.

"Idiot," Jacko said, and came down with his fist on Mike's shoulder, beside the neck, with a blow that would have carried through to his left ankle, and Mike's arm fell, the shoulder paralyzed. The crank fell out of his hand.

Mike stood staring at Jacko with helpless eyes. Jesus, he thought. Jesus, I was going to kill him.

There was too much confusion in his head. His insides were still shaking from the killing, he was half sick, he hardly knew what had happened. In the Philippines everything was always planned, he had always been geared up for killing, on command. But inside his sickness and confusion flickered and rose a yammering yelling of victory, the thing was all his, all his. And in turn the victory was steamed around with a smoke of tears, for beneath the ache of his shoulder was the real hurt that Jacko for the first time in their fifteen years had struck him. But he knew, slowly shaking his head, that it was his fault. He shouldn't have raised the crank. That was the sadness of it. His fault, again. Sorry, sorry, sorry, oh God, when will I be through being sorry? I wouldn't harm you for anything in the world, Jacko, just a little Mickey that wouldn't hurt a fly.

"We've got to get these bodies away from here," Jacko said quietly. "I won't have them found here to bring trouble on my people." He turned back toward the pumphouse.

Mike stood still in the moonlight, a sliver of common sense prodding up through his muddled mind. Here he'd been ready to run, where? in a bloody panic, leaving bodies all over the place to raise a million questions. Jacko would have to think them out of this, lead him out of this. Humbly he followed Jacko into the shack.

"They'll miss Palafox in town in the morning," Jacko said, looking down at the bodies. "And Paz Faz will miss the brothers. The police will be in it. We'll have to fix it so they'll never think of us. We can't be held up by an investigation, if we're sailing tomorrow. If we go. I'm not sure what to do with that thing."

"What do you mean, if we go? The money, Jacko, the money."

"Damn the money," Jacko said. "All I can think of is all this blood and those poor bastards lying there."

With the bodies loaded in the back of the car, rolling back and forth over the potholes, they drove back to Pomona, naked to the waist to save their clothes from the blood, a lunatic spectacle in the moonlight. But who was to see them in the godforsaken countryside? and at ten o'clock, the Pomona station was dead, lights off except for the telegraph office. The square, the street were empty.

They dragged the brothers from the car and arranged them near the trackside waiting-room door, out of sight of the street. The two suitcases lay tumbled beside them. A simple robbery, unfortunately resisted. Palafox's body they laid on the floor in the rear of the car.

They carried fire buckets from the row sitting in their sockets against the station wall and sluiced out the car's backseat and floor, washed their bodies, arms, and hands and put back on their shirts and jackets. They drove away, silent, back toward the city, the hatbox like a third person between them.

What to do with it? Jacko thought as Mike drove fast back down the dusty highway. Throw it in the ocean. But it was not his to throw. Get the $60,000? He didn't want it, not when the thought of it reminded him of the dead law professor, the dead Latin scholar, the useless loss. Should he go bedraggling down to Guaymas, the thing in his hand, begging a reward for three deaths that should never have happened, like some beggar trying to peddle a bag of bones?

"By God, we're lucky," Mike said as they sped along

with the bright moon chasing them, the wind tearing at his words. "All ours. Just fallen into our hands like a gift from God. We're in the clear for $60,000 all our own."

All your own, you mean, Jacko thought, you sweating liar, along with my wife. You think I can't read that nit of a mind of yours? Steal the monstrance and the woman too, is your idea. Well, you're welcome to her, at least as far as the gangplank. All I have to do is get rid of you and her, and then the monstrance, and then what, then what? Cool down, cool down, think.

Mike jammed on the brakes and pulled off the dirt highway onto the grass.

"What the hell are you doing, you idiot?"

Mike pulled a cigar out of his inside pocket and tried to light a match. Jacko knocked it out of his hand.

"Jesus, it's my nerves, Jacko. I got to have a smoke."

"I'll give you smoke. Get out of that seat and let me drive." He shoved Mike out into the road and stepped on the gas. Mike grabbed the rear door as it went by and hauled himself into the back. He sat there hardly aware that his feet were sunk in Palafox's jiggling belly.

"Some friend!" Mike wailed. "Dump me in the sticks!" He got out another cigar and sat there sucking on it, looking bitterly at the back of Jacko's neck. He swallowed some weed juice and felt stronger. Screw you, he thought, remembering his plans. He felt in his pocket for Mrs. Ciro's little bottle of medicine, and suddenly reassured, relaxed and sank back in the seat. Let the smartass captain up ahead throw his weight around for now, he'd end up dumped on his head.

Jacko shoved the accelerator into the floor to try to get the car up to forty. The folded cloth roof was beginning to raise and jump up and down with the wind.

What to do with this thing in the box sitting beside him? Had it fallen into his hands as a sort of trust? His heart sank sick into cynicism; or was it reality rearing its ugly head? You're sick to your stomach, he thought, because your smart-ass tricks have led to three deaths, and all this nobility of rejecting the money, and pious thoughts about trust are nothing but your vanity, struggling in the mud to save itself. Just turn it in for the money, fool, and the Church gets it back and you get paid. If you had ever wanted a decent life, why did you choose working for lawyers? And as for shame and regrets, shut up.

They came over the last long hill and the midnight lights of Los Angeles spread out before them.

"There's a lot to do," Jacko yelled at Mike against the wind. "With Palafox dead we've got to get in his office for the visa stamp, get some money, the letter. We've got his keys in the car lock there. That'll let us in his apartment, and I hope to God he's got a key safe and not a combination." How will I save the hatbox from the cops, he thought, when we catch Mike and the bitch getting on the ship? I can't let the police have it.

They left the Pierce Arrow where Palafox parked it, in the old stable near the Cordova, and Palafox's body face-up on the cobbles in the alley, all his pockets pulled inside out, his wallet torn open in the gutter, its papers scattered. Jacko took what money was in it up the stairs to the apartment and, after a brief dispute with Mike about looting, left it in Palafox's safe, along with the $7,000 already there. He took from the safe the promised $1,000 expense money and all the papers about the monstrance. He got the visa stamp out of Palafox's desk, found a screwdriver in the kitchen and splintered up the front door jamb by the lock to make it look like a forced entry.

He put the keys back in the car lock and they headed for Bunker Hill, keeping to the dark alleys and pausing at the corners to look for cops. Oh, the glorious folly and nonsense of life, Jacko thought bitterly, hurrying along in the dark with the hatbox dragging at his arm. Oh, the stupidity, the accident, the gaiety of senselessness. What did it mean? Nothing. Why should I not be saddled with a crazy trust, he thought, since all of it is crazy anyway. He remembered the time when he stood on the platform at USC with his new diploma in his hand, thinking his life had a fate, a direction, before he became nothing but a straw, the victim of a thousand accidents and secret motives, swirling helpless in a river flowing toward an unknown sea.

Halfway up Hope Street with the La Touraine and safety clear before him, an image of Herculano's face, looking down at his dead brother, suddenly rose out of the dark of his mind. Oh God, he thought, and began to run. No, no, he thought, slowing down. Don't panic, just get your butt on that blessed boat before he figures it out, and you're home free.

CHAPTER ELEVEN

J ACKO, FOLLOWING Mike into the La Touraine apartment, judged from the irritation in the faces of Becky and May, both a little drawn by the midnight hour, that all anticipation of a party had died of waiting at about eight o'clock. Both of them had put on their most extravagant gowns in the hope of inducing some festivity, May splendidly blond in black satin and tulle edged with brilliants, a Barbier copy; Becky quite as striking in an amethyst tube gown of chiffon over a charmeuse slip, with a tunic of lace embroidered with gold, a Poiret copy which May guessed she had bought downtown at the Mart, the least expensive fashion thieves in Los Angeles, for about $15. Becky wore a large brooch of many diamonds, a gift from her father, at her breast.

Their fatigue and boredom with waiting four hours was embittered by the contrast of their finery, so specially perfected, with the wrinkled, dusty suits and stale shirts of their husbands, an affront which had the effect, on May, of making her feel overdressed, but on Becky, who knew her rights as a woman, of making her furious. They bit their lips and murdered their husbands in their minds.

Two bottles of champagne lay in a bucket as though in a coffin, labels floating off like souls detaching themselves from the dead. All the ice had died back into water.

The four stood around the table in the living room looking at the monstrance. The building creaked in the silence as the night deepened. The wicked little yellow coils trembling in the clear glass globes of the electrolier gleamed down enviously on the gold and jewels. The monstrance stood aloof in splendid isolation, like a captive foreigner beset by the shoddy furniture.

"So that's what it's all about," May said. "Is that thing worth $600,000? Why not sell it here? Why does Palafox want it back in Mexico?"

"Because that's where the owner is," Jacko said, keeping his voice civil, and smiled a little tightly to himself. The usual cry for immediate satisfaction. He dealt out on the table the things they had taken from Palafox's apartment.

"How absolutely beautiful it is," Becky said. "It almost makes me wish I had a religion."

"A religion!" May said. "You call that thing religious? Put it away! I can't stand the sight of it. It's a greasy wop piece of Catholic junk, is what it is." She sneaked a side glance at Jacko and when he said nothing, she went on driving in hat pins of nasty thoughts. "Superstition is what it is. All that hocus-pocus and bowing, it's all idolatry and the whore of Babylon. It's probably got a curse on it, a hex like on those barns."

She looked a challenge around at the others. "I say bust it up, sell it here, get rid of the evil papist thing."

Jacko's mouth was twitching.

"How do you know how many devils will come out of it," she cried, "if you play around with that thing?"

Jacko burst out laughing. "Ah, May, you should have been a preacher down in the swamps somewhere, you would have made a million spreading the truth about the dirty Catholics. No, dearest, it's going to Mexico where it belongs."

He turned his back on May and said to Becky, "I'm sorry we were so long in getting back. A lot of complications."

"It doesn't matter," she said sharply, "if you don't mind damp crackers and warm pâté." Who was he, so lordly and tall and full of his male conceit to be doing her the favor of apologizing? Let him keep his apologies! Various nursing-school epithets whispered in her inner ear: Up yours! Stuff it—rectally! She hurriedly squelched this disgusting choir, hating the school which had forever dirtied her mind, and blamed Jacko for it.

Why was she so sharp? he wondered. There were times she was gentle, a sweet little thing, and he was tempted to like her; then all her spines would stick up like a porcupine for no reason at all. What sense did women make, after all? Put on earth for a penance, most of them. But then, poor things, they could not help their immaturity and waverings. Of course he was not such a fool as to consign all women to the category of dingbat, as did so many of his friends in the safety of their clubs. Indeed he had once painfully worked out as an explanation of their minds the formula "acceptable intelligence effectually destroyed by unspeakable atavisms," but discarded it when he realized in a moment of grace that this applied to himself quite as well.

He looked away from her at the flowers she had so tastefully arranged and placed on the table, and thought of the six dollars lonely in his pocket. Time and fatigue had made the reward money less contemptible. He would at least get something out of the wreckage of the evening, even though the money still seemed somehow bought with blood. He fought off the sentimentality of the thought. Scruples made him itch. He certainly needed the money. Maybe a bit of champagne would lighten his gloom. He pulled a dripping bottle out of the bucket.

Becky was rubbing dust off the monstrance. "Don't touch that thing!" May cried, and they began to bicker.

He turned away sighing. His internal screaming protest against the three useless deaths had finally eased into a mental background of fatalistic acceptance. It had taken the dangerous work of burglarizing Palafox's apartment to do this, along with an exasperating argument needed to keep Mike from stripping the whole $7,000 of Palafox's funds from the safe, instead of merely the $1,000 they had been promised.

He realized, with a difficult objectivity, that his sense of shock had been due simply to the suddenness of what had happened. But he could not understand his sense of guilt at what had been innocently unforeseen, almost an accident. Drat the damned bottle! The wire had stabbed his thumb. He began working the cork out as though he were choking somebody. Damned anarchists! Why couldn't those Riveras have stayed in Mexico?

He realized suddenly that what he had felt as guilt was really a nauseous revulsion against what had been his amusement at the affair, as though the pathetic crimes of the Riveras had been a comedy played for his benefit. It was the memory of Ramon's fat face as he attacked Palafox's leg that had pulled his levity down in a bitter crumbling of shame. His life of amusement had stumbled over something hard, dead men, a stink he had hoped to bury for good.

He was sick of the whole thing, and he was stuck with

it. But if he was stuck with the monstrance, which now seemed to him in some way evil, glittering and gleaming on the table, he would get paid for being stuck.

He shot the cork at the electrolier and broke a bulb. May laughed as the glass showered down. Mike set down a fistful of wine glasses on a side table and said, "Gimme that," and grabbed the frothing bottle. "I'm the host here, old Jacko." He turned his back and began pouring. He handed the glasses around.

Jacko took one sip of the wine and set it aside, began checking over the stuff on the table that they would need the next day. Two steamship tickets; the thousand dollars of expense money; two passports which he had stamped and signed with Palafox's carefully forged signature; the letter from the Archbishop's office attesting the reward; the letter prepared by Palafox in readiness for their sailing, appointing him as deputy consul, empowered to exchange for the reward.

"Everything we need, Mike," he said. It was late, he would go home with May after one or two quick drinks. If she was stuck with him at home, how would the crooks work it? He'd have to take the monstrance home with him. Then she would probably sneak out of the house with it and her suitcase, and join Mike. It was too simpleminded, but how else would they do it?

There was only one problem. He could not let her take the monstrance. Linebarger would be along when he caught them on the ship. He couldn't take the chance of Linebarger's grabbing it.

And then again, suppose May had known Lilly was spying? Suppose the Buenos Aires business was all bluff, to fool Lilly, and they were really going to fence the monstrance here, or even in New York? He couldn't gamble on letting them have it even overnight.

He took the monstrance from the table, wrapped it carefully in its white cloth and put it back in the hatbox.

"I suppose as deputy consul I'll have some kind of diplomatic immunity down in Guaymas," he said to Mike, "but I'd feel better going through customs if this were hidden a little. Better not take a chance that they'll want to look at the baggage, if they're still as crooked as ever. Becky, do you have an old hat with a wide brim, something you'd be getting rid of, that we could lay on top in the hatbox to hide the monstrance? Any old thing would do."

"Give him that old thing that looks like a basket of dead pheasants," Mike said.

"How well it would suit you, Jacko!" Becky said. "*Of course* you can have my old hats to wear."

He felt his neck stiffen and his shoulders hunch to start off a stiff right, and immediately pulled himself together again, adopting a languid stance. Drat any woman who could make him mad. He sat on the sofa watching Mike busy with the food at the side table.

Becky came from the bedroom with a hat. He took it from her hand, with a jerk at the end. "I'm going to put this thing where it'll be safe."

He carried the hatbox from the living room through the dining room and kitchen into the studio, leaving the others behind eating and drinking. He took the monstrance out of the box and hid it behind the background of Becky's still-life setup. He picked half a dozen rocks from the collection on the shelf, packed them in the hatbox for make-weights and padded them with the white cloth, then covered them with Becky's old hat. He took the hatbox back to the dining room and left it there, went back to the living room and sat down on the sofa beside Becky.

Mike was standing with his back to them, twisting the wire off the last bottle as though wringing its neck.

"Just what are we celebrating?" Becky asked. "You two are as glum as forgotten heirs. Do we *have* to drink?"

"You're damn right we do," Mike said. He turned with a wide fixed grin and handed a glass to May. "We're going to drink to new prosperity. Doesn't that call for a drink? What's the matter with you? Here, Jacko old boy, drink up." He handed a glass to Becky. "Cheers, my dear."

"Cheers yourself." She was in a bad nurse mood. "This is one hell of a party. Who's died? You jokers come back looking like Custer's ghost and start up this fake celebration like pushing a hearse." She knew she was sounding common, but the nurse world had seized her and she didn't care. "Why don't you go home, Jacko? I'm tired. My eyes are sticking together. I want to go to bed."

"Listen to the little wet blanket," Mike said. "So go to bed, what's stopping you?"

"Well, *I'm* not going to bed," May said, gulping her drink. "What we need is some music. If you didn't want to dance, Becky, why did you roll up the carpet?"

Suddenly, remembering herself kneeling on the floor, Becky felt like crying, and furiously bit her tongue to kill the feeling.

May cranked up Mike's big Victrola and out came the scrape, scrape, scrape of the needle and a sudden blast of tango. She glided over to Mike, and handed him her empty glass. He filled it again and passed the others around.

Jacko sat on the sofa with Becky at the other end and watched Mike and May gliding through a ferocious tango. Becky was holding her glass as though waiting for somebody to take it away.

"So you finally got rid of Mike," she said. "What's taken you so long? Just simple cowardice? It's absolutely absurd to pretend the lawyers object to a little gambling. Even if they are *your* stupid lawyers." Why did she feel so bitter? Was it just anger at this big rooster with his boiled shirt bulging out?

"They aren't my stupid lawyers," Jacko said, "they're everybody's. And I think Mike's rather happy to break us up, look at him dancing." In some ways she reminded him of Mrs. Ciro. But that was his own fault, the result of his telling Becky a dumb joke about women's rights the first time he had met her. After that irreparable error, her spear-pointed fences had gone up, and he had long since quit trying to climb over them.

"How about another slug of this juice?" he asked, smiling. He had had a happy thought, and felt better.

"No *thanks*."

The happy thought was that with Mike in jail, he would be saying goodbye to this nasty little wasp forever. He could afford to be charitable, remember that she had her good side, hidden somewhere. He had seen her tending her little garden in the back, quite touching and humble, and she once had stroked Merlette in a way that made him want to stroke her, in turn. When she kept her mouth shut, she could make a very dear little woman, probably, if that could ever happen. Let's forget her jackass parades and principles, he thought. She could even be quite interesting with her photography, if she would quit turning his polite question or two into a three-hour seminar. The wine was loosening his brains and prejudices. Bless her! She was a dear little thing, in a way. He felt like putting his arm around her shoulders, to comfort her.

"How absurd this whole affair is," she said, ignoring him. "Celebrating a disaster at midnight with everybody's nerves on edge for some reason, Mike and that ghastly gaiety of his. What's the matter with him? Dancing. He never dances unless he's half-tight. What's got into him?"

"Being a little tense is a wonderful reason for having a

145

drink," he said. Be a sport! this can't last long. He lifted his glass. "Here's to masses of money, Becky. Up we go!"

She sat there like a stick, staring resentfully at nothing, the glass warming in her hand. "I find it odd that Mr. Palafox would let that very valuable piece of art out of his sight. Why did he let you and Mike, of all people, take it tonight, instead of meeting you tomorrow with it at the boat? He must be very trusting."

He felt his good cheer go down like a stone. "What do you mean, 'of all people,' " he said nastily before he could catch himself up. "Whup!" he cried, forcing a grin. "Whoa there, Becky my dear. Come on, let's drink to the tango. Do you dance?" He raised his glass once more. "Let's drink to sudden riches, dear." Just like the sergeant. He smothered a laugh.

She took a sip. After all, the poor man was trying to be accommodating, and with the partnership a bust, she wouldn't have to see him again. But the nurse came out of her mouth. "I am not your dear, never was, never will be."

"Never say never, my pussywillow, it's a hostage to future developments. I remember once I said I would never buy a roan horse, and two weeks later I bought a roan horse I hated. What do you think of that? Here's to Mike's new agency," he said gaily, "Mike would be disappointed if we didn't toast it." He raised his glass again.

Something was the matter with his head. He was actually flirting with this woman.

She gave him her dead-eyed look. Was he actually flirting with her? This great boob? Well, he *was* handsome in an ungainly way, too crude, but then. Pity he was stuffed with dead patriarchal ideas. There was, in fact, something almost comfortable about him. Too bad he had so many faults. Pussywillow indeed. Still, she should not be rude.

She took another swallow for civility's sake and pursed her mouth in distaste. "Mike could have done better in a wine. This has a very odd taste. Tell me, why do you insist on being so jolly at a funeral? All these hilarious toasts. Say something amusing if we're going to keep on being so gay and lighthearted."

He tried to think of something amusing. Nothing came. All she could do was complain. Such a charming companion. He wanted to strangle her.

The tango music swerved and dipped, Mike and May sped swiftly back and forth, around the room, swooping, swirling.

Becky patted back a yawn. "Oh, dear," she said and yawned again. Her eyes closed. "I'm really too sleepy to stay up any longer, no matter how amusing you are." She dragged her eyes open again and blinked at him slowly like a sun-dazed owl.

He frowned at her, puzzled. Could she be drunk on one glass? She was drooping like a new widow's smile. He watched her as she watched the dancers.

Slowly his mind became calm, he relaxed. There was nothing to worry about. He'd catch the two tomorrow. He watched the dancers. Dip and swirl, turn and glide, Mike grinning at May. How mysteriously May was smiling at Mike, in the way that had so intrigued him long ago. The Cleopatra act. What was the mystery of woman? Emptiness? Deep design? If not one, then the other. Who would he marry next, to get his children? He could not imagine her.

He smiled benignly at Becky. He smiled benignly at the lovers. How nicely you dance, he thought, and how nicely you'll hang each other tomorrow morning, hand in hand at the pier, the lovers caught, tickets in hand, proof of desertion. Up at seven, get Linebarger. He was beginning to get sleepy. Maybe he had better dance to wake himself up.

What had he wanted Becky to do? He struggled to collect his mind, but nothing happened. What was Becky doing? She had fallen over onto her side on the sofa. He wanted to laugh.

He watched the dancers gracefully dip and sway, swirl and circle. Suddenly the room lurched, the floor tilted, shook itself like a dog and righted again. What's this? he thought, blinking his eyes to clear them. Mike and May glided smoothly down the sloping deck toward him, stood over him staring down. The ship rolled back, he wanted to cry out, Stop! you're making me dizzy! but he was choking. The sea roared in his ears, he tried to raise his arms from the heaving waters to signal to the fast-receding ship, he tried to call for help, but an immense wave rolled over him and he went down, down, burble, burble, and lay, with Becky sound asleep beside him, in the silence of the deep.

"How cute they look, side by side," May said. "Like the babes in the woods."

Mike stood chuckling, looking down at Jacko. He felt fine, bang, clang, he'd hit the prize bell first shot, with Mrs. Ciro's help. His confidence had grown back, he felt up to anything.

His mad dismay of the morning, when he had tried to spit on Jacko's hat, and wept at his disloyalty, had settled down, since he had garnered May, and all his viny tentacles of helplessness, torn loose from reliance on Jacko, as from a stout brick wall, after waving wildly around for half a day, had settled gratefully on his new mistress. All his million little sucking feet now clung as comfortably to her as they had ever clutched at fallen Jacko, and looking down at him now he saw almost a stranger, and not a master. How had he ever been afraid of this sprawl on the sofa? Or had he been? It must have been a dream.

Oh glorious freedom! his heart cried, flying aloft, cock-a-doodle-doo, and he flapped his soul's wings. He looked fondly at May. She'd see how clever he had been. He put his arm around her, she shook it off. His rich mouth pouted for a moment. But just wait till she heard what he'd done, he thought, and smiled again.

"It was easy," he said. "Mrs. Ciro fixed me up with the dope like I said she would. She's always hated him for a lousy snob. He should have patted her butt and tickled her tits, the way I did, and made her friendly. So much for lordly Jacko. Let's get the hell out of here, May darling. I'll pack a suitcase and then we'll go to your place and sleep there."

"Alone."

"Yes, dear."

He went into the bedroom to pack and left her looking down at Jacko as he lay sprawled half-sliding off the sofa. She smiled. It was the first time she had ever seen him rumpled. She put a satin toe under his outstretched leg and gave it a heave. He slid off the sofa and folded softly down onto the floor, began to snore. She laughed.

She turned and studied the assortment of documents on the table. "What about this?" she called after Mike in the bedroom, and picked up Palafox's letter. "This makes Jacko a deputy, not you. What are you going to do when they ask you where he is? And who are you supposed to be?"

Mike came back holding a pair of shoes to his heart and looked at the letter. "What the hell's all the worry about? We got all the papers, that thousand dollars there. I got $3,800 my own money, and I'm going to go back and clean out Palafox's safe, that's another $6,000. I'll just be Mr. Jacko when we get there."

"You mean use Jacko's passport? You'd never get past the customs. If it's wartime down there, the army's taken over the port. You want to get caught lying with a stolen passport and get shot for a spy or something?"

"How about swapping the photos?"

"Too different altogether."

Mike slumped down at the table. "So what the hell do we do?"

She stood over him looking down at his red head with a remotely motherly smile. There was some consolation in having a blockhead for a quasi-lover, management was no longer a problem. A glorious relief after that bastard Jacko, who was always outwitting her. She looked at Jacko, snoring on the floor. Bastard? Now that she was leaving him in the lurch, her heart relented. He looked very uncomfortable, with his coat and vest rumpled up under his chin, his face a pulsing red.

"I think he's strangling," she said.

"So let him strangle," Mike cried. "What'll we do about this?" He stood shaking the letter in the air.

She stooped and loosened Jacko's collar, stripped off his neat bow tie. He snorted once and the blood sank out of his face. "There," she said. "Ittums oppums better, ipsum dishy baby?" She laughed and patted his unconscious nose. "Atsum ittums ittle umawama."

"The hell with him," Mike cried. "What about me?"

She whirled on him and snarled in his face. "The hell with you, you fat jackass. I do what I want, understand?" She raised a delicate fist, his mouth opened in alarm and he ducked, crouching, and she laughed again.

"What'll we do? Why didn't you think of things? Why didn't you get him to make you a deputy too?"

"Are we stuck? Jesus, May, be decent, there's no need to get tough. Let's think this thing out."

"Let's *me* think this thing out," she said. She sat down and tried to read the Archbishop's letter. "What's this say?"

"That promises the reward and describes the monstrance."

She looked up at him. "And you show up with the monstrance in a hatbox at the customs. So they open it looking for a hat and see a fortune staring them in the face. What makes you think they won't dump us in the ocean and get the reward for themselves? From what I know of the greasers in L.A., they'll cut your throat for a nickel any time you're looking the other way."

"All right, all right, what do we do? Jesus, Jacko must have had an answer."

"I'll tell you what we do, by God, we'll fence it right here in Los Angeles. I'm not going to Guaymas with that thing. You know those Catholics put a curse on that stuff to kill a Protestant if they touch it. They're always trying to kill Protestants or give them terrible wop diseases."

"Good God, May, where do you get that horsecrap?"

"Horsecrap to you! My own father told me, he told me about the Catholic witches on their brooms flying through the air, and eating babies, the wives of those damned Polish bakers that killed him. It was Catholic bakers that killed him for his money, damned Poles, and damn them all. I'm not going to Guaymas. If there's a hex on that thing, it will probably sink the ship. I say let's break it up."

"Well, now, you listen to me," Mike said, huffing up and poutering his chest. "I'll tell you one thing—"

"You don't tell me anything, you!" she cried.

The air phewed out of his chest. "Listen," he pleaded, "for God's sake, May dear. You don't know how close the cops are. I got to get away. Linebarger knows about the blackmail. Do you think I can hang around here for a week looking for a fence? I don't know any fences. And another week, dickering? May, I've got to get away tomorrow. And there's $60,000 waiting, more than we'd ever get from some fence."

"More than for those jewels? Are you lying?"

"Look, those jewels aren't even cut right, they're old-fashioned, they'd all have to be recut to be worth anything to a fence. Palafox told me. Look, I'll show you what I mean." He knelt and opened the hatbox, started to take out the old hat.

"Stop!" May cried. "I don't want to look at the dirty thing, I told you it's got a curse on it like all those crucifixes and devil things that they have. Shut up that box, I tell you."

He closed the hatbox and stood up. "Listen, May," he said in a low voice. He wasn't angry, he was sad. "I don't want to break us up. But I got to go. If you won't come, then don't come. But the cops will be on my tail tomorrow." Jesus, he thought to himself, wait till they find those stiffs. And Paz Faz raises a stink when those two greasers didn't come and he I.D.s the bodies and they know we saw Palafox today and the cops will come questioning and they'll say Jacko and me killed those bastards for the—Oh, Jesus.

"Listen, May, yes or no, you coming to Mexico with me, or not?"

She looked at the poor sap. She looked down at the hatbox as though it had a dead man's head in it, and her stomach gave a queasy little shudder. Papists. Witches. Devils. Hocus-pocus. Well, damn them, she'd have to go, if this measly coward whining in front of her wasn't man enough to brave it out here.

"All right. We'll go. But I'll have to be the brains from now on, I can see that. As for you and getting past the customs, Jacko was a deputy consul, you're not. You're a nobody, a stranger. Even if the customs was honest, how would they know you didn't steal it? Who are you, showing up out of nowhere? With a woman. Not married. Good lord, will we have to get married?"

"Not if we were partners in a business, or had some kind of front." He was gathering together the ends of his wits.

"What front?"

"Reporters, maybe, working for the *Times*. Covering the war."

"You got a card from the *Times*?"

"All right, free-lance."

"How about a photographer? You're a photographer."

"Photographer and assistant. I know all about cameras and developing, Becky taught me. Come on, I'll show you the stuff."

He jumped up and led her to the studio, pulled open a drawer and took out a camera. "She's got two of these Kodaks, same size, Number Fours. And a field developing kit. We took it once on a trip to Yosemite when they started the train up there."

He went into the darkroom and began hauling wooden boxes out from under the developing bench. "Here's half a box of developing powder. We'll need that."

He went back into the studio and got one of the two Kodaks. "We might have to take some pictures to make it look good. She's got three field developing boxes. Different sizes. What fits this camera? And rolls of film. Number 123. And fix. And stop. And paper, in case we have to print something. Jesus, what a load."

They packed everything but the camera in one of Mike's suitcases and went back to the dining room.

"What about the Archbishop's letter?" Mike asked.

"Never mind the letters," she said. "All we need is the tickets and the thousand dollars. We can't use the deputy letter, and if the greasers found the Archbishop's letter on us, it would just give us away about knowing about the

153

monstrance. We're free-lance photographers and reporters, we've got the camera and stuff to prove it, and all a reporter needs is a pencil. And when we get there, we just take the hatbox to the priest and get the money. Why would he need a letter from some archbishop when he can see the thing with his own two eyes? Let's go, stupid."

"Yes, dear. There's just one more thing." He put down the suitcases and ran back to the bedroom.

May stooped over Jacko and patted his head. "Goodbye," she said. She stuck one of Becky's flowers in Jacko's open mouth.

Mike came back and stood looking down at his ex-partner. "He's still got six dollars on him. I might need that, May. For cigars. And Palafox's keys, I'll need them to rip off the safe and get a blank passport for you. And we'll just drive Palafox's car down to the ship at San Pedro." He stuck the visa stamp in his pocket.

Mike rolled Jacko over and took his wallet out of his hip pocket. "Ta ta," he said, and rolled him back, dropping the wallet, minus the bills, on the floor.

"I'll take those," she said, yanking the bills out of his hand. "You quit cigars, remember? I think I'll just leave Becky a little note." She picked up the pen Jacko had used to forge Palafox's visas and wrote busily on the back of the ticket envelope. She tucked the envelope neatly into the front of Becky's gown.

"What about that brooch there on her?" Mike asked.

"Isn't there anything decent about you at all?" she said. I'll feed him to the pigs, she thought, as soon as I get that money.

"Goodbye, Jacko," she said, "you handsome son of a bitch. Goodbye forever. Come on, fatso," she said to Mike, and marched out the door, with Mike, loaded down like a mule, following obediently behind with a docile smile meek under his proud nose.

But he paused in the dark hallway once, with his head down, thinking of Jacko, and when he went on, there were tears in his eyes, and the beginnings of resentment toward the woman leading him away. How had she inveigled him into this?

CHAPTER TWELVE

A YELLOW FLAME crept across Jacko's eyelids. He yanked his head away from the blazing demon and his brain crashed against the inside of his skull, echoing bangs of pain as it bounced back and forth. He tried to lift the double-hung windows of his eyelids, but they had been painted stuck. He gave a wrench, they tore loose. He was lying on the floor, looking at Becky, who was sitting at the table looking down at him, her eyes as dead as rocks.

The sun blazed down through the tall window behind her. Steam curled up slowly from a cup of coffee on the table. There was a pillow under his head and a wet rag on his forehead.

"The ideal posture for an idiot," she said, looking down at him. "The complete picture of the total flop, dumped on his ass on the floor, doped, duped by a half-wit. God, to be taken in by that imbecile. God, what a headache," putting her palm to her forehead. "Look at you! Idiot!"

He struggled to sit up. He made it the second time. "Oh Lord," he groaned, sitting with his back to the wall beside her chair, pulled up like a fetus, hugging his knees, resting his head on them. "This isn't a hangover, this is poison."

"A good, clean decapitation would do you a world of good," she said. "God, how you deserve it."

A spasm of rage went through him like a red-hot corkscrew, seeming to twist his brains like a dishrag. He sat up straight against the wall. "Will you shut up, you bloody little witch? Croaking and whining like a busted shutter. A hell of a lot of good *you* were, if you were so smart, why didn't—" He stopped gobbling this verbal puke and sat groaning at the fool of himself.

"And now he's getting away on the ship," she croaked and began crying, gritting her teeth, snuffling and snarling in an anguish of rage. "Oh, if I could only get my hands on him!" She went on blubbering, her eyes squeezed shut, her fists clenched in her lap.

He looked at her for a moment, surprised out of his misery by all this grief, from a woman he had always thought as cold as a fish. She sat there in her rumpled finery, looking like a frowzy morning whore, chiffon tube gown all twisted awry, her diamond brooch tawdry as the heartless virgin sunlight stared down at her with insolent self-righteousness, and he felt a gripe of pity, in spite of his head, at what could become of a woman. Then he shut his eyes and concentrated on putting his pain at a distance.

A clock began to strike, or was it the hammer in his head? Bong, bong, it slowly intoned. He opened his eyes. Yes, it *was* outside his skull. He waited. What was he supposed to do? Linebarger. Get up at seven. What time was it? Bong, bong. Where was the bloody thing? Get Linebarger. Go to the dock. Ah, seven o'clock. He tried to struggle up. But it kept on going. He counted to ten with

157

growing horror, and the foul thing stopped, and he sank back limp.

"Oh God," he said, through the glue in his mouth, "they've got away." He lunged to his feet, grabbed the table to steady himself, and saw the phone hiding on a lampstand in the corner. What the hell was the ship office number? He ruffled through the phone book with trembling hands. What was the shipping line name? Mexican what?

"I already called them," Becky said, wiping the tears from her face with a tatter of lace. "It's gone." She pushed the empty ticket envelope across the table toward him. "There's the number. And a sweet little note from the floozy. Something else you deserve."

He sat down at the table. There was no recourse from the woman; he was too weak to escape. His brains wouldn't work. Were they still in his head? Or had they erupted, leaving only a heaving sea of boiling mush?

They looked at each other, looked away; looked back. The appalling thought occurred to both of them: there was nobody else to look at. They sat in the silence as in a desecrated church, the hideous sunlight glaring in with nauseating cheer.

"How are we going to get them?" she asked in a low voice, guttural with phlegm. It sounded like the growl of a dog.

"We?"

"Well, don't you want to?"

"What?"

"Get them!" she shrieked. "Tear their hearts out!"

"To hell with them," he said. "I've got the monstrance."

"Where?"

"Behind your still-life backdrop."

"You don't care about revenge?" as though offering it for breakfast.

"What for? I'm damned glad to be rid of both of them. Divorce is easy with desertion."

She couldn't believe it. "You don't want to get your hands on her neck and twist it and twist it?"

"What are you, some kind of virgin devil or something?"

"I'll kill him!" she cried. "I'll shoot him! Is it a crime to kill somebody in Mexico?"

"He's gone, Becky. Forget him. Just divorce him."

She began to cry again. God! how the woman leaked! Amazing, he thought, from raging hell-witch to tender little girl in two seconds. "What the hell, you didn't really want that oaf, did you? I mean, ever? You're not that stupid. Why did you marry him, anyway? I've watched you for years. First-class depression. Now I see why. Why *did* you marry the jerk? Loneliness?"

"Don't be comforting!" she said. "So hypocritical!" She stopped crying. She ignored the streaks of tears on her face. "So you won't help."

"I might. I'm going for the reward. I suppose you can come along and kill Mike if you feel that strongly about it. Please, could I have a cup of that coffee, please?" he asked humbly. "If you're not doing anything?"

She got up and walked unsteadily out of the room. He sat alone, bent over the ticket envelope, opening his eyes wide and then squeezing them shut, gradually focusing them.

"Dear Becky," it said in May's knife-sharp slanted writing, "I have taken your husband for a trip. You can have him back when I am through with him, which will be pretty quick, that is, if you can find him. In the meantime, you can have my husband, if you can find any use for him. I don't want him back. Your friend, May."

One glass of cheap champagne and now this. Suddenly his brain swirled and miraculously unfroze; it started moving again. Dope. So that was the part of the plan Lilly hadn't heard. Never mind. Let them try to swap that hatbox full of rocks for $60,000.

Becky came back and cracked a cup of coffee down in front of him, slopping it neatly. He drank the coffee and sat back with a sigh. He shut his eyes. The pain began to fade.

"They listed themselves on the ship as a reporter and a photographer," Becky said, her voice very flat and tired. She had washed her face and straightened her gown. "I feel like an old whore," she said sadly.

"How do you know? And where did you get such language?" he asked, surprised.

"Well, not what you think! Nurse's training. I watched the autopsy of an old whore, I know how she must have felt. I'm a half-ass nurse, you know. I've never told anybody. I flunked the course. That's one reason I married the half-wit. I thought it might be a living." Suddenly she laughed, high and strident, shocking him. "Becky the nurse!" She stopped laughing and looked glumly at the archbishop's letter. "Becky the nurse. May the reporter. That reporter business is just a dodge to get them into Guaymas. I've been looking around. They stole one of my cameras, the rotten thieves, they wouldn't steal some old anastigmat, they had to take the Number Four with the Zeiss lens. He took a lot of roll film, but the camera has a plate back, it won't take roll film." She laughed. "What a horse's ass." Suddenly her face turned pale. "Oh God," she said, and ran out of the room.

In a moment she came dragging back, carrying a small black japanned tin box, its lid flopping open. "My bonds. $40,000. And all my jewelry, that my father left me." She began to cry and then angrily choked it off. "I'm damned if I'll cry. I'll kill him."

"That's the old spirit," he said. "But let's not kill him

until we get your money back. Is there anything to eat?"
He was feeling much better. He spotted a bowl of pecans
on the sideboard, left from the party, got up and brought
them back to the table.

She was shaking her silver mesh purse upside down
over her skirt. "The rotten bloody bastard! He even took my
grocery money. I haven't a penny, and only a week till the
rent's due again. I really don't know what I'll do."

"Did you learn all those words in the nursing school?"

"No, stupid, I learned them from my sainted mother.
Can you make me a loan?"

It was wonderful, he thought, munching four pecans at
once, how being broke made a person civil. "I've got six
dollars cash."

He also had $2,500 in the bank as his share of the part-
nership reserve. And he'd have the whole $60,000 as soon
as he got down to Guaymas. Why not leave her $500 out
of the reserve? Maybe, he dreamed generously, he could
use part of the $60,000 to help her out until she got on her
feet, got a job or something. Idiot, was he?

"I suppose I could get a job, as a practical nurse, but,
oh, those bedpans. No! I'll get down there, I'll get my
money back, I'll cripple the son of a bitch." She began
horning in on his pecans.

"Why don't you go fry us some eggs?" he said, pulling
the bowl away from her.

"Fry your own damn eggs," she said. "Who do you
think you are, the Lord Almighty? Why should the women
always fry the eggs?"

He let her babble on about female rights, encouraging
her with a nod now and then while he ate the pecans. She
couldn't eat them while she was jabbering.

He sat crunching away, considering her face. Small and
dark, sometimes she seemed fairly pretty, in a gentle way;
but sometimes surprisingly ugly. Her face, from the front,

161

was like a sharpened heart. That was her all over, he
thought, pleased with the image. A sharp heart, tough one
minute, gentle the next. Her profile made him think of a
turtle, because of the prominent nose with its Assyrian
nostrils. He had never tried to understand this odd contrast, like the sharp heart, or decide whether she were
pretty or in fact ugly. Or did she have to be one or the
other? Come to think of it, he had once known a woman
who was a Greek beauty from one angle, and looked like
a horse from another. He had never given Becky enough
real attention to have any solid opinion about her at all,
and no feeling except that of boredom, when she got off
on her women's rights song, as she was doing now. He
finished the pecans and dusted his hands together. "There's
some canapés left over there," he said, trying to interrupt
her speech, "if you're hungry, they're probably rotten by
now. How about those eggs?"

The telephone rang. She shut up and went to answer it.
"No, he isn't here just now ... His partner? Just a minute." She turned to Jacko. "It's your bank."

He took the phone. A gentle, courteous voice said, "It's
just that we need to know what to do with your partnership account, sir."

"What about it?"

"Mr. Horton withdrew the $5,000 balance early this
morning, but he didn't order the account closed, sir. So we
have held it open pending consultation with you as the
other partner."

"What are you talking about? What consultation?"

"Well, at present the balance is zero."

"He cleaned it out?" A fit of fury exploded in his head,
the whole world turned blood-red and he went half-blind.

"Can we expect a deposit? You may not remember, our
minimum balance is $200. What shall we do, sir?"

"What shall you do?" Jacko shouted. "What shall you

do? I'll tell you what you shall do. You shall shove it up your ass, you half-wit! I'll sue, I'll sue! You let that bastard clean me out and now you ask me what I shall do! *I'll* tell you what I—" *Blam*, the phone slammed down in his ear.

He slammed down his own. "Oh, God," he said, "I got six bucks. My wallet! Where's my wallet?"

She picked it up from under the table and threw it at him. He opened it with shaking hands. "Look," flapping the wallet at Becky, his cards, his license, old theater stubs, Mexican lottery tickets fluttered out onto the floor, he didn't give a damn. "He took my six bucks! My six bucks!" Anger slunk away, discouraged by too much disaster; his shoulders drooped, his fingers weakened, the empty wallet fell back to the floor.

"What's the matter?" she said. "Run out of money? Robbed? Have a pecan. Fry some eggs. Tell me all about it. I'm beginning to know you, Jacko, you're one of those puffed-up heroes that uses money for guts, go broke and you get the runs. What a man! Get the bedpan!"

She stood and watched him for a moment, shaking her head. Then she said, "I'll cook some eggs, you poor helpless slob," and went out.

That brought his blood pressure back to normal. He sat down and suddenly remembered the $138 in his personal account. He felt better and straightened up. Maybe the little peahen was right, money *was* guts. And there was the $60,000 waiting for him seven hundred miles away, if he could just get to it.

Who could he touch? Linebarger would just laugh at him. How much? $500? The bank? Mortgage the house? No time. Sell his guns, that would do it. But his *guns*? His Parker? His matched Greeners? How could a man sell his children? Gloomily he leaned down and picked up his wallet. If he hurried, maybe he could sell Palafox's Pierce Ar-

163

row to some crook before the cops got to it. Oh God, the cops. How soon could he get out of town?

If he could raise some money, he could get to Guaymas on the train before the ship docked. How long would the ship take? Hadn't Palafox said seven days?

He could phone the station for the next train to Mexico. First Tucson, then Nogales on the border. Leave on the first train out.

She came back in with two plates of eggs, three each, and slid one across the table to him. The flash of her brooch caught his eye.

"I'm going after him," she said as though talking to herself. "I'll buy a pistol. I'm going to finish him off, after I get my money back."

"And how are you going to get down there?" he asked, eyeing the brooch. Were those real diamonds?

"This," she said, unpinning it.

He could hock it on Main Street for a couple of hundred. With his $138 to boot, there would be enough to get him to Guaymas. But she'd turned out to be such a shrew, how was he going to get it away from her?

He got up, went to the studio, came back with the monstrance, set it on the table, and sat down again. It glowed warmly in the sunlight.

"Two hundred dollars for your brooch. I'll go down there and cash in the monstrance and I'll try to get your bonds."

"Don't be silly. I need it to go down there myself."

"Listen, if I go alone, I can do the job for both of us. It's easy for a man."

"Why in the name of God should I trust you? You want me to get a job selling gloves or something while you take off with the one thing I've got? Fat chance."

She hunted around the room for her purse. "That May. I'll thrash her within an inch of her life. Teach her to take away my rotten wretch of a husband. And thrash the hell out of him too. Wait'll I get a whip. And get my money back. Why should I let you do it, even if I thought you could? I wouldn't deprive myself of the pleasure."

He could see her now, hobbling along through the mesquite in her ridiculous skirts, trying to look determined and efficient.

"I'm going to pack," she said. "There's no time to lose. The ship gets there in seven days, didn't you say? I'm going to catch them coming down the gangplank. Isn't there a railroad? Didn't I hear somewhere there is a railroad?"

She grabbed up the brooch and rushed off into the bedroom. She was leaving with his brooch! Where would he get the money? He stood up, started after her, and stopped. He couldn't rob her and tie her up, it wouldn't be legal. He would have to use charm.

He followed her into the bedroom and stood watching her pull two suitcases down off the top of her wardrobe. She began taking out dresses and gowns, laying them on the bed. Organdy, chiffon, a tweed golfing outfit, a split-skirt riding habit, a white tennis outfit, skirt down to the heels.

Good God, he thought, did she think she was going on a world cruise?

She was taking stuff out of bureau drawers without the slightest embarrassment, chemises, camisoles, brassieres, and jamming them into the suitcases. She tramped into the bathroom and came back with an armload of stuff, dumped it on the bed. A pretty little tin box, a perfect cube, rolled off the bed and stopped at his feet. He picked it up. It was colored a cheery green, with red and black printing. On the lid was profile bust portrait of a cow, surrounded by a coil of clover stems with leaves, and five bright red clover blossoms. On three sides it said in red letters "Bag Balm" and "Antiseptic," and on the fourth "Directions."

"For minor congestion of the udder," he read. Good Lord, was she using this stuff on herself? "After each milking, bathe with plenty of hot water, strip milk out clean, dry skin and apply BAG BALM freely."

"What the hell?" he said.

She turned around from her packing. "Give me that!" she said and grabbed the box. "Keep your dirty hands off it."

"What the hell is it for? Since when have you got a cow?"

"It isn't for a cow, you ass," she said, shoving the box into her big purse, along with a roll of adhesive tape and a roll of gauze, "it's for people, it's a great antiseptic. I've used it on dozens of scraped knees on parades when the cops pushed us around. I never go on a trip without it."

"You learned about this in your nurses training?"

"Never mind my nurses training. My grandfather had a cow. He used it on the whole family, cuts, scrapes, the works. It's wonderful stuff."

Bag Balm, he thought, just what the revolution needed. "If you don't mind my saying so," he said, as suave as a bank manager, "one suitcase should be enough, in addition to the Bag Balm. And as for dresses, perhaps just one or two, something simple and solid, like wool or gabardine."

She whipped around at him. "What the hell do you know about it?" and for some reason regretted her roughness. He was trying to be nice. Maybe he was right about the suitcases. One of these days she would get her nurse self under control. Right now she had no time.

"I know a little about war-time journeys," he said. "I wouldn't handicap myself with too much baggage. War-time, you won't find porters."

She thought a moment. She couldn't carry two of them. He was probably right, but she wasn't going to say so. Gritting her teeth, she put one of the suitcases back.

"Do you speak Spanish?"

"No."

He shook his head slowly, sadly. "How do you expect to get about in Mexico? You don't even know how to ask how much the ticket will cost. They'll rob you blind."

She stood looking at her suitcases.

"How will you find Mike?" he continued his litanical dirge. "How will you ask where they are? How will you find food, find places to stay?" He watched her. She was frowning. Frustrated. Good. She believed him.

Why not try the smooth Palafox line? He leaned indolently against the doorjamb. "I don't like to get into such a delicate subject, but a woman traveling alone might be subject to embarrassment—even though the Mexicans are ordinarily most courteous and considerate, and the trains, at least in the first class, are perfectly safe."

He crossed his feet nonchalantly, as though bored. "Morally, the Mexicans are very straitlaced, and would misunderstand the character of a solitary woman. You might be arrested as a prostitute. I am not trying to discourage you, but only to point out some facts. It really would be much wiser to let me do the job for us both."

She slammed down the lid of the suitcase. "I told you, I'm going."

He sighed. "Any attempt to acquire a translator or guide would be misunderstood. You might fall into the hands of some gang. Becky, I have the Spanish, and can offer you a man's help. With the money we have together, we can make it far more easily than either of us alone."

"You sound very convinced of my incapacity," she said sullenly. "The common view of females."

"Not at all. It's simply that your position as a lone woman is so prejudiced. Another thing, I have Palafox's letter making me his deputy, and that gives me a good deal of authority in dealing with officials down there."

She stood considering the idea. "Of course, if we went together, we could use May's idea, the reporter and photographer. I have the equipment and the skill. If we were reporters covering the war, we could go anywhere, talk to anybody, be perfectly free."

He smiled. "But you would need an interpreter, wouldn't you?"

She looked at him doubtfully. "That's the only thing that persuades me. I am perfectly capable of taking care of myself anywhere, at any time. But it's true I don't know the language. The trouble is, I really don't know you very well."

"That's true. But you couldn't be worse off with me than you would be without me."

She looked at him speculatively for a long moment. Then the nurse came back. "But I don't intend to trust you. I'm going to have a pistol. Any funny business, any shenanigans—you'll see in a hurry."

"I'll phone the station," he said. He left her packing.

When he came back from the telephone, he found her in the studio. She put the field developing tank for the No. 123 rolls on a table along with her No. 4 and went into the darkroom.

"There's a train leaving for Tucson at one-fifteen," he said, following her. "It gets there at six P.M. tomorrow, and we wait till the next day for a train to Nogales on the border."

She looked at her watch. "Do they have a diner on the Mexican line?"

"Oh yes, a good one. Excellent wine, the time I went down to Mexico City."

He looked around the darkroom. "We need something to pack the monstrance in," he said. "Something to disguise it. Can we use one of those wooden chemical boxes?"

She pulled one of the boxes out from under the bench.

He went back to the dining room and brought the monstrance. She emptied a box of developer packages and tried the monstrance in it. "Just enough room."

"We can bury it under that stuff," he said. "And film. Where is the roll film you use with that camera?" They put film boxes under the monstrance's gold sun, and developer cartons in three layers on top.

She handed him a black crayon. "Write 'poison' on it."

He wrote: ¡CUIDADO! PELIGRO. PRODUCTO QUÍMICO PONZOÑOSO.

"Now draw a skull and crossbones like the iodine bottle. That'll keep their hands off it."

"Don't you think you're overdoing it?"

"No! Draw it!" She watched him. "Very artistic," she said as he blackened the bones. They packed all but the camera and the chemical box into one of her suitcases. She left him to carry everything and went into the bedroom.

He went back to the living room and folded up Palafox's papers, put them with his passport in his inside jacket pocket. What about hers? Even if he had time to steal a blank passport from Palafox's office, that son of a bitch had swiped the visa stamp. He sighed and shrugged. He'd have to smuggle her in. What if she was arrested? He sighed again, more deeply, shook his head sadly, and forgot about it.

She came out dressed in her verdigris wool outfit, on her head a small cloche of the same wool with a yellow band. Over her shoulder she carried a large bag. "For the pistol," she said. "This is my parade costume. I had this miserable hobble skirt split up the side for walking. Let's go down and hock the brooch. And get my pistol."

He picked up the suitcase and the poison box. "We'll go up to my house for me to pack and you can have one of my guns. All set?"

She looked around the living room. "So much for life

169

with the half-wit," she said, and stuffed a copy of *Camera Work* into her bag. "Goodbye, you rotten trash," she said to the deaf-and-dumb mission furniture. "Goodbye," she said more softly to the cupid guarding the dead fireplace. She bit her lip but it did no good, and as she followed Jacko out of the room she was blotting her tears with her handkerchief.

As Jacko started to open the front door, somebody began pounding on it. "Who is it?"

"Is that you, Jacko? It's Bill Linebarger. Open up."

"Oh hell. Open it yourself."

Linebarger stood in the doorway, looked at him, looked at Becky, looked at the suitcase and the box. Behind him stood two big uniformed cops. Behind the cops he saw Herculano's granite block head, and behind that, two even bigger Mexicans.

"Where the hell do you think you're going?" Linebarger said. He had on his cross-examination face, mouth tight and eyes unfriendly.

"Come on in," Jacko said, hurriedly sorting through a few lies. They crowded him back into Becky, shoving her stumbling back into the living room.

"Have a seat, gentlemen," Jacko said, feeling slightly dizzy in the face of so much power. "Good morning, Herculano. Good to see you again, and so soon. Do sit down. And your friends."

Nobody sat down. Jacko smiled hopefully. The six large men stood in a semicircle, looking hard and steady at him.

"Answer me," Linebarger said. "Where were you going?"

"Now look here, Bill."

"Look here yourself!" Linebarger said, raising his voice and his chin. "Don't Bill me, Jacko. This is an official investigation. Where were you going?"

"I am taking Mrs. Horton down to the station. She is taking the train to Cincinnati. What's this all about?"

"Cincinnati, is it? Why?"

"Mike has left her. Robbed her, in fact. She is forced to go East to live with her relatives."

"She is, is she? What's in that suitcase? Never mind that. Where's Mike? I'm looking for Mike." He was darting his eyes around the room as he had seen it done by detectives in the movies.

"How the hell do I know? He left Becky flat and stole her money. That's why she has to go. The last I heard he was sailing for Mexico this morning. With my wife, by the way. Don't be picking on an injured party, Bill. Anything else you want to know before we go?"

Linebarger started prowling around the room, darting his eyes. "Don't get huffy with *me*, Jacko. There's been a murder. Three murders. Your friend Palafox was killed last night, the night clerk at the hotel saw Mike sneaking up the stairs. And his safe was opened, there's no money left in it. And there were two men shot to death in Pomona that my friend Herculano here tells me you and Mike were supposed to recover stolen goods from. And the goods are missing. Where the hell were you last night?" He quit darting his eyes, turned on Jacko and stabbed with them.

"Why, last night I was lying on the floor right here, knocked out by a Mickey Mike fed me. We were having a party. And he knocked out Becky. All so he could steal my wife, or my wife could steal him, damn fools they are. I never got to see those two men we were supposed to meet, and if Mike did them in for the monstrance, I had nothing to do with it. How could I, knocked out on the floor?"

"That's right, whoever you are," Becky said. "I thought he was dead this morning, lying there like that."

Linebarger's eyes settled on the box on the floor, which

Becky was trying to hide with her feet. "Poison! What's that poison? What are you two doing with poison?"

"It's film developer," Becky said. "Part of my equipment. I'm a photographer, you know, I'll have to make my living in Cincinnati, so I'm taking all my chemicals."

Linebarger picked up the ticket envelope and shook it. "Empty, by God!"

"Well, they took the tickets," Jacko said. "That's what you have to have to get on a ship, tickets. They're escaping."

"Escaping! Where's that ship, Jacko, that ship they're escaping on?"

"You're too late, Bill."

"Where is that ship?"

"San Pedro, San Pedro! It sailed at eleven, Bill."

"Oh, did it? Well maybe it didn't. Maybe it's still there. Come on, you two," he said to the cops, "let's go," and ran out the door with them after him.

That left Herculano contemplating Jacko with his baby-blue stone eyes.

"What a commotion, Herculano," Jacko said. "To think that my own partner ran off like that, with the monstrance and my wife too. I have never felt so betrayed as at this moment."

Herculano said, "May we sit down?"

"By all means," Jacko said, feeling slightly faint. "A terrible mess about your brother, Herculano. I never dreamed Horton was capable of such a thing."

"Permit me to introduce my assistants," Herculano said, sitting down at the table and pulling up his shapeless pants to save what was left of the crease. "This is Manuel," gesturing toward the taller and fatter, "and this is his cousin Braulio." Braulio looked a little faster on his feet, Jacko thought.

Jacko smiled and nodded. Both of them were large and

smooth, with round heads, round cheeks, and double chins. Their tan skins shone softly. Their beautiful suits, evidently made by the same tailor from the same bolt, draped perfectly from their massive shoulders; their cuffless trousers broke exactly six inches above their shining shoes. Fat and sleek, they reminded Jacko of walruses.

Ordinarily Jacko did not think much of fat fighters, easily winded, but the confidence implied by the sleepiness of their eyes, as they looked at him with kindly smiles, almost paternally benevolent, suggested that underneath the fat there was plenty of muscle and that they knew how to use it economically and well. It was quite possible that they won some of their battles simply by falling on their opponents and squashing them.

They made a handsome pair, standing there like a couple of amiable butlers. Braulio's only defect was the buckness of his teeth, childishly clasping his lower lip under his thick black moustache. Manuel's equally thick and black moustache grew down over his mouth so there was no telling about his teeth.

"As a matter of fact," Herculano said, "I have a few questions. The police have gone, we can relax, I can ask them more informally, so to speak."

"Could you rustle up some coffee for our guests, Becky? Sugar, Herculano, cream?"

"Black," Herculano said. The word snapped out like a neck breaking. "You may sit down, boys." His assistants snuggled themselves heavily into the couch cushions. The couch groaned and cracked under the weight.

"So you knew nothing of the robbery of this monstrance," Herculano said. "Or of the murder of my brother. Tell me everything again, Señor Jacko."

"My dear friend," Jacko said, "there is nothing more to tell. Oh, what a disaster, I can hardly believe he is dead, why only yesterday—"

"Enough!" Herculano said, halting traffic with his hand upraised. "You are invited to the funeral, you can express your feelings by attending. That is, if what you say is true."

"But it is true," Becky said.

"So you have said," Herculano said. "But it might not be true. Perhaps, Señor Jacko, you and this Mike went together to Pomona, killed these men and my brother—"

He stopped talking, sat still for a moment, and then made a single sound something like a suppressed hiccup. Could it be a sob? Jacko wondered. Nothing changed in the stone face.

"And stole that monstrance. That pathetic bauble, for a life. Inconceivable. A life for honor, yes. A life for a betrayal, yes, for a broken trust, yes. But not for mere money, for a silly bauble like that thing. That is why I am inclined to believe you, Señor Jacko. You are a man of honor, my brother vouched for that. But then, I am not sure."

He sighed, lifted his hands from his thick thighs, and put them softly down again. "Perhaps this Mike drugged you *after* you both came back from Pomona, after you killed those three, and then he stole both the monstrance and your wife. That is just as believable as the other version. It is all a matter of timing."

"You are right," Jacko said. "A matter of timing. We were having a drink before we were to leave for Pomona, around five o'clock, and that was when he drugged me. Evidently then he went to Pomona with your brother, making some excuse for my not showing up, and committed these crimes. And now he has gone with the monstrance to claim the reward."

"He will never claim it," Herculano said. "I am going to fly down there and wait for the ship. Simply watch the house of the priest and wait. He cannot evade me. Who in

174

the city will not know when this gringo arrives? Who will not know where he goes? The police are my friends, as always, they will watch for me.

"I will catch him. I will take him out into the countryside and break all his bones, one by one. First his fingers, one by one. Then his wrists. Then his arms. Then his feet, possibly with the back of an axe. Then his legs. One by one. I will leave him for the coyotes. It is too bad he has to die, I would like to keep him alive forever, paying with his screams for my little brother, as the years go by, one by one.

"But I must be sure that he is the one, Señor Jacko. I trusted you. I want to be sure you did not break that trust. How can I be sure?"

It seemed to Jacko that the room was growing very warm. A bead of sweat ran down his chest. The sun was behind the three clots, he couldn't see them start a move. "Becky, would you pull the shades, please?"

"Oblige a la señora, Braulio." Braulio heaved himself off the sofa and yanked down the shades, turning the room into gloom.

"Suppose you yourself have the monstrance," Herculano said. "Your version is very plausible. But another is just as plausible. Suppose after you and this Mike killed these men in Pomona, then you killed this Mike and buried him, and took the monstrance yourself. You say Mike has gone on the ship, but who can prove it? It has sailed."

"He took my wife. Why, their names will be on the passenger list in the ship's office. That will prove it."

Herculano shrugged. "Why not? I know many people who will write the names of George Washington and Abraham Lincoln on a passenger list for five dollars."

"But my wife is gone!"

"Or hiding, to make this story good. So this Mike is supposed to have sailed away with the monstrance, but all the time you have it, and Mike is buried somewhere on your father's ranch. Oh, yes, I know all about your family! Now you will see Mrs. Horton onto her train to—where is it?—to her family, then you will take another train to Guaymas with the monstrance. What about that, Señor Jacko?"

"A very clever plan," Jacko said. Wasn't there any way out of this place but the window? A quick leap through the crashing glass, but then, four stories down the cliff into Fifth Street. No.

"Of course the monstrance might be hidden anywhere," Herculano said. He stood up. "But it might be right here, in this place. A good chance, because you have been doped and not thinking well enough to hide it somewhere else."

Jacko got up and stood wishing his heart would not make so much noise. A fat lot of good adrenaline was going to do him with these three monsters.

"Even if I had it, you would have no right to it," he said. "And I didn't kill your brother."

"If you have the monstrance, then you were in on his death for certain," Herculano went on, following out the train of his stone-ground logic. "Suppose I search this place, and find nothing? That proves nothing. In that case, I will fly to Guaymas and wait, and I will get one of you, the one who appears, that is certain. But if I find the thing here, then I save myself time and trouble. Boys?"

The boys stood up and pulled their jackets down neatly.

"Do me the favor of holding the señor."

Jacko backed behind the center table. Manuel picked up the table and tossed it out of the way against the wall. It bounced back upside down and fell on the poison box. Braulio made a dive for Jacko and Jacko aimed a right hook at the side of his jaw, missed, and cut his knuckles badly on the buck teeth. The two boys fell on him like a couple of trees and then dragged him up, holding his arms. All three stood panting, facing Herculano. Braulio spat out two teeth.

"I can see you will not tell me," Herculano said. "So I will have to search. But, forgive me, I feel I must take some payment for Braulio's tooth."

Jacko tightened up, waiting for a blow in the stomach. Herculano stood close to him, breathing in his face. Jacko saw his shoulder hunch and twisted sideways. The rock fist hit him on the side of the hip and Jacko sagged, the leg giving up. Herculano's body had not moved. He hit from the shoulder. The arm was enough. "Is that enough for your tooth, Braulio?"

"There were two, *mi padrón*."

"Hold him up," Herculano said to the boys.

"Stop that!" Becky screamed. "Stop it this minute!"

Herculano pulled back his piston arm and hit again, this time true in the belly. He didn't need a body swing, he could have broken the wall with nothing but his arm.

"Oh, stop that," Becky screamed, shaking her fists in the air, shaking her head in desperation till her hair fell down. "You goddamn bastard!" She grabbed the poker from beside the fireplace and held it up in the air.

"I won't kill him until I'm sure, señora," Herculano said, smoothing the knuckles of his right hand with the palm of his left. "I am not a murderer." He looked at Jacko, who was cramped double, hanging between the cousins, struggling for breath, his eyes bugging from his head.

"That's enough for the teeth," Herculano said. "Just to be sure he doesn't make a nuisance of himself," he said, and swinging his arm sideways cracked Jacko on the side of the head with his open hand. Jacko collapsed and hung by his arms between the boys, his chin on his chest.

"He is all right, señora," Herculano said, wiping his hands with his handkerchief. "I just slapped him. I won't break his jaw until I know for sure. I am a just man. All right, boys. Enough."

The boys let go ofJacko. He went down clunk, clunk, clunk, one bone after another, and lay snoring.

The boys started with the couch while Herculano watched. They tore the legs off, tore out the springs, they dumped the side table on its face and kicked it apart. Becky fell on Braulio with the poker, beating him across the shoulders. Braulio turned and gently caught her wrist, gently removed the poker, and looked a question at Herculano while he held her arm up in the air like the neck of a dead chicken.

"Find a closet for her," Herculano said, and they locked her in the darkroom.

Jacko woke up while the boys were smashing up the dining room, but he decided that he was best off lying quietly on the floor, and stayed there, eyes shut, wishing only for a cushion for his head, which was full of bells mingling with the crashing and smashing going on in the studio.

The crashing, smashing, and ripping stopped. The three smashers came stomping back from their work. Jacko lay still as a possum. He opened his eyes a slit. Becky was standing between the cousins, gently held by each arm.

Herculano said to Becky, "Tell him this when he wakes up. I will wait in Guaymas for the ship and get this Mike for sure. If he doesn't have it, then I will know that Jacko has it, and I will wait for him. If he doesn't show up, I will come back after him. And it would be better for him if he had never been born."

The three of them left quietly, gently closing the door. Jacko opened his eyes and looked straight up into

Becky's. Neither said anything. What had the Carthaginians said, staring at their plowed-under, salted city? Nothing.

The sun shone joyfully through a broken window; the wreckage around them, slowly settling, creaked, cracked, popped, and sighed. Becky began heaving and hauling at the broken-legged table, pulled it aside and lo and behold, picked up the poison box. It was the only thing in the room that had not been smashed.

"How strange it is to see everything flat on the floor that used to stand up," Becky said.

"The artist's eye," Jacko said. "I suppose that's all that occurs to you, the composition of the scene, the shortage of verticals."

"He's going to kill you, Jacko, no matter what you do. He'll find out we've got the monstrance. And then he'll be sure you killed his brother for it."

"He thinks Mike has it, because Mike ran," Jacko said. He was testing his vision. Which of the two Beckys he was looking at was the real one? Suppose he had to shoot a double vision of Herculano? What to aim at, right, left, or middle?

"He'll fly down there and wait like a spider for Mike," she said, "and probably kill him because he *doesn't* have the monstrance. Then he'll know we've got it, and wait for us, and if you don't show up, he'll come back here, or wherever you run, and kill you." She laughed.

"Why are you laughing? Do you think it is funny to have all my bones broken?" The Beckys were slowly coming together.

"It's so neat," she said, chuckling. "You can't escape." Then she began to cry. "Oh, damn this crying!" she yelled and shook her head. "Damn being a woman. I had to stand and watch—" She stopped. She looked around. "My house, my little house."

"We still have time to catch the train," Jacko said.

"What? You can't go now, they'd kill you."

"Listen, I'm certainly no match for Herculano in a fist-fight, not to speak of his boys. But the next time he'll have to shoot. That's a different matter."

She looked at him sadly. "I know you're trying to recover your pride. But it would be three to one all over again. Or six to one. Or ten to one."

He sat up. The room swung around and hit him. He put his hands over his eyes and waited while it settled down.

"Listen, you," he said, "I was worried about the monstrance before, about being mixed up with Palafox's death. Guilt. But I didn't kill him. One of the Rivera brothers did." He got up the way he went down, one bone after another, but slower. He told her the whole thing.

"I don't know if you understand, but I've got to go down there now just because he *is* waiting for me, and I *am* going to cash in the monstrance. That son of a bitch has threatened to kill me, and he always does what he says, I know him. So I've got to kill him." He looked around for a chair. They were all smashed. "And it's smart to kill him in Mexico, not here. Down there, I can buy off the cops."

"So you've got it all figured out," she said. "We go to Guaymas and you get killed, the bonds are gone, I'm stuck down there broke. I can't even get home. What do I do for a living? Be a whore?"

"Don't be so dramatic. Why not wash dishes for somebody? The pay's good, fifteen cents a week. Come on, let's go. You want to stay here and sell gloves for the rest of your life?"

"To hell with you," she said. She began gathering her scattered clothing, packing it back in her suitcase. "Don't just stand there. Get the camera and stuff together. And I want you to teach me to shoot just as soon as you can. Anybody who gets herself mixed up in a mess like this needs all the help she can get." She slammed the suitcase shut.

"Pick it up," she ordered. "I'll carry the rest."

CHAPTER THIRTEEN

"FIVE MINUTES to Nogales," Bisbee said as the old train lurched rocking into a curve. "I'm afraid your passports won't do you much good with General Obregón down south. Once you get across the line, you'll have to go to Carranza's headquarters and get military passes."

Jacko was sitting with Becky beside him, facing the engine and this affable gentleman. Through the window the hot drying breeze of the southern Arizona desert poured a peppering of cinders; outside in the deadly glare a parade of obscene plants wheeled by, cacti towering and tubby, like infernal comedians mocking them with fat uplifted fingers.

They were tired from two days on trains, from sitting up all night in the Tucson station, from eating tamales; their skins shrank in helpless unease from their sweat-stiffened clothing. The little .38 Special Police Positive Colt in its hideout holster on Jacko's ankle was beginning to weigh like a leg-iron. Becky would be doing better with the other hideout he had got her at the house when he had packed his bag. Safe in her big purse.

They were almost broke. Guaymas and affluence regained seemed like a rosy dream-city on the edge of delirium, and in flight from depression they had turned to simmering detestation of each other.

Bisbee was no longer a stranger; rather, after an hour and a half of lolling along on the rails from Tucson, he had become for a time, in the way of travellers, an old and valued friend. But the generous expanse of his advise had begun to teach them chiefly the humiliation of their ignorance; they had encouraged his company to escape from each other, but now were beginning to suffer from the relief. There was nobody else in the car except an upper-class Mexican family of four, with three servants, barricaded incommunicado behind their expensive luggage in the far end.

The faint smell of ancient cigar ashes, buried forever in the faded green bristles of the Pullman upholstery, tingled in their noses like the dust of mummies. Over their heads hung the metal belly of the procrustean upper berth, where Jacko knew he would be tortured that night, somewhere beyond Hermosillo, while his mock wife snored in a mock of death below, as the long green heavy shrouds of Pullman drapes swayed and swung in a giant dance to the bony clacking of the rails.

"And of course you'll have to go through the Mexican customs first to reach Carranza for the passes," Bisbee said. "He's just down the street, by the way. And your box of poison there might cause you a little trouble." He looked with mock gloom at the skull and crossbones staring at him from the box, on the floor between Jacko's feet. "You guard it so carefully. Are you sure there's nothing but poison in it?" He laughed.

They didn't. He stopped, looked apologetic. "Sorry. It just struck me—" His mouth quivered with the onset of another burst of laughter, he rubbed it clean with a forefinger, sighed. "It's just that you don't look at all like Borgias." They looked, he thought, like two students who had just failed an examination.

"Please forgive me," Bisbee said. "Of course I realize it's just film developer, as it says. A good thing to be careful, scare people away. But nobody would take you for a smuggler, O'Donohue. Impossible. Right?" He looked at Jacko brightly, expectantly, the friendliest of confidants.

"A pity you can't fly down. Hitch a ride with a smuggler I know. Very enterprising fellow named Herculano Santana. Ever hear of him? He runs pre-Columbian stuff and church artifacts up here and sells them in Europe. A new racket. I'm sure it's the coming thing, airplane smuggling."

Jacko said nothing, stared into eternity with the eyes of a corpse.

"Right!" Bisbee said, giving up.

He had heard their story. Not all of it, he was sure. He did not believe they were man and wife despite their wedding rings.

They could not be married: she was, he judged from the charming nostril curl of her small, prominent nose, perfectly Jewish, while O'Donohue was your usual ethnically anonymous American, keeping the Irish name while somewhere losing the lip, if ever his ancestors had one, and gaining an aquiline nose from somewhere else.

He might have married her, but not she him, Bisbee knew from familiarity with Jewish attitudes, gained from a welcome to the homes of a number of Jewish friends he had made as a small packer much respected for honesty by the kosher meat houses.

No, hardly married: he could not feel surrounding them

any of that aura of battered unity which he had always sensed around even the most hate-filled of mates. Beneath all the spite and bitterness of war among his married friends he had always been aware that underneath the dust and roil of the battlefield lay the unshatterable bedrock of the vow; that on it, even in the end, the couple perforce lay like prostrate gladiators, left hands handcuffed together till death by their little sworn rings, right hands hiding knives. No such aura with these two. There they sat, as far apart as flesh and milk side by side in a kosher dumbwaiter. Obviously they were each married to somebody else.

Locked up in themselves against each other, they had been all the more confiding in him. Bisbee had been born with the gift of listening; he had only to keep his mouth shut and look civilly at somebody, any stranger on a streetcar, and out would pour the travail of a lifetime, the sufferings, the injustices, endured without cause or any complicity by the martyr himself.

Under the kindly warmth of his eye their troubles had come burbling out like a mountain spring in thaw. Bisbee knew that they would later come to hate him for this unrequited self-exposure, but he could no more stave off the inevitable doom of resentment than he could throttle his idiot talent for opening the floodgates of such confidences.

Who was the man who had stolen her bonds? The same as O'Donohue's partner? If O'Donohue was just a detective, presumably hired for this trip, why did they pretend to be married? And he was a most unlikely detective. He was obviously a man of culture and breeding, with just a touch of the serene brutality of the rich, while detectives, in Bisbee's experience, were usually coarse brutes in checks and bowlers cashing in on muscle and a love of peeping.

Then there was the account of the drugging, the absconding on the ship by the thief. And there was a "they" involved in this flight: who was the mysterious other partner in this "they"? And what about that fleeting allusion to blackmail, winged so swiftly by with just a whiff of nether parts? A great deal was missing from their story.

It all smelled distastefully of Los Angeles hokum, and these two, however broke at present (their clothing showed some past affluence), were typical of the mayfly types who wasted their talents and their riches in the mishmashes one could expect from a town whose extraordinary dullness was enlivened only by political scandal, exposures of public theft, and hoked-up real estate booms. Anybody who lived there long enough was bound to be poisoned by the place. Why didn't these two, themselves so decent despite the mess they had got into, get out? Half the people there were confidence men selling desert land to suckers from the Midwest, who soon learned the game and tripled the price to another trainload of boobs come out for the sunshine.

To Bisbee, Los Angeles was the City of the Plain, the temple of Belial, god of the useless, where men went to fritter their lives away. It had no water. It had no anything. It produced nothing but advertisements, talk, and scandal. The only product it shipped was carloads of oranges, a fruit on which one could quickly starve to death; and to a man who dealt in cattle this frivolity with food consigned the town to the depths of his contempt.

And these two? Typical products of Belial Town, more's the pity. A shame they could not have lived in Philadelphia (where he had been born), a city whose virtues would have soundly enhanced their native worth. Bisbee was convinced that the men of Sodom would have been reformed merely by moving to Jerusalem. But how could these two, trapped in the fripperies and criminal frivolities of Los Angeles, help suffering its effects? to become as silly, improvident, rash, speculative, and deceitful as the town itself? Los Angeles! the whore, the Babylon, corrupter, where the women, as Isaiah said, are "haughty and walk with necks outstretched, ogling and mincing as they go." Los Angeles was a poison box. He glanced down at O'Donohue's box and smiled.

Jacko caught Bisbee's glance at the poison box and thought, So much for our brilliant deception. Obviously Bisbee suspected that they had more than chemicals in it. He felt like a jackass. If he couldn't fool this friendly fellow, what about a nasty, suspicious, evil-minded border guard? He felt his face to be swelling with humiliation. He hated himself for a fool, and finding that unendurable, changed to hating Bisbee, the stuffed-up grinning ape. He looked several miles past the top of Bisbee's head; as Vincent had taught him, inordinate curiosity can only be ignored.

Oh! red tape, passes, bureaucrats! cried Jacko in his soul, damn the hornswoggling pussyfooters, how the hell would they ever get to Guaymas in time to catch the thieves? He pulled himself up and said with the calm of desperation, "About this Carranza and our passes—"

"Of course," Bisbee said, looking doubtfully at the poison notice on the box, "your skull and crossbones might scare off a half-witted *campesino*, maybe some cretin of an Indian. Not the customs boys, though. Red flag to a bull, as they say."

Jacko breathed deeply. "But about these passes, how long do you think—"

"Warnings of danger would only make the *aduaneros* curious," Bisbee said, "or challenge their manhood." He shook his head slowly from side to side. "They will tear your box open in the twinkling of an eye, as they say." Bisbee smiled his charming smile.

Diplomacy! Diplomacy! Jacko prayed in his heart. Impa-

tience would never do. He shifted in his seat, resettled his
mind, and from the well of his despond wound up a bedrag-
glement of dripping cheerful thoughts: altogether a likable
fellow, Bisbee, etc., etc. Helpful, etc. He made a determined
point of admiring Bisbee's poise as he sat in his handsome
khaki jacket and wide-flared riding breeches with one ankle
in its shining dark-brown leather puttee over the other lean
knee, ignoring in perfect balance and comfort the lurch and
sway of the car.

"Now about these passes—"

"Oh, yes, the passes. Hard to tell about Carranza and
passes," Bisbee said. "A dirty fate you are photographers,
and not just plain reporters. He is the vainest man in Mexico, he might keep you as honored guests for months, taking pictures of him, keep you waiting for those passes.

"You might very well become the permanent personal
photographers of His Royal Highness. Snaps of himself,
himself on his horse, himself getting on his horse, himself
getting off it, himself at the head of the dinner parade, or
reviewing several donkeys. You might never get free."

"But we must get to Obregón and the battles, as quickly
as we can," Jacko said.

"And that box. So complicating."

"I wish you would stop calling it a 'poison box,' "
Becky said, trying to muffle her crossness. Charming
though Mr. Bisbee was, she wished he might go to the toilet or onto the platform for a smoke, anything. She had a
desperate need to let down and cry, if only for her appalling ignorance of Mexican affairs and customs, or at least
to have the relief of a thorough-going depression, instead
of trying to be pleasant, as it seemed, for hours. Where
was the wine and the lunch that big fool Jacko had promised? Not on this drunken old cow of a train, wobbling
along forever through this terrible desert. Hadn't her

grandfather told her that the desert was where the devils lived? She was getting to feel as mean as a devil herself.

"Look here," Bisbee said, "there's no use my pretending I believe there's only chemicals in that box. Of course I won't ask what it is, but let's be serious. Obviously it's something you don't want seen. By anybody. So you have a problem."

"Even if that were true," Jacko said, and diplomacy whisked out the window, "it would be none of your business."

"Of course. But I'm an old hand in this country, and it's plain to me that you are brand-new. I don't want to see a fellow gringo in trouble with the Mexicans."

"Very thoughtful," Jacko said. "What do you want? What's our problem got to do with your business, whatever that is?"

"All right, since you're frank enough to ask, I'll tell you. I'm a cattle buyer. The Mexican revolutionaries are rounding up every cow they can find in Sonora. I buy them for Chicago. With the profit I buy arms and sell them to Obregón. You understand, Taft won't sell arms to the revolution, but he doesn't do anything to stop the smuggling, and he won't recognize Huerta. Now I am also a volunteer agent for the State Department, undercover, that is, and my private job of cattle buyer and the arms trading fits in with the government's private policy of helping the rebels.

"Well, you'll be with the army, you'll hear everything State wants to know. Let me handle your stories as your business agent, syndicate them if I can for your sake, and for my sake use them in my reports to the government. And I'll show you how to get that box across."

"All right," Jacko said. "How do we work it?"

"How much money can you spare for bribes? Enough for the private, the sergeant, the chief, and then, who knows, perhaps something for the mayor, a bit for the governor, a smidgin for the president. Fifty dollars would get you across the line."

"How about eighteen?" Jacko asked. "That's it, that's the works."

"Dear me," Bisbee said and looked sadly at the bright brass buckle of his left puttee. "I don't see how you're going to make it down to Guaymas, bribes every time you turn around."

The train rattled over a passage of switches. "Nogales in three minutes," Bisbee said. "If I might suggest—"

"Didn't you know about bribes?" Becky burst out at Jacko. "Why didn't you save some money, then? You didn't *have* to buy tickets all the way to Guaymas. God, the playboy! I always knew you were extravagant, but! You *could* have bought them just to Nogales, but you had to plunk down all the money in one of your grand gestures."

"Smuggling, smuggling," Bisbee broke in, holding up a hand to shush her. "That's the answer. You can cross the line on foot after dark and board the train on the other side."

"When *will* the train leave, Mr. Bisbee? They didn't have a Mexican schedule in Tucson."

"I don't know, I'm sorry to say. The Mexican schedule hasn't been printed for two months. But the train might very well go tonight, they like the dark, it's safer. The trains have been shot up quite a bit lately."

"Shot up!"

"Oh, not badly, just a few holes. Not by the Federal Army, don't be alarmed, that's far away. Obregón has driven most of the Federal Army into Guaymas. It's just bandits."

"Bandits!"

"Well, there are a few, remnants of Orozco's army that Obregón beat up and drove out of the country. Not many."

"Now where is your grand lunch now!" Becky cried at Jacko. "Wine in the dining car!"

"Ahg," Jacko said, gagging over an effort to respond to this nonsense, and shut up. Outside, a tall, cigarlike cactus passed, seeming to wave at him like a finger of fornication. He thought he heard laughter. Fool! a desert spirit cried in his ear. Was she going to be a nag for the whole two hundred and fifty miles? In front of strangers?

"I'm sure everything will be all right, Mrs. O'Donohue," Bisbee said. "But right now we should be making plans. We'll be there in a minute and we should be ready.

"The Mexican customs haul the Pullmans across the line to hook to a Mexican engine, and inspect the baggage right in the cars as a courtesy, not to disturb the rich. Your skull and crossbones will certainly wake them up. We'd better move to the coaches right now and walk. The coach people have to get out and walk across the line to the Mexican customs house. We can join them. But if you're going to sneak across the line, we'd better simply fade into the town."

The train stopped for no reason, and then started up again with a jerk and crept forward. The low, rolling desert hills in their ragged mantle of starved brush and cactus wheeled slowly by. A scatter of adobe huts broke the monotony of Arizona dearth; bleached wooden shacks joined the wretched procession.

More clatters of switches, and a low bawl of cattle groaned through the open window. A thousand beasts appeared in a wilderness of pens, the long red slats of cattle cars sailed by, the mighty chorus of grunting bellows faded. The town suddenly grew up two stories tall each side of the train. The brakes squealed, the car ground to a

191

stop in front of a station that looked like the Alamo, with a twin of itself beside it.

"You see the impartiality of the Southern Pacific," Bisbee said, gesturing at the twin buildings. "Mexico gets as good as we, and Spanish decor for everybody. Let's beat it before they pull us across the line. We'll just walk through the station to Morley Street and have a little refreshment at the Montezuma Hotel. I'll show you the place to cross when it gets dark."

There was no station platform. They climbed down the steep steps and stood in the dirt of the wide oiled street, squinting against the glare of sun at the twin stations, little fake Spanish missions, side by side beyond a second set of rails. A little cur dog sniffed at Jacko's feet, got a swift kick in the ribs, and ran away sideways. Coach people spilled out of their cars and wandered into the American station, a few toward the Mexican; the Mexican border guards loafing in the shadow of the Mexican station saw them coming and, smiling with hospitality and greed, pushed themselves away from the wall and took their hands out of their pockets.

At Jacko's side appeared a small man clothed in a black suit three sizes too big. He lifted his old black hat and stood with his round, olive-skinned face smiling a charming welcome. He was holding a brown cardboard suitcase, broken at one corner and held together by a piece of cotton washline rope.

"Señor," he said in perfect English, "may I speak with you for a moment? Permit me to introduce myself, Roberto Clemente Bustamente y Olaquibel, at your service. If I might presume—"

"Beat it," Bisbee said with typical American courtesy, smiling in a kindly way. "We're not buying any, Señor Bustamente. O'Donohue, let's get to the hotel and get a cold drink for your lady." He picked up the chemical box and started away.

"Hey, hey!" Jacko called, hurrying after him. "I'll take that if you don't mind!"

Becky stood looking suspiciously at Señor Bustamente. His thin, delicate eyebrows peaked up in dismay. He lifted a hand as though to recall Jacko, let it fall in limp despair. His black moustache, its waxed ends all awry, drooped like a bull before the sword.

He looked so disappointed, she thought, and her dead-eyed look softened. He looked so poor, with that broken suitcase. She pinched a dime out of her silver-net change purse and held it out to him. He backed away in horror, raising his hands to fend her off.

Well, she thought, bristling, too proud for my lousy dime? Up yours, she said to herself, and followed Jacko through the station, pushing through the crowd. God knew who all these people were, but whoever they were, there were far too many of them.

On Morley Street cars nosed the curb like hogs at slop, hot-country open touring models, all black as funerals, with cloth tops that scooped in the wind. The stores of the rich small town were fat with goods for the Saturday market crowds elbowing along the sidewalks; troopers of the 10th Cavalry on pass from the army camp; Mexican officers from the Revolutionary Headquarters across the line picking out for themselves what they thought would appear smart as a uniform; ranchers from the country with leather-faced wives and shy, slinky children; drummers of arms from half the world, Winchester, Remington, Kynoch, Dynamit, Nobel, UMC, Western, all making deals with Mexican quartermasters who came loaded with bills from the gambling halls run by their government to raise money for arms. Dark *campesinos* drove their carts slowly down the oiled dirt street through the rivers of cars, re-garding with the patience of stones all this northern bustle.

Beneath the henyard cackle of voices, the backfire and gear-grinding of the autos, lay the continuous groaning roar from the distant loading pens and the crashing of cattle cars shunting in the yards, the clang of iron and the blast of steam from the engines in the great roundhouse. The yellow dust beaten up from the earth by all this human passage glittered in the air, and falling soft as down settled on all like a blessing of riches.

They came out onto International, a broad double width of street cleared like the swath of a tornado straight east to west across the town. Down the center of it ran a file of phone poles as though to mark the line. Where Grand crossed south like a spear into Mexico stood an obelisk, a little taller than the sentry posted beside it. Three others of the U.S. Infantry patrolled the line with Springfields at shoulder arms, looking professional in their wrinkled bloomers. On the other side of the telephone poles two Mexicans in bedraggled and torn shirts and pants, one with a cotton jacket torn half off his back, shuffled slowly back and forth, carrying captured Mausers across their shoulders as though they were shovels. The broad street looked like a battle zone, totally empty of people except for a few crossing the line a block west at the railroad tracks.

"It's easy to cross," Bisbee said, "with the fence gone. The fence got knocked down last March when Obregón captured Nogales over there and beat that devil Kosterlitzsky. Four hundred federals and half the people in the Mexican town charged the fence to get away from the bullets, and simply smashed it flat. A lovely scene." He laughed.

"Just wait till dark. Then all you have to do is walk east a few blocks, cross over and come back to the Mexican half of that crazy double station and board your train. Going over is all very casual, really. Most of the time the Mexicans won't even check your passports. But who knows? Some ass in the *garita* over there who's drunk up all his pay might try to take you for your eighteen dollars. And there's your poison box to cause trouble if he did."

Becky stood looking at the obelisk, sixty feet away, halfway across the barren no-man's-land of the street. "But what's to stop us, right now?"

"Better wait for dark," Bisbee said. "Have you thought this all out? You can't change your mind and come back, once you go, you know, without opening that box for the American customs. They're very nosy with baggage coming this way. They don't care if you go to Mexico or what you take, but they pounce on anybody trying to carry anything back. That's why they cut this crazy big street through the town, they tore out fifty buildings to try to stop the smuggling."

He laughed. "And then along comes this Herculano Santana and his plane. Wily fellow. They can't catch him. But they'd have your box open in a minute." He looked at Jacko. "That wouldn't do, would it? Why not come back to the Montezuma, take a room and refresh yourselves while you wait for it to get dark? And think it over carefully."

Jacko said nothing. You can't come back, he thought. Once you go, you're gone for good until you get rid of it. You can't bring it back and you can't just dump it, not here, not there.

"There's that little man again," Becky said. They turned and saw the small black figure standing forlornly half a block up Morley Street, looking at them. "Can't we see what he wants? He wouldn't take my dime."

"I know what he wants," Bisbee said. "He wants to take some money away from a gringo sucker, that's what he wants. Take my advice and have nothing to do with strangers."

She turned and looked across the street at the Mexican town. "Why does it seem so dismal over there?" she asked. "So messy and dirty. Not like this side."

"It's poor," Bisbee said. "Don Porfirio built Mexico up for thirty years. But now he's gone, and it's all falling to pieces."

He stood looking at Jacko and Becky, smiling his genial neat smile. "Well, I'm glad we met, and to have helped a bit. I might see you down south, you know. If I have to chaperon a carload of ammunition or something like that."

Jacko turned and shook the outstretched hand. "Very happy about our arrangement, Bisbee, and many thanks."

They watched him walk briskly back up Morley Street, his puttees flashing in the sunlight. The little Mexican had gone.

They stood alone. The glaring street was bare of life except for the patient pacing guards. Across the dusty barrier of emptiness the other Nogales lay sullen in the sun, its pleasant street trees seeming to Becky more a cunning disguise than a welcome. She felt very alone, with Bisbee gone.

"Such a *neat* person," Becky said.

"Popinjay. Those puttees."

"I wouldn't be critical," she said, her face turning pink, "you standing there in your silly golfing shoes and your dirty jacket, tamale juice slopped all over your knickers. Typical conceited attitude of male superiority. If you were flat on your back drunk in an alley, you'd still think yourself God's gift to the women instead of the complacent jackass you are. Popinjay!"

They stood face to face under the empty pale blue sky, itching, stiff with dried sweat, smelling dust, oil, horse manure, cow manure on the wind, and themselves.

"Complacent!" Jacko cried. "Male superiority! Six years I've listened to your preaching about the rights of American women. You think you're so abused, you're the most spoiled, cozened, coddled, pampered—if you were in Arabia, by God—" He caught himself up.

"I suppose you were going to tell me in Arabia I'd have a clitoridectomy by now, don't think I haven't heard of them, I'm a nurse, remember, you trying to scare the pants off a nurse, what a joke. And what would you have been in Arabia, eunuch in a harem with nothing in your drawers?"

"Ech, God, I never thought nursing school was such a breeder of vipers, are they all like that?"

"We're tough as nails, we have to be, putting up with fools like you in the beds, half-dead and still making passes, the fools."

"You said you flunked the course."

That hit her, he could see, and was immediately sorry. But it didn't stop her.

"Any more bits of female Arabian desecration you want instruction on?" she cried. "Slavery, chains, beatings, poverty, starvation—"

"For God's sake shut up, will you? you're alarming the sentries."

"Shut up yourself, fatso, don't forget I've got the eighteen dollars, so be nice or you'll sleep in the cattle cars. Pick up the bags and be quick about it." She turned abruptly and headed back up Morley Street.

Jacko watched her small body plow into the crowd. She walked leaning forward, her head down as though butting her way through. Fatso! who, him? strong and lean? And then he realized it was just one of her favorite words, and he suddenly felt like laughing. I suppose, he thought, she thinks she has to be tough because she is so little. He picked up the bags and followed her.

She stopped at the hotel and turned, waiting for Jacko, and at that moment Jacko saw the little black pest with the suitcase, like a large black cockroach, crawling into the rear seat of one of the long black touring cars nosing the curb. In the front sat Paz Faz and Gavira. He stopped short.

"What's wrong?" Becky asked, standing like a rock dividing the stream of the crowd.

"Go in and get a room," he said. "I'll be up in a minute. Here, take these," and plunked the suitcase and the box down in front of her.

He turned into the street, walked four cars up the line to the rear of Paz Faz's car and, hidden by the high black rear of the touring top, stood listening. He looked through the little oval window. The three were facing straight ahead, the pest sitting in back, leaning forward with his head between the others, rattling away like a machine gun. The street noises covered what he was saying, but it sounded as though he were giving orders.

So the little bastard was one of the anarchists. They had followed him to get back the monstrance, they had probably been in the same train.

But why the car? They couldn't have driven it from Los Angeles, it would have taken them a week over those roads. He looked down at the license plate: Arizona, a Tucson dealer. Stolen.

So now he had these three behind him, prodding him toward Herculano, probably already waiting for him in Guaymas with his damned plane.

What orders had the pest been giving? Well, what was the difference? The only important thing was to get away from them. He turned and sneaked away behind the cars toward the hotel.

CHAPTER FOURTEEN

J UST WHO was the rotten little sneak? he thought, stepping up on the curb. He remembered him crawling into the car, like a spider in that old black suit.

The current of the crowd was against him, he waited in an eddy for a break. Just how far would the three of them go to get the monstrance back? And what was he supposed to do about it? Catch the bastards in an alley, one at a time, do them in?

He melted through the flow of people to the opposite stream and drifted with the window-shoppers down toward the hotel. He stopped and stood looking into a store window at buckets of paint stacked in a pyramid. Kill them? As he stood there in the dust, his body seemed to have grown old, his legs too tired. All the memories of the Philippines swirled in a cloud in his head, the endlessness of guerrilla-killing, month after month in the heat and dust, the endless boredom between skirmishes, the shock of ambush, the dirt, the blood, the fatigue of spirit that beset him now. Pull a trigger. The easy way. For what? Money? He wasn't going to kill anybody if he could help it. Just run. The truth was, he didn't have the guts to kill anybody, even if he should, the way he felt now.

He went on, stepped up into the hotel lobby. The place was full of people milling around; potted palms covered with desert dust clustered against thin wooden pillars, turned and fluted by lathes and painted an excrescent brown, holding up a floral-stamped tin ceiling.

Up to the desk. Nobody there. He banged a bell on the counter. Nobody came. In the slowly swirling layers of cigar smoke faces came and went, moonlike, axelike, looming out of the clouds, jobbers in their derbies, city suits, and vests adorned with gold chains, fat watches, elks' teeth and Masonic compasses, thumbs in vest pockets, talking past cigars with lip-lifted important snarls, selling guns, blankets, camp beds, army stoves, all the comforts of slaughter, making the quartermasters jump with kickback joy. No countrymen, no soldiers, no women.

It suddenly occurred to him that the little pest and the others might want something besides the monstrance. Suppose they thought he had killed the twins? Revenge? He stood blank-eyed, contemplating a reflection on the silver bell. The thought of himself being killed by vengeful anarchists didn't particularly disturb him, and this suddenly struck him as interesting. He should feel at least some fear. Did too much death make one lose interest or belief in life? Was that why, ever since those days of bloody bodies huddled in the yellow fields he had looked for the joke in everything, refusing to take anything seriously?

He banged the bell again. All around him men's voices made a steady low roar, like a mountain creek tumbling through a tunnel of boulders. War, death, acquaintances to be avoided. Rather the amusing mild adventure of civil investigation and mildly reprobate trickery in Los Angeles; the big cool restful house on Bunker Hill; his swift little plane, the crowd with ever-open arms at the Yacht Club on the beach in Santa Monica.

How had he got into this mess? standing here broke, stuck with a woman with the temper of a sick weasel, wondering whether to come or go? The monstrance. Nothing but trouble, as though infected with some curse. One touch, then everything had started to fall apart. Suppose he just threw it over the roof? Gave it away to the first beggar he saw? Just surrender it to Paz Faz, forget it? Go back home. Give up and pick oranges.

Where the hell was the clerk? He banged the bell again and beginning to be angry kept on banging. A skinny young man with a little yellow moustache struggling for survival under a bully of a nose came out of a back room wiping his mouth and said Yes?

"Mrs. O'Donohue. What's the room?"

"Two oh three," the other said and stood there leaning on the counter with arms aggressively akimbo.

Something suggestive in the yellow smile sent the blood to Jacko's head, and he thought for a moment of leaning across, grabbing this oaf by the hair, and slamming his forehead down on the hard oak counter. He sighed a deep breath, pulled down his jacket, and pushed toward the stairway. Why on earth should he be sensitive about Becky's honor? What was she to him?

The monstrance was a trap he could not escape. He could not give it to Bustamente, could not sell it, could not abandon it. There was no way he could back out of this crazy trip. The only way he could get rid of it was to return it. He climbed wearily up the stairs.

He lay sweating on the hotel bed, watching a fly circling around the suffocating, half-dark room. He had slept three hours, since he had explained about Paz Faz and the others and she had said, "So what? Why don't you give them the damn thing and get rid of them? All I care about is my bonds." To hell with her and her bonds. He could have slept forever.

Now she suddenly said, as though repenting her sullen silence, "These trains! First in Tucson they say they don't know, then Mr. Bisbee says maybe in the morning, then maybe at night, then finally the desk clerk says seven o'clock. What system! Two more hours of this!"

Was she inviting him to conversation? And just why should he honor her with an answer? Let her rot in her sulks. With the folded copy of the Nogales *Vidette* he zapped the last of the large, furry black flies and brushed the corpse off the bedspread onto the fake Persian carpet where it lay, six legs folded in neat pairs as in triple prayer, with its seven brothers. He closed his eyes.

They had kept closed the tall, skinny windows of the Montezuma's dollar room, to save the final breath of coolness dying immured in the stone walls. The last of the low western sunlight blazed in a fringe of yellow fire around the edges of the cracked green shades, turning the room to the greeny-golden sea cave of some underwater world. In the warm gloom the monster wardrobe rose a dead-faced cliff to the ceiling sky, whose clouds of pressed-tin decorations lost themselves in shadows; the deep brown door, tall and dour, hung dead in the corner; the tall slits of windows gaped like the abandoned embrasures of a vanquished fort, while on the red-brown paper, pale trellises of lilies danced up and down the walls. In the shadows of the coffin room they lay, she in the bony arms of a Morris chair, her feet on the straw seat of the only other one.

However much the stiff chair pained her, she was pained more by the modesty of her gentle side, given an iron spine by the nurse in her, revulsed now to see him lying so familiarly before her, usurping the habitudes of a husband.

Could he not rather have politely sat while she slept, as they waited for the dark to fall? Not that she would ever have lain down before him, not even in full burial panoply; rather than lie before him she would have leaped stark naked from the window into the hurly-burly street.

Half her mind knew she was unreasonable. Yet still the acid of resentment burned that he had not suggested that she do what she would never have consented to do. Where was courtesy? Yet how could she reasonably insist on gentility from someone inherently detestable? She was in no mood to be fair. In her heart she was crying against the terrible strange country, against her aloneness, the dreadful hurt of her abandonment, and most against the terror of her poverty. The mockery of her wedding ring dragged down her heart; from the arm of the chair her hand drooped, too heavy for her wrist. She took off the evil little finger-prison, now just a token of treachery, and put it on the Bible which some maid had established in the exact center of the embroidery-covered table beside her. Beside it lay the thirty-four pesos of Carranza's money she had got for her dollars.

She sat looking at Jacko's long body. He was so carefree, indifferent, lying so comfortably flat on his back, while he tapped the lead tip of a pencil on a front tooth, the only sound in the high room, now that he had killed all the flies. Beyond the window glass the distant world rustled and tinkled, faintly the autos groaned and ground.

He was so carefree! and she so burdened. What right did he have to loll there, as on a bank of flowers in a summer afternoon, staring at the high, dark ceiling, tapping his teeth? She had always detested his lightness, the way he cast off care with an airy cynicism.

What had been her father's word? A *Luftmensch*, an air

man. Forever easy, even when pocket-empty, wearing an aura of wealth, proudly disdaining pride to mingle with brutes like Mike, amused by his petty abuses of the law, amused by Mike's folly. How dare he laugh at her?

Out of the grave her father said within her ear, And why not laugh at you? You didn't have to marry that clown. But don't miss the experience!

A tear welled up in her heart. Why did you leave me? Why couldn't I have gone with you, to lie with you down there, asleep? He asks: Who says, Asleep?

Tap, tap. It seemed to her that there was something dark and secret in both this man and her husband. This one, so well-mannered, so easy and casual, so able, and the other, so coarse, so clownish, so *cruel*, allied in some streak of evil. Both of them went laughing through their lives, as though at some secret joke, like brothers at some mischief.

And his contrary side, his religion, displayed in militaristic rigmarole, what sort of playacting was that? Was he nothing but a stiff, pompous, dried-out pharisee? Was it merely a show for reputation's sake? A mask for his contempt for the law, his tricks, ordering her husband to steal evidence?

It was not for nothing she had gone to Xavier, she knew the Catholic book probably better than he did. Like a robot he marched to mass without fail; groaned out of bed at four in the morning for expositions of the Blessed Sacrament; and yet all the while double-dealing in the streets. To her his faith was as dead as the flies on the floor. Woe to you! she could hear a voice crying, you who proudly pay your tithes on a pinch of parsley while you stand with your heel in the mouth of the poor.

She sat looking at him with the piercing intensity of some small, trapped wild animal, cornered in her chair; not fear, but uncertainty and detestation in her eyes. How could she find the courage to go on with him? It took energy for the nurse to be brave, and she was worn out.

He stopped tapping his teeth, turned his head on the pillow and smiled at her. She jerked her eyes away from the detestable smile; to hide from it she took up the Bible, ignoring the ring as it fell to the floor, opened the book anywhere, and read:

> My breast! my breast! how I suffer!
> The walls of my heart!
> My heart beats wildly,
> I cannot be still;
> For I have heard the sound of the trumpet,
> The alarm of war.
> Ruin after ruin is reported;
> The whole earth is laid waste.
> In an instant my tents are ravaged;
> In a flash, my shelters.

She clapped the book shut and closed her eyes. Green leafy visions of Xavier came back, Dr. Bretnauer's Bible as Literature, the faraway white years of linen innocence.

Jacko's smile faded. He sighed.

"I've been thinking," he said to the ceiling. "About possible dangers on this trip. I mean, apart from Herculano." He had to get rid of her, she was too much of a liability, dead weight, ball and chain. And yet he knew that was not fair; if it had not been for her money, he could never have got this far. And even if he had had the money, could he have abandoned her, broke, in Los Angeles? Forever sucker, he thought nastily, for the helpless female. The only woman he was really safe with was a known thief like May.

"Even if we can lose the Paz Faz crowd and get away without them on the train, there are still other problems."

"Not forgetting Herculano."

"Never forgetting Herculano. But we aren't anywhere near Herculano, yet. There's plenty of trouble down the road before we get to him. Maybe it's true that Obregón has won all the battles as far south as Guaymas. But that doesn't mean full control. I mean, about the trains being shot up, those Orozco people still on the loose."

He swung around on the edge of the bed, sat frowning at his knees. "I had the idea—well, ten years ago I was down here and Díaz's *rurales* police had the country tied up hand and foot, there wasn't a bandit in two thousand miles. Anybody on the roads without a good reason was shot on the spot. But now—" He stopped in exasperation. He simply could not use the word "rape" in the presence of a lady.

He looked up at her, trying to shrivel her with scornful eyes. "That dress! Fixed up for a genteel hike in a city park. Maybe the train will be safe. But *suppose*—" He stopped and sat chewing his lip in more exasperation with the limitations of courtesy. What the hell was another word for "rape"?

"Suppose what?" she said. "Out with it! The train is derailed and the maiden ravished. By the conductor. Just after the fancy luncheon."

"Listen to me," he said, leaning forward. "You may be a general in the suffragette army, but as far as I'm concerned, right now you're just a helpless female about as useful as a broken leg."

"I have a gun!"

"I want you to go home. Get out of this. If you *do* get ravished, as you put it, I'd have to stand by and watch it or get killed trying to protect you, and I don't want to do either one. So cash in your ticket and take your seventeen bucks somewhere else."

She leaned forward, her lip wrinkling up in a trembling

snarl. "My rent's due, you ass! I can't go home. If you're so afraid for your skin, go, leave me, I'll make it on my own. Do you think I'd depend on you? Go away! It's my dollar paid for this room. Get out! I'm here, I'm going. I can't do anything else."

He stared at her for a moment, then got up and walked around to the other side of the bed, as though it were safer. "Jesus," he breathed to himself. He turned and faced her again. "I can't let you. If you go, I *have* to go with you."

She grinned and let out a short bark of a laugh. "I can see you now, scuttling along behind me, terrified for my safety because you think you might have to protect me."

"There's nothing nuttier," he said, restored to calm by her injustice, "than a nut woman. Can't you see I'm *obliged* to bodyguard you if you go? I've got no way out of it? And I don't want to. I don't want my plans fouled up by having to act like some idiot Galahad, and probably get shot for it. Have some consideration! I don't have the time for fooling around protecting some female. I'll get your bonds for you. So take your bag and get the hell back to Los Angeles."

"No," she said, settling into the Morris chair and grabbing the arms as though he might throw her into the hall. She watched him simmer. "Why should I trust you? I'll get my own money. Do what you like."

"Oh God, oh God, oh God," he groaned, "now I understand the wife-beaters."

She laughed. "What a sad sight! The noble knight stuck with his chivalry. How ridiculous you look with your hair on end. You should sleep in a hairnet."

Somebody knocked on the door.

"Who's there!" he shouted, turning in a rage.

"Permit me to announce myself," came a meek, whiny voice, "Roberto Clemente Bustamente y Olaquibel. If I might have a little moment of your time?"

What the hell was the little bastard doing there at the door? Jacko eased the .38 hideout from its ankle holster and held it ready in his pants pocket.

"Oh, the dear little man!" Becky cried. The rotten little thieving anarchist, she would drown him in sweetness, smother him in smiles, until she could get him facedown over a barrel. Then! She swung her feet to the floor and sat up. "Come in, come in!" she trilled in honeyed voice.

Jacko put on his politest smile and began pressure on the trigger. He swung open the door and bowed in welcome. Bustamente came in, his small feet adventuring timidly one after another like a couple of old married mice out of a hole. He stood with both hands holding his black hat in the fig-leaf position.

Jacko looked him over. No guns on Bustamente, at least not yet. He pulled the pistol out of his pocket.

Bustamente stared at the gun. "You were expecting an enemy?"

"Have a seat," Jacko said, swinging the pistol gracefully toward the straight chair. "And let me relieve you of your hat, señor."

"Please do not 'señor' me, señor, for I come to you humbly, to beg a favor."

"You can beg just as well sitting down," Jacko said.

"As a beggar I must either stand or kneel."

Good God, Jacko thought, is this going to be a contest of noble sentiments? He drew himself up. "I beg you to be seated."

"That chair is not wide enough for both of us."

"Then I will go back to my bed," Jacko said, and plumping the pillow, lay down on one side, neatly crossing his ankles in preparation for lying. Bustamente edged his behind onto the chair. His heels hung half an inch from the carpet.

"I want to be your servant," Bustamente said, "and here

208

is why. My aunt in Guaymas has died, and I must go there to settle her will, a small matter of a little variety store, a little house, four hectares of stones and eleven goats, as listed by the attorney, these on the hillside of Cerro la Cantera, where the quarry is. You know it?"

"Not yet," Jacko said.

"I thought you must have relatives there, like myself, to be going at such a terrible time, wars, turmoil. Why else?"

"We are newspaper reporters," Becky said. "I myself am a photographer. We travel over the world for news."

"Adventurers! Well, that explains everything. But I have come to you beseeching a position as a servant, or as in Mexico, a *mozo*, a humble goer and getter, always at your command, if need be to sleep across the doorway like a brave dog.

"You see, I have no passport! But as your servant, they would let me pass. Alas, the consul of Los Angeles, a cruel man named Palafox, refused to give me a visa, so here I am stranded in Nogales. I cannot enter the land of my ancestors, I have been here five days, these pigs at the border, they have stopped me twice now with threats, twice pointing their rifles, calling me Pig or Snake, a son of a jackass, you cannot imagine.

"I am an American citizen, so they call me a foreign dog of a traitor, even though I explain that my parents were Americans before me, refugees from Díaz.

"What will happen to the estate of poor Tía Lucha, and what if I am not there to put a stone upon her tiny grave? What of her goats, her little store on La Avenida Rodriguez, all the varieties? All will be eaten by the officials, nothing will go to her little grandchildren, weeping on the stones.

"If you would let me carry your valises, your pretty little box with the skull on it, they would not molest me, sir, under the protection of such a man as yourself.

"I would attend to all your needs, bring sandwiches on the train, at the stations I would fetch you cool *limonadas*. And how well I know the country! I would be your guide, explain everything about the desert, about Guaymas, the customs, the best hotels, I think there are two now. I beg you, give me your consent, señora, out of the fount of your pity and tenderness of heart."

"Oh, my dear Mr. Bustamente, of course!" she said. Better to keep the little scut close by under control than wandering around up to God knew what.

"Palafox," Jacko said. "I know him very well."

"Oh, but he was hard. But now soft—dead."

"I heard somebody had bagged him," Jacko said.

"And you, sir, will you consent to this act of kindness, mercy, Christian charity?"

"Tell me more about yourself, Señor Bustamente."

"Please to call me by my humble nickname, Beto."

"Beto. Well, go on."

"Born an American, 1873, forty honorable years ago, the son of citizens. I have worked honestly, a tailor, sir, for twenty-five years, beginning as a boy sweeping the clippings of old Rafael Almada of Olvera Street, you know him perhaps? a rigorous master but just, he taught me my trade, sharpening carefully the scissors, straightening the needles, giving to the old bent ones honorable funerals in the poinsettia pot, then tracing patterns, then a little cutting, pants at first, then basting, each art complete, a master by little steps is made, sir, until complete at age twenty I sat beside him cross-legged in the window, until he one day fell forward onto a Prince Albert, who could forget? dead as a dog. That was in 1893. There still I sit, listening to my wife read the papers to me when she has time from her stove."

"You say you have been here for five days." This Beto had let a fly in along with himself. Jacko watched it sailing around. "How does it happen that you met us on the platform with your suitcase in your hand, as though you had been on the train?"

"Oh, the suitcase, I have been dragging it around because I had no money for a hotel room."

Palafox must have known Bustamente was an anarchist, to have refused the visa. But if so, why would Bustamente have asked him for one? Probably the whole thing was a lie.

He sat up on the edge of the bed and rolled up the *Vidette* again. He sat waiting for the fly to land. Why did Bustamente put on this act of seeming so safe, so gentle? Why not come up here with a gun and take the box by surprise, or set up an ambush in an alley?

"Señor, let me kill it for you, as your *mozo*." Bustamente leaned forward with his hand out.

"Well, why not, Beto?" He handed over the paper.

And then he saw it: they could not seize the monstrance because they could not trade it in, they were probably known as anarchists in Guaymas, on Huerta's kill-off list, and in any case, they did not have Palafox's letter of authorization to give to the priest. They had to wait to seize the reward money itself, after the exchange. And in the meantime keep close, make sure the monstrance did not get away.

The fly landed on the Bible.

"Your pardon, señora," Bustamente said and neatly knocked off the fly. It fell on the floor beside the wedding ring.

"Many thanks," Jacko said. So the big fight would not come until the end, with these three and Herculano all waiting for him, watching the priest as though he were a stalking horse. His stomach cramped up. Go home, said common sense. But give it all up? Not now. Something might happen to ease up the odds.

211

The sun had gone down, the room was settling into dusk. He stood up from the bed and went to the window, pulled up the cracked shade. Down below the street was almost empty, everybody home at dinner. Westward the edge of the sky lay white against the black waves of the hills; above, the sky was darkening to a noble blue. It would be dark in half an hour. He looked at his watch. Twenty minutes to train time. All right, let the little spider be their *mozo*. Supposing the reason was that Bustamente didn't want the monstrance to get out of control. That worked both ways: if he had to get rid of Bustamente, he'd be handy. And he wouldn't do anything until he could get hold of the money. In fact, they could travel along as old pals, why not? The only danger was that Paz Faz and Gavira might decide not to wait for the money, and try to take the monstrance. So let them try. Bustamente might do for a hostage. He turned from the window.

"All right, Beto, I'll let you be our *mozo*," he said. "We'd better go, or we'll be late for the train." Becky stood up and straightened her skirt.

"Forgive me for what must look like an impertinence," Beto said, "but there is no train."

212

CHAPTER FIFTEEN

JACKO STOPPED in the doorway and turned. "What are you talking about? It leaves at seven o'clock. The clerk here said so."

"I am sorry, but not today," Bustamente said humbly. "I have been to the roundhouse, I talked with the engineers."

"I don't believe it," Jacko said. What was the little bastard up to?

"Very well, sir, I would never insist against your opinion."

"Let's go, then," Jacko said. He and Becky went side by side down the stairway and through the lobby out into the night, Beto humping along behind them, loaded with the baggage.

"Through the station?" Jacko asked.

"Right through," Beto sighed, "turn left."

They stood in the wide dirt street with the two sets of tracks running empty down the middle, gleaming in the yellow light from the agent's window.

Behind them the ticket office window slammed down, the yellow light went out, the blue night swept over them. In the star-lit dark the agent came out of the station, turned, locked the door.

"Where is the train?" Jacko asked. "The seven o'clock train?"

"There is no train, señor," the agent said. "Not for three days."

"Three days!" Becky cried. "But we must be in Guaymas!"

"If you must, you must," the agent said, smiling with polite regret, "but, I am sorry, not by train. The only engine available is being repaired, boiler tubes were holed by bullets, all the other engines are south with the Army, getting ready for the battle. There might be one returning in a day or two. Who knows?" He started to turn away and stopped. "The only thing I can think of, señor, is that you might rent or buy a handcar at the roundhouse. There are even some with engines! That would get you there." He smiled, bowed, and walked away.

"Is he mocking us?" Becky asked.

"Just a friendly joke," Jacko said, "with just a touch of irony in it."

"What the hell are we to do?"

"What a pity about the train," Bustamente said. "I will not say that I told you so. Will you excuse me? I have to do something." He picked up his suitcase and walked off into the dark.

"Little bastard," Jacko said. "Rotten deserter."

"But the ship will be in Guaymas in three days!"

"Dirty little rat. Don't worry, Mike will wait for me. He'll try to get the monstrance. He's in so much trouble, probably by now he's got the guts to try to kill me for it."

"Don't be silly. Why should he risk his neck fighting

you when he can just sell my bonds in Guaymas and go on with the ship?"

"If they find out that some gringo is in Guaymas with $40,000 in bearer bonds, they'll probably kill him. He'll hide those bonds and carry the hatbox full of rocks to the priest and get the surprise of his life when he sees those rocks. If he hasn't found them already. If we can get there before the ship leaves, we'll get your bonds back. I'll beat them out of him. If Herculano hasn't butchered him first."

"But how can we get there in time, without the train?" She sat down on a bench against the station.

Down the street where International crossed, the little U.S. *garita* squatted on guard, the yellow light from its window shone gold on the double tracks, fading into the dark of the Mexican streets across the line. Across International two Mexican soldiers sat in chairs tilted back against a wall.

"Well, we might as well wait in the hotel," Jacko sighed.

"No," she said, standing up. "I'm not going to sit in that hotel room looking at you for two whole days. Let's go across now. And we have to get the passes, we can do that. Surely there's a hotel over there we can stay in. I'm too tired to go on tonight. I haven't slept decently for two days."

"We can't come back," he said, "not with the box."

"Who wants to come back! What's the idea? Are we going or not? Did we come down here to sit and sulk for three days in a dollar hotel room? Push! Push! We'll force something to come and help us!"

"If we go, we're stuck over there, and I'd rather be stuck in the U.S.A."

"Then stick!" she said. She grabbed her suitcase and started down the street along the tracks. "Just let them try to stop me."

Oh God, Jacko thought, she doesn't speak the language, she doesn't know anything. He ran after her and stood in front of her, blocking her way. "You listen to me, Becky."

She pulled back her arm and aimed her fist at his chest. "Get out of my way, you monstrous boob."

The long rays of a car's headlights swung across the tracks and swept toward them. They stood spotlighted as the car came on. It rolled up beside them and stood rattling its valves and popping muffled backfires.

"It is I, Beto," said the driver. "Have the goodness to join me. We are going to drive to Guaymas in this car. Isn't it beautiful?"

"Where did you steal it?" Jacko asked.

Bustamente laughed. "It belongs to my cousin Felipe. My cousin Felipe is a very wealthy man. He has everything. You don't even have to ask. Just take it. Look at the provisions he gave us!"

Jacko walked around the long, massive car. Its wheels were a yard across, just the thing for wilderness travel, its narrow tires hard as iron. Under the sloping box of its hood its engine rattled smoothly. Its large brass headlights stood out on stems like the eyes of some gigantic bug. And it had Arizona license plates in the frame of a Tucson dealer.

"Splendid!" he said, and climbed into the rear. He sat with feet resting on piles of boxes. Canned corn, beans, to-matoes, corned beef, a sack of *masa* for making tortillas, two cases of beer, two sacks of charcoal, two five-gallon cans of kerosene, two more of water. Where had Busta-mente stolen all this stuff?

Where were Paz Faz and Gavira? Bustamente and those two might be up to something. Riding with Bustamente would be a risk, but he and Becky had to have the ride south, there was no other way. If it came to shenanigans with the three of them, he would simply have to kill them,

216

though with a sigh. The best thing to do was to get the car away from Bustamente quickly, when they were on the road south of town, before anything happened, and leave the other two well behind. Five miles down the road, Bustamente would find himself thrown out in the ditch, and all would be clear. The cotton rope off his suitcase would do. No, the coyotes would chew him up. A good knock on the head would be better, and throw him in the bushes.

Bustamente yanked the car into gear. He waved as they passed the American guard, the other waved back.

As they neared the Mexican soldiers one of them stepped forward into the street, his rifle at port arms.

"¡Alto!" he cried, and Bustamente stopped.

The Mexican came up to the side of the car.

"We are the Ambassador of Austria," Bustamente said, "come to bring recognition from the Court of the Emperor Franz Josef to the First Chief. Stand aside!"

"Oh, Excellency, may I humbly ask the password?"

Bustamente handed him a fifty-peso note. *"¡Viva Carranza!"*

"¡Viva Obregón! And your passports, if you will be so kind?"

Bustamente handed him another fifty.

"All in order!" A wide, beautiful smile under the big hat as he stuffed the bills in his hip pocket. "Pass, friends. And may God go with you!"

"A hundred pesos?" Jacko asked, "How much is that American?"

"Only fifty dollars, señor. A pittance."

"Good *night*! Why so much? I thought you were broke. Where did you get all this money?"

The big car rolled across the line. Becky slumped in the corner, relaxed. Safe! Nobody had asked for her passport. They were on their way, they couldn't go back, they couldn't change their minds, and there was for some reason a feeling of safety in that. The pressure of urgency she had felt died and suddenly she wilted, exhausted.

"Listen," she said, "I told you I've got to have some sleep. Isn't there a hotel down here somewhere?" They were driving under the trees of the Mexican Nogales.

"We've got to get on," Jacko said. The thing to do was to push on out of town, throw Bustamente to the dogs and keep going through the night.

"No," Becky said. She sat up straight with the sudden energy of rage. "Do what I say, you jackass!"

"Damn it," Jacko said, "We've got to go on, you don't understand, there's reasons—"

"No!" she said. "I'm just too tired. Go on, I don't need you. Go to hell. Beto, stop. I'm getting out. I'll find my own damned hotel."

Beto kept going. In Mexico, the *caballero* was the boss. Muttering and cursing to herself in a fury, Becky rummaged in her purse for her pistol and shoved it into Bustamente's ear. "If you don't stop this minute, you little son of a bitch, I'll blow your damned head off." Beto took his foot off the gas and put his hands in the air, but out of courtesy to the *caballero* did not put on the brakes. The car wobbled by itself into the curb.

Jacko gently took hold of the gun and pointed it at the moon. She fought him for it. "Okay, Becky, okay. Beto, find a hotel! Okay, Becky? Okay? We're going to a hotel! Okay?" She quit fighting. He let go of the gun. She sank back in the corner.

What was the use of arguing with her? The woman was like a crazy horse. Hell, they all were. Have to gentle her, gentle her, softly, little by little.

Bustamente began to hum a tune. These American women! He drove on. The headlights shone on the dark trees lining the street, the crowds of people passing under them. "Down there two blocks you see our hotel, the

Escobosa, a fine place. My cousin Felipe says it is full of generals and cabinet ministers of the new government, but surely they will have a room for much-honored American reporters and their humble *mozo*."

Jacko turned up his coat collar. The night was getting cold, with the wind of their passage whirling around him, scooped in by the big black top. He shrugged his coat up around his ears. He sat hunched on the cold, slippery seat, glaring at the back of Bustamente's neck. Crunch. But not yet, not yet, would he choke off that asinine love song. The right time would come, when they would give the little bastard the slip. He smiled at Becky, huddled in the corner. "We'll get a good dinner in a minute," he said, "so cheer up."

She leaned over close to him, raising her lips toward his face. My God, he thought, is she going to kiss me?

"Two rooms!" she whispered fiercely in his ear, the hiss of a snake. "If you can't get two, you can sleep in the street."

Bustamente pulled up in front of the hotel, a three-story building, every window softly glowing. Out of the narrow doorway came a hubbub of talking, laughing, and shouting.

"You let me handle this, friend Beto," Jacko said, getting out. He headed for the door and pushed into the crowd of uniforms and three-piece suits. All the uniforms were informal, personal inventions, pieced together from the Yankee stores across the line, khaki-colored outfits in vaguely military style, puttees, shirts of olive-green or tan, topped off by flat-brimmed Stetsons with four pinches in the peaked crown, here and there a visored military cap, some tan, some white.

"Con permiso, con permiso," Jacko muttered, smiling his way toward the desk through the crowd of men, all talking excitedly, with ebullient gestures hampered by the

crush, all evidently living on a wave of enthusiasm for the war, the new future. He squeezed through to the portly gentleman in white linen behind the desk, leaning back to balance his prosperous paunch, frowning in distress at the confusion of his overcrowded register. Obviously Señor Escobosa; no clerk could look so important.

"Forgive me, señor," Escobosa said, waving his hands in small circles of despair as Jacko came up, "but do not ask for So-and-So, I don't know half of these new officials, and as for who is in or out, who returns the keys any more?"

"Of course," Jacko said, "but I merely wanted to inquire if you have two rooms, for tonight only."

"Two rooms! They are sleeping four in a bed, some have even paid for space on the stairs. How I wish I could oblige! But!" He opened his arms wide, surrendering. "The whole government and half the general staff is in town. Might I suggest a private house? But do not think me inhospitable, señor! Go to the bar in the next room and refresh yourself, tell them Escobosa sent you."

A quick one, Jacko thought, and pushed through the crowd into the bar, shouldered up between a man with a beer and one with a brandy. The brandy man wore a captain's bars on a tailored military blouse, very smart. He glanced at Jacko's creased and rumpled jacket with humorous black eyes, smiled under his neat dark moustache and said, *"Salud!"* raising his glass. "It seems you have made a long journey."

"Salud!" Jacko said, drank and sighed. "I had no idea Nogales would be so crowded. No beds to be had, at least here."

The other laughed. "Nor anywhere else. The high and mighty, the Foreign Secretary, the Minister of War, the Minister of the Interior, six generals, are sleeping four to a room. I myself have rented a corner of the stairway landing, although you would think that one recently honored by a commission would be clever enough to find a better bed. You are welcome to share my landing, there is only one other occupant. Permit me to introduce myself, First Captain Faustino Fabela, assigned to a new company forming in Magdalena. I was an attorney in practice in Guadalajara, so I thought I might be assigned to the headquarters, but it seems they have too many attorneys, so I join a new battalion of peasants who would rather fight than work. And you, are you going to join our cause? We have a few Americans."

"In sentiment, but not officially," Jacko said, and introduced himself. "A thousand thanks for your kind offer of half your landing, but there are three of us, and we would not want to crowd you."

"A reporter, and from Los Angeles! Welcome, we need that the United States should know our reasons for fighting. So you are going south to join Obregón?"

"As soon as we can. Another? Bartender! We were supposed to go by train, but there will be no train for three days, they tell us."

"More likely a week," Fabela said. "But I could offer you a lift as far as Magdalena. My partner and I have the loan of a handcar to take us south. His uncle is a foreman of the roundhouse. What a ride! We have done it before, in timing races. What a sport! This one is a real speeder with a special engine. Come with us, we are leaving at nine o'clock." He looked at his wristwatch. "We can drink for an hour and then we will take you for the finest ride you have ever had."

"I wish I could," Jacko said, "but we already have a borrowed car. A thousand thanks, Captain Fabela, maybe we will have the luck to meet again. Another before I go?"

They drank to the Revolution, shook hands, and Jacko edged out through the crowd.

Outside, Becky was hugging herself in the corner of the rear seat, shivering in the chill of the night air.

"No rooms!" Bustamente said cheerfully, reading Jacko's face.

"We'll have to go back," Jacko said.

"Don't be silly," Becky said, "we can't go back, not now."

"Then you'll have to sleep in the car. You can wear your raincoat for a blanket. Come on, Bustamente, let's hit the road. I'll drive." He stood waiting for Bustamente to move over.

Bustamente laughed.

"What's so funny?"

"Look behind you."

Jacko started to turn, and something hard jabbed him in the left kidney.

"Up with the hands, jackass."

Jacko raised his hands and turned his head. Paz Faz's narrow handsome face smiled at him.

"Well, well," Jacko said, looking down at Faz's old Army .45. "I see you remembered how to cock it."

"Just get in the front beside me here," Bustamente said. "Faz will sit beside us and help you keep calm." Gavira came around from behind the car and climbed in beside Becky. She hunched away farther into the corner.

"So you talked to the engineers at the roundhouse, you knew there was no train, and all of a sudden there you were with a car out of nowhere. Good planning, Bustamente."

If it hadn't been for Becky's damned hotel business, he would have had Bustamente tied in the ditch ten miles down the road by now.

"Well, one takes advantage of a situation, right? Don't worry about a place to say, *mi padrón*. We will go to a little house to wait till I collect a few men to help Faz and

222

Gavira to guard us. And please don't be angry with poor
Beto. I wish you no harm, I only wish to be sure of your
company. I am still your *mozo*. Haven't I proven my use-
fulness? The car? The food? And I will serve you more."

Bustamente turned the big car off Avenida Sonora
through the nighttime crowds, zigzagged east on Calle
Ochoa two blocks to Calle Arispe. Jacko sat trying to ignore Faz's big .45, shoved into his side.

"Where is the monstrance?" Bustamente said. "In the
little chemical box?"

Jacko said nothing. Bustamente headed south again.
Streams of Mexicans moved slowly in and out of the dark
gaps between the single dim streetlights on the corners,
clogging the way and slowing the car; through the soft un-
dertone of Spanish, now and then broke harsh shouts of
drunken Yankee soldiers; the rapid tinkle of player pianos
poured out on the shafts of light from the doors of saloons
and gambling halls. Stalled by the crowd at a cross street,
Bustamente waved off with a snarl a Mexican whore smiling at him over the door. Even uglier Yankee whores
waited hipshot under the corner lights, turning in slow
oxen pirouettes to display their stock. Everywhere the dust
rose from the hundreds of padding feet.

"We are almost there," Bustamente said. "Now be wise,
I beg you. Please don't fight us, don't try to run. Where
would you go, on foot? I assure you, you'll be all right,
and when we're all through with our business in Guaymas,
you can go home in peace. You won't be hurt. Knowing
you, señor, I don't believe you killed the Rivera brothers,
and nobody is looking for revenge, at least not many. I
think I have convinced Faz of your innocence."

Four blocks down Arispe, Bustamente turned right up
Calle Díaz, and as the car began to climb gently toward
the black hills to the west, the crowds began to thin. The
car heaved in and out of increasing potholes, and finally

stopped in the dark where the street tapered off into an alley steep enough for goats. Bustamente switched off the lights.

"We'll have to walk from here," Bustamente said. Jacko stepped out and stumbled into a hole. The last streetlight down the hill behind them shone faintly on the walls of the flat-roofed low adobe houses, stepped up the hill on each side of the alley. Garbage stank in the shallow ditch running down the middle.

They left the forlorn light and stumbled on up the hill in the dark, guessing the way from a rare weak gleam from a shutter or a door. Dogs barked; faintly beyond the blind face of a house in a hidden patio someone was singing; far away in the barren hills coyotes mocked the dogs. Carrying his suitcase with his left hand, the box under his arm, Jacko steadied himself from rut to hole by feeling along the rough walls. Becky panted along behind him.

Up ahead, Bustamente spoke into the dark. He had stopped at the corner of a cross-alley and was talking to a man hidden in the shadow of a wall. Thrust out from the shadow, a worn rifle barrel shone silver in the starlight.

Bustamente opened a door, light streamed out carrying a band of smoke. Jacko and Becky followed him in. Paz Faz and Gavira stood inside the doorway, Faz's gun at his side. An old woman, her face shrunken in a thousand cracks and wrinkles, dark as the old wooden beams overhead, knelt on the dirt floor by the fire in a corner, grinding corn on a metate.

Chickens sleeping in a corner waked up and came out into the light of the smoking open lamp; a sheep in another corner made a complaining baa. The hens squawked flapping into the air and settled clucking on the three rawhide-seated chairs in the room, and on the altar in the corner. Bustamente knocked the chickens off the chairs with his hat, brushed off the dust, and invited Jacko and

Becky to sit down. The old woman continued pulling dinner together, cooking on the open flame in the corner fireplace, fried meat and frijoles.

Bustamente dished up the dinner in old tin pieplates and passed them around. "Enjoy what you can," he said. "Tomorrow we'll have better." He smiled with perfect friendliness at his two prisoners. "Don't feel put out! You know it's a game, sometimes one wins, sometimes another. There's nothing serious at stake here, only money after all. Nothing like lives!"

In silence they chewed their way through the tough meat and scooped up the frijoles with torn and folded tortillas. When they had finished Bustamente said, picking his teeth with a rusty brad, "I told my cousin Felipe, when I borrowed this house for tonight, that you have not been married for long, and he has had the goodness to give you his bed. You can have privacy in the next room, while Gavira and I go for our men and the horses. Guards, you understand. It is not safe now to travel only one or two, we will have four horsemen with rifles to protect us. Tonight we will sleep here, tomorrow will be better. Come on, Gavira." He stood up and the two went out, leaving Faz standing guard in the doorway. The big car rolled off down the hill.

The white walls of the room next door glowed softly in the waving yellow flame of their lamp, a rag pulled through a thin bit of wood floating in a dish of oil. The old woman had been busy: the dusty earth floor had been freshly swept and sprinkled with water, there were sheets and pillows on the big iron bed in the corner. Bustamente had a certain class, Jacko thought, trying to keep what he called a game as pleasant as possible. In another corner stood a Singer sewing machine; in another a table altar with three shelves, with candles and paper flowers.

Jacko looked around the room. There was one small,

barred window high in the wall. The rafters were cut from saplings and branches, the ceiling was of willow wands, and on top of that he knew there was a foot of clay, impossible to get through.

Jacko put the lamp down on a small table beside the bed. "We'll have to get out of here quick if we're going to. There's no telling how long the little bastard will be gone, and we won't have a chance once he gets back." He told Becky about Fabela's offer of a ride. "We'll just have to leave everything and run. I hope to God I can find that hotel again."

"What about that man at the door?" Becky said. "He doesn't know about your little gun. Are you going to kill him?"

"Paz Faz? That sucker. I don't want to kill anybody. I don't have to go that far, at least not yet. Did you bring that split skirt riding habit I saw when you were packing in Los Angeles?"

"And what if I did?"

"Well, put it on! That parade outfit is no good. Don't argue with me now. And put on the boots. God knows what we're going to be getting into from now on."

She got her split skirt out of her suitcase, pulled on her raincoat for modesty's sake. Even with the raincoat on, she felt like asking him to shut his eyes while she got into the skirt, but he didn't seem in the least interested. She thought of the dead whore, lying naked on the slab. So much for modesty. She dropped her skirt.

She watched him squatting on the dirt floor beside his suitcase, picking over things.

"Leave that raincoat," he said, "it won't rain for six months." He pulled out all his socks and began rolling the pairs into balls. "You got any socks? Or just stockings? Here"—he threw her three of the balled socks—"stick

226

those in your bag." He stuffed three more into his left jacket pocket. "Feet, most important."

"Are we going to walk to Guaymas?" She began sorting out her stuff.

"I'm planning to get down to the hotel, that's all. Here, you don't need all that underwear, throw it away. You can carry that big purse of yours, and that's it, and you may have to dump that, if it keeps you from running." He pulled his heavy .44 revolver out from under his junk.

"You're very damn bossy," she said. "I'll take anything I can carry."

"In the handbag." He was looking over his heavy revolver. He tossed her a box of cartridges.

"Carry that." She shoved it in the bottom of the bag under the copy of *Camera Work* and rammed blouses, underwear, stockings on top of that. She crowned it all with the little .380 auto Jacko had given her.

He started wrenching off the top of the poison box. He wrapped the monstrance in a couple of shirts and stuffed it into a pillowcase from the bed.

"Why don't you just shoot him?" she asked, looking at his pistol. "You were in the war. You must have shot plenty of people. If you shot him, we wouldn't have to run and we could carry all our things."

He laughed. "You think killing is easy."

"Then just wound him."

"I don't even want to wound anybody. This isn't war. So far it's a game. If I kill anybody, I turn it into a war, they'll have to try to kill me, for their bloody honor, and I couldn't win, one against three. It isn't the army, I've got no orders, no backup. To tell you the truth, I've never been in a spot like this before. Not even in Los Angeles. I've got no cops to fall back on. I'm in a foreign country, and a lousy one at that, and if I goof, I'll end up in one of their lousy jails, no money for bribes. I've got to keep it a

227

game. To tell you the truth, I'm pretty nervous." He looked up at her and grinned. "Let's just say scared."

"How much time have we got?"

"Two minutes? How do I know. I don't know where Bustamente went. Half an hour? But we have to get to that captain by nine, that's fifteen minutes. That's the most we've got." He stood up. "Let's go."

"I could vamp the guard. Distract him. You hit him over the head."

"Well, that's more like it. You ever vamp anybody?"

"No."

"Okay, try it. He's a sucker for women. Conceited as hell, like all these Mexican macho jerks. You've seen how he pirouettes around like some dancer. And he's crazy about his Spanish honor. You know, you call his sister a slut and he'll kill you to avenge his honor, and then sell her to somebody for four bits. He can't stand an insult. If I ever have to shoot him, that's how I'll spoil his aim—call his mother a whore." Jacko grinned. "Okay, go ahead and vamp him. Or make him mad, fuddle his brains, challenge his manhood, tell him he's nothing but a silly woman with nothing between his legs, that always gets them, that'll drive him crazy." He shoved the big pistol under his belt and pulled his shirt down to hide it.

He led her into the other room. Faz, sitting in one of the chairs, jumped up and got between them and the door, his gun ready.

"Take it easy, Faz," Jacko said. "All we want is a cup of coffee. How about it, mama?" he said to the old woman, crouched on the floor at her eternal job of grinding corn. She paid no attention. One of the chickens was pecking in her dish of flour. She whacked it back-hand and it flapped away. The sheep, standing in the corner eyeing the bowl of corn beside the old crone, ducked its head as though it had been hit before.

Becky sidled up to Paz Faz. She wasn't very good at it; if she hadn't been so small, the sidle would have been a waddle. She pushed up close to him; he backed way like an offended virgin. He wasn't used to macho females.

"Got a cigarette, handsome?" This was a line she remembered from a movie caption.

"What is this?" Faz said, looking down at her, offended and perplexed. "Go back to your husband, woman, behave yourself."

The sheep made three timid steps toward the corn.

"Oh, come on," she said, crowding Faz against the wall, belly to belly, horrifying him. No worse than dissecting a dead whore, she thought. "He isn't my husband. He's my pimp. Come on in the next room. I'm feeling hot."

Jacko stood watching, smiling at Faz. "Go on, Faz, it's free for an old friend. You can tell your buddies in L.A. how you screwed O'Donohue's woman."

"What the hell is this?" Faz shouted.

The sheep made a quick run on the corn. The old woman casually grabbed a burning piece of wood out of the fire and began beating the sheep on the back. The sheep fled in terror around the room, its greasy wool on fire, pouring stinking smoke, the chickens rose flapping and shrieking into the air, their wings batting Jacko in the face.

He lunged for the burning sheep and, grabbing it around all four legs, hoisted it into the air and pitched himself at Faz, falling on him and smashing the smoking, bawling sheep against his face and chest, throwing him against the wall. Becky fell to the side, Faz struggled on the floor under the sheep, which was stamping on him in its efforts to get up. Jacko grabbed Faz's gun from the floor where Faz had dropped it, seized Becky's arm, hauled her up and dragged her out of the door into the night, running for the alley.

"Run!" he said, heading down the hill through the garbage. She kept stumbling. "Let go of me!" she shrieked, yanking free, and sped past him, leaping from rut to crown like a goat.

"Oh, God, there they are," Jacko panted. At the bottom of the hill Bustamente was turning the car up the alley, followed by four horsemen. Still running, Jacko shoved the monstrance at Becky, pulled both his gun and Faz's and began firing over the top of the car. Bustamente dove to the floor, the car rammed into the side of a house. The lead horseman wheeled his horse in a panic as Jacko, running straight at him, fired over his head, the horse fell against the one following and they rolled and slid down into the others; one of them charged back down the hill, the other broke away into a cross-alley.

Becky fell in the gutter. Jacko threw away Faz's empty gun, helped her up and pulled her leaping and hopping the rest of the way down the hill into the crowds of people moving along the street. They hid in the first dark doorway they found. The pillow slip holding the monstrance had torn. Jacko wrapped it up more securely.

Up the hill Bustamente was standing by the stalled car, waving his arms and shouting at his men. The four riders quit milling around, pulled themselves into line and came down to the edge of the crowd, Bustamente stumbling behind them, where they had to stop. They sat there looking helplessly over the heads of people.

"Come on," Jacko said, pulling Becky from the doorway into the stream of people. "We can't wait for them to leave. Just walk slow and they won't spot us." They sauntered along with the crowd until they turned a corner and then cut into the middle of the street and ran.

CHAPTER SIXTEEN

As they climbed onto the little speeder with Fabela and his friend, and their corporal mechanic driver, Jacko saw Bustamente's long car going fast down Sonora, heading south out of town. The speeder was a light handcar with a one-cylinder engine belted onto the front axle. Ordinarily, running on the rails, it could have beaten any car on those dirt roads, but because of the bridges, it had to go slower and would be left far behind.

Half the bridges, little wooden truss affairs crossing dry barrancas rarely more than ten feet deep, had been burned by retreating Federals, and the tracks relaid precariously down across the stream beds so that, going too fast, the speeder would hit the sudden sags in the line almost flying through the air, swooping down and soaring up, sailing half clear of the tracks. Blind in the night, they would not be able to see these dips until they were upon them, and had to slow to less than half speed.

On long, level stretches, the smooth sailing ride of the speeder, rocking a little from side to side, almost put them to sleep; then they would hit a sudden sag into a creek bed and hang on to the seats, swooping and soaring.

They came into Magdalena two hours later, half-frozen by the wind of their speed. The stars like points of ice glittered in the black sky. They sped with the brakes shrieking on the wheels through the dark fields outside the town, fields which bore a hundred little orange fires. There must have been five hundred men sitting in little groups ringed around these flames.

Then blocks of houses blacker than the night rose up against the stars, and they came into the little town seeing faint secret orange lights winking in chinks of bolted doors and shutters flashing by. They slowed into the narrow railroad yards, sneaking past giant overtowering black hulks of boxcars, slowed and stopped beside the maw of a great open shed. Here and there in the yards, and deep inside the shed, a lantern glowed, bringing out of the dark grotesque apparitions of brick walls broken in a battle, angles of crossbeams and burned rafters rising from the sea of black like bits of wrecks of broken ships and shattered gibbets.

The mechanic killed the engine; they sat in the sudden silence still locked in aching huddles against the freezing wind of their flight on the rails. The lantern Fabela had tied to the front of the speeder shone feebly in the stillness, showing beside the gleaming steel rails two short bits of track which were the ordinary home of a handcar. With the wind stilled, their joints thawed, they unfolded from their frozen pupae huddles and sighing and grunting heaved the handcar off the main line onto its perch.

Jacko, still shivering, put out a hand to Fabela. "A thousand thanks. A million!"

"A pity we must part so soon," Fabela said, "but we must hurry off to report to our chief, wherever he is. What a pleasure it has been! I wish we could invite you to our mess, but we have no idea where it is, such a confusion. Four hundred men and nobody knows yet who belongs where! Here's hoping we meet again soon."

In the lantern light everybody shook hands with everybody else in a bowing circle and Fabela turned the wick of the lantern down and out. The darkness plunged in on them, and the two officers with their corporal disappeared into the darkness, the grinding gravel footsteps died away.

"We could have kept right on going," Becky said, gesturing at the speeder, sitting like a spider on its little trackbed. "Why didn't you ask Fabela for it? We can't possibly get it back on the track."

"Never mind the speeder. I want to see if I can find Bustamente, they probably think we're stuck in Nogales waiting for the lousy train and it was safe for them to stop here for the night. If I can steal that car, we can ditch them for good. I want that car, we'll need all that food and stuff."

They crossed the tracks and headed for the lights of the main street. To the west the street ran for five or six blocks of powdery dust and then disappeared in the dark. The dust lay two inches deep, almost white in the dim light from three or four cantinas and a few stores still open to take the pesos off the crowds of sandaled peon soldiers coming in from the camps.

An east wind blew cold and sharp from the jagged ridges of the Sierra Madre, whirling billows of dust up through the light from the store windows to tower into the dark above, or curl away in whirling tilted devils down the street. Hilarious skirts of old newspapers flew up blowzy and sailed away drunk in the air.

A mass of broken adobe bricks blocked the cobbled sidewalks and they took to the street. A little farther, the cannons had blasted a brick building, and the front wall had fallen facedown like a drunk into the dust. A black hole in the shoulder-to-shoulder rank of white adobe fronts gapped like a lost front tooth, ash and soot flew up in the wind from a jumble of black burned beams. But the wreckage was old, the fires cold, the dead all carried away, and held in the teeth of the wind came the sound of the singing cantinas.

A few saddled horses waited hunched in the wind at the stone sidewalks, some wagons, a number of cars, mostly with hastily painted military markings of battalion and company numbers, the usual funereal-looking long black touring models with cloth convertible tops. Jacko walked in the street, reading the license plates. He spotted the car in the second block, with its Arizona license and the Tucson dealer's name, standing empty in front of one of the noisier cantinas.

He handed the pillow slip with the padded monstrance to Becky and moved his big pistol from his back to his belly, just in case Bustamente's crew came out. He set to work on the car.

Small groups of *campesinos* stood about in the street, watching peacefully as he worked. Fabela's battalion, no doubt. More were coming out of the dark fields into the lights of the town, mostly Indians, sandals shuffling through the flour dust. They did not go into the cantinas; they sent single emissaries, who came out loaded with bottles, and then all stood about, drinking slowly, waiting.

He knew next to nothing about these gasoline-fired buggies, which as a Stanley driver he'd always held in contempt. But he knew there was a magneto which, when the engine was cranked, fired the plugs, and there were wires from here to there, God knew where, and the whole circuit was interrupted by a key. The thing to do, logically, he thought, since he didn't have the all-important key, was to cut the switch out, wire around it. But which wires? He fumbled around in the dark under the dashboard, finding

234

three wires running from the switch, or to it, God knew. He said eeny-meeny-miney-mo and hooked two of the wires together, went to the front of the car and started cranking.

The dark Indian faces of the new soldiers regarded him with mild, peaceful eyes, it seemed to Becky, from a thousand years away, with the benign blindness of idols looking up from under an ancient sea. Crank, crank. Jacko took off his coat and sweated in the icy wind. In the cozy cantina, safe from the wind, the Mexicans shouted and declaimed, he could imagine their arms waving, fists shaking with patriotism. He swore and panted, rested, cranked again. Nothing happened.

It must be one of the other wires, he thought, leaning against the puny radiator, panting and sweating. He changed the hookup and started cranking again. God, it was a brute. Who the hell ever invented the thing? He'd never had any trouble like this with the Stanley, which didn't need a crank.

From up ahead came the bray and twang of a little marimba band, broken by the wind, and then Jacko saw them, three musicians standing in a vacant lot, silhouetted black against a fire built against a tall stub of adobe wall, headless survivor of the cannonades. Lighted full-face by the whipping flames stood a fourth man, bigger than the three black humps of musicians, waving a bottle in the air to the time of the music.

One of the Indians, smiling like the sun, came over and offered him his bottle. Jacko took a long swig of tequila and bowing his thanks started cranking again.

But what about the gasoline supply? He stopped cranking. What was he supposed to do about that? He fiddled with various levers under the steering wheel. Cranked. Nothing happened.

He leaned against the side of the car and began swearing. The *campesinos* listened, nodding to themselves, swigging out of their bottles. He knew what he was going to do. He was going to pull his gun and go in the damned cantina and take the key off those three sons of bitches if he had to kill them.

He pulled at his gun. The front sight caught in his pants. He stood swearing at it, tugging. Bustamente came out of the cantina doors, staggered and fell forward, knelt there on all fours, blood dripping from his face.

Jacko stood over him, holding the front sight of the gun next to Bustamente's nose, where he couldn't miss seeing it. "Give me the goddam key," he said.

Bustamente reared up on his knees. "I'm dying! They killed me!"

"I don't give a damn if you're dying. Give me the key."

Blood oozing down from Bustamente's scalp covered the left half of his face, filled the eye. "Friend! *Compadre!* Thank God you have come. Protect me, I beg you. Those bastards will kill me!"

Jacko put the muzzle of the gun in Bustamente's chest and pushed. Bustamente went over backward and sat with his legs sprawled out. "You little pismire," Jacko said, "I'll teach you to kidnap me. Give me the goddam car key!"

"I haven't got it!"

"You lying son of a bitch." Jacko shoved the gun in his pants and dragged Bustamente to his feet.

"Don't be so rough," Becky said, "can't you see he's hurt?" She hurried to hold him up on his other side.

Bustamente stood weaving. "*Compadre,*" he said weakly, "forgive me for what only seemed to be a kidnapping. Protect me, hide me, there's a hotel up the street." His knees gave, they yanked him upright again and began walking him away from the cantina.

"Bastards," wept Bustamente, "they have rebelled. Paz

Faz did this. Think, to be killed with a plate of beans! Those dogs, they won't follow orders any more. They think I am planning to split the reward with you and dump them. They are going to kill you, Jacko. Kill both of us." He began to cry, wobbling along supported under the arms. "We have to protect each other."

"Can you believe this little shit?" Jacko said across Bustamente's bloody face to Becky, who was panting along with Bustamente's arm across her shoulder. "Here he kidnaps us and keeps us prisoner and now he wants to be partners again."

"I have protected you, Jacko!"

"Now he's using my first name, like a brother."

"I made excuses for you, I said Palafox murdered the Riveras, not you. It grieves me, my good friend, that you think I kidnapped you. I was protecting you! I went for a guard! We must work together, *compadre*. Oh, God, I am sick." His knees gave out, they had to stop, he sagged between them.

"Come on, Becky, we'll have to drag him. I've got to get that key off him." Two shops up from the cantina they found what was left of the hotel. Its front windowpanes were blown out, the door propped against a wall with the screws still hanging from the torn-out hinges. In a front room a lamp glowed down on a skinny old man with a white beard, slumped asleep in a chair tilted against the wall.

They stepped up through the doorway into a hall, dragging Bustamente between them. They looked up: the walls rose to the sky, the roof gone. Bricks fallen from the walls lay all over the floor. Bits of charcoal were still falling from the few charred rafters left above. The bitter wind howled over the broken tops of the walls high above, swooped down into the halls and whistled around the corners, in and out of the doorways. The yellow flames of lamps down the hall trembled behind their smoky glass chimneys.

"You are looking for a room?" somebody behind them said. They turned. The old man was standing in the door of his room, holding a lantern high beside his ratty white head. "What have you got there? Another wounded hero from the cantinas?"

Jacko handed him a dollar.

"A dollar! Help yourself! Take the bridal suite. You see"—waving a delicate white hand at the stars—"we have had the roof removed, to improve the ventilation. Should I be mean-minded when I have been so blessed with improvements? I have no blankets, Huerta's men stole them when they retreated through here, but I have sacks. A sack is better than nothing." He brought out an armload of burlap bags from his office and shoved them at Becky. He went back into his hole.

In a room across the hall from the old man, they put Bustamente down on the bed nearest the door. Across the room somebody in another bed was snoring. On the floor beside him lay a tin plate full of tamale wrappings.

Bustamente began to snore through his bloody mouth. Jacko put the monstrance, padded in its torn pillow slip, into one of the tough burlap sacks. He set it on the floor and began to search Bustamente, pulling his pants pockets inside out, going through his shirt pockets and all the pockets of his old black suit coat. No key.

"Damn it, he wasn't lying," Jacko said. "The others must have it. I'm going to have to take it away from them, and I don't much like two against one."

Becky began to spread the sacks over Bustamente. "We can't just leave him."

"Oh, can't I?"

"You can't be so cruel. He'll die of cold. We'll leave

some money with the manager, at least enough for him to
see a doctor. How do you know his skull isn't fractured?"

"What is this?" he asked, following her across the hall
to the old man's office. "The good nurse coming out of the
nasty nurse? You going soft all of a sudden? Okay"—
throwing a hand at the old man as he got out of his
chair—"give him two pesos."

"Five. It's my money."

"All right, five, but hurry up, we've got to get that key
before those two decide to go off in the car. Hurry! By
God, I forgot his watch pocket."

He hurried back to Bustamente while Becky scrabbled
in her bag for the money. Nothing in the watch pocket. He
felt Bustamente's neck pulse. The little bastard was still
alive, anyway. Cruel, was he? He ought to be wishing the
little crook was dead, and here he was being kind. I'll
show her what's kind. He neatly lifted the blanket off the
other sleeper and spread it over Bustamente. He picked up
the monstrance and rushed out of the hotel, Becky following, and headed down the street.

The crowd stood passive in the dust, thoroughly drunk.
The wind had died, and now a great stink rose from the
warm, massed bodies. A block down the street torches
flared. An officer with a sword at his belt and a lot of gold
on his cap and shoulders was standing on the bed of a
wagon, waving his arms in the air. The words came mumbling over the hundreds of men standing becalmed,
charmed by the flaming torches, smiling with peaceful,
drunken eyes.

He led Becky down an alley running along behind the
buildings, to avoid the crowd filling the street around the
ranting general. They came out again onto the main street
and found the Tucson car. He looked over the swing doors
of the cantina and saw Paz Faz and Gavira at a table handy

to the back door. Their usual style, he thought, always with a thought to escape.

"Get your gun out," he said to Becky. She fished the .380 auto out of her bag and he took it off safety, yanked the slide to load it. "All you have to do is pull the trigger. It isn't really big enough to kill anybody, so don't let that worry your tender heart. But it'll hold these bastards in line while I search them, if I have to."

He led her around through the side alley to the rear door, came quietly up the narrow hall, past the stinking toilet. He pulled his gun out of his pants and walked up behind Paz Faz.

"Good evening, Paz," he said, putting the muzzle of the gun against the back of Paz Faz's neck. There was nobody behind him, none of the people along the bar and at the other tables could see what he was doing.

"Do you know what would happen," Faz said, without moving, "if I yelled for help and all these Mexicans saw a lousy Yankee holding up one of their brothers?"

"Certainly I know what would happen. Just before we ran out the back door I'd blow your goddam heads off. Please stand up quietly. And you too, Gavira."

Paz Faz turned his head and looked at Jacko. They stood up slowly. Each of them had a pistol holstered on his belt beside a sheath knife. Faz's mouth twitched with indecision.

"Please don't try it," Jacko said. "I don't want to shoot you, all I want is the key to your car. Goodness, what big knives you two have! And what nice new pistols! Where did you steal them? What a menace you have become, so far from the cops in Los Angeles. Undo your belts, boys. I want all that nice stuff."

No movement. He pulled Faz's knife out of its scabbard.

"Do you want me to cut them off? If you make me, this

knife is damn well going to slip and take a slice out of
your bellies, you miserable bastards."

They unbuckled their belts and handed them over. Jacko
hung them over his arm.

"Let's have the key."

"We haven't got it," Gavira said. "Bustamente's got it.
Go ahead and shoot us, asshole, see how long you last."
He laughed.

That was one advantage these half-breed Indians had,
Jacko thought, at heart they didn't really mind being
killed. What really hurt them was an offense to their so-
called honor.

"I tell you what," he said, "I will turn my wife loose on
you if you don't behave and give me that key. She is a
crazy nurse, she lost her license for poisoning patients who
made too much noise. Now she uses a gun, as you see, or
a knife. She can cut off your balls so neatly you will never
feel them go. So don't push her! She will feed your jewels
to the hogs. Now let's all troop along to the toilet so I can
search you."

He stuck the point of the knife into Gavira's butt and
shoved. Gavira moved.

In the stinking toilet, which was a bucket in the corner
of a storeroom full of cases of beer, he went through their
pockets.

"There was no need for this," Faz said, his voice heavy
with rage. "I told you Bustamente has it."

"Take your pants off."

"Shoot us!" Gavira said.

"Go on, Becky, shoot him, right down there in the blad-
der. It won't kill him, but he'll never piss straight again.
Then I'll knock him on the head and you can cut off his
balls."

"Never mind, Gavira," Faz said. "Why should we risk
anything for the sake of squashing a Yankee cockroach?

241

We can submit now. There will always be a later." He pulled off his shoes and dropped his pants. "Go on," he said to Gavira, "do what the stupid man says. We'll get him later, don't worry."

Jacko picked up their shoes and trousers. "Bustamente better have that key. I'll be back. If I get the key, I'll give you back your pants. If I don't, I'll fix you like a dog. So just wait, unless you want to explain to your friends out there how you lost your pants."

He left them staring at the wall to avoid looking at each other, and locked them in.

"What good will that do?" Becky said. "They'll just shout and bang on it till somebody lets them out."

"No they won't. That lock is saving their pride. You better put that safety on."

"What safety?"

They dumped the pants and shoes in the yard outside the back door and went back to the hotel. Bustamente's bed was empty.

"Where did the little man go?" Jacko asked the manager.

"Little man?"

"The man with the bloody head I paid you five pesos for!" Jacko shouted. "Did you get a doctor?"

"Is he gone? He must have gone to the doctor."

"Where is the doctor?"

"There is no doctor in Magdalena. He went in the army."

"Then how the hell could he go to the doctor?"

"Who said he went to the doctor?"

"You did!"

"I didn't say he went to the doctor. I said he must have gone to the doctor."

"What? Well what for Christ's sake is the difference, he went, he must have gone."

"Well, some say the difference is one thing, some say it is another. But the truth is—who knows?"

"Oh Jesus."

"Come on," Becky said. "He's just gone."

"With the key!"

"Unless those other two hid it somewhere."

"Well, by God, they aren't going to use it. Unless they've gone already."

They ran back down the street. The car was still there, the general was still ranting. The crowd of Indians was swaying and stinking, packed like sardines, drunken faces smiling happily.

"One thing for sure," Jacko said, "if I don't drive this car, nobody does."

The first thing he smashed with the tire iron was the distributor.

A few of the *campesinos* on the edge of the crowd turned from the general and watched him.

"It's easier this time, eh, señor?" one of them said. "Not so hard work."

He stripped the wiring and smashed the spark plugs. "That was you gave me the drink?"

"Yes, that was me." Nod, nod, smile, smile.

"A thousand thanks, friend." He rammed the tire iron into the magneto, gutting it, and threw the last wire onto the roof of the cantina.

"Now we'll get those bastards to put the speeder back on the track."

He kept his gun on the two while they pulled on their pants and put on their shoes, then herded them around to the street. Paz Faz, seeing the hood of the car standing open, stopped and looked at the engine. He turned and looked at Jacko.

"You did this?"

243

"You're damned right I did it. Now where's your key? Go ahead and use it."

Paz Faz lifted a floor board and held up a key. "What a pity," he said. He laughed. Gavira laughed. "How I wish I had seen it! You tearing the car apart with the key right under your nose." He turned to Gavira. "Didn't I tell you he was stupid, like all Yankees?"

Jacko shifted his gun to his left hand and gave Paz Faz a Herculano across the head. Paz Faz staggered. "I'll kill you for that," he said.

"Get going. Down to the railroad yards."

Paz Faz looked at him quietly, no longer angry, no longer amused. "Nobody puts his hand on me and lives," he said. "We will do what you say because now it is certain you will be killed."

"They can't stand being hit," Jacko said to Becky, herding the two in front of him. "They always have to fight with something between, a knife or a gun. The fist is too humiliating."

"That was silly," she said, "simply to humiliate them."

"No," he said, "I didn't do it to humiliate him, I did it to knock the arguing and bullshit out of him. You see now he will do what I say, because he has absolutely made up his mind to kill me for touching him."

The three of them, with Becky holding her .380 ready, got the speeder back on the tracks. Paz Faz cranked, Gavira cranked, Paz Faz lighted the lantern. Jacko took the matches out of his hand, unloaded their guns, returned them in their belts. "Just to keep you from robbing some other poor bastard," he said. "See you in Los Angeles." He gave Paz Faz back his knife. He kept Gavira's.

"I did *that*," he said to Becky as they pulled out of the yards, "to humiliate them. Return their arms, as though I had nothing to fear from them."

"Do you enjoy humiliating people?".

"No. But I like to get them angry. It disturbs their aim."

The handcar gathered speed and began its smooth sailing through the night. He set the engine speed slow enough to be safe from the bridge dips. They sat bent forward like jockeys against the bitter cold wind of their flight.

The lantern, tied to the front of the car, blinded them to the weak starlight, and except for its feeble light, shining only five feet ahead, they seemed to fly through solid darkness. The last boxcar echoed past them, they rattled over a switch, gaining speed as they left the town. From before them the ties flew under the car in a flickering stream, the lantern gleamed on the shining steel rails.

The little car flew on into the darkness as though alive, rocking gently from side to side. The rush of cold air, the smoothness of the speed lulled them into a doze. A row of invisible boxcars in some town roared by in a blast of wind, half waking them, they shot across more switches in a flicker of steel glints, the iron wheels sang around a long curve, their bodies swayed back as they straightened out onto the plain, and they dozed again.

On and on the car flew through the hours, the engine singing to itself. It seemed as though they were being carried in a dream by some strange beast with a life of its own that didn't even know they were on its back, an animal enjoying by itself the delight of its power and speed. They shot over the little wooden bridges, crossing shallow dry washes, with a sudden dull roar of echo, suddenly cut off and left behind, for a moment half waking, then dropping back into the swaying cradle of delicious sleep. They came to the burned bridges and swooped down across the dry creek beds, soared up onto the level plain, and they dozed again.

Suddenly all this ended: the car leaped up under Jacko, he waked as he rose into the air, thrown up bodily from his seat, sailed through the darkness, arms outspread, in a high arc, and came down again with a terrible crash. Stars and red lightning shot through his brain and he lay still, out, his cheek on a rock, his mouth full of sand.

CHAPTER SEVENTEEN

HE LIFTED his head, rubbed sand out of his right eye, spat fine gravel out of his mouth, chewed some, spat more, and sat up. Giant freezing hands shook him. Another enormous hand was trying to squeeze all the blood out of his brain, as though it were an orange. Discouraged, it let go. The brain swelled, blood rushed back in, arteries burst. The hand squeezed again. For a moment he felt like howling, made half a childhood gulp, and then with great effort and concentration began to curse to restore his perspective. Under this violent attack of obscenities his pain lost its universality, attained a focus and settled in the right side of his face, which seemed to be both burning and freezing.

How long had he been out? He looked up at the dark sky. Where nothing but stars had been he saw the moon glaring down, pale as death. Hours?

He felt something tickling his cheek, touched it, felt sand and pain, peered at his finger, saw blood, swore. His cheek had grown a reptilian superskin of fine gravel cemented in a crust of dried blood.

A bit of light caught the side of his eye, he turned and saw the lantern on its side, chimney smashed, smoking little orange flame shuddering and waving in the dark, dimly lighting eroded banks of earth, shaggy brush, broken branches tangled together. At first he thought he was lying in an old sunken road; then recognized the straggling path of sand and gravel, gray-white in the moonlight, as the dry bed of one of those desert creeks that wander ragged down from the mountains to sink dead in the middle of the desert.

In the distance coyotes barked. If this were cattle country, there would be wolves. He felt for his gun. His holster was empty. Then he saw it lying near the lamp. He picked it up and tried the action. It was jammed full of sand. He couldn't even open the cylinder. He threw it into the brush.

Against the stars he made out the rough black balks of a little railroad bridge, crossing the creek ten feet above his head. The speeder lay in the creek bed, smashed into the bank, wheels in the air.

He sat shaking with the cold. Where was Becky? He lunged to his feet, staggered two steps, stumbled over something like a hairy barrel, and fell on his hands and knees. He knelt there swearing.

He had fallen over a dead mule. It lay with its head smashed so that its lower jaw was torn loose, wrenched to one side. Both front legs were broken backward at the knees. It had cast out a large puddle of dung, still smoking faintly in the cold. He felt the carcass: still warm.

He stood shivering in the smooth flow of the icy draft coming down the creek. "Becky!" No answer.

He stumbled around in the creek bed, searched under the wreck of the speeder, in the brush, scrambled up the bank, stood on the bridge looking around. Southward in the moonlight the two shining rails sped straight across a wide savannah, mile after mile of silver grass, high as the knees, waving, glistening far away to the black mountains crouching in the east. Not a tree, not a bush, except the starveling brush along the little dead creek.

Had she walked away, stunned out of her mind, was she wandering down the creek? Then he saw her lying on the edge of the bank where she had been thrown.

He felt her breath on his hand. He picked her up. How light! almost like a child, limp, arms dangling. He held her head carefully against his chest and eased down the bank.

He sat close to the dead mule, sheltering her behind its body from the cold draft of air coming down the creek bed, holding her in his arms to warm her. He felt a hard plaque of dried blood in her hair. The light of the little lamp flickered on her face. He sat looking at her. Between the lids of her almost closed eyes he could see a sliver of white; between her lips, just barely open, the white glint of a tooth. She was so light, a feather to lift. How frail such bones, as light as the wingbones of a bird.

He held her closer, drawing his coat around her. He remembered her stones and rocks, lined on the shelf; her still-life stage, ready for her cameras. What was she like, living so busily, so intensely, with these concerns? And her parades.

He had never known a woman who mocked him as she had done. They were all so meek, or so sly, servants like Lilly, or decorations like May, or saints like his mother. Here was a new kind of woman, flickering and fluttering around her apartment, studying rocks, making pictures, or dashing out to defy the government.

He had always thought, from this performance, that she was an idiot, like all those loudmouthed British bomber-matrons. The tough nurse act, the militance, was that just a front?

Why had anybody so intelligent married a crude dummy like Mike? Had she been simply bat-brained by rough Irish charm, combined, as she had said, with the idea that "it was a living"? But she wasn't that uncouth. Of course a lot of women were just saps—well, like himself for that matter, marrying May.

Or had it been merely to escape from loneliness? She must have known Mike was mainly after her money. She herself not being particularly attractive, maybe she had accepted the humiliation of marrying him as millions of other women bowed their heads and married fools, only to find themselves twice as lonely. And all her greedy activities were merely to fill up the empty pit.

No, not particularly attractive. Looking down at her face, so gentle in the distance of sleep, he realized that he had forgotten the turtle profile, the unfortunate nose, forgotten them in the sense of being unable any longer to see them, at least as misfortunes. If only she weren't such a shrew! If she really were a shrew. Shrews didn't read arty magazines, did they? Make arty pictures? Or feel sorry for treacherous little shits like Bustamente? Well, as the old man said, some say they did, some say they didn't, but the truth was—who knows?

And here we sit, he thought, wrecked God knows where, with nothing left but the monstrance.

He looked at the sack where it had fallen, half buried in the sand. The cold struck him again, he shook helplessly. He had to start some kind of fire. He started to lay her aside, to get up.

"Where are we?" she said.

"Well, thank God," he said, "I thought you had conked out for good."

"I'm so cold," she said, shaking all over. "How sweet you are, Jacko, trying to keep me warm." She got up, stumbled and caught herself. "Oh, it's my knee."

250

Sweet, was he? What next? Maybe the knock on the head had altered her personality. "Sit on the mule," he said. He began breaking sticks out of the tangled flood-rubbish. He piled his sticks by the mule and lighted them with the lantern flame. The trash caught and the oily wood flared up. They sat on the mule side by side, crouching over the fire.

"How heavenly warm. How did it get here? What happened?"

"We ran into it. It must have been standing on the track, asleep."

"Poor thing."

"If it was alive, I'd kill it. Here we are dumped a hundred miles from I don't know where. I know it's the plain of Sonora, but is it the middle or one of the ends?"

"Oh, your face!" she said. "I couldn't see it in the dark." She got up and began hobbling around the creek bed looking for something and came back with her big bag. She sat down beside him on the mule and got out the little green box of Bag Balm.

"I won't try to clean the gravel out of it," she said, "it would just make it bleed worse. But the Bag Balm will kill the germs. I won't even make a bandage, the air will scab it faster. Hold still."

He held still and let her gently smear the stuff on his cheek. "There," she said with satisfaction.

Why did they always say "there"? Even when they made a sandwich, they would give it a final pat and say "There."

He watched her put back the lid of the green box, the firelight on her face, now smiling. The clover blossoms around the cow's head looked like roses. He didn't know whether to laugh or cry. Good God, he thought, here I am in the middle of nowhere with a little girl Florence Nightingale gone cloud-happy with a canful of cow goo.

251

"We can't be far from a house," she said, putting the can back in her bag. "I hear dogs barking."

"Coyotes."

"What are coyotes?"

"Kind of wild dogs."

"Are they dangerous?"

"No. Not if you can move."

"Is there any water?"

"Not here. In the morning we'll find some." Tomorrow we'd better find some, he thought. Where? The track could go on for a hundred kilometers, without a human being. Which way was the closest town? Should they go north or south? Now that he had stopped shaking, his stomach began to grind painfully.

"Would you mind eating some of this mule?" he asked.

She looked down at it, surprised. "You don't mean raw," she said.

"Very thin steaks will cook enough. We ought to eat some of the damned thing, we've got a long hike tomorrow."

"A long hike where?"

"Who knows? We'll flip for north or south." He pulled out Faz's knife and began to whet it on the sole of his shoe. "Mule might be pretty good. Probably a good deal like horse."

"You like horse?"

"Horse isn't at all bad. When the rebels in the Philippines drove off all the water buffalo to try to starve us, we ate horse for a couple of weeks. The dead ones the little bastards shot out from under us. A bit watery."

"I don't care. Horse, cow, mule, what's the difference? What worries me is those miserable anarchists. They'll fix that car, they'll be coming down in the morning. Can't you shoot them as they go past?"

"They'll never fix that car. I smashed the heart out of it,

the magneto. They'll have to catch the next train that comes down."

"You mean we'll get on it with them, and it'll start all over again."

He cut a great flap of hide from the mule's off ham and laid it back, began sawing down through the meat. She stood watching him.

"I fainted at an autopsy once," she said. "Here I am at another, tough as nails."

"So is the mule," he said, and stopped sawing to whet the knife on a stone.

"That's why I failed the nurse course," she said. "Weakness and cowardice. I wouldn't fail it now. Show me anything."

"And what's made you so tough?"

"People like you and Mike, partly. He's a cruel man. And so are you, Jacko. You pretend not to be, but you are."

He looked at her in amazement. "Me?"

"The way you would have left Bustamente broke and sick. The way you hit Paz Faz because you knew it would insult him, when you didn't have to."

He felt the blood heating his face, and it hurt his stone-ground cheek. "A hell of a time to tell me. Couldn't you wait till we were rich and I felt better?"

"I was starting to like you, and then you did that."

"And now you're telling me how much I've missed."

"There, you see, the streak of it in you."

"I've been around you too long!" he shouted. "Didn't you ever hear it said, it takes a good woman to bring out the worst in a man?" He made himself busy with the steaks, wringing the blood out of them as though they were necks. He broke off four green sticks, threaded one through each skinny steak and tuck them in the sand slanted over the fire.

He sat down on the mule. "Come on, sit down. I won't hit you until you grow up."

"See, there you are, the meanness."

"Come on, sit down by the bully, you coward."

"I was being perfectly objective," she said, sitting down. "Nothing personal."

They sat silent, listening to the coyotes, too tired and beat up to argue any more. The mule meat dripped into the fire. When the lower ends began to burn, Jacko passed her a slice and started gnawing at the other. It took a great deal of work, grinding away at the same spot until it came loose and got soft enough to swallow.

"Not as bad as my shoes, I imagine," she said.

He sawed off half a dozen more slices and hung them on sticks to cook. "For tomorrow."

"I suppose you realize," she said, "the ship will dock tomorrow. And those two will sail the next day. And that is the end of my bonds."

"We've still got the monstrance. You'd better try to sleep."

"I couldn't sleep. It's too cold. Let me see it. It would look so pretty in the firelight."

He pushed the sack over to her. They sat between the mule and the fire, huddled against the slow cold flow of air coming down from the mountains. She pulled the bundled pillowcase from the sack and unrolled it. Two bricks fell out on the sand. After them slid a wide tin plate with cornhusk tamale wrappings stuck to it.

They sat silent, looking at the plate. Jacko beat himself on the knee. "I would have *known*," he wailed, "if I'd been carrying it. It was you carried it down to the tracks. I would have known the feel."

"Well, don't blame *me*," she cried. "You gave it to me to carry. Why didn't you carry it yourself, if you're so smart?"

"I should have killed him," he groaned. "I knew it, I knew it, I felt it in my bones, he would do me in. Talk about suckers! When did he do it?"

She picked up the bricks and threw them away into the dark. "You left the sack in the room when we went to give the money to the manager."

He sat with his face in his hands. "I don't know what to do," he said in a low voice. "Where to find him. He may go back to L.A. and break it up and sell it there."

"Maybe," she said. "Except he might gamble on selling it to the priest. There's a lot more money there."

She straightened up one of the meat sticks tilted too low over the fire. "If he goes back to L.A., he's beaten us, there's nothing we can do. If he takes it to Guaymas, we have a chance, he has to take the train, now, and we can catch him."

"If we can stop it," he said. "God knows where we'll be when it comes by." He lifted his head. "I'll tell you something, Becky, never mind the monstrance, I'm worried about water. We aren't thirsty yet, but we will be, and I don't know where we are, or which way to go."

"I just told you. South. What have we got to lose?"

"This time I'll kill him," he said.

"That's what I can't understand about you," she said. "You have a cruel streak sure enough, but you're also a slob. If you really knew what you were doing, you would have brained him in Nogales and stolen the car. And you would have brained the other two, just to get rid of them. But you didn't. You're soft. You're a kind of real cruel Eagle Scout."

"Shut up and try to sleep." He put his arm around her. She leaned against him, her face on his chest. After a while he knew by her breathing that she was sleeping.

Little by little his fatigue dulled his mind. All around him the savannah lay quiet. His chin sank to his chest, his mind floated drugged on a pool of calm, while in a tiny corner of it a last spark sat minutely watching, like a guard, a tiny ear listening to the occasional hushed fall of ember into ash, listening for the rustle of brushed leaves, the whisper of a foot in sand.

He saw himself, sitting there, lost, completely out of place, a wandering beetle. What had he expected, home from the Islands? What vaunting leap to fame and fortune? The brilliant investigator, living the exciting life of a playboy in the lively town of Los Angeles, with all his fashionable friends, deadlocked with his father over a debt. Handsome young husband of a beautiful murdering wife, sullenly waiting for her to screw herself so he wouldn't have to kill her to get rid of her. All summed up here in a lump of meat, two-legged jackass sitting humped on the sand beside his dead brother. Just what did he think he was up to? What had he ever thought he was up to? For a moment he thought to excuse all this as self-pity, but he stopped that lie, knowing it was a judgment. The trouble was that he was nowhere, nobody, and he didn't know what to do about it. All trails ended here in the bottom of a dead creek.

A branch in the thicket snapped with the cold, he opened his eyes. The fire was dying. He laid on more wood, and slowly closed his eyes again. He saw his patient father at his desk, patiently writing in the blue-white room, shepherd of two hundred people.

Why wasn't he himself a kindly person? He remembered his "kindness" to Bustamente, in defiance of her criticism, the kindness of robbing one man of his blanket to cover another. The kindness of getting into a dirty venture and then being too soft to kill when he should. The cruelty of humiliating Faz when he was down.

Out of the dark came the hard brick face of Herculano.

He sat contemplating the baby-blue stone eyes, waiting in the south.

Early in the morning they had left the wreck with the cheeriness of unfounded hope; now, with the sun half-sunk behind the low western mountains and the blue shadows of the sparse brush lying long across the road, they had been walking for seven hours without water, the last in a half-stuporous concentration on putting one foot in front of the other, and hope had died down to dumb patience.

He kept watching her out of the side of his eye as she hobbled along beside him, leaning on the stick he had broken off for her, the limp from the pain of her bruised knee. When the sole of her left boot had come loose, and he had tied his belt around the foot to hold the flapping sole in place, the limp had doubled, and the drain on her strength. She walked bent forward, more and more assuming the shape of an old woman, head down, her steps growing shorter as they slowly approached this long rise. At each step she had to swing the foot outward in a half-circle to keep the belt in place, and he knew the strain was going to put an end to her efforts soon, but there was nothing he could do about it.

Exhaustion would leave them sitting in the middle of the road with night coming on, no water, no food, and against the cold a fire that would only attract whatever evils might be wandering along the railroad.

He had started out that morning carrying her on his back, but his legs couldn't take it for long. She didn't cry or complain; her face just got thinner and more pinched as slowly she seemed to be growing older.

The railroad seemed to stretch forever, dead straight across the plain, which was turning now from grass to scattered scrub where overgrazing cattle were beginning to ruin the savannah. The bright rails running beside the old wagon road shimmered with heat waves rising from the steel; the crooked telegraph poles, cut from mesquite, staggered along with their low looping wire. Ahead of them the road and the horizon wavered uncertainly, and pools of mirage water came and went. Nothing had changed for hours, the same flies pursued them, harassing their eyes, sucking up sweat. Each step seemed to leave them in the same place, until they had begun the slow, barely perceptible ascent of this last low rise toward the yellow horizon where the tracks disappeared into the pale sky.

Hope had turned very heavy, had turned into a curse, as one promise of water after another failed, the distant string of heavier brush that had signaled water, the little railroad bridge ahead that meant a streambed, always dry.

She had never asked to stop and rest because he always saved her the weakening admission of weakness by anticipating her, watching her face, listening to her breathing, waiting for the falter in her walk, stopping to rest at the first sign. Hope was a curse, but much worse was the doubling of his own wretchedness by the constant awareness of hers, and that he had to insist on continuing it.

They had to find some kind of hidden shelter for the night. The railroad, in this country, was the one highway, everything human existed along its line, everything else was death. If help lay beyond the rise, so did danger, but they could not stay where they were.

He had started to explain what he knew must seem like cruelty, his insistence on going on, but she had waved him silent, knowing quite as well as he what they were up against.

The realities of their situation were perfectly clear to him. He knew he had to force her, always easing up just before her breaking point. But at the same time, he had ceased to understand how their situation had come about, even though, if he had had the energy to think about it, he would have been sure there must have been a logic of causes. In the mist of his mind there did not seem to be the slightest causal connection between their departure from Los Angeles and what they were now doing, as though he had been mystically translated from the ease of Bunker Hill to the burning of his feet, the wooden dryness of his mouth, the ache and growing weakness of his body. The cavity of his mouth felt like bone, he could no longer feel his breath on his tongue, he no longer tried to swallow to relieve his throat because there was nothing left to swallow. The floor of his mind seemed to have given way, leaving him floundering for a hold amid a chorus of pains; the clamor of his body rose over the words of his mind, drowning them out.

By the slight added weight on his legs he could feel the road steepen just a little as it neared the top of the rise. As he had done three times before on these miles of rises, he bent and caught the end of Becky's cane in his left hand and went forward again, pulling her along. The weight of the road eased, they were trudging along on the level of the crown at last, and then as they came to the mild descent, the whole plain opened out before him, fifty miles, or a hundred, to the south, the dark blue and purple mountains to the east fading smaller and smaller into palest blue smoke.

Half a mile ahead the railroad tracks bridged a shallow barranca along which grew a narrow woods of mesquite, stretching to the west. Beside the bridge there was a group of buildings, one a low hut and another apparently of two stories.

They went on down the gentle slope, trying to hurry, he pulling her by the hand, holding back as she stumbled. Gradually as they came nearer the details of the buildings separated out and he realized that the two-storied house was not a house but a squat tower, a tank set on a frame of heavy timbers; what he had thought a tall withered tree resolved into the spindly steel frame of a windmill. It was a watering point for the railroad engines. Beside the tower, next to the tracks, stood a small adobe hut, probably the home of the watchman.

As they got closer he saw that the heavy water spout of the tank, hinged at the bottom to be lowered over the tanks of the engines, had fallen free of its hoisting tackle and was lying broken against the framework of the tower. He stopped.

"What's the matter?" Becky said, coming up beside him. "Isn't that a water tank?" She started ahead, he caught her arm.

"It's been wrecked. Look at the spout. They cut the ropes and emptied it." Now he saw the movement low on the ground beyond the legs of the tower, a confused writhing and crawling.

"But there would be some water, a little water!" She jerked her arm free, started forward, and stopped suddenly. "What is that on the ground?"

"Vultures." The pile was just a pile, crawling with the black birds. But separate from the pile he could see sprawled bodies. "There's been a battle."

CHAPTER EIGHTEEN

THE PILE of bodies was about three feet high. A dozen buzzards were flapping and fighting on it, tearing at the fresh meat. All of the bodies were in Federal uniforms, except the four which had been stripped, two of these with intestines already dragged out by iron beaks from bloody buttocks, lying in varicolored loops over the bodies and faces of the others. The birds had barely begun, gobbling and fighting over the dead like old women in their black dresses squabbling at a bargain counter; where heads faced the sky, eye sockets glared red and empty.

In the choking rise of his disgust, he would have shot them all, but he had only the hideout gun left. He left Becky beside the water tower and walked up to the gorging birds, shouting and waving them off. They struggled to rise all at once with a great clatter and rush of wings. In a fury he grabbed up rocks from the roadbed and stoned them, killing two before they could get off the ground, and stood shouting in the storm of black wings as they flapped upward. Over him they sailed in cautious circles, and began to drop down one by one to sit in rows on the top of the water tank, shaking their dusty old maid's feathers of rustling black, settling down to wait.

This heap of crisscrossed bodies, tangled arms and legs lay in the middle of a thirty-foot square of bare earth between the feet of the water tower and the rough adobe wall of the hut. Other bodies lay scattered away from the pile; in front of the wall of the hut, six lay fallen on their faces.

He turned to Becky and saw her looking at the corpses. "You'd better not," he said.

"I've seen all this before," she said. "Only not so many at one time."

They turned away toward the water tower. Above them the birds rustled and complained.

The wooden tank had been shot full of holes, water still seeping out glistened on all the lower half, darkening the staves, held in their rusty iron hoops. The ground had been flooded when the spout had been cut down. Now the earth, churned to mud by many hooves, lay drying in the late sun.

A half-inch galvanized pipe ran down from the tank, along one of the legs of the tower, to a faucet three feet above an old dented galvanized bucket into which it slowly dripped.

Becky turned the faucet and drank out of her hands, splashing water over her face and neck. He filled the bucket a couple of inches and drank from that, handed the rest to her. He watched the water pulse down her throat and when she had finished, emptied the bucket over her head, half-filled it again and doused himself. He studied the bullet holes in the tank. None of them was closer than six inches to the bottom, which meant that there was plenty of water left inside.

Becky stood with her back to the dead men, facing the wilderness of scrub and grass. "We can't stay here."

"We have to stay here," he said.

"They might come back," she said, looking at the hundreds of hoofprints in the mud.

"What for? They won, whoever they were. They went south—or we would have seen them."

He led her to the hut. The door and the one small window faced west, away from the tracks. With the hideout in his hand, he stepped cautiously through the open doorway. The sun's last low rays shone flat through the iron bars of the window. The roof had been burned off. One uniformed corpse slouched in a corner. Stubs of burned willow rafters fanned out from the ashes of a small fireplace in the corner. Along the wall under the window stood an oil-soaked work bench. On it were two rusty files and an old Ford monkey wrench. A mechanic's vise was bolted to the end near the door. There was nothing else in the room. Any watchman who might have lived there had fled the place long ago.

Jacko swung the door on its hinges: sound enough, and the inside bar would hold.

"We'll have to wait here for the train," he said. "Two days. Maybe more." He tried to turn the handle of the vise. It was locked with rust. "You can't walk any more. We don't know where there's any more water. We have to have a fire tonight."

"Then let's build one out in the desert, at least where it's clean." She was holding her bag tight against her side as though afraid of losing it.

"Yeah, and attract God knows who for miles around. The hut will hide the fire and give us shelter from the wind."

"What are you saying? You know people will come here, for the water."

He suddenly turned on her and shouted, "I don't know people will come. I do know we have to stay here. If you don't want to, start walking. Sleep in the bushes. Do what you want. Do you understand me?" He swung open the cylinder of the hideout, looked at the five miserable .38 Specials and closed it again. "Five lousy squib shots. I'd kill somebody for a rifle."

"I'm sorry," she said. "I know you're worried. Listen. The birds. They're at it again." She was shivering.

"Ah, take it easy, Becky. They'll quit pretty soon, when they're full. When it's dark no more will come, they can't see." He went over to the corpse. "Let's get rid of this joker."

She took hold of a wrist. "Still warm. Oh, how I used to hate that lukewarm feeling of the ones just dead. We had to stuff them, in the hospital. When they were cold they seemed further away, more dead."

They dragged the body out, around behind the hut. Jacko stood looking at the little forest of tall mesquite spreading out from the banks of the barranca. Through the branches he could see the posts and rails of a corral. Plenty of wood.

In the hut he arranged the burned stubs in the fireplace. "Your magazine would help," he said.

She took *Camera Work* from her bag and tore out a handful of pages. She handed them to Jacko and without expression watched Gertrude Stein burn away.

He nursed the fire up and handed the magazine back. She looked at the stubs of the torn pages. With the quick violence of impatience and anger she tore out "War on Form" by the Amorphous School of Aesthetics and threw them after Stein. "Yes," she said, "it's very good for starting fires," and tossed the magazine aside.

He went out and stood in the dusk looking at the few birds still feeding. All the dead were Federals except the six in front of the wall of the hut. Two of the Federals had fallen on top of these, who looked like civilians. Of these six, one man was dressed in a black business suit, filthy with grease and dust. He had no shoes. Two were in ordinary bib overalls, three were in dirty *charro* jackets and tight *vaquero* trousers, three wore worn and cracked dress shoes, the rest barefoot or with sandals. Probably bandits, and probably a remnant of Orozco's forces.

The six had been stood against the wall and shot. By the Federals? He hunted around on the ground, looking for empty cartridge cases. Most of them near the corpse pile were 7mm Mausers, the Federal arm. But farther away, beyond the water tank, they were mixed, some Mausers, but mostly .30-30 Winchesters, the round the rebels loved.

What had happened? The six bandits had come for the water, the twenty or so Federals, probably cut off by Obregón in the retreat, had come on them and shot them. It had to have happened in that order, because of the two Federals who had fallen on top of the bandits. Then the Federals evidently had been surprised by the larger party of rebels. This gang, probably on their way south to the battle, had ridden up for water, surrounded the Federals and shot them all down. But why were they in a pile? Had the rebels piled them up to burn them? There was no fuel oil, the usual thing in war. But he had seen men in panic climb over each other, the last trampling the falling onto the fallen in layers. So men surrounded might turn inward, all trying to run, and pile themselves up to be slaughtered.

He walked around the pile, looking at the feet, trying to find the smallest pair of shoes or boots. Most of the feet he could see were bare, shoes stolen by the barefoot or sandaled rebels. He found nothing on the top layer of bodies. Seizing them by the ankle, he dragged some off and hunted in the lower layers. Halfway down he found a tiny man, pulled off his little boots and took them to the hut.

He tossed them through the door toward Becky. "Junk your boots and try these on," he said, and went back to the pile again.

Many of the Federals still had packs on their backs. In the deepening dusk he went through these. Most had been emptied by the rebels, as had the pockets, but he found one, buried deep, that had in it a folded wad of old tortillas. Most of these men must have had serapes; all were gone as loot. There was nothing to use as cover for the night. At the bottom of the pile he found a machete, like a pot of gold.

He stood panting and sweating with the work and looked at the bodies, now disposed in new positions, many still lying on each other as he had dragged them aside, some facedown with arms spread, others looking fish-eyed at the sky with arms outflung as though in praise, others sleeping like lovers, heads lying on breasts. Each one, now relieved of life, of posturing or assertion, seemed to have gained a sort of grace. Dead, they showed no fear.

There were no rebel dead, they had been taken away by the victors. There was little blood on the six executed. All had been shot in the body, the sleek pointed spitzer bullets of the Federal 7mm's had made neat little Geneva Convention holes in flesh, not shattering bone and tumbling. But most of the Federals had been shot with Winchesters, the soft-nosed bullets, meant for game, expanding and erupting in bloody tattered holes. About a third of them, the wounded, had been finished off with a pistol shot in the head, these blowing out chunks of skull and leaving the cratered brains bare to the vultures, or if shot from behind, blowing off eyes, jaws, cheekbones. All this was slowly fading in the dusk. In the west there were three broad bands of yellow above the black mountains. Overhead the stars shone brilliantly, refreshed.

He had seen the same thing in the Philippines so often

that he had learned to see the flesh as meaningless, something merely fallen away from the people and left behind. He turned away sadly and carried the tortillas and the machete into the hut.

She was sitting by the fire with her back to the wall, looking at nothing, *Camera Work* lying in the dirt.

"These'll help out the mule meat," he said, handing her the tortillas. "I'm going to the corral for wood."

At the end of the bare earth of the yard, a path to the corral began in the yellow grass, now turned gray in the growing dark, leading into the little mesquite forest, through it to a pole gate. He shoved this open and stepped inside, started to hack apart with the machete the rawhide strips that bound the gate poles together, and stopped, seeing another lot of bodies, strung out toward the end of the corral toward the railroad tracks, most of them piled up in front of the loading chute that had been used to drive cattle up into the cars. All seemed to have fallen running.

He looked around at the other end of the corral and saw a blanket. He went to take this up, and saw on it dozens of empty cartridge cases, all .45 Colt.

The executioner had finished the game, nobody had gained the chute and got away. Had he left the blanket in contempt? He spat on the ground and yanked up the blanket, scattering the cartridge cases. He went back to work on the gate. He tore off two of the poles and started dragging them back to the hut, the machete clutched in his armpit.

He was only forty feet from the hut when Becky screamed. He dropped the poles and the machete and ran forward, pulling the hideout out of his pocket. He met her running down the path, stumbling past him in the too-big shoes, wide-eyed with fear, and he saw the Mexican running toward him, trying to stop himself as he saw Jacko.

He raised the little pistol, aimed it carefully on the middle of the wobbling belly and held the aim with absolute determination. Skidding and turning, the Mexican put his hand on the butt of his own pistol, and Jacko with perfect concentration squeezed off the shot. The Mexican fell onto his hands and knees, his pistol falling out of the holster. As Jacko ran forward the Mexican, kneeling, collapsed on his face. Rolling heavily onto his side, he fumbled at his empty holster for his pistol. Jacko stood above him, looking down. The shot in the gut had merely stopped him. It would take another to do the job. He put the muzzle of his gun into the black hair of the head. The head turned, large eyes watery in the fat face looked up at Jacko.

He could have fired into the hair. He couldn't fire into the face. He picked up the Mexican's pistol and shoved the hideout into his pocket.

"There's another one," Becky said behind him. Her voice was very high, shaking.

With the pistol cocked, he walked slowly up the path. He stood outside the line of fire from the door and window of the hut, looking around the yard. A horse was tied to one of the legs of the water tower. A second stood off in the desert fifty yards away, looking at him, reins hanging short, probably broken off at the sound of the shot.

There was no sound except the rustling of the vultures, settling down again, and the groaning of the shot Mexican, slow and rhythmical, deep sighs grunted out under pressure.

Becky stood watching him. He was still lying on his side, his right hand covering the hole in his belly. A little blood slowly spread on the shirt. He was a long way from dead, she thought, with pain in her mind. She kicked the machete out of his reach, then picked it up and slowly followed Jacko. The shoes were too big for her, threatened to fall off, her feet seemed to rattle around inside them and the best she could do in walking was to shuffle, dragging the heels to keep the terrible things from tripping her up.

"He's in the hut," Jacko said, "or behind it. I don't think he's got a gun. If he had one, he would have tried to kill me before now. You wait here." He went around the end of the hut to the back, along the railroad. She stood still and listened, hearing only the birds and the groaning. After a moment, he came back.

She stood at the corner of the hut watching him go for the door, ducking under the window. He paused by the doorway, and then with the pistol raised, stepped inside out of sight.

She heard a sharp cry and then a confusion of noises and swearing. She ran to the door. Jacko was lying on his face, straddled by a man beating him over the head with a heavy stub of wood. She stood dumb, watching the arm rise and fall two times and then with a scream of rage she ran in, slashing down on the shoulders with the machete, flaying skin off the top of the shoulder blade. The man twisted toward her, two-handed she chopped the machete down, the long blade caught him along the cheek, lopping it off and baring the teeth and bone of the jaw. Weeping half-blind, grunting with the blow, her lips curled up in a snarl, she hit him again square on top of the head. The blade glanced off the skull, tearing a flap of scalp away, and she saw again in a single flash the dead whore, face covered by her scalp. The man fell forward upon Jacko's body an she stood over him, chopping down at his neck, weeping half-blind, grunting with the blows. The blade chopped deeper, opening up the neck muscles down to the white glint of bone, and suddenly she stopped and stood panting.

Was he dead? she cried in her mind. Oh God, let him be dead. She put the round crude point of the machete on the back and fell on it with all her weight, trying to drive it to the heart. Nothing happened, it was too blunt to pierce. She began to cry again in desperation, panicky with fear that the man would get up, and raising the·blade high, she brought the blade down on the head again. The edge caught and sank in through the bone. She let go of the machete and it stood upright, wedged stuck; then fell over, turning the head like a handle.

Now she was turning sick, her rage fouled on itself. She grabbed one of the arms and rolled the body away from Jacko, knelt on the dirt floor beside him. She touched the back of his head with her fingers, pressed very gently. Under the bloody mat of hair the skull was firm. She brought the bucket and poured the last cupful of water on his head. He lay still.

She went out into the dark with the bucket and in the moonlight picked her way between the scattered bodies to the water faucet. She stood quiet while the bucket filled, her mind stupefied. The tied horse blew through its nose, and as she looked at it, the yard and the bodies settled into a clear focus of sanity and she began to cry again, but not now with rage, now with sorrow, the tears running down her cheeks, sorrow at the world, sorrow at the dead all around her, sorrow at her killing. The bucket filled and ran over.

After a while she opened her eyes and through the glimmer of tears saw in the moonlight the bucket quietly overflowing. She turned off the faucet, dumped a little of the water, and taking up the bail, shuffled back, twisted by the weight, and poured half of it on Jacko.

She stood looking down at him. He was breathing as though asleep. She wanted to sit beside him, but the body of the Mexican was in the way, lying beside him. Detesting it, she seized a wrist and rolled the flaccid body away, sickened to see the head flopping and lolling from the chopped neck as the machete fell out. There was little blood from the wound in the back of the neck. The spines of three vertebrae stood white. One, two, three, she counted down, as though this were a "new one," brought into the university dissecting hall where the student nurses had stood around being lectured on the spine.

She knelt beside Jacko and felt the slow pulse in his throat. She heard again the faint rustling of the birds and occasionally the fall of an ember in the dying fire, and continually the low groan, with each slow breath, of the shot man outside in the path, and fear began to grow in her. She slammed the door to and dropped the wooden bar.

The night wind started up, gently blew over the top of the walls, disturbed the ashes in the little fire. Then she heard a scuffling and panting outside, a whining, a short bark. She stood alert, terrified, and then thought of the gun, which Jacko must have dropped when he fell. She found it in a corner and took it back to where Jacko lay.

She sat down beside him with the gun and the machete in her lap and watched his face. He lay with his left cheek on the dirt, facing her. She watched the one closed eye, waiting patiently.

The cold air breathed through the window, whispered down the chimney. She pulled the old pillowcase out of her bag and laid it over his shoulders.

Slowly the eye opened and looked at nothing; and then it turned up and looked at her. He lay perfectly still, and they looked at each other for a long moment.

She leaned down and said softly, "Jacko." The eyelid slowly blinked closed, opened again and he sighed. He rolled over on his side, raised himself slowly and moved to sit with his back to the wall, holding his head. She moved beside him.

"He was standing on the bench so I didn't see him," he said. He raised his head and looked around, saw the body,

the half-severed neck. He saw the bloody machete in her
lap. "Good. Great. Good for you."

"But I *killed* him," she said.

"For Jesus' sake," he said, his face suddenly twisting
with the pain of his head, "are you apologizing for saving
my life?"

She sat silent for a long minute, thinking. Then she said,
"Yes, I had to." Then, as she thought a moment more,
"But I hated him. I couldn't have done it if I hadn't hated
him. And now he's dead."

"I know it's unpleasant," he said.

"Unpleasant! Oh God." She sat with her head resting on
her forearms, crossed on her knees.

He was beginning to be able to think past the headache.
He pushed the stubs of wood into the fire and little yellow
flames began to flicker up. What was she in for? She
would drag the Mexican with her for the rest of her life
the way he dragged his little yellow man, like a dead
chicken tied to the neck of a chicken-killing dog, and not
all the reasoning in the world would get rid of the yoke of
sadness that was the good man's penalty for taking a life,
no matter what the reason.

"You'll get used to it," he said.

"I'll never do it again. Never."

To him, she sounded like some child promising God.

"Yes, you will, if you have to."

"I won't have to! Never! I'd rather be dead."

"What's the use of dying? When you can save your
friends' lives by killing for them. Be a soldier."

"I can make up for it. I can be a nurse."

"Sure," he said. You never made up for it.

"I'm going back to school. If I ever get out of this. And
if we get that money."

She got up and hunted around for her purse, found it

and knelt beside him again. She took out the green can and began smearing it on the back of his head.

Ah, here we go again, thought the cynic in him, Florence Nightingale and a life of penance, and was sick of the cynic. There had to be something in him better than such dourness.

"Come on," he said, and got up with a groan. "Grab a leg, nurse."

They dragged the body out the door. There was a panicky scurrying in the dark as the coyotes scattered. They laid the corpse with the others. She stood in the moonlight, listening to the groans of the shot man.

"They'll eat him."

"Not while he's alive."

"Help me," she said, and went into the dark toward the groaning.

He stood with the wind blowing around him, all kinds of protests bottled up in his throat; and then gave up. She was standing waiting for him, holding one of the wrists. He took the other wrist and they dragged him into the hut.

"He'll groan all night," he said. He wanted to sleep.

"It depends," she said, putting her bag under the head for a pillow. "He can die of the internal bleeding or peritonitis. He's bleeding very slowly, but it'll finish him eventually and I can't do anything about it. But the infection has started and the pain will get much worse. I hope he dies of the hemorrhage soon, because the other is terrible."

"I should have finished him off."

She looked at him, her eyes very sharp and intent. "But you didn't. Why didn't you? You shouldn't have and you wouldn't have and you know it. Why do you lie? To make yourself tough? I detest such lying sentimentality. You aren't tough. Give me that pillowcase."

She sat in the dirt beside the fat Mexican and began

273

wiping his face with a piece of the pillowcase, wet from the bucket. The big eyes rolled at her and he said something between groans.

"He wants you to hold his hand," Jacko said.

"Then he's dying."

He stood looking at them, sitting together, she holding the big tan hand in her left, the right cooling his face, his other hand covering the hole in his belly.

He turned and went out into the dark, took the machete to the water faucet and cleaned it, rubbing the dried blood away with a handful of the sandy mud. He hacked up the two poles for firewood and carried it in to build up the fire. The fat man had stopped groaning and lay with his eyes closed, but she was still holding the hand.

You could have shot him in the head, couldn't you? something said. No, I couldn't, I had to stop him, I had to hit him where I was sure to hit him, in the belly.

You could have taken just a little more time, couldn't you, to aim at the heart?

No, I couldn't, there wasn't any more time, he had his hand on that gun.

Then he himself said, Why can't you arrange things better? You're the One, aren't you? Why didn't you give me more time? Why didn't you slow him up?

Don't blame Me, you fool. You got yourself into this. You've gotten yourself into everything, folly after folly, because of your stupid vanity, your stupid self-will, your greed, your stupid selfishness. Always feeding your stupid ego.

I refuse to indulge in self-pity, whatever happens, I am a man.

Don't worry about self-pity. Before the end, oh man, you'll howl like a dog.

I will not cry, he said, and turned away.

As he approached the water tower, the free horse, come

in for company, galloped away. The tied horse was glad to
see him and nuzzled his arm. There was an empty rifle
scabbard hung from the saddle, but no gun. There were
two small sacks of corn for the horse tied neck to neck and
slung over the horse's back behind the saddle. He lifted
them off. He dumped the saddle in the mud. He slid the
saddle blanket off the horse's back and began to unfold it.
It was hard as a board, the folds stuck together with
months of sweat, the whole a perfect mold of the horse's
back. He peeled the stinking folds apart and shook out the
blanket as well as he could.

He went back into the hut, carrying the blanket and the
corn. She was still sitting by the Mexican, but had laid his
hand on his chest.

"Let's move him outside," he said.

She looked up at him, saying nothing, listening to the
snarling outside that had started again, and thinking: two
days ago I would have said, Can't you spend a night in the
same room with your handiwork? Now I would bite off
my hacksaw tongue.

She laid what was left of the pillowcase over the dead
face.

"All right," he said, and turned away to build up the
fire. He emptied all but a little water from the bucket out
the doorway, threw a couple of handfuls of the corn in the
water that was left, and set the bucket in the fire. He got
her purse from under the head, took out the thin steaks
cooked the night before and put the purse back under the
head. He threw the steaks in with the corn. He shut the
door and dropped the bar.

They sat against the wall on the horse blanket, the other
one, left by the executioner, over their shoulders, and
waited for the water to boil.

"Shall we go back?" she asked. "Why go on, with the
monstrance gone?"

"I don't know," he said. "I haven't any more reasons. Let's leave it to God." He thought a moment, and then said, "Bustamente might go either north to L.A. or try it the other way and go south to Guaymas. So we'll take the first train we can stop, either way. In the morning I'll tie the horse on the tracks. If the first train's north, then north. If it's south, then south."

"All right," she said. "We'll catch him."

The wind, sometimes coming in mild gusts, sometimes died away, leaving only the hungry sounds from outside. In a little while, he thought, all the coyotes, coming in from miles away, would be full, and there would be quiet until the morning, when the vultures would begin again, joined by more, and then the night would come again and the feast would go on. By the third day the smell would be too thick to breathe.

When the corn was soft, he drained out the water and they ate from the bucket with their fingers. Then they lay down close together, close to the fire, folding themselves into the blanket as well as they could. The wind hummed in the chimney, hesitated, whirled away and whispered like a thousand spirits coming and going, and they looked straight up into the black sky at the worlds of stars.

They could not sleep, but sometimes dozed, forgetting the wind. Sometimes he would wake and pull a little more of the blanket over her, and think of the dead man. Then he had been a fat, lustful fellow with plump belly wobbling toward him, an enemy simply to be shot down. Now he lay so calm and dignified, who having died became a companion for them, riding with them through the night.

Long after the moon had gone down, the ground they lay on began to tremble, and they came up fast out of their dozing sleep. The trembling grew, and then the sound of the train, coming from the south, and in a moment it was upon them, rushing with a roar beyond the wall, the shout of steam and pound of steel passing, shaking the earth, and then the loose rattle and clak of cars following, fading, dying away as the train went on to the north.

"They're going for more men," Jacko said. "They'll be coming back south in the morning."

CHAPTER NINETEEN

T HERE HAD been no need to tether the horse to the rail to waylay the southbound train; two minutes after the engine pulled up and the fireman cut the horse loose, it was clear that the train would have stopped anyway. Half the four hundred new soldiers piled out of the four coaches and six freight cars and climbed down off the roofs and started wandering around looking for loot. The first gang down grabbed the saddle out of the mud, the next shot the loose horse and stripped it; the third gang unscrewed the vise from the bench in the hut and carried it and the rusty files and the old Ford wrench joyfully away to their women singing in the boxcars.

In the first five minutes of this a squad of soldiers under the pistol of a lieutenant had piled the dead up and poured kerosene on them. In another seven minutes the engineer had rigged the fallen spout back up and eased the engine under it. Then they had unlocked the windmill and it had started pumping water into the tank while a dozen men plugged the bullet holes with empty cartridge cases. Another squad was burning the corpses in the corral while another broke down the corral and dragged the poles to the tender. By that time water was pouring into the engine and the engineer was cursing at the water dripping into the fire from bullet holes in the boiler tubes.

They left the crusted saddle blanket in the dirt. Jacko cut the other one down with the machete to make a crude serape and slipped it over Becky's head to cover her Yankee tweed outfit fore and aft.

She insisted on carrying the machete. "It's mine! I earned it!" He didn't argue. He knew how she felt: safe. She could take care of herself. She had proved it. With that thing in her hand, she could face anything. He rescued a belt from one of the dead before it burned up and punched a slit in it to fit her. She slid the machete through it and followed him out of the hut, clumping along in her crazy shoes, her big bag slung over her shoulder.

They climbed the steps into the first coach behind the tender, looking for Bustamente. It was full of soldiers, groups singing, playing cards, drinking. The men sat on the floor where the seats had been ripped out to make room for freight, or perched on crates and boxes which had been dragged in. The glass of the windows had been broken out, half of the window frames themselves were gone, their shades hanging ripped, but even with a mild breeze blowing through, the stink of the men was too heavy to breathe. Outside the dead were roasting, the meat beginning to burn, the fat sizzling and popping and making a black smoke which drifted in choking them with nausea.

They pushed on through six of these wrecked coaches. No Bustamente. As he boosted her into the first boxcar the engine's whistle gave a blast and the people wandering around headed back to the train, crowding into the freight and cattle cars, climbing to the roofs. Jacko and Becky, trapped in the car as the train began to move, settled down in a crowd of women and babies, and listened to them singing and telling stories while the men on the roof shot at the cows and horses along the right of way.

The engine gained speed as the wood mixed with the coal made a fire hot enough to offset the water dripping into it. As the water slowly gained on the wood, they slowed; as more wood was shoved into the fire, the speed picked up; finally they ran out of wood and stopped. Everybody piled out again, the soldiers broke down the mesquite and palo verde thickets along the barrancas, tore down the feeble stick fences, pulled out posts, wrenched the cross pieces off the telegraph poles, and loaded the tender again.

While the train was halted for wood-gathering they went through more cars. No Bustamente. Jumping down from one of them, they saw Paz Faz and Gavira wandering in the crowd. "Don't let them see us," Jacko said, taking Becky's elbow and turning her away. "I don't want any trouble."

"If they're here, Bustamente must be with them," she said. "Why else would they be on the train, unless they know he had the monstrance and was going south?"

"You mean they made it up with him."

A voice behind them said, "Señor O'Donohue! What a relief to find you!"

They turned and saw Braulio smiling at them. The lack of two front teeth made him seem more friendly, maybe because the hole in the smile now made him look stupid.

"Come with me and have some breakfast. I have some good news for you."

"What good news could you have for me— except your boss has dropped dead?"

"Oh, come now, you and I can be friends, if not him. After all, you and I are even."

"Just what is this news?"

"I found Bustamente. Paz Faz told me you would be looking for him. Don't you want to see him?"

"You bet your neck I want to see him." They followed him down the train. Braulio climbed into the last boxcar. With his eyes on a level with the floor, Jacko could see that it was empty except for crates and boxes piled in one end, Manuel in the middle in front of the door, feeding sticks into a small fire burning on a sheet of galvanized roofing. Some ham and pieces of rabbit, cat, or chicken, Jacko could not tell which, were sputtering in a frying pan. Evidently they had thrown the woman and children out of the door so they could have the car for themselves.

"Please join us," Braulio said, smiling down from the doorway. Things were not quite the same, Jacko thought, as they had been in Mike's wrecked apartment. He had the dead Mexican's pistol in his holster and six loads, enough for both the cousins if things got rough.

He suddenly felt quite happy. The gun he had inherited from the Mexican was a double-action, the ones the cousins had in their holsters were single-action. Knife men, like most of the L.A. scum, they had never carried guns at home for fear of the cops, and probably didn't know much about them, so when they got supermacho away from the L.A. cops and picked up these antique cannons somewhere, they had been suckered. He could fire his double-action simply by pulling the trigger, but they would have to cock theirs first. That more than evened the odds. He could get off two shots before these amateurs could even get theirs cocked.

"Why not?" he said. "Whatever's in that pan smells good."

Braulio reached down and gave them a hand up.

"Well, surprise!" Manuel said, looking up from his cooking. The train gave a jerk and the fire fell in. As the train began to roll, he fed it some more sticks.

"We have been looking everywhere for you," Braulio said as they all sat down around the fire, "and you know Herculano, he hates failure. What a relief to find you! He wanted to know if you were coming or not, or maybe stayed in Los Angeles. He isn't patient, you know. If you were coming down, he would wait. But if you stayed in Los Angeles, he would go back and get you there. As soon as your friend Michael told Herculano it was indeed you who killed his brother, he sent us up to find out. We came past the battle disguised as rebels, which means get dirty and stink like a dead dog."

"What the hell do you mean, Mike said I killed Palafox?"

"Well, you did, didn't you? How soon with the rabbit, Manuelito? Hurry it up, don't you see our guests are hungry? Your friend Michael told us after we stuck cigarettes in his belly for a while. You know, he is very hairy down there. How he stank, with the hair frizzling away! That was after our friends the cops caught him and his woman at the priest's house. Trying to collect $60,000 for some old rocks. He had some nice bonds, by the way. Forty thousand dollars."

Jacko looked at Becky. She raised her eyebrows in a genteel shrug and felt for rain with an upturned palm. Bye-bye bonds.

Braulio reached over and tried to pick up a piece of cat. It was too hot for him, he swore and shook his big sausage fingers in the air.

"At first he said one of the Riveras killed El Magnifico, but who would believe that? It was so obvious, you and this Michael had the monstrance, we know that now, so obvious to blame it on a dead lawyer or whatever he was.

Well, we started making a little track of cigarette burns down his belly toward his prick, oh, pardon me, señor, and you know what—Hey Manuel, when do we eat?"

"I know you're a big fat mother-fucking son of a bitch—"

"Tut tut."

"—and a goddam liar. I never had that monstrance. Mike had it."

Braulio grinned and rolled his round head regretfully from side to side on his bull neck. "Señor, señor, we know you had it. Because we found Bustamente on this very train and *he* had it, and he told us he stole it from you in Magdalena, the little shit. So why pretend?"

Manuel stuck the point of his knife into the pieces of cat, rabbit, or chicken, and turned them over, nicely browned.

"We have no tortillas," Braulio said. "I apologize. But the rabbit is good." He picked out a piece with his knife and laid it on the galvanize to cool.

Just to make himself feel better, Jacko felt the butt of his pistol.

"Why waste gestures?" Braulio asked good-naturedly. He bit into the piece of rabbit, showed it to Manuel, pink inside, and tossed it back in the pan. "A few minutes more! We're all friends here, señor. Please believe me! After breakfast we'll give you the monstrance."

What was this jerk's game? Cat and mouse? Play with the Yankee and then try to give him the shaft? Well, then the great speed-draw contest would begin, and the double-action would fill these bastards full of holes.

"Señora," Manuel said, dumping the rabbit pieces and the ham slices out on the galvanize, "please help yourself." Becky took a piece of ham, avoiding what she felt sure was cat. The others piled in and began gnawing. They sat eating in silence with the car swaying and swinging as the train rushed along.

"Delicious," Jacko said, threw the bone out the door and wiped his greasy fingers on his pants.

Braulio threw his out the door too and wiped his greasy fingers on his pants too. He heaved to his feet, staggered across the swaying floor to the pile of crates at the other end of the car. He reached down into some cranny and pulled out the burlap sack, came weaving back.

"Yours," he said, handing the sack to Jacko.

"What's the trick?" Jacko asked, looking at the sack.

"*Here*," Braulio said, shaking the sack at him. "*We* don't want it." He pulled the monstrance out of the sack and put it on the floor. It lay in the sun shining and glittering. "There it is! All yours!" He put it back in the sack again and sat down. He picked up another piece of rabbit and began gnawing. "I just give you back your reason for going to Guaymas. If you didn't have the monstrance, why would you go? I told you we were all friends here. We love you! Herculano loves you! He is dying to see you! Are you enjoying the rabbit?"

"I'm dying to see him too. Where is he, down there?"

"He's living with the priest in the rectory. He invited himself." Braulio laughed. "Where you have to go for the reward. I'll tell you now, to make sure you get there. It's across the plaza from the cathedral. You go to the cathedral, you can't miss that, it is so tall, then across the plaza, and you will see the rectory. It's the only two-storied building in the block. You can't miss it."

"Where is Bustamente?"

"Does it matter?" Braulio asked, biting into another piece of rabbit. "Good, isn't it? Have another piece."

"I asked you, where is Bustamente? I couldn't find him on the train, but you say you did. You know, I like Bustamente. He is a pest and a thief. But there is something about him I like. I think it is because he is the only one who doesn't want the money for himself. He lies and steals all the time, but still he is an idealist. Also, he is an awful coward, but still he keeps trying. Where is he hiding?"

Braulio just kept gnawing away. "When you get to Guaymas, the tracks go along the bay right to the beginning of the town, in the warehouses by the water. Where they end, you can see the cathedral, about half a mile away, all white. You'll see Herculano's plane too, he landed us on the embarcadero."

"Listen, I asked you, where is Bustamente?" Becky, chewing on another piece of ham, watched them both carefully.

"Don't you want to hear the rest about your friend Mike?"

"To hell with my friend Mike."

"Well, that's pretty close to where he is, he's right on the edge of the fighting. Herculano wanted to kill him bang bang right after we finished with the cigarettes, but the police captain wanted the woman, and if we killed him, she might be difficult. So we put him in the Army, figuring he'd get killed somewhere up the line in the fighting. But you know, he is lucky. The Army put him to guarding a carload of Yaquí women prisoners, you know, the ones they are selling to Yucatán, so he's safe. That is a good racket, those women. Some colonel was collecting them off the haciendas where they work, and had them in this cattle car up by Ortiz before the battle started, and up comes the Federal's armored train blocking the way, so they got stuck there when rebels blew up the tracks behind the Federals and they got surrounded."

Braulio tore another hunk off the rabbit leg and chewed for a moment, remembering. "And as the little shithead tells me, up comes this colonel and herds them back down

the line tied leg to leg and some get killed by the stray
shots and the live ones are dragging along the dead by
their heels and the colonel beating them with a whip crazy
for fear he will lose another sixty-five pesos. So he gets
them to another car on a siding down the line he thinks is
safer and puts shithead to guard them with this shotgun.
To hell with the war, he says, I got to save my sixty-five
pesos apiece." Braulio chuckled into his rabbit leg.

"I suppose that colonel is having a fit worrying about
his women there in the middle of the fight. You know
what? In Yucatán they go for four hundred pesos. Well, we
found your friend Michael there when we were hiking up
the tracks with our Federal hats and jackets on, that we
stole off the bodies to get through along the tracks, we
could have gone around on the hills, but it was too tough.
He's even got this shotgun, parading around on guard. We
talked to him, asked him how his belly was." Braulio
laughed. "He said he wanted to get away north but he
can't because the only clothes he's got is a Federal uniform." Braulio laughed again. The grease on his chin
shone in the sun.

"So what will happen to him?" Jacko asked.

"Oh, sooner or later somebody will shoot him. Why
don't you? You can't miss him, right there on the tracks.
After all, he betrayed you."

Jacko took another piece of rabbit. "Oh, I understand
that. He didn't like the cigarettes, so he did the obvious
thing, just like you and me would, lied and told you what
you wanted to hear." Jacko sighed. "I don't suppose you'll
ever believe I didn't kill that fat slob. As for killing Mike,
I'm more likely to kill you, Braulio."

"Why? I didn't burn *your* belly."

"Just tell me where Bustamente is."

Braulio laid his rabbit down on the galvanize, got up
again groaning and went back to the crates. He reached

into the same hole and hauled out a black bundle. He dragged it back to the fire and held it up in the air, swinging at the end of his arm. He looked at it proudly, like a successful hunter. Inside the sagging black suit Bustamente seemed smaller than ever, dangling from Braulio's grip on his neck. The head hung down, the sleeves covered the hands, the pants fell over the feet. His dirty black shoes pointed down, a pirouette in the air. "Just like a chicken," Braulio said, smiling. "He was very insulting when we took the monstrance away from him."

Jacko and Becky sat looking at the swaying body. Braulio stood admiring his accomplishment. Then he sighed and slung the body out the door.

Jacko looked at Becky. There were tears along the lower lids of her eyes. He could see the tip of her tongue between her lips. He knew she was biting it to keep from crying openly. She wasn't going to give these bastards anything.

He looked up at Braulio. Braulio smiled back. They rocked along in silence.

"Now is not the time," Jacko said.

"No," Braulio said, standing above him and shaking his head slowly, "not with the señora, and in any case, it is Herculano that wants to see you, not us. You were never any of our personal business, Manuel and me."

"I am now," Jacko said. They all sat quiet, swaying with the car, listening to the soldiers on the roof shooting at horses and cattle. He would have to stay there and endure these bastards until the train stopped again for wood. He sat and thought about the Philippines and the exigencies of war. He felt slightly nauseated at having accepted Braulio's hospitality, but the rabbit was too good to throw up.

* * *

At the next stop for wood, while squads of soldiers tore down fences and broke up mesquite, they found another car and crawled up into the crowd. By now they had got used to the stink. As usual all the seats had been torn out. Jacko took two of Becky's pesos from her bag and went to see if he could buy something to eat. She shoved the monstrance in its sack back into the corner behind her.

She sat huddled in her serape in a corner, waiting, surrounded by the continual chatter of the bronze-faced women, squatting like hens in their soft, faded dresses with black *rebozos* over their heads. Children squalled, romped, fought, squealed, shrieked, babies sucked at fat breasts while their mothers sucked on corn-husk cigarettes and listened to whining love songs quavered out by some old crones. Beyond them, peon soldiers proud with crossed bandoliers and big hats squatted smoking, boasting and singing. At the other end of the car there was a cockfight going on, hidden by the crowd of bettors.

The train gave a jerk and Jacko climbed in. He picked his way through the women and sat down against the wall beside Becky. He had bought a big Mexican hat off somebody's head.

"Disguise," he said. "Do you think I look like a rebel?"

"From the nose up, maybe. By the way, I think this was a dining car." She smiled a little crookedly and gestured at soldiers playing cards at a table, one end anchored to the wall. The rest had been torn out to make room. He looked around. No more vases in their little holders on the walls. No more gleaming white linen, tinkling silver, wine trembling in the glasses as the car rocked along. In the corner of the smashed-out window next to him there was still a triangle of glass. He looked at the delicate Art Nouveau design etched curling around the corner. "You're right. But I wasn't lying. The service *was* wonderful. The wine *was* excellent." He handed her a dripping tamale. "First gong."

"I listened around the picked up some rumors," he said, carefully unwrapping the corn husks. "One officer says, 'They say the defenses at Guaymas are too thick for us to get through.'

"Another says, 'How thick?'

" 'Well, they say the walls are three hundred feet thick.'

"Then another says, 'Yes, but they are all eaten out hollow.'

" 'Eaten out? How did they get eaten out?'

" 'Mice.'

" 'Oh, you mean those mud-eating mice?'

" 'Yes, the ones Obregón imported from Holland.' "

Becky laughed. "Were they drunk?"

"No, they were making fun of rumors. But I heard a lot more. They say the Federals are stuck at a town called Ortiz. They came up with an armored train and four thousand men and have been stuck there surrounded for five days without any water. Orbregón blew up the track behind them so they can't back out. All the Federals are fighting for now is water, and Obregón holds all the places, the springs. You'd think the jackass Federal general would have brought a tank car, but he didn't. So he's licked. He can't hold his people together without water. They'll just desert. All he can do is abandon his train and try to get back to Guaymas."

"Fine," she said. "We go with them."

"If they go. If they can't get out, Obregón will just cut them to pieces."

"Fine," she said. "Then we get into Guaymas with the rebels."

"Yeah, but the Federals have plenty of men in there and plenty of defenses around the town. There's even four warships in the harbor." He bit off one end of the tamale; the other leaked down his wrist. "These officers were making bets Obregón will just seal up the Federals in the town and bypass it. It's stuck out in the ocean on a point. A trap. So then how do we get in?"

She stopped chewing and sputtered past her mouthful of tamale. "They can't do that!" She sat looking at the car floor, the tamale dripping unnoticed on her boot. "Of all the lousy, dirty tricks."

He sat looking at her. Five feet tall and tough as nails, sitting in her dirty blanket with the machete beside her, the little Paris model cloche hat still on her head. He held back a smile to hide a sudden affection.

"They haven't done it yet. All we can do is just start going and see what happens. For now, go with the rebels and hope they take it. And you look too Yankee, with that hat. Give me another peso."

She dug one out of her big bag. He haggled a *rebozo* off one of the women. She put it over her head. An hour later they began to scratch. She thought it was fleas. He knew it was lice. They sat leaning against the vibrating wall, swaying with the car.

"Jacko," she said, "my little pistol is gone. I couldn't find it in my purse. I think Braulio stole it."

"So it's gone," he said.

She went to sleep, leaning against his shoulder.

In the afternoon they pulled out of Hermosillo with a new engine, rolling slowly south out of the city, across the river and through the groves of oranges toward the desert again. Each deep green tree as it sailed past sank him deeper into thoughts of his father.

He sat hunched in the rocking car, staring at the floor in front of him, his head still a dull ache, his cheek throbbing, and thought of Vincent in that small white office, patiently transferring figures from bill to book, ordering the payroll that supported his two hundred people in the villages. He saw himself again, but now almost as though he were a different person, standing in the doorway looking down at his father at the desk, seeing now bitterly the pride of his regard, a sort of loving contempt, as though Vincent were too old, too naïve, to know any better than to live a life of such servitude. It hadn't been servitude. He saw now that the two hundred had been like his children. He thought of the child he had lost, mourning it as though there were no others.

What would the people do when Vincent got too old to take care of them?

He saw the house on Bunker Hill, a waste and extravagance, and himself in it with sudden contempt at the sentimentality of the fool who sought, in cynical self-indulgence, only the new, the exciting, the spices of life. In his mind he heard his grandfather's voice again: Novelty, the mother of death. He suddenly saw the total selfishness of hanging on to that house, trying to force his father to sell land to clear the debt, the stupidity of it. To hell with the house. Suppose he went back and worked for Vincent in the groves?

She waked up and started scratching again. He said, "We have two hundred people out there at the grove, and a little sort of clinic with about twenty beds. The women who run it do their best, but they don't know much, and we have to call the doctor from Pomona all the time for stuff a nurse could fix up. If you want to be a nurse, why not work there when we get back?"

She looked at him with a faint smile. "Thanks. I'm getting quite fond of you, Jacko. It's that pathetic optimism, so much a part of your charm. Don't spoil it by being practical. I just thought, if the Federals get back to Guaymas, and we get into the city with them, and the rebels seal off the city, how are we going to get out again? If the Federals are trapped, we'll be trapped. For the whole war. Maybe years."

He pulled his gun and began wiping the dust off with the tail of his shirt. He smiled back at her. "You think too much. We just take this business one step at a time."

"Sure," she said, trying to clean the grease off her face with a corner of the *rebozo*. "We take one step with the rebels and maybe get shot by the Federals. Or we steal some uniforms and go with the Federals and maybe get short by the rebels. Nobody loves us, you know."

"You want to quit? We can wait and catch a supply train going back up the line."

She sat hunched over, her legs crossed, her elbows on her knees, studying the rocking floor. "Go back to what? Selling gloves?" She shook her head. "I'm not afraid, Jacko. If I get stuck down here, I can still be a nurse to anybody, rebels or Federals, it doesn't matter. I'm thinking about you. You get your $60,000 and get trapped in Guaymas for a couple of years, you'll just get your throat cut for it."

"I told you, you think too much. Besides, there's a way out of Guaymas, if we do get trapped."

"What?"

"Herculano's plane."

She looked at him. "You'll have to kill him for it."

"I've got to kill him anyway, as long as he's laying for me."

She began to cry quietly. "Oh, Jacko, how did we get into this?" He saw tears just begin to gather in her eyes. "You'll have to fight him. And it's three against one."

"Becky," he said softly, putting his arm around her, "not if I take the three of them one at a time."

CHAPTER TWENTY

L ATE THAT afternoon the train groaned to a stop a
mile north of the village of Ortiz. As the rumble
of the train died there rose faintly from the south
sporadic thumps of cannon and, barely audible, something
like the crackle of dry brush being crumpled in the hands
which Jacko knew was rifle fire far away.

Officers ran down the train shouting at the brand-new
soldiers, they piled off the roofs and out of the cars. Under
the shouts of the officers the mob formed into a long slov-
enly column, their heads passed by the empty windows of
the car; it was suddenly gone, a few laggards hurrying after. All around him the women in the car were gathering
children and bundles, stamping out the fires they had built
on heaps of sand, and with a great stink of swirling skirts
they dropped out of the car and hurried after their men.

As Becky started to rise, he put his hand on her arm.
"Wait. Let them clear out."

"What are we waiting for?"

"For the officers to leave." He waited till the crowd of women had gone and they sat alone in the empty car. "They're bound to stop us if they notice us, they'd seize the monstrance. What we have to do is keep out of sight and sneak through this mess as soon as we can. All we want is Guaymas."

He got up and went to one of the dead fires, scraped up a handful of charcoal. "You look too white. Too young. Not that anybody would rape you. These peasants are rather modest sexually. They'd just kill me and take you over for a new wife." He crushed the charcoal down to dust between his hands and then with a forefinger drew shadows to hollow her cheeks and make pouches under her eyes; finally, two heavy lines from nostrils to the ends of her mouth. He grinned. "I'm really great at makeup. May told me all about it." He wiped his greasy black hands on the front of his shirt and stood up, admiring his work.

"You seem very pleased," she said. "What do I look like?"

"A wonderful old hag. Or dirty old crone. Any other war, I'd have hung a rotten piece of chicken around your neck, but that wouldn't stop these jokers, they smell so bad themselves they'd never notice one more stink. What do I look like?"

"In that wonderful tweed outfit? And that disgusting stubble? An American bum after a three-day drunk, trying to look like a Mexican. That hat! And as for stink, I don't think either of us are too attractive."

He took her hand and pulled her to her feet. "Great preserver of virtue, stink. Come on."

They climbed down the car steps and trudged along the silent train toward the distant firing, Becky shuffling along like an old woman. Between the cars as they passed they could see to the east and south a great plain covered with brush, now darkening as the sun went down, stretching for miles away toward deep blue-purple mountains. To their right low rocky hills, dotted with scattered brush rose steep and black against the yellow western sky. They started to come on little fires in the brush with men around them cooking and sleeping. More and more appeared glowing red in the growing dark, until the plain seemed to sparkle with red jewels.

They passed the engine, hulking above them black against the darkening blue sky, its fires smoldering red in its belly, then another train of boxcars. Ahead of them men were unloading, carrying forward on their shoulders sacks of flour, boxes of ammunition. They fell in with the line and passed four more trains head to tail along the track.

The first in line was a hospital. All along the right of way wounded sat or lay on the ground, in shafts of light from little square windows cut in the sides of the wooden boxcars. On the ground by the tracks, in a great square of light from the wide freight doorway, stood a cart holding a pile of ruined body parts, legs, arms, hands tumbled together, and they had a quick vision as they passed of men above in the car humped concentrated over tables. There was no sound from the wounded waiting by the tracks. There was no sound from these, nor the surgeons' car. As they passed, a boy came to the door and threw a smashed foot into the cart.

They came to a tank car with a long line of soldiers filling bottles, bladders, and canteens with water. They got into line and at their turn, having nothing to carry water in, drank as much as they could hold, dipping from a barrel that from the taste must have held molasses.

They came to the last engine and stood beside it, out of the way of the traffic. As the dark came down torches sprang alight along the right-of-way, kerosened rags tied to the ends of sticks or bits of pipe. They were on the edge of Ortiz, the little village totally dark and abandoned. Four or five miles to the southeast on the plain they could see rising and falling the yellow fire of a solitary battle, but there was no sound. The cannons had gone silent. All around them, as they hid by the engine, men came and went; a ragged company trotted by toward the fighting in the south, wounded straggled toward the rear.

There had been a lot of fighting here around the village. In front of them a cannon lay on its side, one wheel smashed. Rifles lay abandoned. The dead, all Federal, still lay where they had fallen. Squads of men, lighted by torches, loaded bodies into carts. To the east beyond the village there was a great fire. Jacko could smell it on the cool draft of air coming down the plain. The rebels were burning the dead of five days' fighting, the black cloud of greasy smoke rolled southward over them.

They pushed on down the line, leaving behind the crowds around the train and the wavering yellow torch-light. They walked beside the tracks to avoid the awk-wardness of matching stride to the spacing of the ties. As they left the torches, the moon seemed to grow brighter, shining on the wreckage of the battle. Half a mile down the tracks they came to the worst of it. The fallen Federals lay on each side of the track, with the peculiar flat and slumped look of the dead, broken shapes vague in the moonlight. All along the line rebel soldiers were picking over the corpses, pulling their pockets inside out, sitting down on the tracks and trying on shoes and boots where they found them.

They walked through a tinkling litter of empty cartridge cases thrown out in showers from machine guns, stepped around empty 75 mm cannon shells gleaming smooth, the yellow of brass turned white in the moon. Becky stumbled over rifles dropped by the dead and deserters, lying scattered in the way, and they moved back to the tracks. The tracks, sheltered by the stalled train which had now backed south, was clear of all this rubbish.

Even though Becky had to hobble to match her pace to the spacing of the ties, they went a little faster, passing through the wreckage and the heavy smell of the dead. Smashed ammunition carts lay tumbled over, burned-out machine guns lay upside down, dead horses lay stinking and swelling against their saddle girths. Ten yards of papers lay scattered white as snow in the moonlight where cannon fire had blown out a headquarters car. They met two rebel soldiers joyfully carrying typewriters before them, three more with field telephones. One of them wore a Federal officer's cap, heavy with gold braid. Farther down, a burned-out automobile lay on its side, and on his back beside it lay the officer, a full colonel in dress uniform, the wreathing around his choker collar gleaming gold, his mouth a black hole in his white surprised face, his suitcases and his blown-off legs tumbled around him.

The third time Becky stubbed the toe of her clumsy flopping boots on a tie and fell in the gravel, she didn't get up, but sat still between the shining rails cursing in nurse language.

"I can't make it in these goddam boots," she panted. "And I'm not going barefooted in these goddam rocks. Do something!" She sat silent, humped over in defeat.

Jacko stood looking down at her. She looked so small, sitting there in the clumsy blanket serape, he wanted to put his arm around her to comfort and encourage her; but she had never at any time relaxed her isolation. He had always felt it as a sort of universal enmity, not so much against him as against the world in general, an insistence on independence.

He squatted down beside her. All he felt permitted to do was to give her two diffident pats on the shoulder. She surprised him by turning and smiling at him. "Sorry for the outburst."

He sat looking over the dark plain. To the southeast the yellow fire of the battle was still burning.

"That's probably a farm down there, and they're fighting for water. That's all that's left for the Federals. If they don't get water, they'll have to quit."

They could hear, three or four miles straight down the track, the faint crackle of rifle fire. Everywhere else the country lay in a vast silence, made only more deep by the distant barking of coyotes and dogs. To the left lay the moonlit gray-white plain, to the right, close by, the black bulk of the hills rising against the sky.

"If it weren't for that fight down the tracks there," Jacko said, "we could follow the railroad right down to Guaymas. Maybe we could sneak past, but I figure there's a safer way, if you could make it. I've got to fix those boots somehow. It's twenty miles to Guaymas, so they said." He bent over, unlacing his shoes. "I'd kill somebody for a couple of horses. There's plenty of dead ones around, there must be live ones somewhere." He took off his jacket and then his shirt, cut the shirt collar in half with the machete and ripped the shirt down the back.

"There's a better way out, if you can make it," he said, handing her the rags. He ripped off his socks. "Here, put these socks on over yours to help pad out the boots. And stuff the rags into the toes."

He watched her unlace her boots. "It'd be safer to sneak up a canyon and down over the other side of the hills. There's bound to be some way south, down some valley, and there won't be any fighting over there. That way, we could just simply cut around this whole mess and to hell with it."

She sat silent, stuffing her boots. He watched her face.

"We could go very slowly," he said. "The moon would

help us see the way. And maybe down the line somewhere I could steal a horse."

"Where is the train?" she asked. "You said the rebels blew up the tracks to trap it. It has to be somewhere."

He sat up, studying the light of fires down the line. "That's probably it, down there, stuck at the break."

She shoved one foot into a boot and started lacing it up. "All right, Jacko, we'll do what you say, but not yet." She pulled on the other one. "It's Mike. He's down there with the train somewhere. You heard that brute say he was guarding a car. I can't just leave him there, not even knowing we were here. It would be too cruel." He started to protest. What could she want with that son of a bitch? Go down there and get mixed up in that fight just to see him? Say goodbye? He kept his mouth shut.

"I just can't leave him. They burned him. I could at least do something about that."

He wanted to stand up and shout, You mean play nurse with your Bag Balm? Risk everything to put a patch on that horse's ass? But he didn't. He clamped down on the shout and sat smothering himself, his head bowed. He didn't want to hurt her. Ever since he had made the blanket into a crumby serape and slipped it over her head, he had felt that in some way she belonged to him, as though there were a child part of her that he was bound more than ever to take care of.

"You mean you still love him?" he said.

"Oh, don't be romantic, Jacko. I never did love him. I told you that. At least not in that way. But you can't live with somebody six years and not get to feel something for them. Can you?"

"I don't know. I can't remember."

She stamped her feet, trying the new fit of the boots. "I mean, you see them sleeping, you see them sick, you get to know what fools they can be, you see their weaknesses that they're not even aware of. It's mostly pity. It's hard not to love any kind of human, if you know them well enough."

She turned and looked at him. "Didn't you feel anything like that about May? Didn't you ever see her weaknesses?"

He thought about that. Finally he said, "No, I never did. She never had any weaknesses. The only thing I learned was that she was never anything but hard and cold, always on the make. Stupid and selfish. I can see how you'd feel sorry for Mike, because he was kind of dumb and helpless. But May never was dumb and helpless." He wasn't going to tell her about the baby, the jumping down on the floor. "I never prayed for her to drop dead, but I would have thanked God if she did."

They sat silent, listening to the distant battles. From the farm across the plain the tiny rattles of rifles and machine guns rose and fell. Down the line, the same thing, louder, closer. Then she said, "He's down there with his stomach burned and God knows what's going to happen to him. He betrayed me and robbed me and I don't ever want to be with him again. But, Jacko—" She paused a long moment. "Can't we just go down and find him, and let me fix his poor stomach, and say something, say goodbye at least, and then go around behind the hills as you say?"

He realized that for the second time she was asking. Had she ever asked him for anything before? Always she had been fighting him. He knew her well enough to know that if he refused to look for Mike, she would just bristle up and tell him to go to hell and go on down across the tracks on her own. She was as stubborn as oak and brave as steel. Why didn't she just up and go? Why was she asking, as though she needed his consent?

Then he realized what it was. He was beginning to mean something to her. She was treating him like a friend, not just a goddam nuisance she was stuck with. She was giving up something, some independence. And then he realized something else: she didn't want to lose him. And he knew he wasn't going to refuse her, because he didn't want to lose her either.

Suddenly he felt happy. He laughed and got up, picked up the monstrance. The sack swung and struck a rail, the monstrance banged like a piece of junk tin. He took her hand and led her down the tracks.

As they left the battlefield and its clutter behind, they moved from the tracks to the sandy right-of-way where the going was faster. They covered three miles in an hour, Becky clumping along more easily in the padded boots.

The brush bordering the right-of-way grew thicker and taller as they approached the firefight. They could see, a mile away, a stream of tracers from machine guns high on the hill, firing down on the tracks. And then they made out the train against the light of cars burning here and there along its length.

A hundred yards from the train Jacko found the reason for the high brush, a dry streambed paralleling the tracks. He led Becky down into its concealment and fifty yards farther they were walking in mud, then splashing through half an inch of water and pushing through reeds. As they reached the train they left the stream and on hands and knees crawled up the shallow bank till they were looking across the right-of-way through the last of the brush.

In front of them stood two armored engines, now dead-cold, pointed north toward the village. They had backed the whole train out of the battle, down the line as far as it could go. The lead engine was nosed up against two gondolas, and ahead of these was an armored car. They could hear the clang of bullets hitting the steel sides of the gondolas and the plating on the armored car, saw their machine guns firing from the other side of it, their tracers streaming up the hill against the firing coming down from rebel positions above. Other streams of tracers were firing from positions in the gondolas, probably through ports in the low steel sides. Down the line three cars burned, set off by tracer fire from the hill. Where the long line of stalled cars ended, steel rails shone in the light of a burning car, lying helter-skelter where the rebels had dynamited the line to cut off the Federals from Guaymas. Half of the ties still clung to the rails, like the legs of dead centipedes.

All the fighting was on the other side of the train. The side they faced stood in black shadow except where the three cars burned.

"He must be down there somewhere," Becky said. She started forward, and Jack held her back. He studied the length of the train. Four black figures ran past him from the gondolas toward the south, then two more. They dodged past the burning cars, then into the dark again.

Far down the line at the end of the train he saw three horsemen come out of the dark and trot up the line. The running men stopped and turned back, but the horsemen were upon them, arms rising and falling, beating with machetes, and through the cracking of rifle and machine-gun fire he heard desperate shouts. The men on foot fled into the brush, the guards after them, crashing through the brush, rounding them up like cattle, driving them back to the gondolas. Somebody in the brush kept crying and groaning in pain. One of the horsemen thrashed here and there, looking for him. He pulled up his horse and sat quiet. The crying kept on; then a pistol shot; the crying stopped, and the horseman was crashing through the brush again, up on the right-of-way, joining the other two, and the three cantered back to their post in the dark down the line.

"Bastards," Jacko breathed. "Come on. They can't see

us in the shadow of the cars." They started down the train. They passed a car in flames, the roof flaring with burning tar, fire creeping down the sides. The car next to it had burned out, the roof gone and most of the wooden walls, leaving exposed a cargo of flour, now a white mountain barely smoldering. The cloth of the sacks was slowly burning, eaten away by wriggling red lines, letting the flour pour down like snow onto the right-of-way. They left the firing behind.

Ten cars down the line they found the cattle car. Jacko peered through the slats, listened to sighing and muffled moaning. Rows of moonlight ran broken over humped shapes packed close together on the floor. A few women sat leaning against the slats of the car sides. One of them sat so that the moonlight coming through the slats fell on her face. Her eyes were closed, her mouth open, she seemed asleep, perfectly passive. She was probably dead. The smell was a compound of filthy bodies, feces, rotting corpses.

A helpless sad rage rose in him. Somebody was saying over and over, *"Agua."* The Yaquís would never beg. They had probably taken a Mexican woman by mistake.

"Where is Mike?" Becky asked.

"I think the son of a bitch has deserted."

But they found him between the end of the car and the next, sitting on the coupling, the moon shining on his back, bright on the barrel of a shotgun. He jerked the gun up and said, "Get the hell out of here, you bastards, *vamos*, beat it!"

They stood still. "Don't shoot that thing," Jacko said.

Mike leaned forward, peering. "Jacko?" he said in a little voice. He went limp and began to cry. "Oh Jesus," he said, "Oh Jesus." He bent over, the shotgun drooped. "Oh God am I glad to see you." He stood up slowly and coming forward put his hands on Jacko's chest. "Oh, Jacko, I didn't mean it, it was a joke, see? I was always going to split with you. And May, I couldn't help that, she made me take her."

"Where is she?"

"She's dead, Jacko. I couldn't help it."

Jacko stood silent.

"Ah, now, Jacko, don't be angry, don't be mean, Christ, I had nothing to do with it, I was in jail. She left me in jail and went with an officer to save her skin. I never saw her again. It was the officer killed her, they told me. It was a party, they said, in the hotel, she did something or said something, they threw her out of the window, three stories down, or four, or something. Jacko, it wasn't my fault! Don't blame me! Help me! I've got to get away, give me your coat, I can't get through the rebels in this fucking uniform."

He spread his hands out helplessly. He stood looking up at Jacko. "Why don't you say anything?"

He dropped his hands and stepped back. "I suppose you're mad at me." He rubbed the tears off his face with his jacket sleeve. "Oh God," he said, "you don't understand. I've been waiting for days for those bastard guards to kill me. They think I'm a joke. They come up here and point their pistols at me. 'It's orders,' they say, 'the time has come.' Then they click their pistols and laugh. Only one time they'll really fire, Jacko, they'll really do it. I've got to get away."

Jacko stood silent. He could not speak to him. One word would join them, leave Mike clinging to him again. He looked at the man, hardly hearing the words, just the rise and fall of the whining.

He looked inside himself, thinking of dead May, and could not find a single tear, or hate, or anything. What had she done? One time too often with the six for five? The wrong gang, drunk, that wouldn't stand for the way she promised and never delivered? Haven't you got one tear for the poor bitch who killed your child? Instead, he felt like laughing. She was dead, he was free of the woman. Dead? When had she been alive for him?

He looked at Mike. The guilty whining was going on and on, squeezed out by his silence. Why had he been fond of him, with the affection he would have had for a monkey? And suddenly he saw why he had protected him, who had stood for at least five days listening to the women die, begging for water. There was something in Mike that was like himself, or something in himself that was like Mike. How else could he have been fond of him? He stood looking at him in horror, listening to the foolish mouthing.

Mike was looking at the sack in Jacko's hand.

"Is that it?"

Jacko said nothing.

"Listen, Jacko," Mike said, edging toward him again, "you'll never make it. If you get in, you can't get out. Jacko, I was a fool, I know, and I'm sorry as hell. Can't we be partners again? Let's go back to L.A. and fence the thing. You'll never get out of Guaymas with the money. He's laying for you, Herculano. He's got the cops."

Jacko backed out from between the cars and began peeling off his tweed jacket.

Mike came out into the open, leaned the shotgun against the side of the car, and began taking off his uniform tunic. They could hear the sighing and moaning of the women.

"Why haven't you given them water, you bastard?" Becky said. "You seem to have had plenty. Where is it?"

"Oh, there's barrels of it, down by the guards, but oh, Becky dear, I was afraid to open the door. I couldn't hold it if they fought me. If they got out—they're nothing but Indians, Jacko, what would they do to me? What if they got loose? The guards would have killed me if I lost them. Jacko, they're worth sixty-five pesos apiece, I couldn't take a chance they'd get away."

The firing at the gondolas had thinned down, the battle across the plain was dying out. The smell of the women drifted over them. Jacko stood in the moonlight naked from the waist up, the black butt of his pistol stuck in his pants startling against the whiteness of his skin.

"Jacko, why don't you say something? After all these years, why are you so hard on me? What have I done? Just a little joke, Jacko. You've got the monstrance, can't we let bygones be bygones and be friends again? Jacko, let's go back to L.A. Please, Jacko, let's go, let's go."

He came out of the shadows of the car, holding out the uniform tunic.

"Old partner," he said, smiling, coming close and taking Jacko's coat. In the same movement, he seized the butt of Jacko's pistol, tore it loose from his belt and jumped back into the shadow.

"Sling the monstrance over," Mike said, "you stuck-up son of a bitch."

Jacko stood quiet, looking at Mike in the shadow. As he had listened to this low parody of himself, he had heard all his own folly, carelessness, indifference, vanity. How could he have deceived himself so long? Only that in himself, the man who had protected, sheltered, and half loved this brute, was a liar hidden behind a gloss of benevolence, the same twin beast as the one before him. A secret self, smiling hidden as Mike jumped on the bellies, chopped and smashed in the delight of mayhem. Why else had he kept him on the leash all these years, except for a love not of Mike but for his own unknown self living in another? He looked at Mike now with a total hatred for the man, who had mysteriously contained him, and as much for the hidden self he now saw had always been living in him, his own brutality.

He wanted to say, Why did I ever take care of you? I just couldn't see. I couldn't smell the bastard in you because the bastard in you was me. That's why I took care of you, with all your stupidity and cruelty, why I tolerated your jumping on the bellies, why I defended you. Because you were me, the rotten shit inside me, that was enjoying it as much as you, that I didn't know about until I saw you now. Two bastards together, me letting you act out what I was too holy to do, me the kindly father, taking care of the filthy part of himself, in you.

He turned away and went to the door of the car. He reached up for the latch. Let the bastard shoot.

"Don't!" Mike yelled. "I'll kill them if you do!"

He threw the latch. Mike fired the pistol, the shot went wide, he leaned on the heavy door and shoved it slowly open.

Becky was shouting at Mike, aiming the shotgun at him. Jacko grabbed it out of her hands. The women were pouring out of the car, the flood of them knocked him down. He saw Becky disappear under the whirling mass of skirts.

Mike was firing into the women as they ran toward him. Three of them fell. Jacko raised the shotgun. The last of you, he thought, the last of me, and with a terrible hatred and disgust of the man and himself in him, he pulled the trigger. The gun jumped and roared. The women surged over Mike, pounding and battering with stones.

Beyond them Jacko saw the guards galloping up the line. Then they were on the women, slashing and cutting with their machetes, shooting down into the mob as the horses reared and squealed. Jacko raised the shotgun and fired at the first. The guard fell sideways out of his saddle.

He swung the gun toward another guard and saw him covered with a swarm of women, reaching up, climbing, tearing at his clothing. The guard went down, pulled off his horse by two dozen clawing hands, and then the third went down under the women. He lay listening to the pounding of rocks on splintering bones as the silent women beat the guards to death.

And then everything was quiet, the women hurried away, leaving their dead. He could hear them splashing in the creek.

He stood up and in the silence realized that the firing from the gondolas had stopped. He worked his way through the scattered bodies of dead women to where Mike lay half-naked. He stood looking down at what was left of the face, nothing but a bloody mush. The tweed coat was still clutched in his hand.

Jacko looked around for the tunic Mike had been holding out, found it under one of the bodies and put it on. He suddenly remembered Palafox's letter of authorization. He went through the pockets of his tweed jacket and stuffed the papers into the breast pocket of the tunic. He saw the monstrance sack where he had dropped it by the car door, and picked it up.

Two men came running by, then four. He turned and looked back to the gondolas. Men were jumping over the sides and running toward him.

The fleeing mob from the gondolas was upon them. He grabbed Becky's wrist and the panting, grunting crowd carried them along like a river. With the fleeing men all around them, they reached the shining, tumbled rails at the end of the train, bright in the light of the burning car.

He pulled out of the crowd and looked east to the distant battle at the farm. The fighting had died, and in the tiny light of burning buildings he saw streams of men heading toward the beacon of the burning train.

"They've broken," he said, and in himself broke. He pulled Becky into the stream of the mob, seeing through tears the torn, ruined rails wavering brilliant in the firelight. He stumbled on unseeing into the dark with Becky clumping along beside him, clutching her machete.

CHAPTER TWENTY-ONE

FIVE MILES down the line the mob, stumbling along the tracks, met the first of three rescue trains sent up from Guaymas. Jacko and Becky let themselves be carried along with the crowd as it swarmed up into the cars.

They sat silent, crammed among the slumped bodies of the beaten soldiers, listening to the distant battle of the rear guard, waiting in an agony of tension for the train to start its retreat, backing down the tracks. At last it began moving with a great crashing and slamming of couplings. As the train backed slowly down the line, many fell asleep to the rocking of the cars, the rest rode in glum silence, quietly enduring the thirst that had finally defeated them, worn out by five days of battle and fear. There was none of the rebel singing and cheerful chatter.

Many of the bowed heads were clipped bald, prisoners routed out of jails to fill out Huerta's army, many poor and half-starved Indians, derelicts lost in the cities, shanghaied off the streets, absurd in their filthy uniforms always too big or too little, half in clumsy uniform boots, the rest in sandals or barefooted. No one complained. The wounded lay silent.

An hour later the train stopped. To their right Jacko could see the great mile-wide estuary of the bay gleaming in the moonlight, cutting them off from Guaymas, and the long causeway across the water. He knew now they could never have got into the city by themselves. Officers and military police ran along the cars.

The train backed on down the line; trenches and machine guns enfilading the track passed slowly by, cannon in their emplacements defending the approach to the city, then the fields of little fires where thousands of troops were encamped.

They rumbled across the two miles of causeway, then along the Guaymas peninsula at the foot of the steep, rocky mountains that dropped to the edge of the bay, and at last saw the lights of the city coming around the flanks of the savage hills that protected it.

Suddenly they were in the city, at the end of the tracks, looking at the great expanse of the bay, the four warships, black silhouettes against the pale moonlit water. A mile away along the embarcadero the cathedral rose pure white against the checkered gray and black of the lower town.

All around them the soldiers were coming to life; safe, they were talking about tequila, pulque, cerveza, the relief of drunkenness, and came off this last train in a mob, stumbling and hurrying away, ignoring the shouts of officers trying to form them up.

Jacko and Becky lagged behind, letting the tail of the mob dissolve ahead of them up a wide boulevard into the city. Six blocks from the cathedral they turned out of the last of the stream of soldiers into a side street and hid in the shadows of the old Spanish buildings. The panting and mumbling of the stragglers, the clicking of boots and the hushed padding of sandals up the street died away, and in the silence they could hear the lapping of little waves against the stone seawall of the embarcadero.

Across the still water of the bay the reflections of the riding lights of the warships ran toward them like shattered spears, the rich smell of the sea came over them in a gentle drift of cool air from the water. To their right the cobbled street rose steeply from the flat of the old town to the foot of the unpassable stone mountains looming over the city. Their cliffs in the moonlight rose like dead gray faces raked down by immense claws into steep black canyons and crevices.

From the new city came the low grumble of the crowds moving thick in the invisible streets, now and then shouts and shots rose above it; but here in the old town everything lay dead in a frozen checkered pattern of white walls and black shadows. The fortress faces of the ancient buildings stood dead set against the rabble streets; their massive doors, peruked in old stone curves and curls stood locked as though forever, their beady-eyed little windows, set high above aristocratic cheeks of walls, watched from behind their bars.

To Jacko the tall, pale towers of the cathedral, a few blocks away, meant only dread, the end he had shut out of his mind, now inescapable. In his stomach, sickening it, was a solid black ball of fear. He was too tired; as heavy of arm, empty of will, as any of the broken soldiers who had gone before him.

A hopeful dream, pure wish, rose in his mind like a wailing beggar, that all those who should be waiting for him, Herculano and the others, might be unaccountably delayed, arrested, even dead, that he and Becky might somehow meet the priest and make the exchange in civil, quiet conversation, drinking coffee, and then pass on homeward by some magic through the air like the spirits of birds.

But Herculano would have been waiting all these days; Braulio and Manuel would have got through the Federal line on one of the trains just as he had done. And Paz Faz and Gavira, whom he had almost forgotten, those frail threats, where were they? Somewhere ahead, since he and Becky, standing in this shadow, were the last to come, and no more trains behind.

He was suddenly too tired to think any more. He sat down on the step of a deep doorway. "I don't see how we're going to make it, Becky. There's five of them. I could take maybe three of them, one at a time, but how take five that way?" He closed his eyes.

She sat beside him, looking up at his drawn cheek. The white building across the narrow street reflected a faint light onto it.

"How's your face?" She reached up and with her thumb and forefinger turned his head toward her, using his chin for a handle. He opened his eyes and looked at her blearily. The scab had formed nicely over the scraped cheekbone. "It's doing fine," she said. "Nothing like Bag Balm. How's your head?"

"Oh Christ," he said, and closed his eyes again. "I'm too tired." He leaned away from her against the deep stone jamb of the door and went to sleep.

She sat watching the edges of shadow creep slowly across the cobbled street. She didn't protest. She had gotten into this mess all by herself. She was helpless, completely dependent on a man who was too worn out to do anything. She knew he wasn't a coward; if he had been, he would have turned tail long ago.

He grunted and sighed, his body resenting the cold stone. He must have been dreaming he was in bed, and turned away from the cold stone and slumped over against her. She let him slide down until his head was in her lap. He began to snore.

She sat patiently waiting. He would wake up and do something, eventually. She began to smooth the hair on the side of his head with her forefinger, very gently. It lay in small, dirty locks, rather like feathers, rather like, she thought, the shingles on his house; she passed the time, waiting for him to wake, straightening out these little locks with her fingernail.

His head, very heavy on her lap, seemed too big, out of scale; but then, she was used only to feeling her own. She smiled, enjoying the feeling of possessing this heavy weight upon her.

A *Luftmensch*, she thought, the air man. Yet he had lost that lightness now. She remembered him patiently plodding through the necessities at the water tower, carrying water, collecting wood, building the fire, steadfastly robbing the dead to find shoes and food; making her serape out of the blanket, bargaining for her *rebozo*, tearing up his shirt for her. Little by little, her independence had died, and she had found out that in becoming dependent on him, she in some mysterious way had begun to rule him.

What would it be like to kiss him? He was at her mercy now, as she had been at his for days. There was not much space left on his face to kiss, with the wide scab and the short dirty beard.

Something puritanical in her stiffened. But why? Was she still married? Mike was dead, and what there had been of Mike in her had been dead for years, buried under the long self-concealed hurt of being used, the final desertion and robbery. What was she now, officially, with him dead? A widow. But then, she had been emotionally a widow for years. All that was left was the habit of faithfulness. But how, to a ghost?

Perhaps her sudden withdrawal was only because Jacko

was too dirty and smelly to kiss. She imagined him clean, and suddenly with a leap of clarity wanted this clean Jacko to kiss her. Then she knew she wanted him to hold her, as tightly as he could.

At once she sat up straight, backhanding the air to brush all that away, and then thought, Don't be such a fool. When did you become infected with all this puritanical reserve? You are a Jew, it is in your nature to be more honest. If you love him, want him.

All this movement waked him up. He looked at her, his rested eyes now clear and sharp. "What did you say?"

"Hold me."

He began to smile.

"Don't you want to?" she asked. "You did once, I saw your face when you were holding me, when you thought I was sleeping, when we were wrecked."

The smile faded, he looked down.

"Stop that!" she said sharply. "He's dead."

He got to his feet and stood looking away. She stood facing him. "*She's* dead. They're both dead. And I feel as though I had been beaten with sticks, I'm all beaten and tired. Can't you be decent enough to hold me, just hold me?"

"Sure," he said. He held her, folding her in. They stood that way for a long time. Then he said, "I want to kiss you, just once, before we go ahead. Just to have done it, just once, at least. Not more, not until—"

"You don't have to explain. I know what you mean. Until we really feel we're free."

He let her go and turning away picked up the shotgun. "It's not going to be as bad as I thought. We don't have to be afraid of Paz Faz and the other little bastard until we get the money. They won't try to steal the monstrance because they haven't got the papers, the priest would call in the cops, and the cops know these anarchists. So we're safe from them till we get the money at the rectory. And I know Herculano, he won't try an ambush, because he thinks it's all a matter of honor. He wants to see my face when he shoots. So we'll go to the rectory, and after that just see what happens. Here, take the monstrance, I need both hands for the shotgun."

They turned back out of the side street into the boulevard leading up into the new town. Five blocks ahead Herculano's plane sat in the middle of the street like a pale giant moth, two men standing guard beside it. A perfect brand-new design, full cabin, its front ski braced down from the engine, the two skid hoops at the ends of the lower wing. The cabin ran full length, the first cabin plane on earth. It had two seats side by side, their steel pipe frames bolted to the floor. The struts shone in the moonlight.

"Just like Herculano," he said, "to land the thing in the middle of the street as though he owned it. Well, he does own it, he always buys the police wherever he goes."

They walked forward in the shadow of the buildings on the left of the street until the buildings ended and they stood facing a wide esplanade. Two vacant blocks lay as bare as a parade ground between the cathedral and the water, the wide expanse of paving pale gray in the moonlight, the boulevard dividing it. In the middle of it stood the plane; to the right, at the upper end of the esplanade, the cathedral stood broadside to it. Its front faced another block, the plaza, its trees now black, filtering showers of moon flecks through leaves onto pale dried grass.

Jacko stood studying the two guards on the plane. Probably city police loaned to Herculano. All he needed to get rid of these buzzards was money; they never shot anybody until they had picked them clean. Herculano would have money, and no use for it at all with fifteen buckshot in his belly.

A lot depended on who he had to face first. Paz Faz and Gavira probably had rifles. If he met them first, he could get one of the rifles, and then he could deal with Herculano and his people at a distance. But if he met Herculano first, he would have to depend on the shotgun, with its short range, and that meant that he would have to get them from the cover of the trees in the plaza.

He could not see the rectory, the trees cut off the view. But he knew where it would be, on the other side of the plaza from the cathedral, the only two-storied building in the block, according to Braulio. And Braulio would not have lied about that, when Herculano's whole purpose was to bring about a meeting. Braulio had told him exactly where to go, Herculano would know exactly where to expect him.

Even with all this reasonable assurance of safety, he would not have crossed the wide open esplanade for all the money in the world. He led Becky through alleys and narrow streets around the rear of the cathedral, up the street on its other side, and stood in its shadow at the front corner. To his left the steps of the cathedral splayed down across its front.

He stood watching the plaza for movement. The trees were mostly palms, huge-trunked Washingtonias and slender, towering queen palms. Shrubs around their bases, growing along the walks which crisscrossed the block, obscured the buildings across the street beyond the plaza.

In the center of the plaza, half-hidden by the palms and shrubs, stood a bandstand, its low Victorian pierced-wood walls painted white, the lacy gingerbread eaves picked out with colors gone gray in the moonlight.

Counting on the idea that Paz Faz and Gavira would not ambush them until they had been in the rectory and come out with the money, he led Becky across the street and into the trees, following a broad walk toward the bandstand.

The first shot stabbed yellow out of the bandstand. He dropped to the ground, pulling Becky down with him, and crawled on hands and knees into the bushes. The second shot cut twigs close over his head, leaves fluttered down; the third plowed the earth, throwing sand into his face. He stood up and fired, the gun banged and kicked and he could hear the sharp rattle of buckshot on the low walls of the bandstand. Sixty yards away, too far for any shotgun. He heard Paz Faz laugh.

He pulled Becky behind one of the fat palms. They knelt in the dark, listening.

"Why are they trying to kill us?" Becky whispered.

"How the hell do I know?" In his mind everything was topsy-turvy. "Maybe they killed the priest and took the money already. And now they want the monstrance too. Wait here. I've got to get closer to them."

He worked another round into the chamber of the gun as slowly as he could, trying to keep the noise down. It didn't do any good, the damned sloppy old actions always shlicked and shlucked like a hog sucking mud. Two fast shots banged out from the bandstand, one bullet whipped through the bushes beside him, the other glanced off the concrete walk and whining away bounced off the face of the cathedral. Some way to treat a church. He felt like laughing. They were lousy shots.

He moved quietly forward through the bushes. If he could get close enough, they didn't stand a chance, not against the shotgun.

Four fast shots sounded ahead. He stopped. He hadn't heard the whiplike crack of bullet splitting the air; they were firing in another direction.

Then Herculano said from up ahead, "Welcome to Guaymas, Señor Jacko. It's all safe now, they're dead, come on. Bring your little toy and let's go see the priest."

He stood still. The whole thing was going wrong. The

only thing to do was to get away until he could understand what had happened. If the priest wasn't dead, why hadn't Paz Faz waited for the money?

He turned to work back toward Becky. He had to get her away, back into the maze of streets before Herculano and his people could trap him in these stinking trees. He hurried. He couldn't help making noise, brushing against branches, breaking palm fronds and sticks underfoot.

Herculano called, "Don't go away, friend. We're here to help!"

He got back to the tree where he had left Becky. She wasn't there. Then through a break in the bushes he saw her standing on the sidewalk, Braulio beside her, holding her arm. He raised the shotgun, aiming at Braulio's head, and then slowly brought it down. There was too much danger to Becky, they were too close together. Fifteen buckshot would spread too much: thirteen of them might take Braulio's head off, but two of them might hit her.

"Come on out, Jacko," Braulio said. "You sound like a mad ox thrashing around in there."

He moved out through the bushes until he was standing at the edge of the walk. Braulio was holding Becky with one hand and had a pistol ready for anything in the other.

"It's okay, Becky," Jacko said. "Don't let this big ape scare you."

"He doesn't scare me," Becky said, her voice trembling. "He is just bluffing with his damn pistol. Go ahead and shoot him. Don't mind me."

"She attacked me with a machete," Braulio said. "She's pretty good, too. Very brave. See, I have even let her keep her little weapon. What a woman! Here, hand me your shotgun, señor, you know how I am always telling you we are friends here."

Jacko pumped the shells out of the shotgun magazine onto the walk and threw the shotgun into the bushes. No

319

use giving these bastards another weapon. He stepped out into the open and Braulio felt him over for another gun, then said politely, "Shall we go? After you, señor, straight ahead." He followed them up the walk.

At the bandstand they came out of the shadows into clear moonlight. Herculano was standing on the steps leading up to the raised floor, pistol in hand. On the steps beside him, head down as though he had fallen while running out, lay Gavira. On another walk, coming from the esplanade, lay Paz Faz, on his stomach, groaning faintly. Manuel came around the side of the bandstand and stood smiling at Jacko.

"So good to see you, Señor Jacko," Herculano said, and bowed toward Becky. "I was so sorry to have to ruin your apartment. But I am sure you understand. And that, in your sack, it must be the famous monstrance, or should I say infamous? it has caused all of us so much trouble. Well, I am glad we could save you from this trash," gesturing at Paz Faz and Gavira. "Totally irresponsible and therefore totally unpredictable. I see that one is not quite dead yet."

"Please," Paz Faz said faintly. "Water."

"There isn't any," Herculano said.

"Please, water," Paz Faz said.

"What a whiner," Braulio said.

Herculano pointed the pistol at Paz Faz's head and fired. The head jumped a little and Paz Faz said no more. A little blood came out of the mouth, spread in a small black puddle, then stopped. Herculano holstered his pistol.

Somebody fat was running heavily up the walk from the esplanade. Jacko made out a Sam Brown belt: one of the policemen guarding the plane. The fat officer stopped at Paz Faz's body and looked up at Herculano.

"An assassin," said Herculano.

"Ah, my only concern, Señor Palafox, was for yourself. I heard those shots."

"Don't worry, my friend, I am still alive, you will get your money, no fear. Please go back to your post on the plane."

The officer bowed and hurried back down the walk.

"These hyenas," Herculano said, shrugging. "Never full. Well, now, our priest." He came down the steps, pausing on the way to give dead Gavira a kick. "Let's go see the good father and conclude your deal. *Then* we will conclude *our* deal." He punched Jacko lightly on the shoulder and smiled, showing two whole rows of square teeth as though to a dentist. It was the first full smile, or snarl, that Jacko had seen on that concrete block of a face. Mentally he counted the loads in the hideout. Five. None fired yet. A virgin gun. Weak loads, and not enough of them, but they would have to do. If they didn't—well?

"After you, señor," Herculano said, gesturing toward a third path, disappearing into the trees toward the other side of the plaza.

Jacko and Becky led the three down the walk.

"Please don't hunch your shoulders up like that, señor," Herculano said. "It hurts me to think you do not trust me. You know I am a man of honor."

Braulio laughed.

CHAPTER TWENTY-TWO

T HEY STOOD before a great black door, set embrasured deep in the high white wall of the rectory.
Straight into Jacko's eyes looked the blind eyes of
an iron lion. It's head, almost as big as his own, hung on
the door as though decapitated, the jaws agape, the tongue
hanging out, seeming to smile at the memory of an agony.

"You knock," Herculano said. "I want no more of that
priest. I'll wait for you out here, and when you come out
with your $60,000 I'll give you a gun and let you have the
honor of paying for Lorenzo."

Jacko lifted the five pounds of the lion's head and let it
fall with a boom on its iron plate. A night wind came
along the street, blowing papers before it, making the
queen palms in the plaza across the street sigh and gently
bend.

A judas hole in the door slapped open. Somebody said,
"Hock!" and spat; then said, chewing something, "*¿Quien
va?*" in a high, irritated nasal cry.

"Santana!"

"What, you again? Still? Yet?" The heavy door swung slowly open. An old man with white hair like straw sticking out in all directions from under a dirty old German cap stood in the lighted doorway squinting at the five.

"Señor! Oh, how relieved I am, I thought maybe by the grace of God you were dead. We thought you had abandoned us because we had no more chickens to feed you." He stood back, bowed, and waved an arm at them to enter. "How we have been weeping and mourning that you left us! Tears all day, flooding the floor, flowing down the gutter, the neighbors thought it was raining. I have just mopped up the last five gallons. What joy to see you again!"

Herculano let out a single bark of what passed with him for laughter. "The same to you, old fart. You're a brave old bag of bones, though. Don't you know I could kill you with one swat?"

"Go on and kill me, then, you animal, it would be worth dying to know you burned in hell for it."

"Sizzle away, you silly old bastard. It's not me that wants to come in, I've had a bellyful of you and Padre Miguel and your damned beans. It's these two unwashed Americans, with a beautiful gift for His Honor." Herculano turned away.

Jacko and Becky stepped into a foyer which led to a larger patio. The two stories of the house, with their colonnades, ran around the quadrants of a formal patio, dry fountain in the center, lemon trees in the corners, beneath them neglected flower beds, the colors of their poor remains reduced to black, gray, and white in the moonlight. All the doors and windows of the two stories of rooms round the court were dark, the place seemed to be abandoned except for two rooms just to the left of the entrance.

The old man opened the first door and announced, "Two

humble Americans in rags, Father," and went out a second door at the end of the room, chewing away, laughing to himself.

The light of a kerosene lamp shone on the priest, sitting in a black cassock at a large dark table. He turned and looked at them for a moment, then he smiled and stood up, putting down on the table another black cassock. A needle, tucked through the material, shone bright in the lamplight.

Everything in the room was black but the pure white plastered walls: black rafters overhead, the table, five chairs, and a low bed in the corner. The room was too narrow for its length, seeming hemmed in by its massive walls, their thickness revealed by the embrasures of the two windows.

"Come in," the priest said in English, his lean face smiling as he came forward. "I am Father Miguel." He waved a hand at the chairs at his table. "How can I serve you?"

"John O'Donohue, at your service, Father," Jacko said. He bowed and pulled out a chair for Becky. As he was introducing her he saw the priest's smile tighten a little and knew that he was getting a whiff of the war.

"Forgive our condition, Father," he said, "we have been traveling for days with very little water."

The priest shrugged and smiled. "If Guaymas is caught in a siege, we'll all be bathing in the dust like the chickens." He picked up a bronze hand-bell from the table and gave it a couple of clangs. The old man came through the door at the end of the room.

"Well, what is it now?" he said.

"Is there any of the dinner left?"

"Dinner? You mean the beans that Señor Santana left us?"

"Yes, Otilio, and that piece of ham you hid. Warm it up."

"Tsah!" Otilio said and slammed out through the door.

"Don't mind him," the priest said. "He is ninety-two years old. At that age he sees everybody as pesky children. I think you may be a Catholic, Señor O'Donohue? You are very handy with the 'Father.' "

"Right, Father," Jacko said. "Old habit."

"And I," Becky said, not to be left out, "am a Jewish widow." She seemed both proud and a little defiant about it, being outnumbered.

"We are the grateful grandchildren of your faith, Mrs. Horton, it is an honor to have you here."

"We have come to return something to the Church," Jacko said. He lifted the sack from the floor beside Becky and pulled the monstrance out of it, set it before the priest. The jewels glowed and flashed in the yellow lamplight. He took the documents out of his breast pocket and laid them on the table. "And to claim the reward."

The priest leafed through the papers. "I heard from Señor Santana that his brother, or rather half-brother, Palafox, the consul here"—tapping the letter—"is dead. Señor Santana says that you killed him. That is nothing to me, as I have little obligation to the police. But did you get this monstrance by such an act?"

"Not so," Jacko said, folding up the sack, "but he has convinced himself of it. He was very fond of Lorenzo, like a mother and father both. I know who killed Lorenzo, but that man is dead. So Santana has made up his mind I must do."

"I see. So he has been waiting here for you to come for the reward. I am going to take your word for your innocence simply because you are here. If you had really murdered his brother, you would stay far away from Santana, I think. Besides, he has himself been acting like a bandit, forcing himself and his bodyguards on me and Otilio for several days now without any invitation. I have not been able to lock them out until tonight, when they were all gone. Why should I believe them?"

He shoved aside the cassock he had been mending and drew the monstrance toward him. "So much trouble for this piece of clap-trap," he said, inspecting it. "All those clumsy jewels, as though our Lord needed any. Well, it is some people's way of glorifying God. I am sorry to tell you, but there is no reward. The letter from the archbishop is a forgery. The whole thing is a government trick to lure anarchists into the country and kill them. I suppose nobody told your Palafox in Los Angeles. The better to keep the secret."

Jacko sat looking without expression at the letter. Then he looked up at Becky and grinned.

"It's a possibility, of course," the priest said, "that I have stolen the money and made up a lie. But I am sure the police will back me up. But of course, I may have bribed them to do so!" He sighed. "Innocence is so expensive in this country! Well, if it were mine to give you, I would say, take the monstrance back and sell it somewhere. The Church doesn't really need such things, even though it's nice to have them. But it isn't mine to give."

Becky began to laugh. She bent over, laughing between her knees, sat up laughing, bent over again, the tears coming down her cheeks. She stopped herself, wiping her cheeks. She sat still, looking at nothing. Then she hit the table with her fist. "Damn, damn, damn." She sat back in her chair and looked all around the room, seemed dazed. "Oh, how did we get here?"

"Don't be upset," Jacko said, smiling at her with half his mouth. "It was always too good to be true. How could the Church in Mexico give away $60,000, when it has been robbed blind for a hundred years? I just wanted to believe it. Never mind, Becky. You didn't really believe it, did you?"

"No. It's just that you believe anything when you're desperate. Oh, it would have solved so much."

"Who hands out such solutions?"

"So much for easy money," she said. No nursing school now, she thought; well, maybe a practical nurse is enough, doctoring two hundred Mexicans. She looked regretfully down the long road back to the nursing school. Opportunities, opportunities, was there anything else in life for fools but lost opportunities? She had let the bloody scalp of a dead whore scare her away from a good career, only to end up chopping off a man's head. Was that a kind of justice? She, the brave militant! marching her parades down the street, fighting off the memory of cowardice. She sighed. "It's really a kind of relief, isn't it? I didn't really believe it either. A relief to let go."

Otilio came in with a big bowl of steaming beans. He plunked three little bowls down and snapped down three spoons beside them.

Jacko sat still, looking at nothing. You sucker, he thought. It's just what you deserve. You and your elegant hats, your airplane, your alabaster wife, your proud independent career as a snot-nosed snoop, that slick agency, eating anybody's handouts, digging up anybody's dirt like scraping up shit in a dog kennel. What were you ever but a sucker for your own pretensions? He began to smile, seeing himself. Look at you, with your damned homburg hat, sucked in dizzy by an empty-headed alabaster bitch, dragging Mike around, that slaughter-happy oaf, parading the big father act, wiped blind to your own love of evil by your self-cuckolding deceit, who should be more fooled by the Guaymas cops than such a sap? Hell stinks with the frying fat of such as you. Well, he thought, looking down at the beans, that's the end of your dreamworld. I'll go home to where I belong with the mules and the Mexicans and maybe my father will give me a job. He picked up his spoon.

"Why so little in your bowl, Father?" Becky said, pointing to the couple of spoonfuls in the bottom of it.

"I've dined already," he said. "This is just to keep company with your late-night supper."

The lion's head boomed on the great door. In a moment Otilio came shuffling in. "He says, where is Señor-Something-or-Other, why doesn't he come out? He says he is tired of waiting."

Jacko said, "Tell him I will be out in a little while." Otilio shuffled away, making resentful noises.

"You can stay here as long as you like," the priest said. "There are plenty of beans, and he can't keep me from coming and going."

"I don't think it would be that easy," Jacko said. "I know him. He would kidnap you as you went out to the church, steal the keys. He won't stop at anything to get me. He will never give up." He sighed. "The ridiculous thing about it is that it is not really me he is after. He is after what he thinks is justice, revenge, there has to be a dead body to pay for his brother. Another dreamer. Like my $60,000. Who can pay for his brother? Nobody. But he insists on payment."

"Too bad for him," Father Miguel said. He pushed away his bowl and took up his sewing. They watched him. "Well, take as much rest as you can. He can't get in." He used up his needleful of thread and snipped it off with a sharp-pointed ten-inch shears, pulled a yard and a half off the black spool and threaded the needle again.

"Please, let me do that," Becky said. "As a favor."

Father Miguel shook his head. "I need it as a penance," he said, and laughed.

Becky laughed. "So do I. What a mess. Do you really have to use such big shears? Those bunches."

"All the better. Don't worry, I do this from choice. The ladies of the parish would do it, along with repairing the vestments, but I don't let them, the cassocks are too personal."

The lion's head banged again, louder and longer.

Father Miguel ignored it and pulled the long thread through the coarse cloth and high in the air.

They heard Otilio's voice raised in exasperation.

"He curses in Yaquí," Father Miguel said.

Bang, bang, bang, bang, bang, bang, bang, bang.

"You are using too long a thread, Father." Beck said. "A lazy man's thread, my grandmother used to say. Shorter is quicker."

The priest nodded. "I know, I figured it out. The time taken for rethreading the needle is more than made up by the speedier stitches, right? But it seems that when I make it shorter, it is unnecessarily short. I have difficulty finding the middle way. By the way, Jacko, when you are home, what do you do, if I may ask?"

"When I go home, I will be helping my father run an orange grove, I hope. Near Los Angeles."

Otilio came in again. "Padre, he says the same thing, when is the señor coming? It is getting late, he says."

"Don't answer the door again," the priest said, shifting the cassock on his knees. "He has had an answer. One is enough."

Otilio looked at him with concern, then bowed and went out.

"Sociologically speaking, it is a good idea to work for one's father," Father Miguel said. "It tends to keep order in society. The son inherits not only the business, but the craft. That is a very old idea. When I was in Guadalajara, I used to make sermons about much newer ideas, until they decided I was a radical and sent me up here to preach to the trees.

"But nowadays the sons are very ambitious, they feel entitled to high places where they do not have to work at all. That's why they love politics, and this revolution. If they come out on top, in some bureau or other, they can suck the blood of the people and live on taxes. Many of them look at their hardworking old fathers with contempt. Away with the old, they say, anything new is better because it is new, they follow each other, the blind leading the blind, and fall into the pit. Progress! It used to be one man with a rifle could kill one man, now one man with a machine gun can kill a hundred. But I am getting carried away. It has been quite a while since I thought of any of that kind of thing."

"You would like a saying of my grandfather," Jacko said. "Novelty, the mother of death."

"Yes, I like that one. Your grandfather, he lives in the grove with you and your father?"

"Yes, but I wouldn't mislead you. I have been living for years in the city. Not any more, however. I will go back to my father's house."

The priest, with the big shears in his hand to snap off the thread, looked around at Jacko and studied him for a moment. Then he smiled. "I see."

The lion's head banged again like thunder on the great door. The hands of the priest, threading the needle, did not falter.

"They'll break the door," Becky said.

"Yes, it's time for us to go," Jacko said. "Or rather, for me. Becky, you stay here. I'll come back for you when I'm through."

"No," she said, standing up. "I go where you go."

"Yes, sure, when the job's done, but not now. If I worry about you, I can't handle it. You wouldn't be a help."

"What do you mean?" she cried. "Look at the hero, going off by himself! Didn't I help you once with my machete? Where would you be now without that?"

"I know where I'd be, Becky, now lay off." Jacko turned to the priest. "I have to tell you, Father, I have to kill him. I'd better do it before he shoots out the lock of your door. I can't change his mind, and he will never give up, he is that kind of man."

The priest stood up. "I understand all that. The prouder one is, the harder it is to give up when one is in the wrong. Go kill him, if that's the only way. You have the right to defend the life God gives you, and this woman. I am sorry I can't help you. You understand that I myself am forbidden arms?"

"Of course. Is there a way around this house?"

"Yes, an alley goes around it."

"Where is the back entrance?"

The priest led him outside. He pointed across the patio to the rear where there was another great door. "You don't need a key, there is only a bar. There's a stairway to the second floor just to the left. You can see the alley from up there."

"I could use your blessing."

The priest whispered and over his head made the sign of the cross.

He started across the patio as the banging began again, along with furious shouting. He ran up the stairs and from the casement window of an empty room looked down into the alley below and saw Manuel on guard, pacing back and forth. On his head was a pale gray felt hat with a three-inch brim, Yankee style, which was going to make the head shot a little uncertain.

Manuel was using no care. He threw away a cigarette butt, the red coal sailing in a high arc into a stable yard across the alley from the house. He coughed, spat, and walked out of sight beyond the side of the closed window, humming to himself. Why be careful when they had searched the Yankee so well for guns?

Jacko pulled open the leg holster and checked the little Colt. The .38 Special cartridge, proven useless in the Philippines, where you could fire six into a charging, doped-up rebel and he wouldn't even break stride. But one in the head would do for Manuel.

In the stable yard across the alley there were open stalls on three sides, all dark and empty. A buggy and an ancient coach stood abandoned in the moonlight amid a clutter of old barrels and broken bales of rotten hay.

He listened to Manuel's footsteps on the cobbles of the alley, waiting until he had turned and come back in his sauntering patrol, passed under the window and disappeared up the alley the other way. The turn had taken about thirty seconds. Jacko opened one of the casements and folded it back against the outside wall.

He cocked the hideout and holding it in both hands rested it solidly on the sill. The two-inch barrel and the dinky sights didn't make for much accuracy. He heard Manuel's footsteps coming back up the alley. On one of his strolls, he would get tired of walking, and the natural place to stop would be in front of the door. Jacko went over his Tactical Rules. No. 1: the most effective offense as well as the most difficult is to take the enemy by surprise in the rear. No. 2: in the rear from an elevated position. No. 3: from the rear by enfilade. All these West Point abstractions were subsumed under the generic heading of Backshooting. Jacko had never met anybody who preferred any other approach except a few too drunk to care.

The big fat fellow came sauntering into view, two-fingering a pack of cigarettes out of his shirt pocket. He stopped below Jacko and knocked out a cigarette, stuck it in his mouth and went into his pocket again for a match.

Jacko swiveled the gun down, as solid in his grip as a

rock, until its sights were lined up on the hat. If he held on the joint where the brim met the front of the crown, he thought, the bullet should hit at the hairline on the forehead.

Holding hard in his usual dumb-peasant style, he slowly squeezed off the trigger, the little gun jumped like a frog in his hands, and Manuel, with a match flaming in front of his nose, dropped like a wet sock onto the cobbles. The flame of the match, still in his fingers, died out.

Jacko ran for the stairway, jumped down the steps and threw the bar of the door out of its slots. He slipped out, closed the door behind him and ran to the body. He pulled the heavy pistol out of its holster and ran into the stable yard, hid in the nearest open stall. He checked Manuel's gun. It was the same old single-action he had had in the freight car. Six loads ready. He cocked it and, breathing fast, locked his knees against a feeling of weakness. He began to sweat. He had to get through two more of these sons of bitches.

He heard feet running, coming down the alley, and at the same time three muffled shots from beyond the building. Herculano shooting out the lock. Hurry up, Braulio, before that son of a bitch gets through the house.

Braulio hauled up at the body, his gun in his hand, and looked around carefully. He rolled Manuel's body face up, knelt down beside it.

That is what will save my butt, Jacko thought, aiming carefully, the overconfidence of these bastards. Braulio thought he had run away. He held the aim hard and steady, and carefully shot Braulio between the kidneys. The recoil lifted the barrel of the heavy gun straight up into the air. The flash blinded him for a moment. Thank God, he thought, blinking his eyes, for a real gun. Sure as hell, nothing beat backshooting.

He ran out into the alley. Braulio was lying on his face

across Manuel's body, groaning and swearing. He turned on his side, feeling for his own gun, glaring in pain and rage at Jacko as his eyes came around. Jacko kicked the gun out of his hand. Braulio glared up at him, groaning out curses.

"What a whiner," Jacko said. "Here's a kiss from Busta-mente." He aimed carefully down at the nose with his usual micrometer precision.

"Take your time, you son of a bitch," Braulio said.

"I will," Jacko said, and steadily squeezed off the trig-ger. The blast made his ears ring. Braulio's head flopped back into a splatter of its own gray brains. His mouth fell open under the wreckage of his once-was nose, and the black hole of his missing teeth said Ooo at the sky. Jacko grabbed his gun and started for the door.

From the casement above the gun roared and the bullet hit his left ear. He fired blind at the black hole of the win-dow and turning ran for the stable yard, jumping ahead of bullets, around behind the old coach.

He crouched behind it, trying to slow his breathing. Je-sus, he thought, Jesus, Jesus. He felt his ear. His finger went through a half-inch hole in the upper part. How many damned times would he have to explain that in the rest of his life? He swore at the growing pain. He bent over, feel-ing just a little sick at how close his head had come to it. The bastard had come straight through the house. What had he done with Becky?

He peeked around the corner of the coach and a bullet whacked through the woodwork above his head.

He went to the other corner of the coach and shot a fast one at the window. Herculano laughed, safe in the dark.

She had picked up the shears and run out into the patio in time to see Herculano leaping up the steps to the second floor. She ran across the patio and quietly followed him up the stairs. She could hear him yelling at Jacko and followed his voice. He was in one of the empty rooms. She stood in the doorway looking at his back. He was kneeling at an open casement, the barrel of his gun on the sill, aimed at something she could not see.

"You stay there, son of a whore," Herculano shouted. "Cops coming pretty soon with all this shooting. Just take it easy. You move and I'll get you, you know."

She opened the shears, thinking that one blade would slide in easier than two; then realized she didn't have enough grip on it. She had to cross ten feet of wooden floor. She had to have a noise, to cover the creaking.

A gun fired, a bullet from outside drove into the ceiling above her, plaster trickled down.

The way he was kneeling, she thought, his spine curved somewhat to the left, sheltering his heart side. She stood unmoving, waiting for one of them to fire again, and brought back her memory of the anatomy of the thorax. If she drove the shears in from the left and up slightly through the fifth intercostal space, she ought to hit the heart, and the shears were more than long enough to go through the lung and heart both. She judged the location of the space between the ribs. Two inches to the left of the spine would miss the transverse process. She would have to hold the shears strong in both hands to keep them from glancing off a rib and spoiling her aim.

Another shot came through the window and as Herculano fired again, under cover of the blast, she crossed the room swiftly. Not stopping, with the shears held hard, she crouched and drove them between the ribs straight through. Herculano stood straight up in front of the window, his arms held out a little as though he were starting to fly. She put both hands in the middle of his back and, as he started to collapse, pushed him hard straight out of the window. He fell over the sill, his feet flying up, and she heard the soft crunch of his body and the clatter of his gun as they hit the cobbles. Then she sat down on the floor and held weakly onto the sill, her forehead on the backs of her hands.

The pounding of her heart slowly eased, the pulsing in her head died away. She got slowly up and looked down into the alley. Jacko was standing by the bodies, looking down at Herculano's broad back and the shears sticking out.

She went wearily down the stairs and out into the moonlight.

"Oh God," she said, seeing the blood on his neck, "He shot you."

"Only a hole for a hell of an earring," he said.

"Let's go," she said, "oh, please, let's go. I can't stand any more. Oh, hold me, Jacko."

"Half a minute." He stooped and pulled Herculano's wallet out of his hip pocket. "For the guards. Come here." He put his arms around her and held her up, and looked at the shears sticking out of the broad back.

"Is this a life?" she said into his chest.

"It's a life," he said. "Wait till you're running my hospital. Come on, let's get the plane."

They left the dead and walked away down the alley.

"Wait till you're running my hospital, Becky," he said quietly, soothing her, "all this will be nothing, a dream. And when we're old, it will never have been, you'll see, you will have forgotten everything."

The way he had forgotten, all at once, now, with half a smile on his dirty face, with his arm around something better to think about than the child, the castle, the wife, the moose, the little yellow man, and the bones, the bones of O'Hearn.

BESTSELLING WESTERNS
BY RICHARD S. WHEELER

"No one does it better than Dick Wheeler."

—*The Round-up Quarterly.*

☐	51071-2	SKYE'S WEST: BANNACK		$3.95
	51072-0		Canada	$4.95
☐	51069-0	SKYE'S WEST: THE FAR TRIBES		$3.95
	51070-4		Canada	$4.95
☐	51073-9	SKYE'S WEST: SUN RIVER		$3.95
	51074-7		Canada	$4.95
☐	50894-7	SKYE'S WEST: YELLOWSTONE		$3.95
			Canada	$4.95
☐	51305-3	SKYE'S WEST: BITTERROOT		$4.50
			Canada	$5.50
☐	51306-1	SKYE'S WEST: SUNDANCE		$3.99
		Coming in October '92	Canada	$4.99
☐	51997-3	BADLANDS		$4.99
			Canada	$5.99
☐	51297-9	FOOL'S COACH		$3.99
			Canada	$4.99
☐	51299-5	MONTANA HITCH		$3.99
		Coming in December '92	Canada	$4.99
☐	51298-7	WHERE THE RIVER RUNS		$3.99
			Canada	$4.99

Buy them at your local bookstore or use this handy coupon:
Clip and mail this page with your order.

Publishers Book and Audio Mailing Service
P.O. Box 120159, Staten Island, NY 10312-0004

Please send me the book(s) I have checked above. I am enclosing $ _____
(please add $1.25 for the first book, and $.25 for each additional book to cover
postage and handling. Send check or money order only—no CODs).

Names _____
Address _____
City _____ State/Zip _____
Please allow six weeks for delivery. Prices subject to change without notice.

Tor Books presents

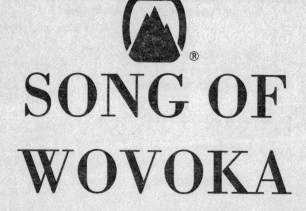

SONG OF
WOVOKA

a story of the last hope of the
Sioux

from **Earl Murray**
the author of
Free Flows the River
and
High Freedom

52091-2 $10.99